"Ambassador Lang is asking for medical supplies, not quantum torpedoes," Kira said. "How does taking a hard line, making it difficult to save Cardassian lives, benefit Bajor?"

"Your attitude surprises me, Colonel," Asarem said pointedly. "You of all people should appreciate the need to ensure that Cardassia is never again in a position to harm Bajor, or anyone else. Perhaps the reports of your patriotism are exaggerated."

Kira's eyes narrowed. "Have you even been to Cardassia since the war?"

"No," Asarem said. "I haven't."

"Then what right do you have to dismiss Ambassador Lang the way you did just now?"

"The rights given me by the people of Bajor who elected me to serve them."

"And the people of Bajor elected you to be their avenging angel? To single-handedly make the Cardassians pay for fifty years of wrongdoing?"

Asarem slammed her case on the table. "I decided to hear you out because as the commander of Deep Space 9 you're owed a measure of input. But I'm done."

Kira persisted. "For all the horrors inflicted on us by the Cardassians, half our population wasn't executed and millions of our children haven't died since with flesh melting off their bodies due to radiation sickness. We didn't emerge from the Occupation drowning in our own dead. Where is your compassion, Minister?"

"With the generations of dead and brutalized Bajorans who committed no crime save being born Bajoran. The Cardassians allied with the Dominion. They brought destruction on themselves. Now get out of my way before I call First Minister Shakaar and inform him that we need to reconsider your position as commander of this station."

STAR TREK
DEEP SPACE NINE®

MISSION: GAMMA

BOOK TWO OF FOUR

THIS GRAY SPIRIT

HEATHER JARMAN

Based upon STAR TREK®
created by Gene Roddenberry, and
STAR TREK: DEEP SPACE NINE
created by Rick Berman & Michael Piller

POCKET BOOKS
New York   London   Toronto   Sydney   Singapore   Andor

This book is a work of fiction. Names, characters, places and incidents are products of the author's imagination or are used fictitiously. Any resemblance to actual events or locales or persons, living or dead, is entirely coincidental.

An *Original* Publication of POCKET BOOKS

POCKET BOOKS, a division of Simon & Schuster, Inc.
1230 Avenue of the Americas, New York, NY 10020

Copyright © 2002 by Paramount Pictures. All Rights Reserved.

STAR TREK is a Registered Trademark of Paramount Pictures.

This book is published by Pocket Books, a division of Simon & Schuster, Inc., under exclusive license from Paramount Pictures.

All rights reserved, including the right to reproduce this book or portions thereof in any form whatsoever. For information address Pocket Books, 1230 Avenue of the Americas, New York, NY 10020

ISBN: 0-7434-4562-7

First Pocket Books printing September 2002

10 9 8 7 6 5 4 3 2 1

POCKET and colophon are registered trademarks of Simon & Schuster, Inc.

For information regarding special discounts for bulk purchases, please contact Simon & Schuster Special Sales at 1-800-456-6798 or business@simonandschuster.com

Cover art by Cliff Nielsen

Printed in the U.S.A.

"What do you fear, lady?" he asked.

"A cage," she said. "To stay behind bars, until use and old age accept them, and all chance of doing great deeds is gone beyond recall or desire."

—J.R.R. TOLKIEN,
The Return of the King

*For my husband, Parry, and my father, Jeff—
because they handed me the key*

and

*In memory of my brother Tad:
"Not all those who wander are lost."*

ACKNOWLEDGMENTS

If it takes a village to raise a child, it takes a family to write a book. Many deserve thanks.

First, I would be remiss if I didn't express gratitude to the *Deep Space Nine* family of actors and writers who gave us this incredible universe to play in. Long after this book is garage sale fodder, *DS9* will endure.

My husband continually pushed me to aim higher; without his encouragement I never would have tried, let alone succeeded. He and my daughters—Sara, Ally, Rachel, and Abby—showed admirable patience and positive attitudes throughout this process. My parents, Marge and Jeff Clayton, must have wondered how they grew a geeky daughter in the midst of my cheerleader sisters, but they have always supported me with enthusiasm. My siblings deserve notice as well: Laurie reintroduced me to *Star Trek* after years of hiatus; Jane was my steady support; Tad shared my love of sci-fi and fantasy; and Julie was a bud. My brother Peter is a marvelous thinker, genetics researcher, and social policy innovator who gave me the tools for the Andorian backstory. My sister-in-law Amy inspired me with her bravery. Peter Jarman's loan of his laptop assured there would be a book.

A tender thank you to my fellowship of writers, all of whom own part of this book. My incredible writing partner, Kirsten, might not have co-written this with me, but she's been with me in the trenches the whole way—middle of the night, weekends, deadlines. She's the godmother of the project. Jeff Lang, whose wit, wisdom, and open arms saw me through rewrites, incessant whining, and everything else. A gifted writer in her own right, Bethany Phillips is the reason the outline was eventually completed. Thanklessly, she proofread, talked plot points, and offered advice whenever, wherever. Jim Wright, a comrade in arms, who, in a way, started me on this road when he said, "You should write a column for *The Starfleet Journal.*" Keith DeCandido was the voice of pragmatic experience who talked me off a few proverbial ledges!

Dena's blanket hugs and prayers kept me warm through long hours at the computer. My dear MIA Mikaela brought the funny whenever I needed it. Both of you deserve smooches.

The amazing Susannah just gets it: *Law, hîr nín, ú dollen i Rîw. Anírach, nui lû, gwannad uin gwaith lín?* Cathy, Marsha, Betsy, Eden, and the toytrucks gang supplied the cheering section. The team at Oak Hills School that supported the girls has earned special thank yous—Wendy, Chris, Heidi, Ashley, Tammy, and Cynthia. My resident genius, Dr. Fraser Smith, brought the tech hooks that made me look good. Without Patti Heyes, Katie Fritz, Sara Wilcox, and my friends in PTF—D'Alaire, Julie, Monica, Janet, and Marianne—I never would have made writing *Star Trek* fiction a priority.

To the "father" of this project, Marco Palmieri: for your brilliant instincts, incredible talent, unfailing patience, and daring to take a chance on this new kid, I owe you my deepest gratitude. Thank you for giving me the chance to build foundations for my castles in the air.

I am a part of all that I have met;
Yet all experience is an arch where through
Gleams that untraveled world whose margin fades
Forever and forever when I move. . . .
. . . And this gray spirit yearning in desire
To follow knowledge like a sinking star,
Beyond the utmost bound of human thought.

—ALFRED, LORD TENNYSON,
"ULYSSES"

I

"qablIj Hi'ang!" *Ngara snarled the traditional challenge at the approaching Son of T'Mokh. She crafted a dance of fast precise spins to the tempo of her anger. Sweat dripped off the glistening ridges of her forehead, beading on her eyelashes. "I will toast my father's honor over your corpse, you sniveling p'takh!"*

A master of the spear, Lughor did not fear her. Blow for blow, he would match her dazzling display of warrior-craft. "qabwIj vIso'be!" *he growled, revealing himself as one well schooled in the ways of battle. In one deft motion, he rent in twain her sleeve from shoulder to wrist. She roared in anger.*

Weapons clashed. Lughor pushed against her. Ngara deflected each blow. Grunting, she gained ground on him. She raised her spear over her shoulder, heaving the point into Lughor's thigh. In pain, he staggered backward. Calling upon Kahless, he found the strength with which he could combat her fiery fury.

The struggle began in earnest: thrust, parry, spin away. Weapons locked as the combatants matched rippling muscle against rippling muscle.

Her pulse, pounding through her ears, deafened her to

Lughor's mocking provocations. She cried, "On this night, I will stand in hot black pools of your blood, spilled when I slit your throat!" Ngara flew through the air, her spear before her, aiming for his throat.

Lughor's eyes narrowed. In a feline crouch, he leaped up to intercept her chonnaQ *with his own. Ngara's weapon snapped in two. Roping his arm around her waist, Lughor wrested her to the ground. In one swift movement, he stripped her of the knife strapped to her thigh.*

A battle cry rang from her throat. Ngara broke free of Lughor's grip. Flipping him onto his back, she straddled his waist, curling her sharp fingernails into his skin. Lughor bucked, but Ngara bored him down, pressing his shoulders to the ground. The sticky sweat-slick cohesion of their bare limbs fused their bodies together as they wrestled on the forest floor. Pungent air, heady and thick with their mingling musks fed their desire.

The smell of Lughor's blood on her hands suffused Ngara's senses; she longed to flick her tongue in his wound, greedily lapping the droplets from his skin. Hunger for her burned in his dark eyes. Pinning her arms above her head, Lughor slid his d'k tahg *beneath the lacings of her leather corset, blade against breast. "I will have you!" he growled. And with a swift up-thrust—*

"Nog, what the hell are you reading?"

The padd Nog had been holding with white-knuckled intensity almost flew out his hand when he heard the voice in his ear. With a clatter, he slammed the padd facedown on the mess hall table and rested his arm on it protectively. All things considered, *Defiant*'s embarrassed chief engineer felt like he'd come precariously close to leaping out of his own skin.

Nog looked up to see Ezri Dax's upside-down face smiling mischievously at him as she leaned over the top of his head. "At ease, Lieutenant," she said. "I can only assume that wasn't the engineering status report I asked for."

Eyes still fixed on Dax, Nog felt around the top of the table with his free hand, past his bowl of tube grubs and his Eelwasser, and

2

found the padd in question. "Umm, no. That would be this one," he said, handing the padd to Dax. *Blessed Exchequer, please spare me this humiliation . . .*

"Thanks," Dax said, straightening up to examine the contents of the report. "I've got Bowers running a diagnostic from the tactical side. With any luck, we can identify where those false readings are coming from when we line this data up with his."

"I'm sure we will," Nog agreed. *She's not gonna embarrass me! Oh, thank you, thank you, thank you . . .*

"That must have been some fascinating reading on that other padd," Dax said at length. "You don't often encounter references to leather corsets in Starfleet's engineering manuals."

Ears flushing, Nog winced. *The jig, as Vic might say, is up.*

"Oh! *Burning Hearts of Qo'noS!*" exclaimed Engineer Bryanne Permenter, pointing at Nog from across the mess hall. Bringing her tray with her, she plopped down in the chair beside her boss. "Have you gotten to the part where Ngara has the *bat'leth* duel with the minions of the House of Rutark?"

Nog looked up at Dax. She folded her arms and raised a teasing eyebrow as she waited for Nog's answer.

"Yes, all right! I'm reading *Burning Hearts of Qo'noS!* There, I said it! Are you happy?" Turning to Permenter, he said excitedly, "That was great! I never thought she'd make it past the bewitched targs guarding the moat, did you?"

Dax rolled her eyes and shook her head. "Is this what all engineers do between duty shifts?"

"Hey, not fair, Lieutenant," Permenter said. "I got it from T'rb in sciences. So they started it. And if the text was in the library computer and not copy-protected, none of us would need to pass the same padd around from one person to the next." Turning to Nog, she said, "Didn't Richter have it before T'rb?"

"No, Richter asked me to pass it to her when I was done," Nog said. "Ensign Senkowski gave it to T'rb."

Retrieving his chef's salad from the replicator, Jason Senkowski announced loudly, "Don't you dare bring me into this. I wouldn't waste time on that poorly written excuse for a novel. Imagine it, Lieutenant," he said, addressing Dax, "a Klingon *bodice ripper.* I tell you, it's the end of literature as we know it."

Permenter snorted. "This from the man who practically begged me to read *Vulcan Love Slave*."

Nog looked at Senkowski, surprised. "Really? Which version?"

"The classic original, of course," Senkowski said. "By Krem."

"That's never been proven," Nog pointed out.

Senkowski shrugged as he sat down, one table over from the group. "Never been *dis*proven, either. I know Iskel is the popular favorite, but I'd say the evidence that Krem was the original author is compelling. Regardless of who actually wrote it, though, I'll take *Vulcan Love Slave* over *Burning Hearts of Qo'noS* any day." Senkowski turned his attention back to *Defiant's* first officer. "And for the record, Lieutenant Dax, I happen to *like* Starfleet's engineering manuals. I find them pithy, concise, and thorough."

"I appreciate your candor, Ensign," Dax intoned solemnly, trying not to smile. Senkowski had made no secret of his ambition to earn a second pip by the mission's end.

"Still miffed Mikaela got the shift chief promotion, eh, Senkowski," Permenter noted.

"I take my engineering duties seriously," he said, raising a forkful of salad.

"As well you should," Dax said, elbowing Nog.

Taking the hint, Nog added, "You're an invaluable member of the team, Ensign." Pulling the padd close to his chest, he sneaked another look.

Ezri laughed.

"What!" Nog protested. "I'm at the good part!"

The mess hall doors opened, admitting Lieutenant Sam Bowers. "Lieutenant Dax," he called when he saw her, waving a padd.

Whew. Dax can bug someone else for a few minutes. Nog returned to his novel. *I just need to see what happens when Lughor's brother . . .*

"Results of the tactical systems diagnostic?" Dax asked, weaving around several empty tables to meet Bowers halfway.

Reluctantly, Nog tore his attention away from Ngara and Lughor's heated encounter. Though he was off duty, the weapons systems problems could spill into the next shift; an advance notice of what he was facing could be helpful.

Holding up the padd triumphantly, Sam told Dax, "Turns out we had a redundant programming problem. Nothing serious after all."

Dax took the padd and scrolled through the data. "That's a relief. Last thing we need in a firefight is a malfunctioning torpedo bay," Ezri said.

Sam nodded in agreement. "Tell me about it. I like to think I'm good at improvising, but I prefer having a full arsenal at my disposal."

Satisfied that the *Defiant*'s most pressing problem had been resolved, Nog settled in to find out whether Lughor had yet managed to break Ngara's clavicle. Permenter leaned over to see what part he was reading, "oo-ing" and "ah-ing" appropriately.

Unexpectedly, the lights dimmed. Every crewman in the mess hall froze in anticipation.

Nog's sensitive ears heard EPS conduits changing amplitude before plummeting into unhealthy silence. With *Burning Hearts of Qo'noS* tucked under his arm, Nog was on his way to main engineering before the call from the bridge rang out over the comm system: *"Red alert! All hands to battle stations! We're under attack!"*

Acrid smoke filled the corridor, stinging her eyes. Half blind, Dax and Bowers rushed onto a bridge in chaos. Along every wall, stations flickered and sparked as crewmen worked to contain fires and route control of key systems to other consoles, only to contend with new malfunctions at those stations. "What the hell happened?" she muttered, unable to hear her own words over the cacophony.

Through the smoke, she made out Vaughn standing in front of the command chair, issuing orders to engineering over his combadge. She stumbled over burned panels thrown aside to facilitate repairs, crunching pieces of shattered control interfaces and carbonized isolinear circuitry. The dim lighting wasn't making it any easier. She heard Sam curse when he saw the condition of tactical.

"Captain," Ezri said, raising her voice to be heard over the Klaxon.

Vaughn pointed toward one of the pulsing red alert lights as he struggled to hear the report coming in. Ezri got the message and found a working panel from which she could mute the Klaxon.

Nog's voice was suddenly audible to her, but he sounded frantic. *"—targeted our energy systems with millions of nanobots. They're eating through our EPS system like acid, bleeding our power. Warp core's down and we're running completely on the auxiliaries. But at the speed the nanobots are working, it won't last long."*

"Understood," Vaughn said. "Do what you can, and keep me posted on your progress. Vaughn out."

"What do we know so far?" Dax asked.

"We tripped some kind of sensor web. The instant we penetrated the field, the nanobots just shifted out of subspace and converged on *Defiant,* entering through the plasma vents. We didn't know what hit us until it was too late. I want a shipwide status report immediately." Turning to Bowers, Vaughn said, "Sam, make sure that whatever we've stumbled into is the end of something and not the beginning."

Seeing that sciences was vacant but at least partially functional, Ezri took a seat and attempted to assess the scope of the damage. Nearby, Prynn Tenmei knelt beside an unconscious Ensign Leishman, the bridge engineer on duty when the attack came. Judging from her injuries and the condition of her station, Ezri concluded at a glance that Leishman's console must have blown right in front of her.

Ezri moved to initiate a site-to-site transport to sickbay, but discovered transporters were down. She relaxed when Ensign Richter entered the bridge, carrying a medkit. Tenmei moved aside to give the nurse room to work. Satisfied that Leishman was being taken care of, Dax returned her attention to coaxing information from the uncooperative ODN.

"Lieutenant Dax," Richter said, removing hyposprays from the kit. "Dr. Bashir wanted me to let you know that high-level radiation is flooding every deck. The whole crew will need hyronalyn inoculations. But we don't have the medical staff to cover."

"I'm not sure who's available," Ezri said.

"I can help," Tenmei offered.

Richter gingerly eased Leishman up off the floor, attaching a neuromonitor to the back of her head. "I don't think she'll need surgery, but Dr. Bashir will have to make that call."

Dax called to two crewmen working by the aft wall of the bridge. "Rahim, M'Nok—get Leishman to the medical bay." Dax looked at Tenmei. Her face and hands were smudged black, and she looked as though she had a nasty burn on her jawline. "You sure you're up to volunteering, Prynn?"

"I'm fine. Honest," Tenmei said.

Richter shrugged at Dax. "It's her call."

Ezri nodded to Tenmei as the two crewmen saw to Leishman. With Rahim on one side and M'Nok on the other, they lifted the unconscious engineer between them and draped her arms around their shoulders. Richter followed right behind them after handing a hypospray to Tenmei, who stayed just long enough to administer hyronalin to Vaughn, Dax, Bowers, and the remaining bridge officer, Ensign Cassini.

Ezri finally succeeded in calling up the engineering stats. Preliminary readings indicated that the nanobots had become inert. *So they were designed to cripple us, not necessarily to kill us,* Dax mused. *The question is, how much damage have the little monsters done?* The diagnostic results, illustrated by green bars, one block stacked upon another, flashed onto her screen, but the data stream stalled with only two or three bars lit. "Come on, you can do it," she urged the damaged *Defiant.* She watched, waited, and after a few moments that felt like eternity, her heart sank. "Captain," she shouted, trying to keep the panic out of her voice. "We've got a situation."

Vaughn, working with Bowers on tactical, crossed over to the science station.

"Report," he said, resting a hand on the back of Ezri's chair.

"What you're looking at on this screen is the sum total of our power resources, including all backup and auxiliary systems," she said soberly.

Vaughn frowned at the readings. "Three or four hours tops?"

"I'd put it closer to three, but if we shut down all nonessential systems, we might be able to squeeze out a bit more time."

"Do it," he ordered. He returned to the captain's chair. "Mr. Bowers?"

"Yes, sir," Sam responded.

"Send out a broadband distress call—"

"Sir," Cassini said, working from a sensor display. "There's a ship approaching, four-hundred thousand kilometers and closing."

"On screen."

The viewer sputtered reluctantly to life, and Dax's first thought upon seeing the starship was that it looked like a fat metal wheel preparing to roll over them. An oddly configured drive unit formed two flat slabs mounted on the aft curve of the wheel, one atop the other. The part of Ezri that was Torias and Tobin, a pilot and engineer respectively, began to appraise the ship's design for visible signs of its strengths, weaknesses, and functions. *How fast can it fly? Are those weapons ports? Friend or foe?*

"They're deliberately skirting our trajectory, sir," Bowers reported. "My guess is that they're trying to avoid triggering the sensor web that got us. That may mean they're the ones behind it."

"They could have seen what happened to us and are just looking to avoid the same fate," Cassini pointed out.

"Except that they're closing on us. Down to one hundred fifty thousand kilometers and slowing."

"Hail them," Vaughn ordered.

Sam tapped in commands, waited, and tapped in more commands. He slammed his fist into the console. "Our transmitters are off-line, Captain," he said.

"We're being scanned, sir," Ezri announced, watching the *Defiant*'s internal sensors register the probe.

"What's our tactical situation, Sam?"

"Phasers and torpedo launchers off-line. Cloaking device and deflector shields nonfunctional. I'd have to say we're sitting ducks, sir."

Vaughn scowled and tapped his combadge. "Bridge to engineering. This would be a good time to tell me our propulsion systems are back on-line, Nog."

"Eighty-five percent of our EPS system is shot, sir, and power levels are plunging. We're doing what we can, but the truth is, we're not going anywhere anytime soon."

"Unknown ship now ten thousand kilometers and closing," Bowers said. "They're hailing us. Receiving a message, but I can't make heads or tails of it. If we have the algorithms necessary for decoding, the universal translator can't find them."

"Audio," Vaughn ordered.

The guttural gibberish blaring over the comm system sounded like no language Ezri had heard in any of her lifetimes. Intermittent static contaminating the stream didn't help matters.

"Unknown ship is coming to relative stop above us, *z*-plus three hundred meters away, matching our momentum. Distance is now constant." Bowers suddenly cursed and announced in a rising voice, "Transporter signal detected inside main engineering!"

Phaser in hand, Vaughn was headed for the door before the word "engineering" had escaped Bowers' lips. "Dax, you have the bridge. Sam, you're with me."

Cold and dark as a tomb, thought Nog, wishing he could trade his hypersensitive hearing for better night vision. Between the plasma coolant leaks and the EPS system, Nog had enough work to keep his entire staff—hell, the whole crew—busy for a week.

"I need more light here," Nog said, up to his elbows inside an access panel alongside the main engineering console. If he could get the primary EPS junction functional, the *Defiant* might stand a chance. Flat on his back, he gazed up at the singed circuitry, searching for reasons to be optimistic. A sharp, barky cough caused his hands to shake; the hyperspanner clattered to the floor. "Dammit!"

Lying beside him, Ensign Permenter flashed her own light in his direction. "You doing okay, boss? That last burst of plasma got you in the face," she said, concerned.

He coughed. "Without power, coolant is the least of our problems. Pass me that laser drill."

She slapped the tool into Nog's hand, retrieved the hyperspanner from where he dropped it and replaced it in the toolkit. "Heard from Nurse Juarez. Mikaela's gonna be fine."

"One piece of good news," Nog sighed deeply. "See if Senkowski and his team have managed to shore up the auxiliary power."

"Yes, sir," Permenter said, scrambling to her feet.

In the midst of the hum of tools and engineers speaking in hushed whispers, a shimmering light appeared, emitting a metallic buzz.

"Transporters!" Permenter shouted, slapping her combadge. "Intruder alert! Security to engineering—!"

Two tall alien figures in luminescent environmental suits materialized, carrying a coffin-size box between them. Nog peered in the half-light, trying to see behind the dark-tinted face shields.

One of the aliens panned the room with what to Nog's eyes looked like a scanning device, then pointed at the primary EPS junction where Nog had been working. They lifted the box between them and started forward.

"No you don't," Permenter said through gritted teeth. She held her phaser threateningly before her and stepped in front of the aliens, blocking them from approaching the junction. "Drop that thing and back up. Now."

The aliens stopped and looked at each other. One of them jabbered something incomprehensible to Permenter. He unhooked something from a utility belt and pressed a button, causing the device to glow green.

"Turn that off!" Permenter shouted.

Dammit! Nog stepped forward, drawing his own weapon. "Stay back," he warned. "Take another step and I'll fire." The alien continued to speak in its unknown language as it eased closer to Nog. *I don't want to do this, I don't want to do this,* he chanted in his mind.

The alien kept coming.

He fired his phaser. The intruder approaching him jerked and collapsed to the ground.

The shot distracted Permenter, giving the intruder she was covering the opportunity to lunge forward and spin her around. The alien hooked an arm around the engineer's neck, pulling her head back against his shoulder, using his free hand to wrestle the phaser out of Permenter's hand. Suddenly the phaser was pressed against her temple. Nodding his head toward Nog's phaser, the alien made a guttural noise. The message was clear. *Drop the weapon.*

Unwilling to risk Bryanne's life, Nog complied, then kicked his phaser off to the side.

The main doors suddenly opened and every face turned.

"Stand down!" Vaughn barked.

Bowers pivoted into the room after Vaughn, holding his phaser out in front of him. Three security officers and Dr. Bashir came racing in after Bowers. Perhaps overwhelmed by the superior numbers, the intruder threatening Permenter dropped the phaser, released her, and dove for cover behind the warp core.

Dropping to his knees beside the wounded alien near Nog, Julian Bashir opened his tricorder and performed a scan. "Our environmental conditions are suited to his physiology," he reported, easing off the alien's helmet. "Their biology is . . ." Bashir frowned and trailed off, looking as if he'd just seen something on the tricorder that puzzled him. The doctor abruptly removed a hypospray from the medkit, applying it to the alien's neck.

"Will he be all right?" Nog asked, crouching beside Bashir.

"Should be. I'll know in a minute," Bashir replied.

Okay, so who or what did I just shoot? Nog wondered. From what little he could discern in the half-light, their alien guest had leathery, hairless brown skin, a mouth as wide as his eyes were apart, and filmy membranes over his eyes. He looked amphibious, down to the ridges of cartilage where humanoid ears would be. *Weird.* Earless humanoids always looked odd to Nog.

"The stun hit him pretty hard," Julian announced to his shipmates, all of whom watched him intently. "It was close range, but fortunately his environmental suit diffused most of the blast."

Hidden in the shadows behind the warp core, the alien who had assaulted Permenter had found a ripped-out section of damaged EPS conduit and hefted it over his shoulder, obviously screwing up his courage to attack anyone who approached him. He jabbered away incoherently.

"Why are you here?" Vaughn asked, cautiously approaching the agitated alien. "What do you want with us?"

The alien responded by swinging the conduit out in front of him and shouting something long but totally incomprehensible. Vaughn backed off, maintaining a respectable distance between them.

Bashir's patient inhaled sharply, sputtering and coughing; the membranes over his black-brown eyes lifted. He lurched up, bent over and retched on the floor. Soothingly, Julian patted his back.

"I'll give you something for the nausea." He scanned his patient once more with the tricorder, frowning again before applying another hypospray. The intruder's head swayed and tipped backward. Julian braced his fall, easing him back onto the floor. Searching the medkit, he found an emergency blanket to cover the alien. "You're going to be fine. When your temperature stabilizes, you'll feel better."

"*Nijigon boko nongolik* attack us?" the alien gasped, wiping its mouth with the back of its gloved hand. "We were trying to help."

"Finally," Bowers muttered, relieved that the universal translator had succeeded in decoding the aliens' speech.

"We haven't understood your language until now," Vaughn explained to the pipe-wielding alien. "Our ship has recently come under attack. For our own protection, we had to assume that you set the weapon that damaged our vessel, and that you and your companion had hostile intentions. I'm glad to find out we were wrong.

We have no desire to hurt anyone." Vaughn holstered his phaser and spread his hands, stepping forward. "I'm Commander Elias Vaughn of the *Starship Defiant,* representing the United Federation of Planets. We're on a peaceful mission to this part of the galaxy."

The armed alien dropped the conduit and detached his helmet from his environmental suit. No, Nog saw, *her* spacesuit. Save her greenish-gray skin, she closely resembled her colleague. She ran long, knobby fingers through a profusion of violet colored braids attached to a headpiece. Skin pockets hanging off her jaw alternately inflated and deflated with each breath.

"We saw what happened to your ship," she said, her voice low and percussive. "When the snare activated, it registered on our sensors. We're quite familiar with what these weapons can do, so we came to assist you. We brought with us an energy source and were about to integrate it into your power systems when that one—" she pointed at Nog "—attacked my partner."

"Lieutenant Nog, chief engineer," he said. "And I'm very sorry. After what we'd just been through, I had no way to know you were trying to help us."

A long silence elapsed. The alien riveted her attention on Nog. She took a cautious step toward him. "If you couldn't translate our message, it was an understandable error." Her lashless lids moved up and down over her eyes several times. "I, also, am my vessel's technologist. My name is Tlaral."

Nog grinned. Her statement told him all he needed to know. Suddenly he was at her side, examining her equipment. "As engineers, we already speak the same language. Show me how this device works," he said, tipping his head back to look up at Tlaral. "Is this a duranium casing?"

"Looks like we're done here," Bowers shrugged.

Folding his arms, Vaughn chuckled and shook his head as he watched Nog and Tlaral commiserate. "Witness here, first contact—engineer style."

Within the hour, the alien technology poured energy into *Defiant's* auxiliary systems. As Vaughn learned from Tlaral, the temporary fix would power environmental and computer systems until they could reach a safe port. What would come after? Vaughn called an impromptu strategy session in his ready room to make that determination. He invited Tlaral to join them while her companion, a "technologist" named Shavoh, recovered in sickbay under Julian's watchful eye.

As the meeting progressed, Vaughn realized their options were slim.

"Other than your world—" Vaughn began.

"Vanìmel. Where there are repair facilities, supplies—whatever resources you might need," Tlaral interrupted. "I've been authorized by my chieftain to offer your ship and its crew our world's hospitality. He awaits your decision."

"You've stated my crew has few alternatives beyond Vanìmel," Vaughn said, repeating Tlaral's assertion. The technologist had been adamant that the *Defiant* come to her homeworld. From Dax's review of the sensor logs, Vaughn had learned of multiple M-class worlds with warp-capable civilizations located within a few days of their current locale. Why Vanìmel and not one of the others was a question Tlaral had yet to answer.

"Of course there are other worlds—most are some distance from here—that might be willing to offer aid to strangers. Assuming they didn't first shoot you down for trespassing," Tlaral left her chair to point out several planetary systems on the starchart displayed on Vaughn's viewscreen. "Here, and toward the Wiiru system. And that's hoping you make it that far without encountering another one of the weapons that caught you today."

From a padd, Bowers examined the preliminary data Tlaral had provided on the web weapons. "What are the odds of us being hit again?"

Tlaral explained patiently, "This whole sector is webbed. Vanìmel and my people, the Yrythny, are under siege. That's how we know these weapons so well. They are meant to ensnare *us,* but they do not distinguish between our ships and others. You might not see any ship-to-ship combat, but make no mistake, this is a war zone."

Vaughn folded his hands together, rolling the day's cumulative knowledge around in his head. The stopgap power bridge Tlaral had installed in engineering had already proved the effectiveness of Yrythny technology. Even Nog had been impressed. Pragmatically, the *Defiant* was days away from the closest advanced civilizations, assuming they could restore warp drive without further assistance. Vaughn disliked having limited options to choose from, but from appearances, Vanìmel was a solid one. He made his decision. "We gratefully accept your chieftain's generous invitation, Tlaral. From there, we'll determine how to go about repairs."

"Our government will be very accommodating," she said earnestly. "The present struggle has isolated us from our neighbors. I know our leaders will be grateful to have an ally."

Ally, Vaughn thought, musing on Tlaral's word choice. *Perhaps these Yrythny have motives beyond offering aid and comfort to weary travelers. Which begs the question . . . what will they expect in return?*

2

Before Colonel Kira Nerys opened her eyes, she resisted the impulse to thump the walls or kick the panels of her quarters, though part of her suspected that if she uttered the phrase "Computer, end program," the world as she sensed it would dissolve in an instant. Or that she would awaken from an exhausted sleep on the frozen Dakhur ground to be told it was her turn on watch. Or, even better, that she had dozed off, midconversation with Odo, and when she finally emerged to consciousness, she'd feel the warm flow of his embrace.

Sprawled diagonally across her bed, mussed covers tangled around her legs and pillow smothering her nose, Kira rightly guessed that whatever reality she was in, she slept solo. Her own smells and the definitive silence testified to her aloneness. But maybe, just maybe she wasn't actually on the station any longer, maybe she was . . .

"Ops to Colonel Kira."

So maybe she was still at home.

Deep Space 9, home? That was a place her mind couldn't go this morning.

Throwing aside the pillow, Kira sighed, rolled over, twisted her shoulders to loosen the stiffness and spoke to the ceiling. "Kira. Go ahead." She could hear a hint of a tremor in Ensign Beyer's breathy voice. The coolest heads had gone with Vaughn to the Gamma Quadrant, leaving the jumpy ones behind; Kira was learning patience.

"Um, we've just received a subspace transmission from the Cardassian ship Trager, *sir. Its captain has requested to speak with you."*

"Put it through to my quarters, Ensign. Audio only." She suddenly felt remarkably alert for having not yet partaken of her morning *raktajino.* She addressed her unseen visitor, steeling herself for her stomach's inevitable lurching. "Colonel Kira, here. Go ahead, *Trager."*

"Colonel." The rich baritone voice poured into the room, and despite being braced for it, Kira found she still had to rein in her emotions.

"Gul Macet," she said evenly. "What can I do for you?" Kira reached for her robe and cinched the waist tie extra tight. Ruffling the hair on the back of her neck with her fingers kept her hands occupied. Intellectually, she knew Macet wasn't Gul Dukat, the hated former prefect of Cardassian-occupied Bajor. Cardassia's provisional government had vouched for him, even sent her his DNA scan in an effort to reassure her and any others who might question his identity; unfortunately, scientific technobabble failed to overwrite years of conditioning. She tried repressing her gut reaction to Macet, but instinct was not easily assuaged by intellect.

"And how is life on Deep Space 9 this morning? All's well, I presume?"

"Nothing out of the ordinary. Why?" Kira took a seat in front of her companel, hastily skimming the last shift report. The tone in Macet's voice made her wonder what he knew. Like something awful might be hurtling toward the station at warp speed and he thought he'd give her a friendly heads-up.

"With all that's gone on lately—resettling the Europani, Fleet Admiral Akaar and his group coming to Bajor, your first officer leaving for the Gamma Quadrant—I know you've had your hands full."

"Goes with the territory, Gul Macet. We're a busy outpost."

"Busy supplying aid to my people among your many tasks, Colonel. We certainly appreciate all that Bajor has done for us. The last shipment of medical supplies could not have had better timing."

"I'll convey your gratitude to First Minister Shakaar the next time I speak with him." No point in telling Macet that after the Europani had been resettled on their planet, Kira had worked to bring the Cardassian relief efforts back up to their previous levels. *There must be a point to his contacting me,* Kira thought. *I hope he gets to it soon.* Chitchat wasn't typically Macet's style. On the other hand, she didn't really know what Macet's style was.

"Perhaps I can offer my thanks in person."

Abruptly, Kira straightened up. "You're on your way to Bajor?" *So much for today being uneventful.*

"To the station, actually. We should be arriving this afternoon."

"We?" Alone, Macet would be tricky; if he brought a battalion of soldiers with him, Kira might be facing a logistical nightmare. Such as how to prevent a station full of Dukat-loathing Bajorans from killing Macet on sight.

"Myself, my men, Ambassador Lang, her staff—"

"Ambassador Lang," Kira repeated. "Natima Lang?"

"Ah, you remember her."

"You could say that." Once a resident of the station, Lang had been a correspondent for the Cardassian Information Service during the Occupation. After the withdrawal, Lang's advocacy of controversial reforms on Cardassia had forced her and her students to seek political asylum back on the station. Familiarity with Lang's virulent anti-Occupation stance had always lent her a modicum of respect in Kira's mind. And then there was the Quark factor: Lang had exhibited a knack for bringing out the latent nobility lurking beneath Quark's profit-oriented paradigm. Now she's returning as an ambassador from Cardassia's fledgling democratic government.

"Ambassador Lang is on an errand from Alon Ghemor. She requests a meeting with First Minister Shakaar at his earliest convenience. You can arrange that, can't you, Colonel?"

"I'm not his secretary, Macet," Kira said tersely. "And I should probably tell you, he isn't on the station. He's in Ashalla working out the details of Bajor's admission into the Federation."

I think if you conveyed the news of our visit to Admiral Akaar, he would be pleased that Minister Shakaar has accommodated us. It's possible the Admiral might appreciate the opportunity to discuss the status of the Federation's protectorates in Cardassian territory."

Kira's eyes narrowed. "I'll be happy to pass word along to the first minister and the admiral, though I believe they might be better able to accommodate you if they knew what Ambassador Lang's business was."

"It's not my place to explain Ambassador Lang's mission. I'm merely serving as her transport and protection at the behest of our government. She will make her purpose known to the appropriate parties in due time. Meanwhile, if you could present our request to Minister Shakaar, we would be in your debt."

"I'll do what I can." *Though how willing Shakaar will be to reorganize his life around a surprise Cardassian visit is yet to be seen,* Kira thought, grudgingly giving Macet credit for excellent timing. Shakaar risked appearing to be unwilling to forgive old grudges if he failed to give the Cardassian diplomats proper attention, something the Federation delegation would certainly frown upon. "Meanwhile, why don't you transmit the specifics as to when you anticipate arriving, what kind of accommodations you'll require, supply needs and so forth."

"You're most gracious, Colonel. Transmitting requested specifications now. And I look forward to seeing you again."

"Good day to you, Gul Macet. Kira out." Kira waited for the light on her communications panel to indicate the termination of the subspace link before she contacted ops. "Ensign Beyer, how is the station's workload looking around 1400?" Kira tapped an inquiry into the computer requesting the arrival and departure schedule even as she waited for Beyer to provide the big picture. "Pull together stats on docking crew support staff, available security officers   whatever it takes to host a vessel the size of the *Trager.* And check the Habitat Ring for vacant guest quarters. I know a lot of our meeting spaces have been appropriated by the Federation delegations, so long-term conference room availability might be a concern."

"The Chamberlain—"

"The Cardassian relief vessel?" Kira read aloud from her desk screen.

"Yes, sir. The Chamberlain is set to leave at 1245 off upper pylon one. Starfleet's Kilimanjaro is off at 1315 from lower pylon three," Beyer prattled on. *"Regularly scheduled Bajoran shuttles leaving for—"*

"Ensign."

"Yes, sir?"

"I can read the schedule. What I need you to tell me is whether or not the station has the resources to accommodate the *Trager* based on the specs just transmitted to ops."

"I think we're good to go, sir."

"Transmit the appropriate docking specs to the *Trager* and notify Lieutenant Ro about its arrival. Wait. Belay that last one. Have Ro meet me at my quarters in twenty minutes."

"Yes, sir."

"Kira out."

Kira leaned back in her chair, steepled her fingers together and brought them to her lips. *The Trager comes to pay a social call . . . whatever the Ghemor government has in mind must be explosive, otherwise Macet wouldn't have been so cagey about Lang's mission . . . and what if Macet has his own ulterior motives? Time to plunge in and hope I'm not drowning in palace intrigue by day's end.* She sighed and headed for the shower, for the moment satisfied by the reality thrust into her brain by coursing adrenaline.

Accustomed to briskly exiting her quarters, Kira avoided spilling her double *raktajino* by instantaneously thrusting the mug away when her boot nearly connected with Lieutenant Ro's skull.

"You mind telling me what the hell you're doing down there, Lieutenant?" Kira asked.

Ro looked up at her. "I'm sorry, Colonel. You obviously haven't been out yet."

Kira crouched down to see what held Ro's fascination: a small, opalescent ceramic urn with a torn piece of parchment sticking out of it; two spent sticks of incense and what looked like a cheap, bronze religious icon—something one might find in the marketplace stalls around the temples. She removed the parchment from the urn and immediately recognized the ancient Bajoran calligraphy. Scanning the words for something identifiable, she felt puzzled until her eyes locked onto the characters for the word "Ohalu." She looked over at Ro whose tight-lipped expression indicated she, too, had recognized the text.

"I take it these things don't belong to you," Ro observed.

"No," Kira confirmed. "But it might be a good idea to know who they do belong to."

"My thoughts exactly," Ro said. Removing a tricorder from her belt, she scanned the items for DNA and stored the readings in the tricorder's memory. Then she touched her combadge. "Ro to Shul."

"Go ahead."

"Send someone with an evidence bin to Colonel Kira's quarters. There are some religious artifacts sitting on the floor outside her door that I want collected. Return the bin to my office and I'll handle it from there. Ro out." To Kira, she said, "It's probably nothing, but better safe than sorry."

Some minutes later, after Corporal Hava arrived to gather up the items, the two women walked toward the crossover bridge. Kira wasn't surprised by Ro's familiarity with her routine; Kira's alpha shift walks to ops were part of the station's rhythm. The walks began many years ago, taking on special significance when a stop by Odo's office became more than an excuse for exchange of gossip. Though Odo's departure might have given her a reason to take a turbolift, Kira found comfort in going through the same motions she always had, as if holding on to this one remaining vestige of an old routine would somehow help keep her grounded.

"Any idea who might have left those items?" Ro asked as they walked.

"How would I know? Since I made Ohalu's book public, I've more or less been out of the religious loop," Kira said, more testily than she intended. "Maybe an extremist crackpot thinks his tokens will prevent my evil influence from tainting the faithful."

Ro appeared to be exerting effort not to answer Kira's annoyance in kind. "Sorry, Colonel. I assumed that perhaps this had happened before. That maybe we're dealing with a precedent."

"No. I'm just as puzzled about it as you, Ro," Kira said. "But I don't plan to lose any sleep over it."

"Wasn't suggesting you should, sir. Like I said, it's probably nothing. But you do understand that nocturnal visits to the door of the station commander's quarters need to be investigated?"

Kira nodded. "Fine. Just keep it discreet. Last thing we need around here is another religious crisis."

By the time they made their way to the Promenade, the place

was already crowded and noisy with merchants opening their store-fronts, parents hustling reticent children to school, Bajorans heading for morning shrine services, Starfleet personnel attending to the business of bureaucracy and overnight shift workers flooding into Quark's. Earthy smells of roasting Andorian flatroot, a delicacy presently popular with the ops staff, seeped onto the walkway.

Kira observed Ro's apparent obliviousness to the confusion swirling around her and wondered what the security officer might be mulling over. Ro's brow wrinkled more deeply as she studied the floor.

Her head came up and she looked at Kira. "It occurs to me that since I'm not in the religious loop myself, maybe in-depth surveillance of our local faithful might be a gap in our intelligence. I'll find one of my deputies who isn't offended by my agnosticism or your Attainder to keep us briefed as to the goings-on among the prylars and vedeks," she said, with thinly veiled sarcasm. "We could be facing a religious uprising and neither of us would know about it."

Kira smiled grimly. "All right, Ro. Point taken." At least Ro felt comfortable enough to make light of her current predicament. It wasn't as if *not* talking about the Attainder would make it vanish. She paused, stopping in her tracks when a fact she'd dismissed a week ago suddenly seemed relevant to the present. "Maybe I do know something."

"Oh?" Ro said as she nodded to Chef Kaga, who was carrying a basin filled with a squirming mass of *gagh* as she and Kira passed the Klingon Deli.

Kira continued. "When I was talking to Captain Yates a few days back, she mentioned something about rumors of a schism in the Vedek Assembly."

Ro's eyebrows shot up. "Really? That's interesting. At least I know what to listen for during the next week or so."

"You could always put Quark on it."

"And give him one more reason to think he knows more than the rest of us?"

"Bad idea."

"Agreed."

Kira noted that as she and Ro walked the crowds parted a bit too quickly to be spontaneous. She never thought she'd miss the jostle and muttered-under-the-breath 'excuse mes' that used to mark her morning strolls through the Promenade. Now, it was the station visitors who offered polite pleasantries. When she appeared, Bajorans averted their eyes, finding that the goods in their arms, the padds in their pockets or the posted station schedules required their immediate attention. Kira understood they had no malicious intent; were she in their position, she couldn't honestly say that she wouldn't do the same. But she missed the smiles in their eyes, the wave of a hand, the sense of community that united them.

"Ensign Beyer mentioned a Cardassian ship arriving this afternoon?" Ro asked.

"Yes," Kira answered, grateful for the diversion from her thoughts. "A Cardassian warship called the *Trager* bearing a diplomatic delegation will be visiting the station. Its commanding officer is a Ghemor-loyal gul named Macet."

"We have semiregular visits by Cardassian ships. This one warrants special attention because—?"

How do I say this delicately? Kira thought. "Let's say that Macet bears an *extraordinary* resemblance to his maternal relatives, the *Dukats.*"

"I see," Ro said. "Exactly how Dukat-like does he—?"

"Nearly identical," Kira said grimly. "On his previous visit, understanding our people's sensitivity to his appearance, he stayed aboard his ship."

"Thoughtful of him."

"Send out a security notice alerting station residents of Gul Macet's arrival. Include a picture from his file. Explain that he's here on official business." Kira imagined panicked Bajorans stampeding to Ro's security office or whispered gossip wafting about the station causing needless fear.

"Our residents are generally reasonable people, but Macet's appearance is a surprise I doubt they'd handle very well."

"Agreed. Another layer of security presence might be a precaution worth taking."

Ro rolled Kira's words around in her head. "Plainclothes deputies. Specifically assigned to areas being utilized by the Cardassians."

"A good place to begin," Kira said. "When Ensign Beyer finishes assigning quarters, I'll have the details sent to your office."

They arrived at a turbolift. "Then with your permission, Colonel, I'll take my leave of you here."

"Dismissed, Lieutenant," Kira said. She watched Ro head off for the security office, waving to Quark who was posting the morning specials near the front door. Why her security chief would consider seeing the Ferengi socially in any capacity puzzled Kira. Maybe it had to do with keeping your enemies close.

Maybe.

Or maybe not?

Another thought she couldn't wrap her brain around this morning. At least not until she'd had another *raktajino*.

As soon as Kira stepped into ops, Ensign Beyer thrust a padd containing the minute details regarding Macet's visit into Kira's hand and began a recitation of her most recent accomplishments. Instead of waving her aside, Kira commended the anxious ensign's efforts and hastily retreated to—

—*my office,* she thought, still amazed by the twists and turns of her life that had brought her here. The more Kira flexed the muscle of her position as station commander, the more she enjoyed it. Hell, she'd be happy if the only perk of being in charge was not having to indulge every whim of the egomaniacs populating the upper echelons of the Bajoran Militia and government. Most days, her job title allowed her to skip implementing stupid directives passed down by bureaucrats. On Deep Space 9, *her* word was law.

Still, she marveled at how quickly self-interest supplanted concern for the collective good that marked the Occupation era. Former comrades-in-arms who, in earlier days, would have shared food off her utensils, wouldn't bother to acknowledge her pleas for personnel or supplies if it didn't benefit them personally. As hard as the resistance days were, Kira missed how basic Bajor's needs were then—how simple the goals. Shakaar's tireless efforts since the end of the war to make Bajor a more active participant in the community of the Alpha Quadrant were steering the people into a new and much more complex age, compelling them to face the question of how to move forward anew as Federation citizens. Bajor could reclaim its former greatness, of that Kira was confident, but not without the growing pains innate to any change. Part of Kira's job, as Deep Space 9's commander, was to help ease those pains by tackling her share of unpleasant tasks. And she knew as soon as she signed off with Macet that one of those unpleasant tasks would be awaiting her arrival in ops.

She sighed: she couldn't put off contacting Shakaar any longer. Kira took a seat behind the desk, cleared her throat and told Selzner to open a channel to Bajor.

After several annoyingly long delays as her request to speak to the First Minister went up the chain of government underlings, Shakaar appeared on the viewscreen, frowning. *"Nerys,"* he said, curtly. *"We're quite busy here."*

Kira understood his unspoken message: you'd better have a damn good reason for disrupting me during these delicate and politically sensitive negotiations. *Well, things are about to get more delicate,* she thought.

"First Minister," she began, proceeding to outline what little she knew of Macet's mission and a few of the details of his impending arrival.

Shakaar absorbed her report without surprise. *"Thank you for this news, Colonel. I admit we suspected something like this was coming. The timing is rather unfortunate; whatever the Cardassians want, it will best be dealt with on the station, I think. The talks with the Federation could easily be upstaged and we can't risk that. Make whatever preparations are necessary to properly host them."*

"Of course. Can I tell them when you'll be available to meet with them?" Kira crossed her fingers, hoping Shakaar wouldn't expect her to babysit Macet's group for an indefinite period of time.

"Give me a few days to wrap up some loose ends here. I'll be back on the station before the end of the week."

Kira hoped she didn't look too relieved. "Thank you, Minister. I'll get back to you when—"

"Come to think of it," he interrupted, *"a reception would be the polite way to receive them."*

"Excuse me?" Kira said, uncertain where Shakaar was taking this line of thinking.

"We need to facilitate their introduction to Admiral Akaar, Councillor zh'Thane, and the other dignitaries in the system. We

can't assume they'll randomly bump into each other in the habitat ring." Shakaar was gesturing animatedly with his hands, a trait Kira recognized as something he used when he was conveying his plans for a surprise assault on a Cardassian patrol. *"We need to do this properly. Show how we've mastered the finer points of diplomacy. Bajor, after all, is a citizen of the quadrant."*

"That's a fine idea, First Minister. Just let me know what kind of support you'll need from my staff. I'm assuming Lieutenant Ro will provide security—"

Shakaar smiled broadly. *"No, Nerys. I believe you're misunderstanding me. I'd like you to take charge of this event."*

Kira stared. *Be calm, Nerys. Don't let him dare you into saying something you'll regret,* she thought, biting back a curt reply she longed to deliver coupled with a vivid scatological epithet. "I'm hardly qualified to work on issues of interstellar protocol. I'd probably end up seating the Romulan attaché next to the Klingon delegate and then where would we be?" She smiled insincerely, curling her fingers into tight fists.

"Colonel, I don't need to remind you how fully occupied my own staff is at this time. Not to mention that most of the Militia is still cleaning up the vestiges of the Europani matter." Shakaar shrugged his shoulders. *"At the moment, I can't spare the personnel. You're familiar with the parties involved—you and your people have had more direct dealings with Lang and Macet than any of us—I think that qualifies you perfectly."*

Taking a deep breath, Kira rose from her seat and laced her hands behind her back, keeping her expression as neutral as she could. "Really, First Minister, I have to protest. I believe this is a case of misplaced belief in my abilities."

"My aide Sirsy will be at your disposal. She'll contact you with the list of Bajorans I believe should attend. She'll also give you our tentative schedule over the next week or so," Shakaar said. *"Have some faith, Nerys. Shakaar out."*

When her desk screen abruptly reverted to its standby pattern, the most profane word Kira knew tore itself from her throat. *He's not going to let me forget who's really in charge here. That he could use my religious situation to punish me. On his whim I could be back on Bajor planting crops before the next moon waxes.* She gritted her teeth. *And who in the hell decided I needed to moonlight as the station's social secretary?* As she touched her combadge, the inklings of a plan began forming in her mind. What was the first rule of leadership? Know how to delegate. Ensign Beyer seemed anxious to please. A crash course in diplomatic reception planning would keep her busy and out of Kira's way. And the Cardassians? She'd be damned if she had to be the only one yanked around by this unexpected visit. "Kira to Ro."

"Yes, Colonel?"

"You learned something of diplomacy when you served on the *Enterprise?"*

"Excuse me, sir?"

"The Cardassians, Lieutenant. You've been appointed to head Deep Space 9's welcoming committee."

When Beyer notified Ro that the *Trager* would be docking within the hour, the lieutenant used her remaining time to review any information Odo might have accumulated about the ship's passengers. Only Lang and Macet proved to have substantive entries in the station's database.

Because Macet's military career apparently had never taken him to Bajor until recently, the most information she found on him was in a Starfleet Intelligence file that had recently been uploaded to the station from Command. Presumably Kira had requested the file following her encounter with the gul during the Europani evacuation. Among other things, it included Captain Picard's official report on the *Phoenix* affair that Macet had been involved in, plus some recent updates by Kira and Vaughn. But little else.

Lang was another matter; Ro found the name cross-referenced in more than a dozen files outside her own. While Ro appreciated Odo's thorough but terse summaries of facts and observations, she found his subtext most illuminating.

For example, the contents of Odo's "Natima Lang" file, compiled during the ambassador's second visit to the station, fascinated Ro. She was impressed by Lang's unorthodox political views and active resistance against Cardassia's Central Command. Why the Ghemor government had selected her to run errands to Bajor was obvious. What took Ro a moment to figure out was the relevance of Odo's inclusion of cross-references to stationwide crime reports in Lang's file. She focused on a few specific items that caught her attention.

Forty-two percent reduction in illegal trafficking linked to Quark's

Six complaints regarding quality, swindling or thievery re: bar service (twenty-seven in same time frame previous year)

Dr. Bashir: dabo girl w/sprained finger from stuck dabo wheel; no harassment involved

The conclusion was obvious: Odo attributed the crime rate drop to Lang's influence on Quark. So Quark had ties with Ambassador Lang, probably romantic ones. *What did Lang have that he wanted?* she wondered. Ro might be considering her possibilities with Quark, but she wasn't stupid about him. Quark, characteristically, wasn't one to plunge into a relationship without a profit motive hovering in the background. If some mutually beneficial emotion passed between interested parties, so much the better, but love alone never justified any transaction. His steadfast belief in the 229th Rule of Acquisition, "Latinum lasts longer than lust," assured that.

She considered Lang's holo. Unless one found exotic reptiles desirable, Ro never understood what might make Cardassians attractive to anyone outside their own species: she found them brutes who gloried in the slow, sadistic kill. Never distinguishing between those who could defend themselves and the sick, weak or young, Cardassians in Ro's experience gloried in calculated brutality simply because they could.

But Lang . . . If the eyes, indeed, were the windows to the soul as the old Terran adage went, Lang's eyes lacked the chilly veil of superiority all Cardassians seemed schooled in. Rather, Lang evinced a steely softness Ro believed characterized those who knew and practiced compassion, but understood that protecting goodness required a willingness to go into battle when circumstances required it.

Her viewscreen's chronometer reminded Ro that she had less than twenty minutes before the *Trager*'s arrival—and she still had an errand to run before she greeted the station's latest guests, if "guests" was the right way to reference them. Usually guests didn't require more than uneventful arrivals, pillow pastries and quiet quarters to find comfort aboard DS9. The Cardassians might be comfortable, but the rest of the station was another matter.

After reviewing the potential pitfalls of hosting a warshipload of Cardassians, Kira and Ro determined that the station status would have to be pushed up to security level yellow. Impact to the day-to-day tasks occupying most civilians would be minimal: other than permitting only scheduled trips to and from the station, internal communications, commerce and activities would continue as normal. Those affiliated with the diplomatic delegations, Militia members and Starfleet personnel, would have to provide retinal scans in addition to the usual voiceprint ID in certain secured areas. All ships would be subject to random security checks and no last-minute flight plans would be authorized. The cargo pilots would complain, but Ro felt the inconvenience would be mitigated by the decreased likelihood of some militant anti-Cardassian group deciding to use the station as a staging ground for an act of revenge.

Reassured that her people were in position and that all available measures had been taken to guarantee an uneventful remainder of shift, Ro closed Lang's file, hoping she could glean a final insight into her guests by visiting the one person on Deep Space 9 who might know more than Odo.

Quark polished the last in a set of exquisitely crafted Gamzian crystal snifters (an idea he'd thought of after reading last year's bestseller on Ferenginar, *Packaging Your Way to Easy Profits*) when Ro sidled up to the bar. She smiled cryptically.

"After we talked the other day, I went ahead and reserved the holo-suite for tonight. Hope that wasn't too forward of me," Quark said.

Ro shook her head and shrugged. "Tonight isn't going to work. Station business."

"Come on, Laren. Tell that slave driver of a boss of yours that all work and no play makes for perpetually irritable employees," Quark said, and muttering under his breath added, "and if she's not walking evidence of that truism, I don't know who is."

"I have a feeling you'll want to be behind the bar tonight, not in a holosuite."

"Hmmmm. Must be some kind of show you've got planned if it's better than gazing at you across a candlelight dinner for two, the moonlight etching your profile in silver against the velvety night sky."

"Quark," Ro warned, her eyes narrowing.

"Fine, fine," he groused. "I'll have to unload the holosuite time, though at this late hour that might be hard to do without deep discounts . . . Then again . . ." He craned his neck around the corner and hollered into the storeroom. "Hey you, Treir!"

Treir appeared in the doorway, a two-meter statue cut from jade. "Try again," she suggested, gazing placidly down her green nose at her boss.

Rolling his eyes, Quark gestured for her to come closer. "Check the attitude in the back, Treir. This is business." He waited, looked back over his shoulder and saw his number one dabo girl still fixed in the doorway, clearly unimpressed by his dictum. And what was with the outfit? Wearing scanty and provocative exercise attire instead of scanty and provocative work attire. Disgusted, he dropped his hands to his hips. "I could fire you for being out of uniform during business hours."

She folded her arms across her chest, yawning. "Try again, Quark."

"I don't—This isn't—I refuse to—" he sputtered. Glaring, he gave an annoyed sigh, squared his shoulders and took a deep breath.

Resting her chin in her hand, Ro's eyes danced with amusement; she unsuccessfully suppressed a smile.

Insulted, Quark spun around and said, "Try to remember you're on my side, Laren." He turned back to Treir and said very slowly, "If you have a moment, Treir, I have a business proposition I'd like your input on," he punctuated his amiable sentence with a decidedly sardonic smirk.

"Sure, I have a sec. What do you want?" she said, hopping up on the counter. She threw her bare green legs out in front of her, braced her hands behind her and arched her back in a stretch.

She's trying to distract me—and it's working, Quark thought, noting how equally effective she'd been in blocking his preferred escape route. "As your employer, I shouldn't have to recite a damn sonnet to get answers to my questions. You signed a contract. I could fire you—without cause."

"Yeah, but we both know you won't. I'm too valuable to the bar," Treir said pleasantly, removing a pair of metal bracelets from her pocket and bending to snap them around her ankles.

"Hey!" Ro jumped up from her stool and circled round to where

Treir perched on the bar. "Are those new grav weights? I saw some of the Starfleet people using them during their rec periods."

Treir nodded affirmatively, unsnapped one and handed it to Ro. "They're great for extra resistance. Improves the workout like you can't believe. Just press this button here and it enhances the artificial gravity by—"

"Ahem," Quark cleared his throat. "Were we not having a discussion, Treir?"

Pressing her face between her calves, Treir grabbed her ankles and flattened her back. "You were talking. I wouldn't call that a discussion."

Quark looked pleadingly to Ro for support, but Laren was preoccupied tinkering with the grav weights. *So it's just me and Treir's fantastically pliable limbs . . .*

"Be careful with that, Ro. It can be tricky if you aren't used to them. Increase the resistance gradually," Treir advised.

Ro nodded in acknowledgment and locked one of the grav weights on her wrist.

Distracted by Treir's point-flex-bounce rhythm, Quark paused, straining to recall what started the discussion in the first place. He admired Treir's unapologetic advocacy of her own interests, but her unpredictable demands certainly slowed the pace of doing business. Then his brilliant idea reoccurred to him. "Due to an unforeseen change in plans, the bar has three hours of available holosuite time."

"Didn't I tell you that last-minute date scheduling is a surefire way to end a relationship before it starts?" Treir rolled over onto her stomach, grabbed her foot with her hand and pulled it up to her shoulder. She repeated the stretch with the other leg, maintaining her balance between the counters all the while. "Ro, I think you might have the setting on that weight too high . . ."

"My evening with Lieutenant Ro has been *rescheduled*," Quark clarified. "Leaving us with a prime business opportunity."

Ro activated the grav enhancement field with a quick flick, sending her arm plunging to the floor like a falling rock, dragging her along with it. "That was predictable," she said to the tile pressed against her cheek.

"Can we please focus?!" Quark growled.

An uncharacteristic silence descended on the bar. Servers

paused, protectively hugging their drink-filled trays since Quark deducted broken glassware and spilled beverages from their salaries; gamblers peered from behind the *tongo* wheel and over the *dom-jot* table, hoping for a front seat view of any fight that might break out; diners tossed tips onto tables, eased out of their chairs and closer to the door. Even big, brawny Hetik froze over the dabo wheel.

"As you were, everyone!" Treir said, dropping off the counter. "The house announces a complimentary round of Orion ale!" A cheer went up through the bar as she ordered several pitchers from the replicator and began filling mugs. Servers whisked by to collect the libations as swiftly as Treir poured.

Quark extended a hand to Ro and helped her up off the floor. "We'll send out a stationwide notice advertising that we're auctioning off this rare and valuable holosuite time—" he said to Treir.

"In half-hour increments," Ro suggested, brushing smudges off her uniform.

Quark continued, "Highest bidders have the company of the dabo girl—"

"Or boy," Treir said.

"Yeah, yeah. Whatever. The dabo *person* of the customer's choice. We'll have a stampede by day's end."

"Good idea. If you want me to proofread the notice, let me know." Treir finished pouring the last round of complimentary drinks and strolled toward the door.

"The idea was for you to write the notice!" he shouted at her back.

"Break time," she said apologetically. "I've got a few laps around the docking ring to cover before my next shift.'

Watching as Treir disappeared into the Promenade crowds affirmed Quark's deep belief in the incompatibility of females and finances. No sense of timing in females. A business proposition required tending, to be cultivated like a rare cheese. How typical for Treir to run off, just as the real work started. She confirmed why females proved most useful when naked, in the mud, wombs rented out. Quark retrieved another Gamzian glass snifter from the box and began polishing it. "I do *not* need my notices proofread." Ro would validate him. As females went, Ro was surprisingly like a male.

Ro shrugged. "Last time—"

"Weren't you here on business, Lieutenant?" Quark said, irritably. Maybe she wasn't as malelike as he'd hoped.

"Right. Business." She checked her chronometer. "Damn! I'm running late," she said, rising from her barstool. "Wanted to give you a heads-up. The *Narsil* won't be able to dock until tomorrow."

Quark blessed his excellent eye-hand coordination when the glass he held threatened to slide out of his grip. "What is it with bad news and station management today. You collectively wake up on the wrong side of the bed?"

"The captain of the *Narsil* didn't file a flight plan until an hour ago. We're not permitting any unscheduled dockings or departures until further notice," she said as she headed for the exit.

He followed after, walking beside her. "I have a load of Matopin rock fungi on that ship, Ro. It festers if it isn't put into proper storage so if the *Narsil*'s cargo bay needs decontamination—"

"Oh, yeah," Ro said. "Speaking of food, Colonel Kira requested that you send up a catering menu to Ensign Beyer. Minister Shakaar assigned her to oversee the planning of a diplomatic reception."

The portrait of Kira as a domesticated female doing female business—for once—at the bidding of her male superior had a certain appeal to Quark. "What's the occasion?"

As Ro outlined the parameters of Kira's latest assignment, Quark ran his thumb up and down the glass stem, mentally calculating the number of VIPs and high-powered individuals likely to be in attendance; he found the potential bottom line very attractive. "We're talking a lot of guests then. Starfleet, Cardassians, Bajorans, Trill, Andorians, Alonis. . . . Numbering in the two- to three-hundred range?"

"More or less. I suppose," she answered.

The list of high-priced, exotic delicacies he could dazzle the delegations with boggled the mind. And the bill? The Bajoran government would have to loot the temple treasury to cover his costs . . . unless . . . unless he could parlay this catering job into a more lucrative business opportunity.

So what if Bajor succumbed to all the money-free, hearts-and-flowers flourishes forced upon them by joining the Federation? Quark was confident that Cardassia would never embrace the Federation's do-gooder ideals. The Great River wasn't dammed up, merely diverted. Granted, there were issues with starvation and disease, but soon enough the Cardassians would be ripe for the picking. He'd dealt with them before (a bit on the chilly side—every client had its quirks) and being a good Ferengi, he'd adapted. Ply them with a little *kanar* and he could sell them anything.

This could work.

If Ghemor—or Shakaar for that matter—planned on hosting many more occasions like these, their governments certainly would want the finest food services in the sector. Quark's Bar: Official Hosting Services to Wormhole Worlds. Had a nice ring to it. He could have a snazzy logo designed. Maybe wrangle an honorary title of some kind or another. This little party had the potential to provide a means of securing his future (not to mention unloading more than a case or two of *yamok* sauce that wasn't too far past its expiration date to be palatable). The Material Continuum always provided to those willing to navigate its rapids. A toothy smile spontaneously filled his face. "I'll send the menu up immediately. I'm certain I can come up with something especially pleasing to all the parties."

"Thanks, Quark." She took his free hand and squeezed it appreciatively.

"You know, Laren, I'm acquainted with more than a few Cardassians," he said, hoping he already had an "in." "Who's Ghemor got coming?"

"Someone Colonel Kira worked with in the Europani crisis, a Gul Macet," she paused, studying Quark's face closely. "But the delegation is being headed by a woman, Natima Lang."

He gulped, glanced at Ro, and hoped he'd had the presence of mind to avoid gaping at the mention of *her* name. *Of course she knows about my special connection with Natima. She's playing me like a Trill* syn lara *and doing a damn fine job of it to be sure,* he thought, shivering in delicious anticipation of their upcoming night out. The potentialities of a woman who could outmaneuver him had a powerful allure.

"You might want to take care of that," Ro said, gesturing at his palm.

Quark looked down and discovered he held a handful of shards, the rest of the snifter a pile on the floor. Glass-punctured fingers drizzled blood onto his ruffled shirt cuffs. "This is a custom-made suit of the finest Tholian silk, I'll have you know. I hope you're handy with mending, Lieutenant, because I'll be dropping this suit by your quarters as soon as this shift ends."

Treir, sweaty and panting, jogged past Quark, carefully sidestepping the broken glass. "Had a bit of an accident, huh?"

He gave his star dabo girl a look. "Break time over?"

"I needed my other weight," she said, by way of explanation. "Then I'm going back out."

"On the bar," Ro said. She flattened a palm on Quark's chest, straightened and smoothed his shirt ruffles, and smiled. "I'll send Dr. Girani if you don't get that hand attended to."

And she left.

Quark watched Ro walk away, finding the confident way she threw her legs out in front of her, her hips swinging steadily, oh so alluring. When the turbolift doors closed behind her, Quark turned back into the bar, his wound reminding him of unfinished business. He retrieved a napkin from the countertop and fumbled behind the bar for a medkit. Hopefully, that stupid dabo boy had recharged the dermal regenerator after that exquisitely tasteless episode with the fingernail lady last week.

"Treir! Get this glass mess taken care of!" Quark shouted.

"Try again, Quark," Treir said sweetly, dabbing at her forehead with a bar towel.

3

Captain's Log, Stardate 53471.3

    The Defiant *has taken up temporary residence in the main storage bay of the transport ship,* Avaril. *Our hosts, the Yrythny, have offered us their resources and supplies to help restore* Defiant *to full functionality. According to the Yrythny,* the "web weapon" we encountered was designed for the express purpose of disabling Yrythny ships.

The Yrythny are embroiled in a conflict with the deployers of the weapon, the Magisterial Cheka Kingdom. The Yrythny describe the Cheka as militant imperialists who dominate this region of space. The Cheka employ a twofold strategy in maintaining their civilization: they enslave species to serve their empire, and subsequently augment their technology base through their conquests of those species. The Cheka apparently have neither the ability nor the motivation to innovate, relying primarily on the inventiveness of other species. Thus far, the Yrythny have successfully resisted Cheka conquest.

The Cheka's current goal is to genetically engineer a servitor species to act as their army (possibly as the Founders created the Jem'Hadar), and this seems to be the source of their fixation with the Yrythny. The Yrythny, they believe, hold the key to the genetic breakthroughs the Cheka seek. And because the Cheka have no compunctions against experimenting on living subjects, the Yrythny understandably refuse to cooperate.

Doctor Bashir has informed me that the Cheka have likely chosen the Yrythny for experimentation due to the unusual nature of our hosts' DNA. His scans have revealed that Yrythny genetic material is artificially enhanced, and Bashir has hypothesized that at some point in the Yrythny's distant past, an advanced species such as the Founders or the Preservers tampered with Vanìmel's evolutionary process with chromosomal segments that hastened their evolution from amphibious animals to sentients. The Yrythny call it the "Turn Key."

In an effort to coerce Yrythny cooperation, the Cheka have mined all the sectors around Vanìmel with their web weapons. They've succeeded in destroying numerous Yrythny starships as well as cutting them off from most interstellar commerce. The long-term impact of such isolation could be dire for the Yrythny, and they eagerly seek peaceful, cooperative solutions to their present dilemma. We hope our exchange of information will allow both our peoples to bet-

ter detect and defend against this unseen enemy. Our ability
to safely resume our mission may depend on this alliance.

Standing before the observation window, Vaughn watched Vanimel, a sparkling aquamarine gem of a world, become progressively more distinct as the *Avaril* advanced. The planet's ring glowed luminously beneath the light of its sun. Expecting the ring's ice, rock, and frozen gases to soon come into focus, Vaughn gasped aloud when a structure of modules, domes, and towers resolved instead.

"A city!" he said, feeling childlike awe.

Tlaral nodded. "Almost half our population inhabits Luthia. Our seat of government, our universities—all of it resides within the ring."

The closer the *Avaril* drew to Luthia, the more astonishing the ring city's design became. As civilizations build atop one another, so had the Yrythny built the ring. Older, crudely crafted units comprised Luthia's interior with little segue to the elegantly designed units mounted along the ring's exterior. Docking platforms fixed on elongated spindles extended from the edges, defining the farthest perimeter.

Doors buzzed open admitting a pale-green Yrythny who wore a headpiece of cascading rainbow colored braids, interwoven with crystal beads and metallic ribbons. His three Yrythny escorts resumed positions in the corners of the observation deck, eyes trained deferentially on the ground.

"Chieftain J'Maah," Vaughn addressed the *Avaril*'s captain. "Thank you for allowing me to take in this stirring vista."

"I wish I could have brought you to the bridge, Commander Vaughn, but I assure you the view from here is equally magnificent," J'Maah said, walking toward Vaughn, arms extended. In greeting, he grasped Vaughn by the elbows; the commander reciprocated the gesture.

Stepping behind Vaughn, Tlaral bowed her head subserviently, waiting to be addressed by her superior. The chieftain rapidly tapped his tongue against his teeth, a signal to the technologist, Vaughn guessed, that she could resume her former stance.

"We have word from our leadership. Assembly Chair Rashoh bids you and a group of your officers join him for a meal," J'Maah said, officiously. "You will dine while the *Avaril* docks, clears quarantine and other such matters. Our crews will relocate the *Defiant* to a docking bay at the port, where your people may undertake repairs. Our government is also arranging accommodations for your crew within the city."

"Your generosity is deeply appreciated, Chieftain."

"Tlaral will take you to our shuttlebay as soon as you have assembled your team."

"We'd be happy to transport down if it would be easier," Vaughn offered.

Sternly, J'Maah shook his head, vibrating the skin pockets hanging off his jaw. "Our transporters have limited range. It was the reason *Avaril* need to come so close to your ship before our technologists could be beamed over. The assembly chair's private shuttle has been sent for you. Quite an honor. Quite an honor. Go on then." J'Maah shooed Tlaral and Vaughn toward *Avaril*'s tremendous cargo bay where *Defiant* and her crew were ensconced.

Vaughn exited without protest, rightly sensing that J'Maah was accustomed to calling the shots. As per J'Maah's instructions, he would gather his senior staff and he would meet with the government leadership. But, like it or not, he would return to his mission as soon as possible.

On *his* terms, naturally.

After what seemed like a protracted trek down the docking spindle, the transport doors opened, admitting them to a customs-security area. With a Yrythny escort on either side of each member of the away team, Ezri followed behind Vaughn, Shar, Julian, and Lieutenant Aaron McCallum, security officer, as each of them submitted to full body scans and routine medical screening. For a passport, the Starfleet officers had retinal patterns entered into the Yrythny database. When security issued an "all clear," their guides led them into the public square, crowded with the trappings of Yrythny life. Merchants hawking bleating animals; food vendors with copper frying vats, their aprons splattered with oil and batter; students clustered around a fountain in heated discussion.

Ezri was content to allow "her" Yrythny to guide her through the sea of bodies, jostling this way and that. Her attention was drawn above the confusion to the lacy, carved arches, lined with enameled tiles, and the delicate curlicues painted up the pillars. Squinting, she could make out dainty flowers and vines twining around the base of the domes, made translucent by the warm light of Vanìmel's sun. She wanted to pause for a moment, to study the graceful lines and forms, but her Yrythny escorts continually ushered her along.

Choruses of Yrythny voices thudded around her, punctuated by grunts and moans as bodies crashed into each other. With Julian in front of her and her tall Yrythny guides to the side, Ezri was effectively blocked in; she allowed the crowd's momentum to propel her forward. Other than ceilings and heads, she saw only the walls, seemingly carved out of rose-colored sandstone instead of forged metal. She continued to walk, face upturned, until she crashed into Julian's back.

"Sorry, Julian, I wasn't paying . . ."

Piercing screams cut through the plaza. A crash of a tipping cart. Weapons fire.

Throwing arms out, their Yrythny escorts turned their backs on their Starfleet charges, shielding them from whatever was going on. Blocked by the wall of tall Yrythny, Ezri ducked down to look beneath their linked arms.

Up winding staircases, through ornate doors and elaborate archways, panicked Yrythny fled, tossing aside whatever they carried. But as many Yrythny swarmed out of the plaza, others streamed in through adjacent streets wielding anything from crude metal bars to beam weapons.

A mob. Heading directly for the away team.

More weapons fire. An escort next to her went slack, tumbled to his knees and toppled to the ground. Then another. Then still another. Whipping out his tricorder, Julian went to work. Vaughn shouted. Ezri couldn't understand him over the din. She heard another of the escorts trying to reason with the rioters, screaming, "Stop! These are our guests, not our captives!" But his appeals were ignored as one of the rioters clubbed him across the head with a pipe. The escort fell, whether unconscious or dead, Ezri didn't know.

So it's a lynch mob, Ezri thought. *These people are so eager for Cheka blood, they'll do anything for a taste of it, even turn against each other.*

She spotted one of their attackers making a beeline for Shar.

"Shar, watch out!" she shouted, spinning around and reaching instinctively for her empty holster. *Damn diplomatic protocols.* Weaponless, she charged forward. A Yrythny forearm hooked around her neck, yanking hard against her throat.

Complying with the beam weapon pressed against his temple, Shar swallowed hard and dropped to his knees, clasping his hands behind his head, his antennae tensed. Fury and the smells of fear stimulated his senses. The click of safeties being released seemed unnaturally slow and loud in his ears.

A guttural exclamation. The metallic sound of weapons fire. More screams. Blue gray smoke obscured his view.

Several Yrythny off to his side argued. "—reports said our defense perimeter was compromised—"

"—Cheka sending their spies—"

"—our chance to make an example—"

"—say we kill them now—"

Shar fought not to be sickened by the dull thud of metal against tissue and cracking bones. Senses threatening to overload, he fought to ignore the scent of singed flesh, the sweat-sour clothes worn by assailants, the bioelectric surges of pain.

Shar looked around him. The away team's escorts had suffered a brutal assault. Vaughn and McCallum appeared uninjured. He glanced behind him to check on Julian and Ezri, but his assailant swung the butt of his weapon across Shar's face. Blood, warm and sticky, drizzled down his cheek. His breathing became a hiss.

"Move again and I'll blow your head off," his assailant said, pressing the weapon into Shar's wound.

A companion grunted approvingly.

His emotions intensifying toward violence, Shar's eyes panned up to his assailant's face. The Yrythny was slow, clumsy. Shar's antennae spread wide, triangulating on his target—

"Fire that weapon, U'ndoh," a new voice rang out, "and I vow you'll never see the light of day again. The same goes for anyone who harms these innocent people."

His assailant paused. Shar remained still. The gun fell away from his cheek, and his assailant abruptly ran off. Slowly, Shar's need for violence receded and his breathing returned to normal. He searched the nearby crowd for his rescuer, but it seemed she had departed.

"Listen to me, Wanderers!"

Shar jerked toward the now-familiar voice, distinctive among the angry rumblings.

A Yrythny, about his height, hair twisted into a topknot, shoved authoritatively through the crowds. Ignoring their taunts, she slapped away hands and shrugged off any who dared try impede her. When she reached a pillar near the plaza's center, she flattened and rubbed her palms against the pillar's smooth surface to attain adhesion, and without a backward glance, shimmied up, kicking away a rioter who grabbed at her ankle. When a solid meter separated her from the tallest Yrythny, she anchored her legs around the pillar, tightly linking her ankles. Her coarsely woven skirt rucked up around her knees.

Cupping her hands in front of her mouth, she shouted, "Listen to me or suffer the consequences! As your Lower Assembly delegate, I speak as the law. This gathering is illegal!"

One by one, the mob turned their gazes upward. Pottery and fruit hurtled through the air, smashing against the pillar. Rioters shouted protests; others watched warily.

"Wanderer caste caught bearing weapons may be subject to punishment by death," she continued, ignoring the glass shattering above and below her.

In response, some Yrythny cast aside weapons; pieces of pipe, tools, and sidearms fell like stuttering raindrops. A few rioters disbanded, but others persisted in catcalls.

From her high perch, Shar's defender surveyed the remaining agitators haughtily. "Disperse now if you wish to avoid arrest!" she cried. "An armed patrol is on its way and is prepared to take all of you into custody. Save your energies for actions that will change our world for the better, not ones that will doom your cause and yourselves."

Her pronouncements ignited quarrels, both with her and among themselves. Primitive, hivelike contention heated the plaza as Yrythny fought with Yrythny. Head swimming, Shar saw coal eyes dark with rage; knobby fingers, grabbing, scratching; wide, gaping mouths rimmed with glistening teeth. Fevered chaos spun faster and faster around him . . .

The distant, rhythmic thud of boots thundering toward the plaza proved their leader's claim. Panicked, the crowd pushed and shoved every which way, stampeding over the fallen. Terrified shouts drowned out cries for help.

Fear reigned.

Holding her post on the pillar, the Yrythny leader watched closely, waiting for the ground situation to stabilize. Slowly, the mob dispersed, leaving only the injured and infirm. She eased her way back down, waiting, her eyes turned toward the patrol pounding slowly closer, ever closer. The mob retreated. Shar discovered that, like Vaughn and McCallum, Dax and Bashir had survived, unharmed.

Rushing down the stairs with weapons drawn, the patrol peeled out of formation to secure each arched entrance into the plaza.

"No one move!" the patrol leader bellowed. "You there," he pointed. "Stop what you're doing!"

Shar followed the gesture to Bashir, who crouched beside several of their fallen escorts. Pale, but unscathed, Ezri sat close by, monitoring one of the wounded Yrythny with the doctor's tricorder.

"I'm a physician. These are your people I'm treating," Bashir snapped, clearly agitated after their ordeal. "They sustained their injuries protecting us, so you'll have to arrest me to make me stop," he said, and continued mending a laceration.

That seemed to bring the patrol leader up short. "Fine, then." Carelessly, he kicked away refuse cast aside by the fleeing mob. He approached Commander Vaughn, who was facing him expectantly. "Are you the leader of your group?"

"I'm Commander Vaughn."

"Chief Enforcer Elkoh," the patrol leader said. "Can you explain what happened here?"

"I was going to ask you the same question."

The patrol stopped all Yrythny lingering in the plaza, demanding identification and conducting spot searches. With arms straight up in the air, civilians suspected of lawbreaking waited their turn to have their belongings inspected. Other enforcers retrieved the weapons thrown aside by escaping rioters.

Vaughn provided what answers he could to Elkoh's inquiries; perhaps they looked to him, as an alien, to offer an objective account of the incident. For his part, Vaughn was more interested in what the Yrythny female who dispersed the mob would have to say. She stood by quietly, watching, awaiting her turn. She'd removed a small computing device from her shoulder pack and was clicking through the contents when the chief enforcer thanked Vaughn and turned to her. "Delegate Keren?" he asked.

She nodded, unruffled, and replaced her computer in her shoulder pack. Shoving her hands in her pockets, she said, "Enforcer?"

The officer subvocalized something into a metal nodule mounted on his throat and then paused, listening intently to his earpiece until frown wrinkles creased his spotted forehead. "You had something to do with this?" he said accusingly. "After the last time, Assembly Chair Rashoh said that if you were discovered to be involved, directly or indirectly with any act of Wanderer rebellion—"

"I read the censure," Keren said, raising a hand to hush her inquisitor. "I caught word that there might be trouble, after the Assembly received the news of the aliens' visit. I came here to greet the Assembly Chair's guests."

"From whom did you 'catch word'?" the officer sniffed.

"That doesn't matter," Keren dismissed him breezily.

"Assembly Chair Rashoh will beg to differ. He—"

"Stop, Elkoh. *I* speak on behalf of our esteemed leader," said a Yrythny newly arrived on the scene.

To Vaughn's eye, the towering, dark-skinned newcomer resembled the chieftain of the *Avaril* in mien and garb. But where J'Maah had been thick and stumpy, this Yrythny was lean and tall, his neatly braided chestnut hair falling out of an elegant headpiece, adorned with bronze and silver embroidery.

"Yes, sir, Vice Chair Jeshoh." Elkoh offered his superior a bow before ducking away. "I may need to question you and your people further," he cautioned Vaughn.

"I'm not going anywhere," Vaughn said mildly, keeping his attention fixed on Vice Chair Jeshoh, who had turned toward the away team's benefactor.

"Ah! Delegate Keren. Why am I not surprised to find you here?" Jeshoh trained his ebony eyes on the smaller Yrythny.

"You owe these strangers your gratitude, Jeshoh," Keren said, pointing at Vaughn's crew, who continued to see to the injured escorts. They'd been joined in the last few minutes by several Yrthny medics. "The honor guard you sent to bring them to the dining hall would all be dead were it not for their medical assistance. Your own enforcers are more interested in finding the guilty than helping the wounded." Keren tossed her cloak off her shoulder.

Jeshoh turned back to Vaughn, and in a gesture Vaughn was beginning to know well reached for the commander's elbows. Vaughn responded in kind. "I bring the deepest apologies of our leadership. Please know we will do all we can to assure your continuing safety."

Before Vaughn could reply, another enforcer tapped him on the shoulder. More questions. Could he identify any of the agitators from a digital image? The soldier handed Vaughn a tablet and showed him how to scroll through the contents. While he perused the Yrythny "Most Wanted" lineup, Vaughn listened to the conversation resuming between Jeshoh and Keren.

"You risk violating your censure, Keren."

"My fellow Wanderers listen to me! The violence could have been much worse."

"For your sake, I hope an investigation proves you right."

"It will. The truth bestows confidence, Vice Chair Jeshoh."

"So you always say. I still win our debates."

"That's a matter of opinion," she countered.

"You haven't passed a single resolution this legislative session."

"My most recent is stalled in *your* committee."

"If it was a good law, wouldn't we pass it?" Jeshoh walked away before Keren could protest. "Commander . . . Vaughn, is it?"

"Yes," Vaughn said.

"The leadership awaits us. Several of these enforcers will escort us to dinner." Taking the tablet from Vaughn, he called out to Elkoh, passing the device to him. "You will proceed without further inconvenience to our guests, Chief Enforcer. Assign your best people to accompany us."

Silently, Shar and Keren walked side by side down Luthia's long, streetlike tunnels past shops, laboratories, supply depots and military checkpoints to a pathway that ran along an artificial river. Swift currents hurried along beside them, foaming and crashing against red coral barriers and boulders, which were weathered smooth. He found the soft random sounds of the water calming.

With each twist of the path, with each bridge they crossed, Shar became increasingly amazed at how much more of a "city" Luthia was than any of the Federation's space stations. No matter how much time he spent on Deep Space 9, he never forgot that he was swaddled in metal and conduits. Here, the life pulsing through the city might wholly push aside his disbelief.

A dense, mixed population of civilians, government and military personnel created a stimulating mix of textures and scents: salt-water-filled bins of fish; tangy, unwashed clothing and rotted wood; butter-soft slippers made of skins; homespun cloaks, gaudy baubles, tubs of congealed cooking fats. He was reminded of some of the more rural communities of Andor.

Shar avoided looking directly at Keren, trying instead to study her unobtrusively. Not nearly as muscular as many of the Yrythny they'd encountered so far, she had a slender build. Her charcoal and cocoa-colored facial stripes blended in with the nondescript head-piece she wore. Her clothes were suitable for farm work, and yet apparently she was some kind of government leader.

Keren shoved her hands into her pockets and hummed a discordant tune while she walked. Shar lengthened his stride so he could keep up. Surprisingly, he felt not the slightest bit winded as he chased alongside Keren; he'd grown accustomed to his body taking time to adjust to the gravity or the atmosphere of a new world, but Luthia already felt comfortable to him.

"Thank you," he said finally.

She raised calm eyes to Shar's frankly curious face. "Are you addressing me?"

"You saved my life," Shar offered by way of explanation. "Thank you."

She shrugged, adjusted the ties on her blouse. "The fools who attacked misunderstood the news from the *Avaril*. They thought you were Cheka spies, captured when you encroached on our perimeter. Of course, it may be that you *are* spies, but we've no proof of that. I'm afraid that our ongoing conflict with the Cheka has many of our people on edge. The helplessness, the anger sometimes feeds the mob mentality and overwhelms common sense."

"I see. Then, may I ask . . . Why me, Delegate Keren? My shipmates—"

"You have me at a disadvantage," Keren interrupted. "While you know me, I don't have the benefit of your name."

"I beg your pardon. Ensign Thirishar ch'Thane, science officer, *U.S.S. Defiant.*"

"Thank you. I liked the look of you, Ensign ch'Thane. Kneeling there, you didn't seem fearful." She studied Shar. "More curious."

"I have many questions," Shar said honestly.

"As do I. In exchange for your life, may I ask the first?"

When he realized Keren appraised him as candidly as he did her, he felt his face become flushed. *For what other reason have I come on this journey, than to ask questions and seek answers?* "Please," he said.

"Dammit!" Ezri whispered, hopping on one foot. The thud of her boot resonated through the cavernous hall of the massive government building into which the away team had been led.

Startled, Julian looked up from his tricorder. "Are you hurt?" He glanced at their soldier-escort, offering a smile. No need to panic the local constabulary.

Wearing a pinched expression, she grunted, "I walked into that bench over there. My shin hurts like hell." She shook out her leg, rolled her shoulders.

Julian scrutinized her nervous fidgeting. Yes, Ezri had assured him, several times, that she felt fine. Aside from heightened adrenaline—entirely normal, considering—and a few minor bruises on her throat, his tricorder readings bore her out. Maybe. Her blinking, her jerky movements—uncharacteristic clumsiness . . .

"Don't say it," she said perfunctorily.

"What?"

"I could tell you were going to say it."

"Say what?"

"You had that look," she said, screwing up her face. "The look you reserve for an infected specimen."

"Not fair," he protested, shaking his head. "I'm always concerned about you." He suppressed the desire to put his arm around her. *One doesn't squeeze the X.O. on duty,* he reminded himself. By mutual agreement, he and Ezri were keeping their relationship in their quarters for the duration of their mission. "We've had a rough day. We're all exhausted. We're on an alien planet in a strange environment—"

"So why aren't you looking at Commander Vaughn that way? Or Shar? Or Aaron?" she challenged.

He considered her, and by some not-genetically-enhanced instinct, Julian knew that Lieutenant Colonel Travis had stood a better chance of defeating General Santa Anna at the Alamo than he, in this moment, had in winning an argument with Ezri Dax. "Shall we go to dinner?"

"You're trying to change the subject."

"As a matter of fact, I am," he admitted, following their group into an expansive dining hall. Rich, spicy smells instantly assaulted him, very reminiscent of a victory celebration General Martok had once hosted aboard the *Rotarran*. A few of his non-Klingon guests had lost their appetites (and their earlier meals) after prolonged exposure to the gamey buffet. He hoped his crewmates could avoid such queasiness now, especially Ezri, who in the past had struggled with nausea.

The thought reminded him of something. "Being in Luthia doesn't make you spacesick?"

She snorted indelicately. "I beat that months ago."

"So far above a planet's surface, with all these twisting hallways? And that bowl over there appears to be filled with something akin to *gagh*." He peered more closely at a passing plate. "Possibly a tangerine-colored sea anemone."

"Keep it up and you just might *make* me sick."

Modestly dressed in rough linens and bland earth tones, Yrythny attendants guided the Starfleet guests to the head tables. Twenty or so Yrythny, dressed similarly to Jeshoh, stood beside benches waiting for their guests. When the officers from *Defiant* assumed their places, the attendants scurried to the back, eyes cast down.

The strong social parameters he'd observed since meeting the crew of the *Avaril* led Julian to believe that the Yrythny were a caste-based society. The basis of those castes wasn't readily obvious; he wondered if their unusual genetics figured into their designations. Headwear, it seemed, denoted rank. Turbans, hairpieces, skullcaps and scarves in vivid colors, some with beads, others with elaborate embroidery contrasted sharply with the nondescript veils and hooded cloaks he'd seen in the plaza and streetways of Luthia.

Thus far, everything he'd learned about the Yrythny, whether from observation or while treating their wounded, intrigued him.

At the front of the room, an Yrythny wearing sky blue robes clapped his hands together three times. He lifted his arms to the heavens and chanted an invocation. Joining hands, the other Yrythny focused eyes upward in imitation of their cleric. When the chant concluded, hosts and guests alike sat down.

Servers with heads swathed in scarves carried in plates of cold yellow and green vegetables drizzled in creamy sauces, flat, wide noodles and pots sloshing with shellfish broth. Commander Vaughn directed the servers to Julian, who scanned each dish for metabolic compatibility. After a brief analysis, he signaled Vaughn with the all clear. The commander scooped a generous helping of noodles tossed with pieces of a purple squidlike life-form onto his plate; the others followed suit.

Ezri reached toward a plate of kelp-colored fishcakes.

Julian cleared his throat sharply.

She sighed. "What now?"

"If you feel your spots starting to itch . . ."

Ezri rolled her eyes. "I know the drill, Julian. I don't need you to mother me."

He frowned. "Did it ever occur to you that I'm simply looking out for the welfare of *Defiant*'s first officer?"

She scooted over, placed a quick kiss on his cheek and whispered, "Tell you what. After food and a shower, we can climb into bed and you can conduct a thorough examination of *all* my spots. In the meantime, *relax*."

Julian laughed and shook his head. Admittedly, he tended to overcompensate where Ezri was concerned, but he had no desire to embarrass her or undermine her authority. Perhaps he could ease up. He kissed her back, pleased by the prospect of a leisurely late night. And spot #514 was a particular favorite.

Copying the Yrythny, Ezri used her hands and fingers as utensils, rinsing them in the water basins when she changed from one item on her plate to the next. The efficient servers periodically passed by to swap out dirty basins for clean ones. The food supply, comprised mostly of marine life, seemed endless. Whenever she cleared one plate, another appeared. Julian had escaped to speak with Vaughn three plates ago. Finally, she cleared a plate filled with pulpy fruit and syrup-soaked biscuits and no plate replaced it. Grabbing her stomach, she slumped over. *I've eaten enough to last me the rest of the day,* she thought, *and considering that the replicators on* Defiant *won't be working anytime soon, that's not a bad thing.*

On her immediate left, the Yrythny she remembered as being called Jeshoh was finishing his own meal.

"If you don't mind, I'd like to know your people better," she began, hoping he wouldn't find her curiosity offensive. "Vice Chair Jeshoh, isn't it?"

Dipping his fingers in the basin, he rinsed the last of his meal away and dropped his hands to his thighs. "Yes. I understand we have similar roles."

"Oh?"

"Like you, I am—" a filmy lid dropped over his dark eyes before abruptly opening "—second in command. Talking may prove enlightening for both of us."

The servants cleared off the tables, brushing crumbs to the floor and wiping the surfaces in front of the guests. Jeshoh spun away from the tabletop giving the workers more room; Ezri did the same, so they sat knee to knee.

"I heard Delegate Keren use the term 'Wanderer,' and call them 'her people.' To what was she referring?" The slavish servility she was witnessing piqued her interest. She respected the cultural values of other worlds, but being fawned on by attendants who didn't dare meet her eyes or accept "thank yous" made her uncomfortable.

"You're perceptive," Jeshoh said, bemused. "We are two peoples. I am Houseborn, meaning after my sea time as a hatchling, I returned to the place where my parents laid me. I was reared in House Perian, the First House of the Yrythny, on the shore of the north continent off the Black Archipelago.

"The Wanderers have no home. Like the Houseborn, they, too, are swept into the sea as hatchlings, but when the time comes to make the transition to the land, they fail to return to their place of origin. Lacking the proper instincts to heed the voice of the water, the Wanderers are proven to be weak. They work harder to attain the same knowledge we Houseborn come by naturally."

Ezri refrained from commenting. Instead, she asked, "But where do Wanderer hatchlings end up, if not at their own Houses?"

"They come ashore to other Houses, where they are taken in and raised as servants."

"And this Delegate Keren," Ezri said, recalling the slightly built, feisty Yrythny leader who scaled the pillar and effectively dispersed the mob. "She is—?"

"Delegate Keren is a Wanderer. A representative elected to voice Wanderer interests in the Lower Assembly. She is also trouble," he added quietly. "Over time—in the last two centuries especially—the Wanderers have attained more rights and privileges. Keren, I'm certain, would try to convince you otherwise."

"I wouldn't mind hearing both sides of the story," Ezri said truthfully.

Jeshoh smiled and shrugged. "I suspected you wouldn't. You seem very inquisitive, which is a trait my people admire. But I feel I should warn you, she'll make it sound worse than it is. With their advanced educations, Wanderers have earned positions in the sciences and arts. They were chiefly responsible for the building of Luthia, originally as an escape from planetside living. Now, Luthia hosts half our population. Wanderers still live separate, primarily congregated in the oldest part of the ring. They call it the Old Quarter."

"I take it the mob in the plaza were unhappy Wanderers." *Unhappy was putting it mildly. Maybe enraged? Perhaps even seething with retribution?*

"The Wanderers believe the Houseborn will use the war with the Cheka to rescind their rights—or use it as an excuse to avoid advancing their rights. Either way, they're misguided." While he spoke, a servant knelt beside Jeshoh, poured oil from a small pitcher onto his arms and massaged it into his skin. He carried on without acknowledging her presence.

Ezri pursed her lips, considering the best way to phrase her next question. "From what you've said, it sounds like the Wanderers have tremendous opportunities. What else do they want?"

Jeshoh sat silent, submitting his limbs to the servant's ministrations: the other arm, a lower leg, the other leg. Ezri hoped his silence meant he was considering her question, not that she had overstepped her bounds.

Finally, he clicked his tongue, dismissing the servant. He said softly, leaning closer to Ezri, "They want arms—to serve in our military. They don't trust the Houseborn to defend them," he shook his head. "They want to join the Houseborn in the waters and have offspring. But they fail to see that passing on their flawed instincts will weaken our species."

"And in spite of progress toward more equal rights for the Wanderers, you still have a hard time living together, I take it?" *If the groups in the front and back of this dining room not mingling are any indicator, I'd have to say the answer is "yes,"* Ezri thought.

"The Cheka barricades magnify the problems. Since we began associations with other species, our society has reconfigured itself around interstellar trade. Supply shortages and economic setbacks make people afraid and angry." Jeshoh paused, looked around to make sure no one was listening before whispering, "Rumors of a Wanderer underground movement are being voiced in committee meetings, not just gossiped about in the marketplace."

And the real reason we were almost killed in cold blood starts to emerge. "That's a very serious situation."

"And we've yet to find a practical way to resolve it. Neither side trusts the other," he paused again, looking around to see who might be listening in on their conversation. "We haven't had war on Vanìmel in 200 years, but . . ."

Ezri grasped the Vice Chair's meaning. Though the Yrythny had lived in relative peace for two centuries, Jeshoh feared conflict was imminent. *What have we stumbled into?* She wondered what Vaughn and the others had learned.

Unbidden, she remembered how Curzon's deft maneuvering had prevented one of the early Proxcinian crises from exploding into war. "You say you traffic with other species routinely. Have you thought about utilizing third party mediation to open up talks with the Wanderers?" she said finally.

"Explain," Jeshoh said, puzzled.

"Bringing in a neutral party to facilitate talks between the warring sides. Oftentimes, someone from the outside—one who isn't invested in one side or the other—is better at determining what points are negotiable and what points each side needs to be flexible on." As she spoke, she drew an imaginary diagram on the tabletop with her fingers. "A third party functions as the apex of a triangle, balancing the single line binding the conflicted parties together by drawing lines among all three."

Jeshoh smiled indulgently. "Unfortunately, economic relationships being what they are, our neighbors may be counted upon only to act in their own best interests. Actively helping to stabilize the situation on Vanìmel would damage their standing with the Cheka, who are the dominant economic power in this region."

From the table behind Jeshoh, the Yrythny cleric turned around abruptly, throwing aside a bowl of fish noodles to gape at Ezri. "A third between the Wanderers and the Houseborn," he said, eyes wide with excitement. He didn't bother to plunge his dirty hands into the basin, instead electing to rub them on his robes.

Sipping from a water glass, she reiterated, "Third party mediation is hardly a new idea."

"The third forges a whole peace?" the cleric persisted.

Ezri looked at the cleric, then at Jeshoh for clarification—he had none—and then back at the cleric. "I suppose," she said, wondering what he was getting at.

The cleric grabbed Jeshoh by the shoulder and shook him. "It's the Other. What she says follows the pattern of the Other."

Jeshoh's confusion gradually dissipated. "Perhaps," he said, prying the cleric's fingers off his shoulder. "It may be worth considering, at least."

By now, loud Yrythny voices clamored on all sides of Ezri; benches were shoved back as individuals of all ranks squeezed into the spaces around her, and with shoulders and elbows bumping, gesticulated madly. Julian shot her worried looks; she ignored him. Contrary to what he might suppose, she did not start whatever this thing was and she wasn't about to be blamed for it. He was a little too quick to fall in with Benjamin and his "She's a Dax. Sometimes they don't think, they just do" aphorism. *Had Benjamin ever had the nerve to say that to my face? Hah!* No matter what anyone might think, she didn't go looking for trouble all the time. Especially not *this* time.

Another Yrythny beside Jeshoh stood up, raising a hand, asking for acknowledgment from the Yrythny leader, Rashoh, who was seated beside Vaughn. "Assembly Chair, our good cleric has a rather startling idea that merits immediate consideration!"

With one swift movement, the cleric hefted Ezri to her feet, threw a food-speckled arm around her shoulder and clutched her to him as he approached the head table. "Good Master, Lensoh speaks truly. This one—this visitor from far away—has been sent by the Other to finally bind together our fractured world." He squeezed Ezri for emphasis, his fingers bruising her upper arm.

"I never said that," Ezri protested. "That's *not* what I said. I said that the Wanderers and Houseborn should consider third-party mediation . . ."

Vaughn looked at Ezri quizzically; she shrugged her shoulders as if to say, *I swear to you I don't know what he's talking about.* Still, with virtually every pair of Yrythny eyes fixed on her, she knew she'd be doing some accounting to Vaughn later but she hoped it would be for laughs. Vaughn had a decent sense of humor. Usually.

To the cleric, Rashoh said, "Explain further." But his frown remained focused on Ezri.

"This one has suggested the introduction of a Third. To complete the triad of Wanderer and Houseborn. To balance our people and facilitate peace," the cleric said. "And I believe this one, this Ezri Dax who stands beside me, has been sent from the Other to help us. She will be the Third!" In benediction, the cleric raised his arms to the ceiling. "Praise the Other!"

The crowd murmured a disjointed chorus of honorifics to the Other before the drone of chatter consumed the room. Trays clattered to the floor and benches toppled as they eagerly discussed this latest development.

"There must be a misunderstanding here," Vaughn said, attempting to quell the excitement in the room before it spread any further. "Lieutenant Dax will share our knowledge and experiences with you, but any other role would be inappropriate." He gave Ezri a meaningful look.

"I have to agree," Ezri chimed in at once. "It wasn't my intention to involve myself in your internal affairs."

"You cannot deny the Other's intervention," the cleric insisted.

Many Yrythny politicians, including Keren, had left their tables to assure themselves a position where they could better hear and be heard. A few tried to worm their way closer to Ezri, hurling questions at her faster than she could answer them. She rotated toward each voice in succession, trying to match what was being said with the speaker. *What I wouldn't do for Jadzia's height about now,* she lamented. Ezri saw Vaughn's hand above the crowd, as he jerked his thumb back to indicate he wanted her at his side, posthaste. Squeezing her way past the servants and politicians and clerics, she walked up to her CO, carefully placing her back to the crowd.

Vaughn said, over the cacophony of Yrythny voices, "If you'd excuse me, Assembly Chair, Vice Chair, Honorable Cleric, we must take leave of you and your good people at this time." The murmuring quieted, the Yrythny waited respectfully for Vaughn to continue. "My officers and I need to check on the status of our ship and those we left behind. Please accept my thanks on behalf of all of my crew for your gracious hospitality."

Perhaps realizing the uncomfortable position their guests were in, Rashoh and Jeshoh interposed themselves between the away team and the crowd as Vaughn led his people toward the exit. The cleric, who originally fingered Ezri, included himself in the leadership, staring after her with reverential wonder. She groaned inwardly. At least the other Yrythny were clued in that they needed to allow their leaders—and their guests—to proceed without interference.

In the spacious hall beyond the dining room, the Yrythny leaders offered the entire *Defiant* crew guest quarters, far removed from the civilian areas; reduced trade and tourism in the wake of the Cheka conflict had left their hosting facilities completely empty. The away team learned that one of Rashoh's aides would escort them to the docking bay harboring *Defiant,* where further instructions would be provided.

The discussion proceeded without Ezri commenting. She thought that was best.

On their way back to the *Defiant,* Ezri related her conversation with Jeshoh and how her neutral comments had been seized on by the cleric and twisted into something unintended. "At least I haven't been elevated to an Yrythny deity," she quipped. *Though godhood would have appealed to Curzon.*

"For all our sakes," Vaughn replied, "you'd better hope it stays that way."

* * *

In the complex of guest accomodations where the bulk of the *Defiant* crew had been housed following the away team's return to the ship, Shar tried to concentrate on the database terminal his hosts had provided each member of the crew. Unfortunately, he was finding it hard to focus.

Shar gave up counting the number of times he'd heard Vaughn, Dax, and Bashir's doors open and close over the last hour. He didn't need to eavesdrop on their conversations to miss the tension in the air; his antennae hadn't stopped itching since Vaughn and Dax had met with Nog back at the ship.

Working with Yrythny engineers and his own team, Nog had made supply lists for the *Defiant*'s repairs. The Yrythny had—or could get their hands on—most of what Nog needed to fix the ship. How to defend the *Defiant* against the Cheka nanobots was proving to be the challenge, one that might take longer than the actual repairs. Even their hosts admitted they didn't know how extensive the web network was in this sector; the Cheka apparently redeployed the webs frequently at random coordinates in order to make space travel as dangerous as possible for the Yrythny. The only reason *Avaril* had been able to come to *Defiant*'s aid at all was that the particular web that had snared *Defiant* was one the Yrythny had recently discovered. With the web weapons invisible to sensors, the commander didn't want to make a move until they developed a workable countermeasure.

Not one engineer had yet shown up at the guest quarters. When it became clear Nog wasn't planning a dinner break, Vaughn finally sent Lankford and T'rb up with food. Shar expected that Nog would catnap on a cot by the ship: the situation was that critical.

Everyone without a specific assignment had been ordered to comb the Yrythny database for information on the Cheka and their web weapons. So once Shar had retired to his quarters for the evening, he settled in front of his terminal and tried to go to work—except that the continuing discord among his senior officers had proven very distracting.

Of course, he knew that something else was causing his mind to wander this evening, something that had nothing to do with the stir Lieutenant Dax had inadvertently caused. Ever since he'd examined the tricorder readings Dr. Bashir had taken of the Yrythny back aboard *Defiant*, Shar had been preoccupied with their genetic

"Turn Key." The opportunity to research it in the Yrythny's own database was proving too great a temptation. In delineating its nature to Commander Vaughn, Dr. Bashir had described it in human parlance as a "skeleton key," designed to unlock any gene, even reconfigure it, to hasten the evolution of a species. The implications of the Turn Key had a particular allure for any scientist with an interest in cytogenetics. Especially one from Andor.

The climate of Luthia suited Shar well. Healthy Yrythny skin required high levels of humidity, he'd learned, an environmental condition that also suited Andorian physiology. Though the Yrythny didn't sleep in beds, but rather, cushioned depressions in the floor of their sleeprooms, Shar found the accommodations lavish, almost decadent for a species whose technology was still about two hundred years behind that of the Federation. Overstuffed couches and planter boxes flowing with flowering vines were mounted on every wall except the one that opened into a round courtyard. A burbling, multitiered fountain surrounded by gardens textured with ferns, trees and lacy crimson ground cover provided a pleasant view from every apartment.

The three stories of the *Defiant* crew's rooms extended off the courtyard like spokes of a wheel, providing them easy, private access to each other. Dax and Vaughn's quarters were on the level above Shar. Several times already, the commander and the lieutenant had ascended and descended the stairs situated off to the right of Shar's courtyard wall. Many of his crewmates had lounged by the fountain reading or chatting, enjoying the view of the stars through the clear dome overhead. General consensus seemed to be that the housing conditions were making this unplanned mission detour more palatable.

As had tended to happen on this mission, Shar's thoughts strayed home whenever he had empty time. Every day since last seeing his bondmates on Deep Space 9, he found himself yearning for them, and for the intimacy of the *shelthreth* that he'd denied the entire bondgroup by accepting this assignment to the Gamma Quadrant. And Thriss . . . if he allowed his thoughts to linger too long on her, he knew he'd lose his ability to think. *Thriss would love it here on Luthia* . . . He stopped that thought before it went any further: staying focused on his research into the Cheka and their weapon was his best recourse against loneliness.

The courtyard doors parted, admitting the sounds of bleeting avians, trickling water and the brush of soft footfalls. Shar expected to see Nog and started when he recognized his rescuer from this afternoon, the Yrythny delegate. In the lavender light of Luthia's dusk, Keren stood in shadow, the edges of her face eerily translucent, but her energy—unmistakable. *What could she possibly want? Maybe she's mistaken my quarters for Ezri's, right above me,* he thought.

"I've come with answers, Ensign ch'Thane," she said airily, her draping clothes rustling as she walked. She first opened the sleep-room door and then the closet.

"My roommate isn't here, Delegate," Shar told her, wondering what she'd come to tell him that required privacy.

"Excellent. Then you can come with me without being missed."

After the dinner-hour controversy, Vaughn had ordered all personnel to minimize unsupervised contact with the Yrythny until the "Lieutenant Dax situation," as it had come to be referred to, was resolved. "I need to check with my commander, he'd—"

"Don't." She held up a hand. "Please trust me. All I want is for you to see the other side."

"The other side of what?"

"Of this. Of Luthia. Of my people." Keren dropped down on the couch beside him. "Our city is abuzz with talk about the Other sending a Third. There are those who see it as a sign, others as a Houseborn trick. It's not your commander's fault that you've only dealt, thus far, with the Houseborn leadership. They know little of my people's truth, our history, our concerns. And that's why I've come."

Shar could see why she was a politician: she was a persuasive orator. Perhaps this was what his *zhavey* had been like when she was younger. She didn't seem duplicitous, and she *had* saved his life. Commander Vaughn's instructions notwithstanding, perhaps this was an opportunity to find other resources in Luthia, outside official channels, that might help his shipmates. Shar decided to trust her.

"Very well," he said.

She tossed a thin, heather-brown cloak at him; like hers, it featured a large hood and fastened at the neck. She also provided him with Yrythny-style footwear in lieu of his boots. The thin slippers, comprised of fabric tops laced together with roughened, leathery skins for the sole, would be virtually soundless as they walked. The need for such attire was obvious: to avoid drawing attention to himself or to Keren. Once he'd fastened the cloak and pulled the hood up over his head, flattening his antennae among his locks as he did so, Keren brought a finger to her lips and gestured for Shar to follow her. Slipping through the courtyard, the leaf fringes of rangy trees provided additional cover. Vanìmel's second moon had risen, casting cold pale light over their path.

"You can't seriously think this idea has merit, Dax," Vaughn said, extending his legs onto the coffee table. He sipped his brandy and waited for her reply.

Ezri, hands knotted behind her, walked the room.

Was this the third or fourth time through this conversation? For his part, Julian seconded Vaughn's opinion, but wasn't about to do so in front of Ezri. She would see it as a personal betrayal, when in reality it was a question of propriety. Starfleet regulations, to say nothing of the Prime Directive, provided narrow criteria for any kind of intervention in a non-Federation world. Because he outranked her, technically, Julian could voice his objections without subverting her position, but he knew Vaughn would do a far better job than he would at pointing this out.

"Look, I know this is a little out of the ordinary," Dax said, continuing to pace. "But I've been going over this in my head since dinner, and I'm just starting to wonder if maybe we're being a little too quick to dismiss the idea. After all, they were the ones asking for my help. Given the aid that they're providing us, is what they're asking really so out of the question?"

"You're talking about helping to facilitate a fundamental change to their societal structure," Vaughn said. "There are protocols in place for such an undertaking, and for good reasons."

"But according to Jeshoh, that change has already been taking place for centuries. Whatever the underlying reasons for this schism between the Houseborn and the Wanderers, these people know they have a problem. They want help solving it. All I'd be offering is the benefit of an outside perspective."

Vaughn sighed. "Let's not kid ourselves, Dax. Your 'outside perspective' is going to be viewed by these people as *guidance.* They already see you, you'll pardon the expression, as a prophet. Someone who's come to impart otherworldly wisdom. That just seems like the wrong place to begin a relationship with the Yrythny. If there's to be a solution to their internal dilemma, wouldn't it be more meaningful for them to find it, rather than as a pronouncement from on high?"

"The Yrythny are facing crises on many fronts," Ezri persisted. "We're already working with them to develop a defense against the Cheka. How is what I'm proposing to do any worse? And besides—if Julian's right, the Yrythny species owes its very existence to outside intervention. Hell, we all do, don't we? As individuals and as entire species, the people of the Federation are who they are today because of how they've influenced each other. That's not interference, that's *life.*"

Vaughn rubbed his temples. "God, I hate arguing about the Prime Directive." He looked across the room. "Well, Doctor? You've been uncharacteristically quiet this evening. Do you have an opinion on this?"

From the look on Vaughn's face, the commander knew precisely what he was doing in asking for Julian's opinion. Without meeting Ezri's eyes, Julian cleared his throat. "I think there are valid points on both sides of the argument," he said neutrally. "If we go forward with this idea, I believe the best course would be simply to make the Yrythny aware of their options by showing them historical precedents from our own databases, and then leaving the decision up to them as to whether any of those is right for Vanìmcl."

Vaughn looked back at Ezri. "That actually sounds reasonable to me. Dax?"

Ezri was frowning at Julian. "If it comes up tomorrow, sir, I'll follow the plan we've discussed."

"Thank you, Lieutenant," Vaughn said, rising from the couch. "I'm going to check in with Nog before I call it a night. Get some rest, both of you. Tomorrow will be a long day." He let himself out the balcony door.

Julian steeled himself, waiting for Vaughn's footsteps to fade away, knowing as soon as they did . . .

"Thanks for your support there, *Doctor!*" Ezri slouched into an overstuffed armchair designed for the long-legged Yrythny. Her feet dangled above the floor.

"Let's distinguish between my support for you as my first officer and my support for you personally—"

"Don't you dare hide behind our relationship! You should have more confidence in me!"

"What are you talking about? Of course I have confidence in you. But what does that have to do with . . . wait a minute." Julian stared hard at Ezri; he could almost see her mind spinning a plot. "You think you could mediate this conflict, don't you?"

Ezri didn't answer.

"You do!" Julian exclaimed. "I can't believe this. You really think you can do it, don't you? No challenge is too great for Ezri Dax."

"I don't know what you're talking about."

"Oh, I think you do," Julian said. "This whole thing started when Commander Jast was killed. Ever since then, you've been relying more and more on your past lives. This isn't you, Ezri!"

"And just how the hell would *you* know?" Ezri snapped. "Let me clue you in on something: Before I was joined, I was a damn good officer. Maybe not as stellar as the superhuman Doctor Julian Subatoi Bashir, but as Ensign Ezri Tigan I was levelheaded, assertive, even ambitious. Then I become the unplanned ninth host of Dax, and for the first time in my life, I don't know who I am anymore. *That's* the Ezri you got to know, my love. And now, when I've finally figured out how to integrate my past lives and apply them to my own personal evolution, you think I'm not myself. But what you're not getting is that the Jadzia you were getting to know that first year, the one who hesitated, and got nervous and spacesick all the time—*she* wasn't me."

Julian looked away for a moment, then forced himself to meet her eyes. "You said Jadzia," he said quietly.

"What?" Ezri snapped.

"You referred to yourself as Jadzia just now."

Ezri stared back uncertainly, obviously replaying the conversation in her mind. "That was an honest mistake."

Julian nodded. "I know it was. Because as a doctor who's spent years studying Trill symbiosis, I know that in an unplanned joining, it can take quite a while for the host to find her equilibrium. So I'll ask you just one question, and then I'll let the matter drop. Do you really think you've found yours?"

When Ezri declined to answer, Julian wondered if he'd made a mistake confronting her with this tonight. "Look, it's been a stressful day for both of us. Maybe we're both not ourselves tonight. We'll be more clearheaded in the morning. Let's go to bed."

"Excellent suggestion." She shuffled off to the sleeproom.

Julian waited for a proper interval to pass before following after her, knowing he probably wouldn't be counting her spots tonight. He heard her toss her combadge on a table, kick off her boots, unfasten her uniform. *Now would be good.* When he reached the doorway, Ezri was waiting. She threw a cushion at him.

"What?" He clutched the pillow against his chest.

"Get some rest. Captain's orders," she said, and locked the door.

Shar tripped on the uneven floor gratings. Every other step, he bumped into cloaked Yrythny, streaming out of homes and work. The Old Quarter hummed with night activity. Shar and Keren descended a wide stair into a central plaza, joining the sea of people flowing in and out of archways. Shoppers lined up at merchant stalls and booths; artisans and performers squeezed into spaces not occupied by food carts boasting leaf-wrapped fish grilling over sage-fragrant coals or ropes of bulbous root vegetables dangling on hanging racks. A hidden puppeteer manipulated his carved, brightly painted creations for a group of enraptured children, while a lute-playing musician accompanied his tale. With their hoods up and in the poor lighting, no one noticed Shar or Keren.

He followed Keren to a tapestry shop tucked in a crooked back alley. Pushing aside the weighty rug-door, Keren and Shar ducked inside the dusky shop. With tables and cabinets piled high with fabric wares, Shar could barely see around the pyramids of dry goods emanating mildew and dust. The Yrythny attending the virtually empty store ignored them, continuing to enter information into a computer terminal on his countertop. Keren picked through hanging tapestries lining the back wall, lifting a particularly worn-looking one, examining a price marked on the back and moving to the next one. What she hoped to accomplish by taking him shopping wasn't yet clear to Shar. He opened his mouth to tell her so, when, after she'd studied a massive, wall-size tapestry with rotted out fringes, she vanished. Peering under the tapestries on both sides and behind him, Shar failed to locate her. He duplicated Keren's actions: lifting a corner of the massive, moss-green tapestry, tilting his head to read the price and—*swoosh*—the floor spun, and he found himself standing in a corridor crammed with Yrythny, cloaked like him.

Uncertain as to what he was supposed to do next, he hung back until he felt Keren's hand gripping his arm. The crowd propelled them into what must be the tapestry shop's warehouse, where the Yrythny sat on a dozen or more metal benches. Other than the scrape of bench legs on the floor, the rustling of cloaks and the occasional whisper, the room was quiet. Though the mottled light obscured his ability to distinguish bodies, Shar guessed there were almost a hundred in the room.

He and Keren secured a spot near the back, and waited as the seats slowly filled to capacity. Finally, when it appeared that not one more body could be squeezed into the musty room, an individual seated close to the front rose.

"Aliens have come to Luthia," the leader began. "We have been assured that these strangers are not agents of the Cheka, and there are those who believe the strangers—one in particular—have been brought here by the Other to help us find peace with our Houseborn siblings. I for one am skeptical. This could very well be yet another Houseborn attempt to lull us into passivity so they can find our group and institute a crackdown. We need to have a strategy in place for dealing with either possibility."

A woman in front of Shar stood up. "We should at least consider the possibility that the situation is exactly as it's been described to us—that these aliens have come to us in need after being caught by one of the Cheka traps meant for us. As strangers to this region of space, they're uniquely positioned to view our dilemma impartially. Perhaps the Other did indeed lead them to us. In which case, the rash actions our people took when they arrived may have already damaged our cause. Perhaps as they learn more about our plight—"

"And how precisely will they do that?" someone else jeered. "The strangers won't be allowed to see us. The Houseborn will keep them away from the Old Quarter because it is squalid and dirty. The strangers won't talk to the house servants and the *shmshu* herders and the fishers. They'll be trotted around to the intelligentsia who, fearing the loss of their lifestyles, will minimize the seriousness of our plight."

For the first time, Shar wondered who from the mob was in the room. He hunched over, tucked his feet under the bench and hoped his alien presence would go unnoticed. His antennae twitched with the conflicted emotions in the room.

A new speaker began, "I came out of House Fnorol in the East Sea. Until twenty years ago, the Elders eviscerated Wanderer females as they came of mature age, justifying their actions because it prevented them from joining their 'superior' Houseborn sisters in the spawning waters." Shar could hear the sneer underlying his bitter words. "Those that weren't maimed, died. There's no way our esteemed Assembly Chair will share that part of our history with the strangers." And he sat down.

"What about the burnings! They came through our villages and burned them to the ground!"

"Our younglings were starved—"

"—beaten with clubs when they were found to be Wanderer young—"

One after another, speakers rose, testifying to mutilation and slaughter with such matter-of-factness that Shar could barely imagine the scope of their experiences—their histories. As quick as his mind was, Shar found himself struggling to process what he heard. He searched for something inside himself that would allow him to understand such atrocities.

"Information about atrocities committed against us can't come from us directly," the meeting leader argued. "The Upper Assembly can discredit it as the ranting of militants, and not history. The fact that we can't carry arms or defend ourselves, even when we serve on starships—is obvious. Starvation, repression—during the Black Time, slavery—those things will be even harder to bring to light."

A Yrythny sitting several benches away from Shar sprang to his feet and rushed to the front of the room, his body quivering with anxiety. "I say we forget about the strangers. They're of no consequence. We may have another Black Time if the Cheka barricades don't come down soon. The Houseborn *will* starve us to save their own, be sure of it."

"Or they'll kill us. Round us up and slaughter us so our hungry mouths don't take food from theirs," another agreed.

The last comment provoked a wave of whispering, stopped only when the meeting leader demanded order by rapping a scepter against the podium. "Enough! We have eyes and ears in many places. Mass murder won't come upon us unawares, but the Houseborn may appoint these strangers to decide our fate before tomorrow if we aren't careful."

Keren stirred beside him. Shar wasn't surprised when she worked her way down the row, through the center aisle and to the front. She threw back her hood, revealing her face. Audible gasps sounded from every corner.

"I make no pretense as to my identity. You all know I am one of you," she said, calmly. "I believe that the strangers coming may be for our good. We have struggled since the Archipelago Wars to wrestle rights away from the Houseborn and we are still far from finding equality with them." She paused, directing her gaze at the floor for a moment before returning her attention to the crowd. Her eyes moved from row to row, seeking personal contact with each listener as she spoke. "My time to go into the waters is coming, but because I am a Wanderer, I will be denied that opportunity during the Homecoming fifteen days hence.

"Instead, I will present myself to the physicians, receive my injection and go about my life pretending that I don't want or need to go into the waters," Keren's steady voice was heavy with sorrow. "And I will be living a lie. I deserve to take a consort, to add to the next generation. I believe our contact with the strangers may make that and many more things possible."

"How do you know they can be trusted?" the leader asked.

She stepped behind the podium. Resting a hand on each side of the rostrum, Keren surveyed the crowds. "I've dealt with them. They don't even come from this part of our galaxy. They live tens of thousands of light years from here. Knowing nothing of our history, they can look at both sides impartially. Who else among those that we trade with, that we exchange culture and knowledge with can make that claim? None." Her eyes finally found Shar, willing him to lift his eyes and meet hers; he complied and held her gaze, unwavering.

"Who knows if these strangers have been brought here by the Other? There's no question that we face perilous times. The blockades may turn Houseborn against Wanderer after centuries of relative peace. We have neither the arms nor the resources to fight them, but we are being swept by currents that will decide our fate, one way or the other. The strangers may be our last chance." Keren spoke as if to Shar directly, as if she sat at his elbow and whispered her words for him alone. He was transfixed.

4

When the turbolift doors closed, Ro requested the Promenade. She scowled at the universe in general, wanted to bang her forehead a few times, but settled for resting her head against the wall and closing her eyes. Seeing Gul Macet, Ambassador Lang and their "delegation" of soldiers had triggered a brain stem reaction: being hunted like prey. That her next turn would find her face-to-face with a resettlement camp guard prepared to clamp holding irons on her wrists and haul her off to be beaten. It was easier with the Maquis because she'd rarely had to stare down her enemy; the covert, anonymous nature of their war assured that. Now, she counted on the traveling time between the outer edge of the Habitat Ring and her upper core office to cushion her jangling nerves.

Conditioned response, Ro reminded herself. The reason her advanced tactical instructors gave repeatedly while drilling the class through every permutation of every worst-case scenario conceivable—so when you're staring your worst nightmare in the face, your training, not your instincts, takes over.

"Welcome to Deep Space 9, I'm Chief of Security, Lieutenant Ro," she recalled saying as she nodded a courteous greeting to the Car-

dassian, Macet. *Kira wasn't kidding about the family resemblance.* When he opened his mouth to speak it was every propaganda holovid from her childhood. The same elongated syllables she'd heard announcing "the unfortunate need for ration cuts" or that "strained resources forbade the distribution of vaccines to afflicted provinces." And she pushed back an instinctual inclination to spit at his feet.

This. Isn't. Dukat. She'd repeated the words in her mind each time she found herself staring at him. She tried focusing on the tufts of hair on his chin, as if the cosmetic difference could trick her psyche into accepting Macet. Her mouth had parroted all the proper polite inquiries she'd heard employed on occasions such as these. Maybe she'd picked up niceties via osmosis from Troi and Picard. The whole *Enterprise* crew had been so damn polite! *"I hope your trip went well." "Radiation in the Denorios Belt often sends false sensor readings this time of year." "We've secured quarters in the habitat ring for the senior members of your party—oh no, it isn't any problem. More convenient access to the meeting rooms than having to come down from the docking ring every few hours."* What she wanted to say was "Get the hell off my station and stay off."

She had searched Macet's face for evidence that justified her fears and found nothing there but even-tempered professionalism—maybe even good humor. Did those traits prove he wasn't Dukat? She'd seen the propaganda. Dukat allegedly loved children and small animals. He was an excellent father. Surely he couldn't authorize the wholesale slaughter of an entire camp accused of aiding the resistance? Hah! Wasn't Lang a former member of the Cardassian News Service, a.k.a. the empire's propaganda machine? All of it felt a bit too coincidental for Ro to be comfortable.

Give her a day alone with him. Hell, give her an *hour* alone with him and she'd figure out the truth. Assurances from the Ghemor regime and DNA tests might support Macet's claim to be who he said he was, but in a universe that already contained changelings, mind-altering entities, and even less explainable phenomena, how could anyone ever be truly sure of him?

Ro's stare must have lingered on Macet for a long while before she noticed the small, slender figure clothed in a vivid periwinkle blue gown standing beside him. She didn't recoil from Lang's proffered hand. The gesture surprised her: Cardassians didn't, as a rule, shake hands. In Ro's experience, such a greeting came more commonly among Federation types than from the austere Cardassians. Clasping both her hands around Ro's, Lang thanked her for accommodating them on such short notice. Strangely, the ambassador's fingers on Ro's wrist recalled the pleasant touch of cool water. In her experience, cold Cardassian hands usually meant death, or at least the promise of it.

Lang had issued the order to Macet's men to disarm before she would permit them to continue beyond the airlock. Ro had witnessed their puzzled expressions as Macet walked down their line, equipment satchel proffered—their barely camouflaged resentment when he sealed the bag and sent it back into the *Trager* with one of his men. Understanding that Macet could have just as easily disarmed his men while shipboard, Ro recognized the gesture for what it was: a move to placate her defenses. They had submitted, Ro imagined resentfully, to Lang's demand for absolute silence while the party moved from the disembarking area to the habitat ring. As she guided the group through the least traversed corridors, Ro observed the ambassador surveying each doorway and dark hall ahead of them. And while Lang's hands rested, deceptively relaxed, at her sides, the tension in her thumb and forefinger indicated she wasn't quite as willing to embrace the passivity she required from Macet's men; Ro would bet the house that hidden beneath the rustling folds of her gown, Lang had a weapon. *She's on as high alert as we are. She's as concerned about Bajorans coming unhinged as Kira is about possible Cardassian treachery.* Ro had made a conscious decision to let her guest's infraction of protocol pass without comment—carrying weapons aboard the station was forbidden save for Militia and Starfleet personnel, and authorized visitors.

Ro had found her guest's wariness reassuring: at least neither party labored under the pretense that a meeting between former enemies was anything normal.

Lang must have noticed Ro's scrutiny because she had quickly said, "Reconnaissance is an old habit. You don't live most of your adult life under the threat of arrest or assassination without assuming an enemy with a weapon lurks in every shadow."

"I know something of that myself," Ro had answered.

Lang's expression had softened, a touch of humor in her eyes. "Somehow, that doesn't surprise me."

A smile crossed Ro's face now as she replayed the scene in her mind, realizing that was the moment she decided that she liked Lang. Once their mutual mistrust had been established, Ro had felt freer to make small talk, mention Lang's previous experience on the station. Traversing a particularly obscure access tunnel crossover bridge, Lang had recalled how she used this route to deliver confidential reports to her underground contacts. Ro made a mental note to add semiregular sensor sweeps of the corridor to the surveillance profiles. In her turn, Ro reciprocated with an anecdote or two about her Maquis days. Lang had laughed at more than a few of her tales. Fringe rebel groups, regardless of ideology, tended to have characteristics in common.

Macet had remained quiet for the duration of their walk, something Ro felt grateful for. He must have sensed her reaction whenever he spoke; she hoped she didn't physically recoil for that would be an undeservedly rude response to a guest. But until the cadence and timbre of his voice stopped causing her blood to boil, she was glad Macet kept his mouth shut.

Upon arriving at their quarters, Ro had briefed Lang and Macet on the extra security precautions Kira had ordered. Neither seemed particularly surprised; they exchanged a glance that informed Ro the Cardassians had contingency plans of their own. Layers upon layers of fear would have to be peeled away before her people and their former oppressors could have uninhibited rapport. Whatever mission Alon Ghemor had assigned Ambassador Lang must be critical to Cardassian interests. Otherwise, how could he justify a high-profile visit while relations between the two worlds remained tenuous at best? Shakaar's humanitarian initiatives had been a solid first step toward finding common ground, but Ro wasn't sure they were prepared to expand past them, especially with the Federation talks underway. *Damn Cardassians always have the worst timing.*

A metallic hum overtook the almost silent whirr of the turbolift. Ro turned toward the sound to see Taran'atar shimmering into visibility.

Ro frowned. "Don't I recall an order coming down from the colonel about your being shrouded in public places aboard the station? Namely, that you aren't supposed to be?"

"The enemy is here. I needed to assess them," he said, checking the charge on his phaser.

Ro shook her head. "The Cardassians aren't our enemies any longer. They've never been *your* enemy. Your people served alongside them in the war."

"Do you know their minds?" he asked, returning his sidearm to its holster.

"Bajorans aren't telepaths, if that's what you're asking," Ro said, hoping her glib answers would irritate Taran'atar enough that he wouldn't pursue this line of questioning.

If Taran'atar sensed Ro's discomfort, it didn't stop him from peppering her with questions. "Do you have knowledge of their goals—their strategy?" he persisted.

"I'm assuming they're here to meet with the First Minister, but outside that, no, I haven't tapped into their database or spied on their private discussions."

"Then they are your enemy. The unknown is always the enemy, Lieutenant," he said as if there was no arguing with his conclusions.

Much as his cold pragmatism felt far too absolute for these "enlightened" times, Ro had to admit she agreed with him. How else had she survived during her years with the Maquis? Most of her Maquis friends had been slaughtered by Cardassians or arrested by Starfleet. And yet, by the grace of some unknown power that she refused to believe was the Prophets, she stood here, in a Bajoran uniform, alive, free and physically unscathed. It was her steadfast refusal to trust anything or anyone that saved her. Or so she believed.

"All possibilities exist until a choice is made," Taran'atar continued, accepting her silence as a tacit endorsement. "Until the moment of choice, it's strategic to anticipate and plan for any potential outcome. It's how survival is assured."

"The odds of Bajor obtaining a safe, beneficial outcome will decrease if the Cardassians think we're luring them into a trap," she said, playing the opposition card.

"You are naïve, Lieutenant, if you assume that the Cardassians aren't luring *you* into a trap."

A soothing voice announced their arrival at the Promenade. Ro turned to look at the Jem'Hadar before she exited the lift. "Do you have business here? Or do you have more innocent civilians to spy on?"

"There is nothing here that concerns me. I will report my observations to the colonel at a later time." He appeared to be conducting a quick weapons assessment before, presumably, shrouding again.

How could he assume that blatantly disregarding orders was fine? Taran'atar was breaking a dozen rules Kira had laid down for him. "I'm telling her about your clandestine operation during my end-of-shift security briefing." She felt like an older sister tattling on an errant sibling.

"Do you think I would have showed myself to you if I had not wanted you to inform the colonel?"

Damn it all if he didn't just make me look stupid, Ro thought. The turbolift doors closed, leaving Ro a little bit grateful she didn't know where the Jem'Hadar was headed next. She didn't know whether to be comforted that someone, namely Taran'atar, on her side had sidestepped propriety for expediency, or annoyed that she hadn't had the guts to do it first. As she wove through the Promenade crowds toward her office, she continued contemplating his words. The unknown is always the enemy, he'd said. These people weren't unknown . . . but everything she knew about them told her they were the enemy.

Sergeant Etana thrust a stack of reports into Ro's hand as she passed through the doors of the security office; Ro barely acknowledged her. Making peace with her own confused thoughts proved harder than wrestling down a Vicarian razorback. She hated admitting that Taran'atar more or less espoused her own suspicions. All her training, her years in Starfleet were supposed to have quashed her xenophobia. Nice to know her enlightened education amounted to something. She found her chair by rote, tapped in her passwords and called up her workfiles.

Inwardly, Ro sighed. She sorted through the memos queued up on her viewscreen. Opening those designated "urgent," she shuttled the others away until she was in the mood to deal with them. She'd always been cynical toward the old Federation philosophy about forgiving and forgetting because there were rarely assurances ahead of time that the enemy had replied in kind. Even the great negotiator himself, Jean-Luc Picard, had been deceived on occasion because he believed that those across the table from him told the truth simply because *he* told the truth. Hadn't she seen his dangerously trusting nature on their first mission together? And hadn't she herself exploited it on their last?

What a strange day this had become! A philosophical alliance between a Bajoran lieutenant and a Jem'Hadar soldier wasn't something Ro could have predicted a year ago. What isn't known is the enemy until proven otherwise. Ro had little experience to prove to her that Cardassians weren't the enemy. Even this group had yet to provide any details about why they had come.

She called up Lang's file to amend it with information about her present visit. Ro now had a lilting alto voice accompanying her mental picture of Lang. The viewscreen picture failed to capture Lang's incisive intelligence, her graceful carriage or ability to elucidate her hopes for the future of her people.

Ro would be lying if she didn't admit to enjoying her brief chat with Lang. After a few minutes of animated discussions with the ambassador, Ro considered that her own view of Cardassians as an aloof, calculating and cruel people might warrant an exception. Lang had a sense of humor; she questioned her people's nearly universal adherence to officially sanctioned views of government, religion and ethics. Her misgivings about Cardassians weren't entirely unlike Ro's concerns about the Bajoran tendency to mindlessly accept whatever the vedeks passed down to them without critically thinking through the rightness of those edicts. She found herself nodding in agreement with Lang's ideas without pausing to consider that these ideas came from a Cardassian.

In an impulsive moment, before she'd left the Cardassians to settle into their quarters, Ro had asked Lang to join her for drinks at Quark's sometime after dinner. She conceded her own naughty curiosity about Quark's reaction to seeing his old flame, elegant and beautiful as ever. But there was also her hope, however small, that she could, once and for all, eliminate the bitter taste of suspicion from her mouth, by proving Taran'atar, herself, and all those who lived in a place of mistrust and ignorance, wrong.

Councillor Charivretha zh'Thane sat taller in her chair, hoping to create the impression that she was listening attentively to the Bajoran trade minister. Her seasoned experience in surviving such meetings aided her attempts to focus, but enduring Minister Kren's nasal monotone for extended periods of time required more than her usual self-discipline. Unwilling to risk appearing impatient, Charivretha deigned to check the time; she guessed Minister Kren's accounting of Bajor's trade relationships with non-Federation worlds had been going on for two hours. His proposed solutions to amending those trade relationships once Bajor entered the Federation would account for another two hours. A suggestion to Second Minister Asarem Wadeen, who peripherally supervised Bajor's monetary and trade policies, that Minister Kren submit his remarks in text for subsequent sessions might be in order. Charivretha's two dozen or so counterparts appeared to be focused on the speaker. Perhaps it was the dual impact of Kren's nervous energy and vocal tones on her Andorian senses that made her restless. Or perhaps not: out of the corner of her eye, she noted the meeting's chair, Trill ambassador Seljin Gandres, dozing off in spite of Gandres's years dealing with the Pakleds on behalf of the Trill diplomatic corps.

Charivretha's antennae alerted her to her aide's presence; Thanis's relaxed energy patterns were distinctive in this tightly wound room. He whispered something in her ear, stepped back and waited for her response. *Damn. We're already working on the station instead of Bajor to accommodate my personal circumstances,* she thought. *If I keep asking for favors, I'll prompt more questions and curiosity—exactly what I'm trying to avoid. But this situation can't be helped.* She raised her placard, asking for recognition from the chair.

Gandres started, too relieved at Charivretha's interruption to be properly discreet. "Excuse me, Minister Kren, Councillor zh'Thane has asked to be recognized."

"A matter of personal concern has come to my attention. I'd like leave for the remainder of the hour, with the chair's approval," Charivretha asked.

Gandres picked up his wand and tapped the bell sitting on the table before him. "Chair calls a recess for all delegates. Session to be resumed at 1330."

While her colleagues and their aides milled around her, some lining up at the replicators, others starting preparations for their own remarks, Charivretha gathered her things and followed Thanis to the wardroom's antechamber where her visitor awaited.

Uncharacteristically, the usually composed Dizhei paced the length of the room. Her antennae tense, eyes bright with worry, Dizhei flew to Charivretha's side as soon as her elder entered. Before Dizhei could speak, Charivretha raised a hand for calm. "I'm assuming we have a situation with Thriss."

"It's not *a* situation, *Zhadi,* it's the ongoing situation. I'm so sorry to disturb you, but there was an incident with the cloth merchant an hour ago and I'm uncertain how to proceed," Dizhei said through short bursts of breath.

Sighing, Charivretha took a seat on one of the benches lining the waiting room. She patted the spot beside her, indicating to Dizhei to join her. Charivretha rested a hand on Dizhei's shoulder, making small, soft circles on her back. "Slow down, Dizhei. You'll faint."

Clenching and unclenching her hands, Dizhei leaned closer to Charivretha, allowing the young one to whisper her concerns. "I thought a distraction would help. She's done little but taunt poor Anichent about the lack of progress in his research—if you were to ask me, I think she's tampering with his data just to see if she can make him as irritable as she is, but I have no proof to support such allegations and even Thriss tends not to be cruel—"

"Dizhei, *shri'za,*" Charivretha implored, hoping her use of the endearment softened what she imagined was her own impatient tone. She also hoped it reminded her son's bondmate that they were not alone in this place, that discretion was paramount. "When your students misbehave, are you always so flustered?"

"I'm sorry, *Zhadi.* I see more than mere misbehavior from Thriss, and I fear where I see these behaviors leading."

"Explain," she prompted.

"We went out shopping today. I had read in the station announcements that a group of craftsmen from the Musilla province would be displaying their wares. I thought it might take her mind off—" she paused "—everything. She likes mingling with those of other cultures. Her *zhavey* is a textile artist and I thought she'd find an outing pleasant."

"And . . . ?"

"She found a piece of cloth—handwoven, exquisitely rich in

color and detail. Seeing that it pleased her, I asked the merchant discreetly for a price—I thought I would surprise her with it as a gift. When he tried to take it away from her, telling her at my request that it wasn't for sale, she raged at him. 'How could he deny a soul her burial shroud? Was cruelty to widows part of his way of doing business?' I paid him the litas you left me and removed her from the shop as soon as I could."

"You did well. What do you require of me?" Charivretha squeezed Dizhei's leg affectionately.

"I believe we need to reconsider our plan to wait here until Shar returns," Dizhei answered confidently. "Anichent agrees."

Charivretha imagined how long Anichent and Dizhei had been planning on bringing this proposal to her before Thriss' behavior forced the issue. *The intimate associations of bondmates . . . I miss them,* she thought, remembering her own experiences. But sometimes bondmates lacked the objectivity to perceive the wisest course of action. "Didn't we all decide that being here when Shar comes back will improve the chances of his returning to Andor for the *shelthreth?*"

"Thriss is pained by the reminders of Thirishar that surround us, and yet she wallows in them. She, of all of us, insists on sleeping in his bed every night," Dizhei shook her head. "I can't help but think that perhaps, if we go home, Thriss can lose herself in her studies. Complete her medical training and start her residency sooner."

Charivretha considered her child's mate, imagining not for the first time how effective Dizhei must be in dealing with her pupils' overly concerned families. Not one for impulsivity, Dizhei had the most responsible nature of the four of them. She could be counted on to be rational under the most trying circumstances. And yet, here she sat, her flushed forehead and bloodshot eyes tangible evidence of emotional distress. If gentle Dizhei felt this undone by her predicament, Charivretha could hardly fathom what the moody Thriss might be capable of. One misstep and Shar's future could be jeopardized. The stakes could hardly be higher. *I wonder if all zhaveys go through this . . .*

As much as she appreciated the honor of Shar's being matched with a bondgroup, Charivretha found herself wishing, not for the first time, that Shar's DNA might have been compatible with one less volatile than Shathríssía zh'Cheen. Yes, Thriss's willowy fragility, unusual by Andorian standards, suited Shar's tendency for appreciating the unconventional. He enjoyed being unique, embracing the less obvious choices, and Thriss certainly embodied that. Together, Shar and Thriss brought out the best and worst in each other. At the time she met Thriss, a scrawny, wide-eyed thing of seven, Charivretha had no idea what a force to be reckoned with was sweeping into her life.

It was during Shar's Heritage studies. The students were learning the first forms of an ancient festival dance, one they'd be called on to perform at the Time of Knowing. Sitting in on her *chei's* class, Charivretha had remembered her own Knowing ceremony—the subsequent celebration after she'd learned the names of her bondmates; her life had been redefined during those hours. She had recalled her own youthful excitement while observing her *chei* and his classmates, including Thriss, standing off to the side in the shadows. Considering the group as a whole, Charivretha had noted how Thriss's plainness, her homeliness, distinguished her from the rest. And then, on her cue, Thriss had assumed her place in the form, had risen up onto her toes and had curled her arm over her head with such delicacy and loveliness that Charivretha's breath caught in her throat. Dozens of pairs of childish eyes had focused on the ethereal Thriss, each wondering if she would someday belong to them.

Subsequent years brought Thriss official reprimands for misbehavior in class—mostly for inappropriate displays of temper—but she had remained well liked by her peers, gaining a folk-herolike reputation for speaking out against perceived injustice. All her peers valued her opinions and desired her approval as they copied her hairstyles and the clothes she wore. When she staged a sit-in protesting Andorian communities encroaching on animal habitats, half the students joined her.

Except Shar.

Shar's seeming obliviousness to Shathrissía ought to have been Charivretha's first clue that he felt differently about her than he did about his other bondmates. He never sought out her company, never invited her to study. For her purposes at the time, Charivretha found Shar's disinterest a relief: it decreased the likelihood that her *chei* would find the trouble that followed Thriss wherever she went.

When, five years later, Shar received Thriss as his bondmate, Charivretha still refused to worry because the bondgroup was a strong one. Shar instantly adored Dizhei, as everyone who met her did; with Anichent, he found a kinship of minds unlike any he'd ever experienced. Anichent and Shar quickly became inseparable. Charivretha often saw Shar and Anichent shyly holding hands during study time; Shar's tender displays of affection warmed Charivretha as few things did.

Though he treated Thriss honorably, Shar appeared indifferent to her company. Because Shar tended to run counter to whatever trends and fads existed among his peers, Charivretha assumed he ignored Thriss because of her popularity. Thriss tried, but failed, to provoke any substantive reaction from him. In retrospect, Charivretha could see that Shar had conscientiously avoided Thriss, taking deliberate steps to assure their school schedules, their extracurricular hours and mealtimes didn't intersect. *As his zhavey, I should have known intuitively why he behaved the way he did: Shar ignored Thriss to avoid confronting the powerful attraction he felt for her. Years, I wasted years that I might have used to derail what proved to be the inevitable explosion between my chei and his lover . . . if I could have stopped them, if I could have foreseen what they would do and how irrational they could be . . .*

Knowing all of the situation's complexities, Charivretha had played a dangerous card in bringing Thriss to Deep Space 9. Ideally, Thriss' ability to insinuate herself into Shar's emotions should have given him an incentive to bow out of the Gamma Quadrant mission. Instead, Thriss's appearance had reinforced the very decision Charivretha hoped to reverse. Shar had accurately perceived that his best chance at pursuing his misguided quest to find an external solution to the Andorians' spiral toward extinction—as if he, brilliant as he was, could solve a problem his people had struggled with for so long—was to go as far from Thriss as possible, as fast as he could travel. *The Gamma Quadrant certainly meets those criteria,* she thought bitterly. *Now what to do with Dizhei? If Thriss' outbursts threaten Dizhei's equilibrium, we might face losing more than Shar. . . .*

Thanis discreetly crouched down beside Charivretha, informing her that the trade agreement transitioning session would be resuming shortly. Did she need to ask for more time from Ambassador Gandres? Charivretha shook her head no. With all the tenderness she could muster, Charivretha gathered Dizhei in her arms, cradling her against her shoulder. Beneath her own trembling hands, Charivretha felt the labored breathing that marked Andorian keening. Resisting the impulse to give into her tumultuous feelings, she focused her energy on reassuring Dizhei, cursing her selfish offspring. Where had she failed in conveying to Shar the seriousness of his obligations? "I will do what I can," she whispered into Dizhei's hair. "I promise."

As Ro prepared her end-of-shift report, she noted grimly that while the Cardassian presence on the station hadn't produced a marked increase in security problems, the imposition of yellow-alert protocols had. One of her corporals had just been admitted to Dr. Tarses' care. The Klingon captain of a vessel loaded with Cardassian humanitarian aid had charged the security officer with a *d'k tahg*, when, under orders, the deputy prevented the *J'chang* from launching. Other than reissuing her earlier statements about changes in station security, adding random, full-body scans, and making certain that all pilots arriving at or departing from the station were aware of those changes, Ro felt there was little else to do until everyone adjusted to the new rules. People typically hated change.

A beep from her console alerted her to the approach of a visitor to the security office. Ro recognized her through the door windows immediately: Councillor Charivretha zh'Thane.

Ro rose from her chair as the councillor entered, but zh'Thane quickly indicated she expected Ro to sit down. The councillor took her place in the visitor's chair, sitting regally straight, hands folded in her lap; she exemplified poise.

Before today, Ro had spoken to zh'Thane only a handful of times, and on all those occasions she found the diplomat to be pleasant enough, but imperious. She could only imagine what Shar must have felt growing up with such a formidable presence to contend with. Even now, in her office, Ro felt zh'Thane was holding court.

"I bring the accolades of Admiral Akaar, Lieutenant Ro. He's pleased with Colonel Kira's decision to increase security. He also admires how swiftly and capably it's been handled," she said, a slight tremor in her voice.

Knowing Akaar's reservations about her competence, Ro found zh'Thane's words to have little more substance than polite pleasantries. What intrigued her was the crack in zh'Thane's perfectly composed veneer when, for an instant, she showed vulnerability. *In good time,* Ro thought. Not wanting to offend her guest, she offered a half-smile.

Zh'Thane replied by deliberately closing her eyes, allowing her long gray lashes to flutter politely. "I'm sorry to hear of your corporal's injuries. I hope it's nothing serious."

Ro was impressed with how in-the-know zh'Thane appeared to be: the incident with the *J'chang* had occurred in the previous hour. "Dr. Tarses will release him to his quarters this evening. Just keeping him under precautionary observation for the time being. Thanks for asking." Assuming zh'Thane had more pressing concerns than passing on Admiral Akaar's compliments, she made the opening move. "Now, what can I do for you, Councillor?"

"The yellow-alert status. It's my understanding that all starship departures and arrivals require a day, sometimes longer, for clearance," she said, perusing a padd she'd apparently had tucked inside her sleeve.

"That's correct. We felt that we needed to screen for potential security risks, biohazards or other illegal activities that might threaten the various diplomatic goings-on." And her staff—already putting in extra shifts since Akaar's arrival—felt burdened by the pressure of their added responsibilities. *Councillor zh'Thane had better not add to their load,* Ro thought defensively.

"A plan must exist to accommodate emergencies. Something involving Admiral Akaar or First Minister Shakaar, for instance." Her antennae curled slightly forward.

"Not going to happen. The same rules that apply to the lowliest scrap scow apply to the admiral and the first minister. Barring full-on military assault or medical emergency—"

Zh'Thane pounced. "I require a medical exception for my vessel, Lieutenant."

"Why?"

"That's a private matter."

Ro refused to budge. "Without signed medical orders, your ship will have to queue up behind everyone else."

"I'm a Federation councillor, Lieutenant," zh'Thane said quietly, though the warning in her tone was implicit. "You can take me at my word." The councillor leaned forward as she regarded Ro challengingly across the desk.

Placidly, Ro met zh'Thane's stare. Tough talk and aggressive body language never phased her. "If I had a bar of latinum for every VIP who asked for special privileges, I'd be retired on Risa by now. We're in a state of heightened alert." Why was it that important people always assumed the rules didn't apply to them?

"The war's over. I think we're reasonably safe. Aren't you being overly cautious?" zh'Thane snapped.

"If I hadn't experienced an unprovoked Jem'Hadar attack fairly recently, I might agree with you. Our known enemies might be accounted for—it's the unknown enemies we need to guard against." The casualties, the damage to the station's primary systems, and the ensuing panic all loomed large in her recent memory; none of it would Ro want to experience again. If safety required inconvenience, she would happily be the enforcer.

"Perhaps I should speak with Colonel Kira," zh'Thane said.

"That's certainly your privilege. But if you have a genuine medical concern that may require bypassing our security measures, the colonel will require the same answers I do."

Zh'Thane appeared to waver indecisively. "This isn't—" she began, then started again. "Lieutenant, believe me when I tell you I'm not insensitive to the station's security concerns or your responsibilities. But the situation—" She cut herself off again and closed her eyes, then took a deep breath as if to calm herself. When her eyes opened again, they seemed pleading. "Please don't require this of me."

"With respect, Councillor," Ro said gently, "I can help you only if you can help me to understand the situation."

"I know," zh'Thane said. Hands squeezing the armrests, the councillor's upper body and antennae tensed, until she exhaled deeply. "It's simply that I've been trying to convince myself that taking an outsider into our confidence wouldn't be necessary. I realize now how foolish that was. But you must understand that that level of trust doesn't come easily to many of my people, Lieutenant. If I am open with you, can you assure me that what I say will remain between us?"

Ro stared at zh'Thane, a little stunned to see how fragile and powerless she suddenly seemed. *Whatever's going on, it's obviously mortifying her to do this.* "I have no desire to violate your privacy, Councillor. Perhaps you *should* speak with the colonel directly—"

"No," zh'Thane said firmly. "It's my understanding that you're Thirishar's friend. He admires and respects you. That will make this easier for me, but I need to know that you'll keep this in confidence."

With a deliberate move of her hand, Ro tapped in the commands engaging her office's privacy shields. She rarely used the shield, saving it for interrogations or clandestine informants reporting in. "I will, unless doing so somehow compromises the safety of this station."

Zh'Thane nodded. "Acceptable. . . . You're aware of Thirishar's bondmates being aboard the station?"

"Yes," Ro said. "I was the one who arranged for their stay in Shar's quarters during his absence, per his request."

"For which I know they're most grateful. Having any small aspect of his life to cling to has been a great comfort to them these past weeks. You see . . . by accepting his current assignment, Shar has put his well-being, and that of his bondmates, at risk."

Ro frowned. "In what way?"

"He was supposed to come home!" zh'Thane hissed. "I don't speak of a cultural obligation that's at odds with his Starfleet career, although that aspect of it certainly can't be overlooked in all of this. I speak now of biological necessity."

Ro tried to intuit from zh'Thane's hints what she might be implying, and became alarmed. She knew that some life-forms had an imperative to return to their place of birth in order to continue the reproductive cycle of their species, only to die if they failed. "I've heard that Vulcans—"

"This isn't like that," zh'Thane said. "You're perhaps imagining that Shar has put himself in danger by denying an inner drive to procreate, but that isn't the case. In fact, the situation is, in many ways, far more grave than that, with potentially farther-reaching consequences.

"The Andorian species, you may know, has four sexes, none of which is truly male or female as you define them. Our interactions with the many two-sex species that comprise the majority of sentients with whom we traffic has led us to accept male and female pronouns for simplicity's sake, and because it helps us avoid unwelcome questions about our biology.

"Because our procreative process requires chromosomes from four parents, it is, as I'm sure you gather, a very complicated matter for four individuals who are compatible—genetically and emotionally—to come together to produce a child."

Complicated is an understatement, Ro thought. *It sounds damn near impossible.* "Councillor, forgive me, but . . . I don't understand how such a biological system could sustain itself."

"It doesn't," zh'Thane said quietly.

That was when Ro began to understand what the Andorians were facing, even as zh'Thane continued to spell it out.

"Our species is dying, Lieutenant. It wasn't always this way, but certain . . . changes . . . have led to our present dilemma, which neither Andorian nor Federation science has been able to solve. The best we've been able to do is adjust ourselves to our circumstances. Our culture is now defined by the need to do whatever is necessary to ensure the survival of our species. Successful conception requires careful planning. As many variables as can be controlled, are. But matching together the most viable quads is difficult undertaking. This is so much more complicated than . . . Do you know that within minutes of Shar's birth, his DNA map was entered into our master files with the express purpose of being matched to those he was most compatible with, genetically? He belonged to something bigger than he was before he even had a self-concept!

"Thirishar believes we are simply delaying the inevitable. And he's right. We take our obligation to produce offspring more seriously than any other aspect of our lives because our species is headed toward extinction. We have to do all that we can to assure our kind's survival until a solution can be found."

Ro watched zh'Thane's antennae twitch sharply with her every word, the councillor's agitation palpable.

"That's why you needed Shar to return home," Ro realized. "To join his bondmates in producing a child."

"Yes. In their late teens and early twenties, all fertile Andorians are obligated to return to Andor for the *shelthreth*—a period of time and a ritual akin to a wedding. If all goes well, the *shelthreth* results in conception and the bondgroup's obligation to reproduce will be met. But time is an important factor as well. Individually,

Andorians have only a five-year window of fertility. Thirishar and his bondmates are nearing the end of theirs. His stubborn refusal to come home and instead waste precious months in the Gamma Quadrant is putting them all dangerously close to missing their last opportunity to conceive.

"Perhaps you're wondering how tragic it can possibly be if one less child is born to us. But to my kind, every birth is important. Every new life is hope. And yet Thirishar, my own *chei,* doesn't see it this way." Zh'Thane shook her head. "There has never been a time in his life that he didn't have these obligations, and yet somehow, he thinks he's the exception. That the needs of his people have no hold on him!"

"Councillor, please—"

The knuckles of zh'Thane's hands turned white-blue. "He goes off on this quest of his, thinking he's doing what's best for all of us, without stopping to think that it might destroy everything his life is about! If the worst happens, all of it—Dizhei's students, Anichent's research, Thriss's medical studies, my career will be worthless! Our work will have no meaning because we will have failed in our greatest purpose and obligation to our people."

"Has something happened medically with one of Shar's bondmates that compromises the *shelthreth?*" Ro prompted gently.

"My *zhri'za.* One of Shar's bondmates, Shathrissía. The stress of Shar's decision is having unforeseen—consequences. She has become emotionally unpredictable—possibly even unstable. I worry about what she might do if she loses control. If her equilibrium destabilizes any further, she will have to return to Andor."

"Why not make the arrangements and depart now, if you're so concerned?"

"Because it is still the best choice for the three of them to wait here until Thirishar returns," zh'Thane explained patiently. "Should the situation change, however, we might have to move swiftly, without having time to make the proper applications."

"Our medical staff has training in the physiologies of most Alpha Quadrant species," Ro offered kindly. "They might be able to help."

Zh'Thane's voice cracked and a wail-like sigh escaped her throat. "If only it were as simple as asking Dr. Tarses for a hypospray. Or finding a project to keep Thriss busy—perhaps sending her on a cultural tour of Bajor or to Cardassia to offer medical service. She tends to be mercurial, to change her mind at a moment's notice. If we can persuade her to listen to sense, she might agree to go home."

Ro considered how best to handle the situation. She'd always sensed something conflicted in Shar, simmering below the surface of his steadiness. And it was uncharacteristic of someone as skilled in negotiation as Councillor zh'Thane to become so overwrought without good cause. She went with her gut. "Without betraying your trust, I'll take this to Colonel Kira and let you know what she says. I'll get back to you once she's made her decision."

Likely embarrassed by the intensity of her outburst, zh'Thane refused to look at Ro. "Thank you, Lieutenant." She exited without a backward glance.

Ro spent the remaining few minutes of her shift considering how best to present zh'Thane's petition to Kira when her relief reported in. Sergeant Etana Kol nodded to Ro but scarcely said a word as she took Ro's place at the security desk. Etana hadn't been her usual jovial self since the *Defiant* departed; like several others in the station crew, the deputy had someone aboard *Defiant* whom she missed terribly. And from what Ro knew of the relationship, three months would be the longest time Kol and Krissten had been apart since they'd gotten together. That must be hard. Still, Etana's not stupid. She must have known getting involved with a Starfleet officer might mean prolonged time apart. "You okay, Kol?"

Etana looked up with a smile. Ro was impressed by how easily it seemed to fall into place. The sergeant shrugged. "Hate sleeping alone."

Ro smiled back. "Don't worry; when she gets back, you'll be annoyed you don't have the bed to yourself anymore."

Etana laughed. "You're probably right. Night, Lieutenant."

"G'night, Kol."

As she left the security office, Ro saw to her surprise that zh'Thane was still just outside, chatting pleasantly with Hiziki Gard, the Federation's security liaison and aide to the Trill amabassador. Ro nodded to Gard as she passed them, and gleaned from the few bits she overheard that zh'Thane's earlier angst had passed.

Was that whole thing an act? Ro wondered, stopping in front of the turbolift. As she reconsidered what she would say to Kira, Ro found herself wondering how much of zh'Thane's performance had been staged and how much had been genuine.

"Lieutenant."

Ro looked over her shoulder and saw the councillor standing alone again near the security office, Gard having apparently moved on.

"Thank you," zh'Thane mouthed soundlessly. Her eyes brimmed with pain for the briefest of moments before the composed politician's facade descended like a mask. Then she turned away, disappearing into the humanoid tide of the Promenade.

5

"Commander, I can't access the Defiant," Nog hissed.

What the hell is Nog doing in my room? Vaughn thought, eyelids fluttering as he bounced back and forth between half-sleep and wakefulness. He couldn't recall his dream save that his hair was the brown of his youth and there were swaying palm trees in the background. He thought Ruriko was there, but as always, he was unable to reach her.

"Commander, are you there?"

Blindly, Vaughn felt his way to the end table, groping for his combadge. When he clutched it in his hand, he pressed it and said, "The door won't open, Lieutenant?"

"Sir, there's a contingent of Yrythny soldiers here—with weapons. And they pointed them at me when I tried to board the ship."

Fully awake, Vaughn swore and sat up, reaching for his uniform. "I'll be right there, Nog. Vaughn out."

What a difference a few hours make! After the night's last debriefing, Vaughn had felt comfortable with how things stood—at least with Nog. The *Defiant's* problems seemed cut and dried: if it's broken, fix it. Repairs would be complex—taking far longer than any of them desired—but the Yrythny had pledged to be generous with cooperation and resources. Maybe that was his mistake: assuming that the worst was past them. He'd served in Starfleet long enough to know that whenever a situation looked bleak, it was bound to be a veritable black hole before it improved. Nog and his team had even addressed his most pressing concern, the development of a theoretical model for a defense system against the Cheka weapon. *That alone should have tipped me off that this whole thing would be shot to hell before breakfast.*

Vaughn recalled that, after midnight, Julian had wandered up to the repair bay. Bashir, he knew, didn't need as much sleep as most humans, so Vaughn didn't look askance at the doctor's middle-of-the-night proposal to inventory sickbay. Anyone willing to work was welcome. In a flash of inspiration, Julian had suggested using the humanoid immune system as a model for a defensive weapon. The ideas tumbled out from there.

If the Cheka nanobots represented invading viruses and bacteria, then femtobots—even smaller and designed by the *Defiant* staff—could be used be like the CD8+ T and B cells deployed by humanoid bone marrow to gnaw through the viruses. Nog's plan called for maintaining a cloud of femtobots in stasis just beneath the ship's shield envelope. If *Defiant* tripped another web weapon, the femtobots would activate and attack as soon as the nanobots pierced the shields. Brilliant.

In theory.

The trick, of course, was that although it was well known that molecular cybernetics didn't stop at the nanite level, creating femtobots able to withstand the stress of the shield matrix *and* hard enough to pierce the nanobots was uncharted territory. The *Defiant* simply didn't possess the structural materials Nog and his engineers would need to make the plan work. Their computer simulations, run using variations of readily available materials, had all failed. Either the femtobots disintegrated in proximity to the shields, or the ship sustained critical damage due to delayed or partial deployment. The femtobots required something more resilient than *Defiant*'s replicators or her engineers could fabricate.

Even though a significant challenge awaited Nog, Vaughn hadn't been too worried. Nog's resourcefulness and innovative abilities never ceased to amaze him. Vaughn had instead assumed his biggest problem would be his hosts' hastily conceived notion that Dax should facilitate some mediation process between warring Yrythny factions.

Prime Directive and first contact issues aside—and his concerns regarding those protocols weren't exactly minor—Vaughn had reservations about letting Dax get mixed up in the Yrythny's internal politics. Despite her zeal and seriousness about her transfer to command—and the fact that her past-life experiences gave her unique advantages as his XO—nothing in the lieutenant's Starfleet background or his own interactions with her shouted that she ought to have her responsibilities broadened to include diplomacy. Granted, her counselor training lent her legitimate, professional expertise in the area of xenopsychology, but Vaughn still remembered Curzon Dax's questionable judgment during the Betreka affair, and the choices that had nearly gotten them both killed. Ezri wasn't Curzon, of course—not exactly—and while she was a quick study, Vaughn wasn't about to turn over the fate of a world poised on the brink of civil war to her, no matter what gods appeared to have ordained it.

Sprinting up the stairs that led to *Defiant*'s docking bay, Vaughn saw the problem immediately. Just as Nog had reported, a squadron of armed, uniformed Yrythny soldiers blocked the ship's airlock. Nog was huddled with several engineers some distance away. The chief engineer's face relaxed visibly when he saw his CO; Vaughn hoped the situation hadn't worsened since he left his quarters.

"Report, Lieutenant."

Nog launched into his story at once. "I arrived at 0600 to resume command of the repair team, accompanied, as you can see by Ensign Senkowski, Ensign Leishman, and Ensign Gordimer."

At mention of their names, auburn-haired Senkowski, smiley Leishman and stocky Gordimer in succession, straightened up and nodded a polite acknowledgment to their commander.

Nog continued, "We discovered the troops you see here blocking the airlock; they denied us access to the *Defiant*. Lieutenant McCallum, Ensign Merimark, Ensign Permenter, and Crewman M'Nok are still aboard. I've already contacted them and they haven't been threatened, or had their work interfered with. They didn't even know they were trapped inside until I told them."

"What do these guards have to say?"

"Nothing, sir, except that they're acting under orders to secure the ship."

There must be a point to this. Even implied threats aren't arbitrary. "Have you contacted the Yrythny authorities?" If Vaughn were to guess, he'd assume that one of their friendly dinner companions was responsible for their armed visitors.

"Sir, we've tried to raise our concerns with the Yrythny government, but our inquiries have been rerouted, ignored or gone unacknowledged," Nog said.

I just bet they have, Vaughn thought. *They want us to stew in our worry a little longer. Makes us more pliable, more readily agreeable to their demands when they finally get around to making them.*

"And for that, I apologize, Lieutenant Nog," Assembly Chair Rashoh's rumbling voice came from behind them. "I had hoped to contact you myself, Commander, before your engineers arrived for duty this morning, but obviously my good intentions came to naught."

So you've decided we've waited long enough, or you've grown impatient. Which one is it? "As you say Assembly Chair," Vaughn said placidly, turning to face Rashoh and his party. None of their identities surprised him, just the failure to bring their token Lower Assembly member, Keren, along as a spectator. Accompanying the Assembly Chair were Vice Chair Jeshoh and another Yrythny official Vaughn didn't recall meeting. He considered them cautiously, wondering what ill tidings they brought. "Imagine my concern at discovering my crew had been denied access to *our* ship." *Let the games begin . . .*

"*Your* ship, certainly," the Assembly Chair said with a toothy smile, his never-blinking eyes glinting like obsidian. "As your lieutenant has no doubt reported to you, we haven't violated your sovereignty and boarded your vessel. Rather, we have some concerns that we wanted to discuss."

"Concerns?" Vaughn raised an eyebrow. *What trumped-up excuses have you spent the night dreaming up?* He offered Rashoh a warm smile of his own.

"The radiation contamination inside is immense. We require assurance that our own people won't be impacted," the Assembly Chair said soberly.

Vaughn smiled tightly at Rashoh. "Mister Nog?"

Taking his cue, Nog opened his tricorder and panned it in the direction of the airlock. After a moment he turned back to Vaughn and held up the results of his scan.

To Rashoh, Vaughn said, "I encourage you to verify these findings with your own instruments, but according to this, you and your people have nothing to fear."

A pointy-faced Yrythny wearing billowing muted green pants and a gaudy macramé headpiece stepped forward with outturned feet, bowed, and said in a hesitant voice, "I am Science Minister M'Yeoh. Let me come to the point, Commander."

"By all means," Vaughn said pleasantly.

Threading his lengthy, bony fingers together and flexing his fingers rhythmically—as one might tap one's toes—Minister M'Yeoh waddled closer to Vaughn. "As I see it, you have three options," he said. "Clearly, your ship can't fly or sustain life for long. Should"— he gulped—"you decide that it's irreparable you might wish to trade your ship for one of ours. Or you might decide that our world suits you as a place to rest temporarily. Perhaps contact your own people in the Alpha Quadrant and wait for them to come and bring you home."

"Or they can repair the *Defiant* using our resources—personnel, raw materials and so forth," Jeshoh interjected. "As we *promised* our guests yesterday."

At least Jeshoh's not pretending to go along with this charade. "Vice Chair Jeshoh offers the only option I'm willing to take," Vaughn said, waiting for the word he felt certain would follow.

"But that's our problem, Commander."

There it is, Vaughn thought ruefully. *The "but."* Would that someday sentient nature surprised him even a little, but it often seemed as if all species—all thinking beings—functioned on similar paradigms, even this far from home.

Assembly Chair Rashoh clucked, jiggling the pockets of skin hanging off his jaw. "We want to be generous with you, but the reports from your chief technologist indicate that your ship will require extensive—and expensive—resources. Much of what you need we obtain from foreign trade, and as we've already explained, our conflict with the Cheka has limited our supply runs. How can we possibly give you what you need without risking shortages to our own vessels?" Assembly Chair Rashoh's sad expression lingered on Vaughn for a long moment, allowing his words to hang in the air.

"I understand completely," Vaughn said. "Would you consider a trade?"

Smiling, the Assembly Chair took Vaughn by the elbows. "I believe we would be open to such a proposal."

"Hmmm. I have some suggestions, but perhaps you have something in mind?"

M'Yeoh said, "We've reviewed this model for a defensive weapon that your Lieutenant Nog designed and found it has merit. But like you, we lack a raw material suitable for construction of the femtobots."

Hearing mention of his work on the defense system, Nog sidled up close to M'Yeoh. Vaughn had momentary concerns about how the Yrythny government had been privy to Nog's technological innovations, but then he recalled that a group of engineers from the *Avaril* had asked if they could help out. In spite of their rough first contact, the Yrythny engineers had bonded with Nog and his staff.

"Among the trade avenues still open to us, we have a membership in a matter Consortium several sectors away that deals in unique and rare materials," the Assembly Chair explained.

"Matter Consortium?" Vaughn asked.

"A nexus of free trade situated near a natural particle fountain in this sector. The Consortium harvests the outflows of the particle fountain. The matter emerging from the fountain has undergone intense gravitational pressure and temperature fluctuations. Its molecular and subatomic structure is fundamentally altered by these forces. We believe it will meet your requirements."

Nog was rapt with attention. Technology that facilitated particle fountain mining, while found in the Federation, such as the one at Tyrus VIIA, was still primarily experimental. Vaughn could see the cogs in his mind spinning furiously as he processed Rashoh's words. When Nog leaned forward, as if he were preparing to question the Assembly Chair, Vaughn touched his shoulder, wanting him to hold back until he had the complete picture.

"You're saying we can obtain the structural materials we need from this Consortium?"

Rashoh smiled but shook his head. "Unfortunately, trading is closed to nonmembers. However, as members ourselves, we would be willing to act on your behalf. You could travel on *Avaril*, with your ship, allowing your crew time to work on your repairs during the journey. Our long range probes have recently verified a route to the Consortium that is still free of web weapons."

"A generous offer," Vaughn said, relieved that the game was nearing an end. "But what could we possibly offer you in return?"

"Allow your first officer, Lieutenant Dax, to stay behind and mediate talks between the Houseborn and the Wanderers."

And your first instinct was right, Elias. The situation with Ezri is the real problem here. He exhaled deeply, considered the group standing before him and saw in their faces a resolute determination to do whatever it took to bring their will to pass.

"Agreed," Vaughn said. "Threats weren't necessary, Assembly Chair, Minister M'Yeoh, Vice Chair Jeshoh. Reasonable people negotiate and I am nothing if not reasonable. Your soldiers will now leave and my engineers will go to work." He smiled coldly at his blackmailers.

The Yrythny delegation didn't bother to hide their relief at Vaughn's answer. *Why hadn't they just asked?* In his more than eighty years in Starfleet, whether it was dropping into a war zone or playing cat-and-mouse games with the Tal Shiar, Vaughn had learned that desperation drives otherwise sane people to do crazy things. *The time for asking whether Dax should do this is probably past—the question now is whether Dax can do this. For all our sakes, I hope her plucky determination—and the cumulative wisdom of all her lives—will be enough.*

Shar waited impatiently as the troop transport in which he rode crept slowly through the narrow needle, toward the massive docking platform. Through the windows, he could see Luthia's winking lights diminishing as he inched closer to the *Avaril*. Would that he could have joined the others an hour ago when the crew checked out of the guest quarters! But he—along with Candlewood, Juarez, and McCallum—was remaining behind to assist Lieutenant Dax. Loading the shuttlecraft *Sagan* with the away team's supplies and piloting the ship to a bay closer to their guest quarters had left him little time for a pressing personal errand. He still hoped he had enough time to pull Commander Vaughn aside to make a private request. Shar rarely made such requests; he hoped Vaughn understood that.

If Commander Vaughn followed the pattern established thus far, *Defiant* would send its official weekly report to Deep Space 9 while at the Consortium. "Letters" from the crew to their friends and families were transmitted on an "as time and equipment permitted" basis. At present, both were in short supply, but he didn't wish to let another week pass. When the next report was transmitted to Colonel Kira, Shar hoped to include a message to his bondmates: not only because they expected one, but because he deeply regretted the last one he had sent.

His first letter home had been stilted. Still smarting from the sting of his *zhavey*'s ploy, he'd been at a loss as to what to say. She had staged her ambush—bringing his bondmates to the station all the way from Andor to persuade him not to join the *Defiant*'s mission—because she loved him and believed his choices would lead him to unhappiness. But that didn't lessen his frustration with her tactics. There was a fine line between "force" and "guilt" to Shar's way of thinking. Especially since she *had* succeeded in making him feel guilty. He missed the days when their relationship was less adversarial.

All these feelings had filled Shar when he'd recorded his first message to his *zhavey*. He finally settled on a matter-of-fact recitation of his experiences coupled with brief well wishes and words of affection. Had he sent what he had recorded on the first pass, Shar expected that Charivretha might have come chasing through the wormhole after him. Saying the words, however, had been enough to make him feel better, so he erased the inflammatory accusations in favor of his proper letter. He might send his first draft later on, when the *Defiant* was too far away to catch . . .

> *Zhavey:*
> *I am sorry to have disappointed you. Please believe me when I say that I would not have chosen as I did if I didn't believe that I was doing what was best for* all *concerned. Has not your whole life been about the greater good of Andor? Is it too hard to understand that I've become what I am by learning from your example?*

Even more difficult was the letter to his bondmates. All his words were *just* words. Empty. Hollow. Failing utterly to convey the heartache he felt, or to acknowledge the heartache he knew he'd caused them. Why were pain and love coupled so tightly together?

Dearest Thriss, Anichent, Dizhei—I love and miss you all, but this mission must come before my return to Andor for the shelthreth. I hope that someday you understand my choices and forgive me. While it might seem I'm being selfish, I'm doing this for you, for all of our people. Our people's present course merely postpones the inevitable—we must explore new possibilities if we are to defy our fate. And if a few aren't willing to make sacrifices for the many ... Unfortunately, because you are matched to me, you are among the few. You didn't choose this for yourselves and for that, I'm sorry.

In the early weeks of the mission, Shar had watched Vaughn and his daughter, Ensign Tenmei, tentatively feel their way back to reconciliation after years of estrangement due to her belief that Vaughn had put his duty to Starfleet before his love of her mother. Shar wondered if someday he would have to make a similar reconciliation with his bondmates.

Early this morning, he had come up empty as he fumbled for the right words to express his thoughts to those closest to his heart. Never mind that he had years of practice recording such messages, having spent so much time away from them, communicating solely through subspace letters. No matter where his Starfleet assignments had taken him in the past, maintaining his ties to his bondmates had been a priority. Infrequent were the times when, as a group or individually, they could take leave from schooling or work.

While Dizhei's teaching responsibilities tethered her to Andor, both Anichent and Thriss left home for personal and professional reasons. Anichent's research and conferences had provided him with opportunities to visit Shar at the Academy. Thriss regularly went from Andor to Betazed with her own *zhavey,* a visiting professor from the Andorian Art Academy to Betazed University. During the war, Thriss had managed to meet Shar for weekend leave on three occasions. In the war's darkest hours, each of her visits had buoyed him up and renewed his resolve to press forward in the face of reports enumerating Starfleet losses. Her dreams of a post-war future underscored his determination to make the most of every duty shift, helped him avoid discouragement when the casualty reports listed the names of friends and officers he had served with.

Damn it, Zhavey! I had reconciled myself to not seeing them before I came home from the Gamma Quadrant. I had prepared myself and knew I could make it for another few months and then return home for the shelthreth. *But you couldn't trust me enough to accept my choice without questioning.*

Of all of them, he thought Thriss would have most appreciated this voyage. She never shied away from new experiences, always living close to the edge, plunging into the unknown when the rest of them cowered beneath their covers. Since they were children, she had always been the first to take a dare. More than once, her risks had landed her in the infirmary or before a disciplinary council, but her passion never dimmed. She never ceased to surprise him.

He still remembered the look on his bondmates faces as they stood by while Charivretha demanded he return with them to Andor.

Ever the optimist, Dizhei had tried to look cheerful, but her cloudy eyes and too bright smile betrayed her true feelings. Anichent's silence during the argument had disappointed Shar. After so many years of closeness, Shar assumed that he, even more than Thriss, would know why Shar needed to join this mission. Anichent had been Shar's first love, the one who, early on, had encouraged his academic pursuits, fed his ambitions to attend the Academy. Hadn't it been Anichent who, in his pragmatic, methodical way, outlined the sacrifices Shar would have to make in following the life path he had elected to take? But in their last encounter, he'd barely said a word.

And Thriss . . .

How many sleepless nights had they spent lying on their backs, mapping the constellations in Andor's heavens, interspersing their stargazing with talk about their goals and dreams? His absurd aspirations didn't sound quite so absurd when she brushed her lips against his ear, whispering words of encouragement. She, more the others, had always defended his choices, even when those choices were made at her expense. After everything they'd been through together, after he'd opened himself to her incandescent spirit and saw his own yearning for a better future reflected back at him . . . How was it that she, of all people, could come to him making that final desperate appeal as he was about to board *Defiant? Oh, Thriss . . .*

The shuddering transport groaned to a halt. Shar sprang through the barriers and ran up the steps to where the *Avaril*'s crew prepped for launch, *Defiant* once again nestled inside its cavernous bay. Hoards of Yrythny shuttled storage lockers of supplies into exterior hatches; officers with electronic tablets ran through pre-launch checklists. Shar surveyed the crowded platform until he found his own crew. Dr. Bashir was giving last-minute instructions to Ensign Juarez, who would stay behind as medic for Lieutenant Dax's team. Spotting his commanding officers engrossed in conversation, Shar worked his way over to them. He assumed a position at Vaughn's elbow, waiting for his turn.

"Transmit on subspace channel delta—" Vaughn was saying.

Ezri's brow furrowed. "Delta? That requires security encryption."

"Right. I want our communications kept private, just to be on the safe side."

"All right," Dax said, and then smiled. "Any last words of encouragement?"

"Yes. Try not to start a war this time."

"Very funny. I'm not Curzon, you know."

"Try to remember that and I'm sure you'll do fine." Vaughn surveyed the dwindling activity in the launch bay and said, "I expect we'll be departing shortly. Has your team finished offloading your supplies?"

Lieutenant Dax threaded her hands behind her back and stood up a little straighter before turning to Shar. "Ensign?" she said in her firmest command tone.

"Yes, sir. An hour ago."

"Excellent work, Ensign," Vaughn smiled, placing a hand on Shar's shoulder. "Since I won't be here to consult with Lieutenant Dax, feel free to offer any insights you might have gleaned from having a professional politician for a mother."

Never mind that I've spent most of my life trying to avoid being overtly associated with Zhavey . . . "Yes, sir." Shar took a deep breath. "Sir, if you don't mind—"

"Yes, Ensign?"

Shar fingered the isolinear chip in his hand. "Commander, I realize this is unorthodox, but I have a personal request to make . . ." His antennae tightened and twitched.

"If you'll excuse me," Dax interrupted, "I need to say good-bye to Julian."

Respectfully, Vaughn waited until Dax was out of earshot to speak. "You were saying, Ensign."

"When you transmit your weekly report to Colonel Kira, would it be possible to attach a personal letter to my bondmates?"

Vaughn smiled. "Of course, Shar," he said gently. holding out his hand to accept Shar's chip. "Though I can't guarantee that the report will go out on schedule, I'll make a point of adding your message to the data stream. Rest easy, Ensign."

"Thank you, sir," Shar said, flushed with gratitude. "And good luck."

As he walked away to look for Nog, Shar spotted exhausted Ensigns Senkowski and Permenter and knew his friend would be close at hand. Neither officer had been far from the *Defiant* since the *Avaril* docked. Earlier this morning, Shar had observed Permenter curled up on a storage locker, snoring. He turned a corner around stacked cargo canisters and as he suspected, found the chief engineer speaking animatedly. Enthused about the task at hand, Nog didn't notice that both ensigns stared at the padds they held, their bloodshot eyes looking like they were propped open with toothpicks.

"—and make sure that the cables we're running down the new EPS conduits are free of irregularities. The shield augmentation might destabilize if—Shar!" Nog exclaimed. "Want to hitchhike to the Consortium with my engineering crew? Lieutenant Dax won't care."

"You know how clumsy I am with a hyperspanner. I'd probably couple a flat ring to a trisk wire." Shar recalled more than a few near-misses during the Core repairs back at DS9.

"Hey! That was almost a joke. Not quite ready for stand-up at Vic's, but you're coming along nicely."

"Stand-up?"

"Never mind."

Shar had been gradually assimilating his shipmates' sense of humor on this trip. They tended to sprinkle humor into almost every conversation. He supposed that with practice, it would eventually come naturally to him.

"There's someone I want you to meet," Nog said. "Hey, Tlaral! Come over here." He waved her in their direction.

A Yrythny was bent over a communications unit, using a microlaser to fuse the last array component in place. She lifted her eyeshield. "I'm busy!" Tlaral shouted.

"I want you to meet my friend and shipmate, Ensign ch'Thane," Nog shouted.

Tlaral nodded politely, dropped the eye-shield and resumed her work.

Nog whispered, "She was one of the ones who beamed aboard to help us after we tripped the web weapon. If I could find a way to get Commander Vaughn to let me invite her to stay with the *Defiant* permanently, I would. She's a whiz with the cano pliers—and I've never seen an engineer who could diagnose a circuit board faster. Except maybe my father."

"Is she going with you?" Shar asked, wondering if the glow in Nog's face indicated that he might find true love, or at least serious infatuation, on this journey.

"Her husband—they call them consorts here—is a bigwig in the government. He's going to be on board, too. He's like the science minister or something? Mutters a lot."

"M'Yeoh. Yes, I've met him. Why is he going with you?"

"We need a senior government official in order to be able to trade at the Consortium. He was the only one who didn't need to be here for Ezri's gig."

Shar knit his brow quizzically. "Gig?"

"We need to go to Vic's more when we get back, Shar. You'll pick up the lingo in no time. You need to get into the groove."

Shar felt confident he could live a fulfilling life without knowing what a "groove" was, let alone getting into one.

The *Avaril* had been gone from Luthia for less than a day when the Yrythny General Assembly summoned Ezri to appear before them. She shouldn't have been surprised—they'd been anxious from the beginning.

Vaughn had only just launched when a messenger appeared with her nonnegotiable schedule, loaded with committee meetings from breakfast to bedtime. Having only a cursory knowledge of the Yrythny, she hardly had enough information yet to make any substantive pronouncements as to the merits of each case. She had wasted no time in assigning the entire away team to research while she'd locked herself into the makeshift office space provided her by the government. After a few minutes standing on her head (which seemed to settle her nerves) she had begun mapping out strategy, searching Curzon's memories for any relevant experiences he might have had. What she concluded was that whenever circumstances hurtled Curzon into the unknown, he was phenomenally gifted at faking it. *Some help you are, Old Man.*

So she had treated her meetings as she would a surprise exam or a red alert. Focus. Breathe. Study the situation. Act, not react. And try not to panic. It worked for the most part. A thirty-two hour diet of position papers had filled her head with facts. Whether she could put them together in a useful fashion was another issue altogether.

She was about to find out.

Nothing like having some prep time, Ezri thought, shuffling through the padds loaded with Yrythny history, law, customs and geography brought to her by Candlewood and Shar. She read as quickly as she could, catching the main points and leaving the fine print for later; hopefully, no one would be quizzing her. She'd just finished perusing a treatise on Wanderer rights when Shar appeared in her doorway.

"The escort's here, sir," Shar announced.

"Already? They're early!" Ezri moaned. "Help me gather all this up. And find me something I can carry it in. I don't know when I'll be coming back here today."

Shar quickly procured a shoulder bag and loaded it up with any and all items Ezri might need. *"Coral Sea Wars,* then *Black Archipelago Conflict,"* she pronounced finally. *"First Proclamation on Rights* came with the *Peace Talks."*

"I think *Black Archipelago* comes before the *Coral Sea Wars,"* Shar commented, then added "sir."

"After! Let's go!" She marched out of the office and into the exterior corridor, where the escort to the Assembly Hall awaited her.

* * *

Since he'd first set eyes on it, Vaughn knew that the *Avaril* rivaled even a Romulan warbird in size. After living aboard her for only a day, he decided that she conformed less to his notions of a starship than she did to a warp capable space station. Finding his way around identical spiraling corridors and dozens of transport car tracks proved challenging. If their wide-eyed expressions of confusion were any indication, his crew felt similarly.

Because *Defiant* was still, to all intents and purposes, uninhabitable until repairs were completed, the crew had been provided accomodations aboard *Avaril*. Bowers, who had been supervising the removal of personal crew gear from *Defiant*, had mistakenly guided a group, arms laden with duffel bags, to the *Avaril*'s engine room. Wisely, Chieftain J'Maah had designated several large empty rooms close by *Defiant*'s bay to serve as living space, minimizing the square meters in which the Starfleet crew could get lost. To facilitate intercultural understanding, Chieftain J'Maah had provided them access codes to the unrestricted portions of the ship's database. The voyage to the Consortium was expected to take four days in each direction, so Vaughn had issued a standing order that all *Defiant* personnel were to spend at least two hours daily exploring the political and social contexts of the sectors they were traveling through. In addition, attendance at scheduled inter-crew mixers was mandatory (the exception being Nog and his engineers: repairing the *Defiant* took precedence over all activities for the duration of the journey). For himself, he was determined to memorize the layout of the *Avaril*; he hated getting lost.

But there were practical concerns that required adaptation, such as the sleeping accommodations. Because the rooms given over to the *Defiant* crew weren't actually designed to be quarters, nothing remotely resembling a bed was available. Bashir and Prynn had been assigned to collect sleeping bags, blankets and pillows from *Defiant*. After the first night sleeping on the *Avaril*'s decks, Vaughn expected the crew's tolerance for noise, snoring and quirky bedtime routines to increase markedly.

With Bowers, Bashir, and Prynn still fine-tuning housekeeping and his briefings with Chieftain J'Maah completed, Vaughn was left with a block of time before he was scheduled to join the

Avaril's senior staff, including Science Minister M'Yeoh, for dinner and a discussion of what to expect at the Consortium.

From what Vaughn had gathered so far, M'Yeoh, in his ministerial position, would secure credentials for Vaughn to conduct trades under the Yrythny's sponsorship. Vaughn's impression of the science minister since their first encounter was of a sniveling career politician. Descending from one of the oldest and most prestigious Houses on Vanìmel had been enough to secure M'Yeoh a high government position. Developing a constructive working relationship with him over the next few days might prove challenging. Vaughn had never had much use for inheritors of power; they were too often more trouble than not in his experience.

Checking the time, Vaughn noted that he had about half an hour before he was to present himself in J'Maah's quarters. Having heard that the crew had organized a poker game for later in the evening, Vaughn decided to go on a personal errand now, before the meeting with J'Maah, freeing him up to play a few hands after dinner.

Though he knew unscheduled hours might be infrequent in coming days, he decided to forgo practicality and download the next volume of *The History of Terran Civilization* from the *Defiant*'s library into a padd for recreational reading. He'd finished the volume on Alexander the Great the day before they'd encountered the Cheka weapon; he was eager to revisit the rise of the Roman Empire.

With most of the crew settling into their new living spaces, Vaughn wasn't surprised to find the corridors outside *Defiant*'s bay empty. He entered his personal access code into the doorpad and strode across the bay, the hollow clap of his shoes against the deckplates echoing through the chamber. Like a recovering patient, *Defiant* rested on her seldom-used landing legs. Supplementary power modules attached to external access ports and long, snakelike umbilicals trickled energy into the ailing vessel's environmental systems. Vaughn patted her hull affectionately, hoping for her quick recovery. He ordered the hatch to open and he climbed aboard. Given the chance, Julian would lecture him about unnecessary radiation exposure, but the hyronalyn would cover him for more than the fifteen minutes the task required. Besides, decontamination was progressing at a good clip, and Vaughn wanted to sit in the captain's chair, feel the armrests beneath his hands, take in the view from the center of the bridge. He might not be *Defiant*'s first love, but he felt their courtship was going well and he missed being in her company.

He hadn't taken ten steps down the corridor beyond the airlock when he swore he heard the sound of a door closing. Tensing, he kept still and waited for any further sounds, but heard nothing. He didn't dare ask the computer for information. At the closest functional companel, he initiated internal and external sensor sweeps; both yielded nothing. As far as the computer was concerned, Vaughn was the only organic being in the repair bay. Still, he couldn't shake the sense that someone or something had been here—if not when he arrived, then certainly just before.

The *Defiant* had been boarded illicitly—he was sure of it. He wished the violation were unexpected, but the only unexpected part was how soon into their journey it had happened. Though his hosts had been gracious since achieving an "understanding," Vaughn knew intuitively that he needed to be wary.

Thus far, all his interactions with the Yrythny, save the manipulative tête-à-tête with the Assembly Chief, had been nonconfrontational and cordial. Vaughn had collided with enough admirals and politicians in his day to recognize that getting a job done sometimes required playing hardball. Since the unpleasantness back in Luthia, the Yrythny had facilitated his every request and resolved every concern he raised. That alone troubled him. Though it wasn't unreasonable to assume that the Yrythny's unhesitating cooperation had been bought with Vaughn's concession to allow Ezri to mediate, Vaughn had become too old and suspicious to take anything for granted. He found himself wondering what the next round of demands would be. *If any more unauthorized visitors come aboard, I need to know how, and why, and who's being so bold— without needlessly worrying the crew. I will* not *be surprised again.*

With great reluctance, Ezri tore her eyes away from the ceilings, and offered a courtly nod to two door attendants awaiting permission to admit her to the Grand Assembly Chamber. She had assumed upon seeing the hexagonal domes, the vaulted ceilings trimmed in gold, the filigree archways and the kilometer of inlaid marble floor, that she had reached the Chamber, but her escort, with some amusement, had informed her this was merely the lobby. She had gasped audibly when she saw the exterior chamber walls were encrusted with mosaics made of salmon, red, black and melon-colored corals, gemstones and burnished metals. Her escort, upon seeing her interest, explained that the pictures told the tableaux of Yrythny mythology and religion. How the Other had come from a faraway world to stir the primordial oceans of Vanìmel with its magic, thus allowing the Yrythny to leave the dark depths where they had always dwelt and be quickened into warm-blooded sentience. Within the artistic flourishes, exaggerated proportions and motifs, Ezri recognized the various stages of Yrythny evolution from amphibious animals to upright sentients, to a space-faring people who had constructed Luthia and developed warp drive. The picture-book story spread out above her was a helluva lot prettier than the pages of text she'd been force-fed. Certainly studying the mosaics could qualify as job related; she resolved to request the time to do so.

Shar cleared his throat and she realized the door attendants had placed their ceremonial scepters in a wall rack in preparation to admit her to the Chamber. Breathing out, she smoothed her uniform and waited for her cue. She could do this. Of course she could do this. Hadn't she made dozens of presentations before her classes at the Academy? This would be a piece of cake. She could tell that joke about the human, the Klingon, and the Romulan who walked into the Vulcan embassy, and then . . .

Upon seeing close to a thousand stern-faced Yrythny, dark eyes fixed on her, Ezri's mind blanked. She gulped. All the representatives stood in unison—a thunderous sound in the vast chamber—acknowledging her entrance. Those sitting closest to the center dais, the Upper Assembly representing the Houseborn, wore heavy robes of sapphire; those sitting on the balcony levels rimming the oval-shaped room, the Lower Assembly representing the Wanderers, wore green robes. She climbed a small number of stairs onto a rostrum of the presiding chairs. A backless bench was placed in front of a long flat table where Assembly Chair Rashoh, Vice Chair Jeshoh, Lower Assembly Chair Ru'lal and Lower Assembly Vice Chair Keren sat, soberly waiting for her.

As soon as she sat down, the entire Assembly resumed their

seats. Ezri shifted on the bench, trying to remember whether sitting with her legs crossed or tucked neatly together with ankles linked was more dignified.

The Assembly Chair touched a control, illuminating one of the closest representatives. Ezri guessed this was how the chair recognized a speaker. Her guess was confirmed when the delegate stood and addressed the Assembly.

"We have discussed, Assembly Chair, the matter of this outsider, Lieutenant Ezri Dax, functioning as a Third, and both assemblies have agreed by a narrow margin, to accept her input. I propose a resolution, which I am now sending to my fellow representatives." He thumbed a switch, ostensibly sending the text of his resolution to the other desks in the Chamber, ". . . that this Ezri Dax take up residence, planetside, in the House of my birth, Soid, where she can best learn the manner of our people and then render a judgment. I move for a vote."

He hadn't been sitting more than a minute when hundreds of lights began flashing on every level of the room. The Assembly Chair recognized a delegate seated near the Yrythny who had just spoken, but without permission another delegate on the opposite side of the room stood up and began speaking until yet another delegate stood and began speaking over the words of the other. Ezri jerked back and forth, trying to keep track of what was being said, the speakers, the lights, the points of order and resolutions, but found it impossible. The Assembly Chair's fingers flew across his desk panel, his jaw clenched, but none of those clamoring for recognition heeded his points of order. Jeshoh, Keren and the others looked on helplessly.

From what little she did follow, Ezri learned that members of each House protested any House but their own being designated as the one she would visit first. In turn, the Lower Assembly representatives felt that focusing on the Houseborn issues would prejudice her before she had a chance to hear the Wanderer side. As lights from the top of the Chamber went off and on, voices grew more heated, argumentative rhetoric stopped being funneled through the Master Chair and instead went directly toward the "enemy" party. Several delegates, robes catching on balustrades or on chairs, climbed over barriers separating delegations and further punctuated their arguments with their fists. Jeshoh shouted for order, as did Keren, but their calls were ignored.

And Ezri discovered that many hate-infused faces directed their venom at her. Seeing contempt and mistrust wherever she looked, she hoped the leadership had a plan to protect her, just in case she was mobbed. Thinking she could even attempt something of this magnitude was such a mistake. *Have you lost your mind Ezri? This is crazy!*

And then she remembered. A crumb, a fragment of a memory and she rooted around for the rest of it.

. . . Lela felt their hostility, their scorn, as she made the long trek from the door to her seat. As if being a woman, being young and being her symbiont's first host weren't enough to prejudice them against her, she knew she had a controversial proposal to make. Most of her colleagues would vehemently disagree with her idea, and it stood little chance of passing, but she knew that she had to make the proposal anyway because she couldn't live with herself if she didn't. Further, she knew that she would deserve their sneers and mocking whispers if she couldn't stand on the courage of her convictions. She knew that courage wasn't the absence of fear, but rather, acting in the face of fear. Rising from her desk, she lifted a hand, requesting the president pro tempore's attention and when he refused to see her, with a shaky voice she said . . .

". . . I am here because I believe in the cause of peace," Ezri began. "Because I believe that my unique perspective gives me the ability to see through the thick forest of rhetoric and rivalry and find the clarity that lies beyond the dark and shadowed path." And as Lela's words flooded back to her, Ezri's confidence increased, her voice ringing out more clear and strong, striking a chord with the quarrelling Yrythny until gradually, they settled down, resumed their seats and prepared to listen.

Of course I can do this, she thought triumphantly. *I'm Dax.*

6

"What is this, the eleventh time you've searched Jake's quarters?" Ro observed, the door hissing closed behind her.

Sitting on the couch in front of a storage box, Kira looked up from the antique book she perused. "These items were transported from B'hala. I think I've only looked through them three or four times." She took a sip from a mug sitting on the coffee table. "A fifth time can't hurt."

Ro sat down in a chair across from Kira. "Nothing new, I assume." In the course of her duties, she, too, had examined the contents of every box stacked against the walls. Anything he'd left behind had been systematically analyzed and catalogued. Though foul play wasn't readily evident in the circumstances surrounding Jake's departure, Bajoran and Starfleet security were treating the disappearance like a criminal investigation.

"I thought maybe knowing Jake's frame of mind when he left might give us some clues. I've been thumbing through the book the investigators found on his nightstand, but so far," she paused, examining the spine of the novel and reading aloud, *"The Invisible Man* hasn't proved to be much help."

"The forensic behavioral specialists from headquarters combed through his personal logs, his books, his schedule, who he was eating dinner with—his diet even—and they didn't draw any conclusions."

"But I *know* Jake. I should be able to see nuances that the experts might not," Kira said, dropping the book back into the carton. Replacing the lid, she pushed the carton aside and moved on to open another numbered container. She examined an insert listing the carton's contents. "Looks like work clothes and family pictures in here."

The depth of Kira's loyalty never ceased to astound Ro. To her, it appeared that Kira spent every minute she could spare from her regular duties focused on solving the mystery of Jake Sisko's disappearance. Ro didn't find fault in Kira's single-mindedness. Jake's vanishing coupled with Captain Sisko's mysterious disappearance and Odo's departure made for a major string of losses. Kira's behavior was more than justified to Ro's way of thinking.

"I've followed your updates throughout the day and the situation generally appears to be under control. I'll send a strongly worded memo to the Klingon ambassador reminding him that docking on Deep Space 9 is a privilege, not a right." Kira reached into the box, flipped through a pile of photos, and pushed aside a neatly folded sweater before removing a padd. "What did you think of Ambassador Lang and Gul Macet?"

"Lang surprised me," Ro confessed, smiling as she remembered. "We started talking—even had a few laughs—and we're meeting for drinks in a few hours. I think she's curious about what's going on around the station . . . to see if anyone from the old days is still around."

"You know about her history with Quark?" Kira circled her hand two or three times to indicate "the rest of the story."

Ro shrugged. "Quark doesn't kiss and tell unless it gives him more room to maneuver. The look on his face when I walk through the door with Lang should be pretty revealing."

"I imagine it will," Kira said dryly. "Anything else come out of Macet's presence aboard the station that I should know about?"

"Minor accidents. An unfortunate incident with a *jumja* stick when Macet made an unexpected appearance near the arboretum."

Kira winced. "Prognosis?"

"Dr. Tarses said a few sutures and an analgesic would cover it. A fainting here and there. An irate prylar who swears we're seeing the second coming of Gul Dukat—based on an obscure passage from the *Larish Book of Prophecy.*"

"Macet . . ." Kira said, absently tracing shapes on the coffee table with her finger. "Do you have any thoughts?"

"Yeah. I want to run my own DNA tests because it's too bizarre to be believed." Ro had been eager to say those words aloud since she met Macet. Standing face-to-face with the physical reincarnation of Dukat had catapulted her thirty years into the past. From her days on Bajor, she recalled waiting in the soup line, staring at the screens bearing the prefect's holo, wondering if the image was of a real person or something the Cardassians invented to scare their slaves. The way Bajoran mothers would invoke the *pah-wraiths* to warn their disobedient children. Ro never bought the folklore about the *pah-wraiths* anymore than she now accepted what she'd been told about Macet.

"Ro, your reaction's understandable, but—" Kira said, doing her best to sound like she believed what she was saying.

"Colonel, there have been no confirmed sightings of Dukat since your own experience with him at Empok Nor," Ro stated emphatically. Believing Kira was about to protest, Ro pressed on. "And I know the rumors about the fire caves. Without concrete confirmation, they're just that—rumors. Dukat could be anywhere, doing anything," Ro argued. "He's insane! Who's to say he hasn't developed some alternate personality and it's this Macet."

"Akellen Macet was known to the Federation even before the Occupation ended," Kira said patiently. "Starfleet Command sent me his file right after I notified them of his role in the Europa Nova evacuation. And Alon Ghemor transmitted the gul's DNA records as well as his own personal assurance of Macet's identity."

Why Kira insists on sticking to the official party line, I don't get, Ro thought. *But I suppose being in charge means you have to appease the brass. That doesn't mean I have to.* "Asking Gul Macet to submit to a station security ID verification wouldn't be out of line considering our current alert status." Ro wanted her shot at him. Have him in her office on her terms.

Kira's eyes drilled into Ro's. "While I have no doubt that Macet would agree to it, I won't authorize it. Consider this issue closed, Lieutenant."

Knowing the debate was over, Ro pursed her lips and said, "Yes, Colonel."

"Anything else?" Kira took a deep breath and leaned back against the couch.

"In direct violation of your orders, Taran'atar has been shrouding and spying on our Cardassian guests." Ro conveyed the details of the Taran'atar incident to Kira with more objectivity than she felt. Part of her was glad Taran'atar might be out gathering the intelligence that would, with any luck, put her own lingering doubts to rest.

"I'll handle Taran'atar," Kira said, her expression pensive. "But continue to note any disruptive behavior. What's next?"

Kira's lack of reaction to Taran'atar's disobedience surprised her. Ro paused, wanting to ask how Kira planned on managing the Jem'Hadar. How could Kira be comfortable with Taran'atar playing by his own rules? Under usual circumstances, she'd pass off responsibility for Taran'atar without a second thought. This time, Ro had to trust that Kira had a plan to prevent him from provoking the Cardassians. Macet and Lang she didn't worry about. Macet's soldiers were another matter. If Macet's soldiers reciprocated Taran'atar's undisguised animosity, trouble was inevitable.

"Problem, Lieutenant?" Kira asked.

Shaken out of her thoughts, Ro answered, "We do have a delicate situation involving Councillor zh'Thane." Without sharing the finer points of Andorian physiology, Ro explained zh'Thane's end-of-shift visit and the resultant request to Kira.

Kira nodded. "How do you want to handle this?"

"Perform in-depth background checks on zh'Thane's staff. Send a crew to scan every centimeter of her ship. Everything checks out, she gets a pass off the station."

"All right. I'll update Admiral Akaar on zh'Thane's request. He shouldn't have any objections if he's in the loop from the beginning."

"Good point." There came a moment in every conversation when enough had been said; for Ro, it was the mention of Akaar. Until he had shown up, Ro had been able to put off sorting through her issues with Starfleet. His presence triggered many unhappy memories. *At least Kira's dealing with him.* "Will there be anything else, Colonel?"

"You're dismissed. Oh. Wait." Kira looked sheepish. "Just to satisfy my own curiosity, but you wouldn't know how the reception plans are coming along, would you?"

"Would that be why Quark was following Ensign Beyer around begging her to sample his tube grubs with icoberry sauce? Come to think of it, she had tablecloths draped over her shoulders and a mouth full of food last time I saw her," Ro said.

"The tube grubs must be for Ambassador Gandres—he has a fondness for all things Ferengi, or so I'm told."

"I'm impressed, Colonel. You managed to delegate party planning duty pretty quick."

"Shakaar insisted on having the job done correctly. As station commander, it's my obligation to find the individual who can best meet the minister's expectations."

"Whatever you say, Colonel," Ro said, grinning as she turned toward the door.

"Oh—and if Ambassador Lang says anything you think I might find useful—"

Ro paused. From appearances, Kira's evening would consist of replicated *raktajino* and a cold floor. *I bet Kira would enjoy a night out. I should . . . no. I wouldn't want her to feel like she had to accept my invitation, and it might be awkward to turn me down. Maybe another time.* She finally said, "Goes without saying, Colonel."

Kira had removed another box from the stack before Ro made it to the door. Persistent as she was, Ro couldn't imagine starting and restarting the tedious process of searching for answers in those boxes—especially since she was confident there were none to be found.

The difference between a believer and an unbeliever, Ro thought.

When Charivretha entered Thirishar's quarters, Anichent raised his hand to request that she refrain from interrupting his conversation. She recognized the Vulcan on the viewscreen as a well-known scientist. It pleased her to see that Anichent was working on his post-doctoral research instead of frittering away his time, moping as Thriss seemed bent on doing. How capably Anichent navigated his technically dense conversation with his colleague! All their talk of rips in space-time fabric fascinated her, but she doubted she could explain it if called on. Science had never been her forte.

During her student days, Charivretha had taken only the minimum requirements in physics, chemistry and biology, choosing instead to fill her schedule with extra courses in political science and government. Still, she found the physical sciences exciting in a mysterious way. In relaxed, intimate moments, one of her bondmates, a warp propulsion theorist, whispered to her the subtle poetry of swirling galaxies and interstellar fusion—a unique ritual between lovers to be sure. Her devotion to him was not unlike

Shar's love for Anichent. In this one way, she and her *chei* were similar.

Anichent deactivated the subspace link and turned to her. "Thank you for waiting, *Zhadi*. I meant no disrespect."

Thinking about how pleased Shar would be to see his bondmate immersed in the work he loved, Charivretha affectionately squeezed Anichent's shoulders. "You amaze me, Thavanichent. You should apply for that fellowship at the Daystrom Institute."

"As you say." He flushed, and looked away, focusing on gathering up the bioneural circuit sheets and isolinear chips scattered over his work surfaces. The Vulcan he'd been conversing with was engineering a device to be retrofitted on starship arrays; Anichent had decided to see if he could build a miniature model of the device in order to verify his own findings.

Charivretha could imagine Anichent, one day, deciding to join Starfleet engineering as a way to facilitate spending more time with Shar. They could request joint assignments. Both of them would be less lonely. Charivretha believed having a bondmate by his side could only help Shar, stabilize him, reinforce his obligations to the Andorian Whole.

Feeling conspicuous for not helping, Charivretha dropped to the floor, working to assist Anichent in gathering his things. "I've come with a plan for the evening. I think it would be good for all of you. Don't give me that look, Anichent. Even you need to rest from your work—to recreate."

"Dizhei must have talked to you," he said sagely. He leaned over the desk and chairs, searching for any components he might have missed.

And that's not the half of it . . . Unwilling to revisit the humiliating discussion she'd had with Lieutenant Ro, Charivretha avoided following up on Anichent's words. He could draw his own conclusion. "How many days has it been since you three did something fun? Dizhei has been correcting her students' projects, you've been tinkering with hyperspanners and laser drills and Thriss has been preparing her residency applications—"

"Not many of them," Anichent muttered.

Those two, quarreling again? Do they ever stop? Poor Dizhei! Taking sides might disturb the precarious bondgroup dynamic, so she resolved to avoid any topic that might result in a conversation about Thriss. "You all deserve to be rewarded!" Charivretha said, reassembling a toolkit. "There was quite a bidding war over these holosuite hours. An attaché I work with was our most eager competitor, but in the end, I succeeded. I'm not about to let such a valuable opportunity go to waste."

Anichent placed the last of his items into a nearby case. "I suppose we should ask Dizhei and Thriss if they feel up to going out."

"Come with me, would you?" Charivretha asked. Anichent nodded stiffly and arm in arm they went to find the others.

No one will notice, Thriss thought, her hand hovering over the control panel. The temptation to increase the volume overpowered her fear of being caught; she made the adjustment. Out of the corner of her eye, she watched Dizhei. When her bondmate continued working without interruption, Thriss relaxed.

From the time they were little, Shar's voice had always hypnotized her. He wasn't prone to long speeches or flowery language but the tone in his voice made her shiver deliciously. She recalled "borrowing" school supplies from his desk just so he would have to ask her where she'd put them. Once, during their exercise period, she'd casually thrown a foot out in front of him during a foot race, sending him sprawling to the floor. Of course she'd volunteered to escort him to the nurse. That was the first time she'd touched him: dabbing a lumpy bruise on his forehead with a cool cloth. Oh, how annoyed he'd been with her! She smiled a little sadly at the memory. *Now he's thousands of light years away without me to take care of him.* She rubbed her eyes, hoping Dizhei didn't see the beginnings of tears.

Notwithstanding Dizhei's unfailing kindness, Thriss knew she became impatient with the weepiness. The high rounded back of her chair shielded her somewhat from Dizhei, though, so she hugged her legs tight against her body, rested her chin on her knees and settled in to watch the recording.

Several days ago, she'd been browsing through Shar's database when she discovered his journal—what Starfleet people called their personal logs. At first, she watched them after Anichent and Dizhei were asleep, fearing their disapproval, selfishly wanting to hold something of Shar's for herself. Both her bondmates fussed about propriety, about respecting personal boundaries. Thriss knew that delving, uninvited, into these recordings might be construed as a violation, but she couldn't help herself. And it became harder and harder to wait until the middle of the night to spend time with Shar. So she decided to risk viewing them now, even though Dizhei, who listened with earpieces to her students' assignments, was in the room with her.

From what she could see, he appeared happy. This latest assignment to DS9 agreed with him. Seeing his contentment, however, always led her back to questioning why he couldn't be content with *her*. Why not come back to Andor for the *shelthreth* and then she'd go wherever he wanted her to. They simply had to put their obligations behind them.

Voices in the background cued her that others had joined her and Dizhei. *Why did Anichent have to come in now? I want to finish watching this day first, the day he received my gift.* She saw Shar looking at the elaborate model of Andorian DNA, constructed with rounded, highly polished, multicolored crystals. It pleased her to see he kept it on the shelf closest to his bed.

"Thriss!"

Abruptly, she spun her chair around and before she could protest, found herself facing Charivretha.

Dizhei, sprawled on the bed studying childishly drawn maps illustrating Andor's geography, startled when Charivretha addressed Thriss, her earpiece dropping into her hand. Anichent plopped down by Dizhei, leaning over to whisper in his bondmate's ear.

"Computer, halt playback," Charivretha snapped. "Do you have authorization to examine Shar's logs?" she asked Thriss.

"He gave us access to his quarters. Access is access," Thriss explained. She respected Charivretha. Honored her. Feared her. But in this one place, where their personal interests intersected in Shar, Thriss and Charivretha were forever at odds. Charivretha accepted Thriss because she matched Shar's genetics, but his *zhavey* made no secret of her preference for Anichent, or her admiration for Dizhei. Further, Charivretha resented Thriss' unconditional support for Shar's decisions, especially those decisions that conflicted with the priorities Charivretha believed Shar ought to embrace. And with Charivretha, duty defined life. Duty and obligation. When Thriss refused to use her influence to pressure Shar into accepting

Charivretha's edicts, the barriers between Thriss and her *zhadi* grew, but Thriss didn't care. She loved Shar too much to see him unhappy, even if it meant sacrificing her own happiness. And there was that little tendency of hers—a tendency to resent being told what to do.

Charivretha specialized in telling people what to do. She had made a career of it.

"Personal logs require passwords." Charivretha grabbed Thriss by the chin and, treating her like a child, tipped her face up.

"I know his passwords," Thriss said. She met Charivretha's pointed stare, her stormy gray eyes revealing nothing.

"You stole his passwords," accused Anichent.

Dizhei placed a steadying arm around Anichent's waist, trying to soothe him.

"I don't steal, Anichent," Thriss snapped, jerking her head out of Charivretha's palm. "I know these things about Shar. He's used the same password for his private files since he was fifteen. If he hadn't wanted me to read them, he would have changed the password. He didn't, so I can do as I please. With his blessing." Because she understood Shar's deep affection for Anichent, Thriss hated arguing with him; she tried avoiding it—another way she honored Shar. Too bad genetic matches didn't mean good personality matches. If it were possible to be more opposite from Anichent than she was, Thriss didn't know how. They were fire and ice.

The antennae on Anichent's head twitched and flexed, his eyes darkened. "You behave as if this blessing extends only to you, and not to Dizhei or myself. How do you know I don't have knowledge of Shar's passwords?"

Why was he always seeking a fight? "View the logs. I don't care."

"I respect my *ch'te* enough to allow him the privacy of his own thoughts," Anichent snapped.

She tossed her hair. "Or perhaps you're afraid that those thoughts aren't of you."

Charivretha shushed them both, sending Anichent into the other room to check on the featured menu at Quark's. Thriss complied with Charivretha's orders to keep peace. One more argument with Anichent would mean ending her day with another headache; Thriss wearied of fitful sleep. She moved away from the desk and dropped down onto the edge of the bed; Dizhei alternated between massaging her shoulders and stroking her hair.

Taking Thriss' place in front of the monitor, Charivretha exited Shar's logs and then explained her intended evening plans.

Thriss bit back a complaint. Well-intentioned as she was, Charivretha always wanted to fix things even when, given time, resolutions might occur naturally. The thought of spending a night pretending to have a good time so Dizhei and Anichent wouldn't have one more reason to be irritated with her. . . . Anichent especially. "I have applications to finish," she said, offering the first excuse she could come up with. "And you know me and holosuites."

Before Charivretha could retort, Dizhei tenderly placed her head in Thriss' lap, linking her fingers through hers, stroking the back of her hand with her thumb.

Oh, all right. Guilt works too, Thriss thought.

"We could visit the Palace of Zhevazha or take roles in one of the Sagas," Dizhei suggested. "You always enjoy swordplay. Or maybe we could visit a favorite spot. You love Casperia Prime. You told me yourself that the days you and Shar spent climbing there were the best vacation you'd had in years!"

On rare occasions, segments of the bond would section off in a pair or trio. Thriss and Shar had gone away together once—after he graduated from the Academy and before he assumed his wartime assignment. She cherished those days as belonging to her and Shar alone, never sharing any details of their time together with either Anichent or Dizhei.

Thriss leaned down to touch her cheek to Dizhei's. "You go, *sh'za.* You and Anichent deserve to relax away from me. I'm not good company right now. Enjoy food that's not replicated. You told me last week you wanted to learn to play *tongo,* this is your chance!"

Almost imperceptibly, Dizhei shook her head. "I'll stay with you. It's not good to be alone. Anichent can go with *Zhadi.*"

Thriss eased Dizhei up from her lap. Cupping Dizhei's face in her hands, Thriss touched her forehead to hers. They entwined fingers through each other's hair. Dizhei was like a *zhavey* to her. Thriss decided she could yield—make an honest effort to get along with the group. "I believe the last time we fenced, you beat me.

Every game. Don't assume you'll have an advantage this time."
Thriss smiled and Dizhei reciprocated.

In the doorway, Anichent appeared holding Quark's evening
menu; he sighed, visibly relieved.

Thriss assumed that Anichent was happy he didn't have to take
her on; their "discussions" usually ended after heated words or
thrown furniture—and it wasn't always her doing the throwing.
Neither of them enjoyed being pitted against the other in the battle
for Shar's affection; both resented, justifiably, having to defend
their places in Shar's life.

She wasn't entirely so self-absorbed that she didn't know what
Anichent really thought: he believed Shar's unusually strong attachment to her would fade after the *shelthreth* because he saw her
and Shar's relationship as being comprised of physical urges, sexual chemistry. He clung to the hope that in the long run, Shar would
choose a mindmate over a bed partner. *What Anichent doesn't see
is that I am both,* Thriss thought triumphantly.

Neither she nor Anichent spoke of what would happen to Dizhei,
who nurtured and loved them all, regardless of what her own future
held. She cared more about their collective concerns than her own.
Thriss' own *zhavey* had chastised her once for their overlooking
Dizhei's needs, chalking it up to youthful myopia. As time passed,
Thriss recognized her *zhavey* was right: Dizhei was the stabilizing
influence that held their bond together.

Thank the gods for Dizhei, Thriss thought. *One of us needs to
keep their wits about them.*

Quark leaned against the bar, both lobes focused on table 5
where Natima and Ro sat conversing. Normally, the layers of bar
noise never interfered with his ability to follow whatever conversations were underway. He'd grown accustomed to filtering out the
dings of the dabo wheel, the clatter of latinum at the *tongo* table,
clinking glasses and the clicking heels of the servers as they raced
across the floor to pick up their drink orders. But tonight, he swore
Ro must have brought some privacy device to protect whatever fe-
male-talk she had planned with Natima. It was like that nightmare
he had where he showed up at his vault to collect his latinum only
to discover his vault was a front operation for a Bajoran Orphans

Charity Fund. He'd given away everything he'd earned without realizing it. Talk about feeling naked before the universe! That same panicked sensation threatened to wash over him now as, try as he might, he couldn't figure out what those conniving females were up to. *But oh, they're lovely to look at, aren't they?*

Natima, her thick hair sparkling with merlot-colored gems woven into the twist down her back and extending to her waist, wearing that crisp, shimmering red-black gown, the square neckline showing off enough of her fine, feminine assets to bring back pleasant memories of springwine and *oomox*. And Ro, zipped to the neck in some stretchy blue thing that looked far too Starfleetish for Quark's preference, still had that dark, sexy tomboy aura going for her. Too bad Garak wasn't around to offer Ro some off-duty wardrobe advice. He might have been able to persuade her to try something more flattering. Quark shuddered when he recognized the lunacy of that last thought. *A female reduces me to missing Garak?* Quark poured himself a shot of whiskey, threw it back in one swift motion and waited for the burning sensation in his eyes to recede. With all the chattering, he could only pick up the slightest hint of the timbre of Natima's voice or the higher notes in Ro's laugh.

At least she's laughing.

But what if she was laughing at him?

He'd thrown back a second shot before he'd even had a chance to consider how his staff might take advantage of his panic by pocketing their own tips. Quark made a mental note: *Conduct locker and body searches before staff clocks out.*

Several stools away from where he stood, he noticed an unfamiliar Starfleet officer sitting quietly, sipping spoonfuls from a bowl of what looked like plomeek soup and reading the latest edition from the Federation News Service. He scoped her out. A thin, platinum band on her left hand, fine age lines around her eyes and a centered sensibility evidenced by how easily she focused on her reading in this noisy room. Discerning her descent (she was a bit too—pointy?—to be all human) proved challenging. Before he'd drawn any conclusions, he found a pair of steady green eyes fixed on him.

"Hello," she said. "You must be Quark."

"And you must be a new customer I need to impress. Can I get you something to drink?" He sauntered down the bar and cozied up

113

to the new kid on the station. Pretty. Nice hands. Definitely on the curvy side of female. Add a plunging neckline and she'd be a dabo girl to be reckoned with.

"Thanks. But the soup is fine until my husband gets here," she said with a polite smile, and resumed reading.

And what in that padd could possibly be more interesting than me? Maybe it was his approach. He tried again. "I've quite a selection of otherworldly delicacies. Can I get something going for you and your husband, Lieutenant Commander—"

"Matthias. Actually, I believe he's already eaten with our children. We're meeting here before we attend Prylar Kanton's B'hala lecture."

"A lecture?" Quark couldn't hide how underwhelmed he was by her choice of entertainment. "A spin at the *dabo* wheel or a hand of *tongo* wouldn't be more fun? Who knows—you might get lucky."

She tucked a loose amber-blond tendril behind her ear and took another spoonful of soup. "I'm certain the lecture will be very pleasant."

Pleasant. We wake up in the morning so our day can be pleasant? What a sad, sad life. He sighed. With Bajor about to join the Federation and the Militia poised to be assimilated into Starfleet, the fun quotient around here will plunge. One more reason to search for business options elsewhere . . .

. . . A search that might be aided by one Ambassador Natima Lang, Quark suddenly realized, and reminded himself that he needed to keep her under his watchful eye.

"My house specialty drinks are the perfect way to toast your *pleasant* evening," he suggested to Matthias. "A Warp Core Breech? Black Hole? Triskelion Tidal Wave?"

"I'll pass. After all, once I'm done with the lecture—a *pleasant* part for him since he's an archeologist—the *excitement* begins in the atrium with a candlelight dinner for two. The Chateau Mouton Rothschild we're being served will be my drink quota for the night."

Quark grimaced. "Why settle for something as pedestrian as a Rothschild when I can offer you the seductive delights of a thousand worlds?"

"That's a risk I'm willing to take."

Quark *tsked* and left Matthias to her soup. *Having Natima around must be throwing my game off,* Quark thought. He couldn't remember the last time he'd gone zero for five on a sale. He resumed his perch within eyesight of Natima and Laren.

"You must be very fond of her," Matthias observed, ostensibly attending to her padd.

Quark twisted toward the officer, but realized she wasn't looking at him. "Are you talking to me?"

"You were involved with the Cardassian at that table, what, five or more years ago." She paused, pondering her next words thoughtfully. "Things didn't end well. You're watching for an opening to go over there to find out what they've been talking about."

Oh please don't let me be dealing with a telepath. I'll never be able to fix the wheels again! Panic threatened to flood him.

Matthias must have noticed his discomfort because she quickly clarified her comments. "I spent five years doing field research in inter-species anthropology. Studying the body language patterns and brain stem physiological reactions of a number of Alpha Quadrant sentients. Most individuals fail to realize how much their unconscious reactions reveal about them."

Being a man whose work it was to know what his customers wanted without asking, Quark appreciated her area of study. "Remarkable that you can know so much without reading my mind."

"I didn't say that," she teased. "I have some Vulcan ancestry, but it's a few generations back on my father's side. Your secrets are safe, Quark."

"Secrets? I have no secrets. My life is an open book."

"True. Ferengi aren't particularly complicated to decipher."

"Not particularly complicated?" Quark felt like he'd just been insulted.

"No," she said, unapologetically.

"So you can just look at whoever happens to walk into the room and after a relatively short observation figure who and what that person is about."

"More or less. Some sentients are more obscure than others."

"You don't say?" *Now that's a talent a good businessman could learn to exploit.* "What about him?" Quark asked, indicating Morn, who sat in his usual seat, nursing a tall mug of frothy ale. The Lurian turned toward Matthias and blinked blearily.

"He falls into the obscure category," she said.

Impressed, Quark considered asking Commander Matthias if she could share a few tips that would enhance his already formidable skills in the fine art of behavioral profiling, but before he could open his mouth, in walked a Bajoran man with smooth pate and a thick, but neatly trimmed brown-black beard. Decently tailored clothes for an academic. Quark watched as the man cast a glance around the room, smiling when he spotted Matthias; he moved speedily to her side. *The husband, I presume.*

Their animated whispers held no interest for Quark. Before he could ask the husband if maybe he wanted a spin at the dabo wheel, Matthias pushed away her half-emptied soup bowl. *Holding hands like newlyweds,* Quark thought cynically, as they left the bar presumably to hear Prylar Kanton's scintillating lecture on the wonders of B'hala.

Morn watched him, straight-faced.

"What are you looking at Mr. Obscure?" Quark snapped, sending his best customer scurrying off for cover behind the new dabo boy, guessing correctly that Quark's glare wouldn't find him there. Quark spent a good part of his day pretending he didn't have a dabo boy.

"Table 6 wants the Dabo-Dom-Jot Special," Treir said, sidling up beside him.

Quark also spent a good part of his day pondering those staff members most likely to exploit any weakness on the part of management. "We don't have a Dabo-Dom-Jot Special," he answered, waiting to see what angle Treir was coming from. She had to have one: she wouldn't be Treir if she didn't.

"I invented it after I realized that the gentleman at table 6 will cough up one bar of gold-pressed latinum for the Dabo-Dom-Jot special." She indicated an assorted group of humans, smuggler or mercenary types, huddling in a corner of the bar.

Quark grinned. Holosuites going for five times their usual rates. Latinum for bogus package deals, and two gorgeous females sitting right in his eye line. Maybe things weren't going so bad, even if he couldn't understand *a single word those females were saying!* He composed himself. This was business, after all. "By all means, offer them the Special."

"See, the thing is, if I become the Dabo part of the Dabo-Dom-Jot

116

special, I want fifteen percent instead of my usual five percent," she said, dropping seasoning tablets into half a dozen Black Holes.

Treir, there isn't a tar pit big enough or dark enough to hold your evil mind. "No deal." He wasn't in the mood to take more punishment at female hands than he had to. He'd figure out his own bogus package deal and charge more.

"Fine. I'll tell them to check out the Fifth Moon Casino on their way home to New Sydney. Their Dabo-Dom-Jot special is only 45 strips, anyway."

"Ten percent," he countered.

"I would have settled for eight, but thanks for the bonus."

An incongruity in Treir's tale occurred to him. "How could the Fifth Moon Casino charge 45 strips for their Dabo-Dom-Jot special if you invented it?"

Her white teeth shone against her jade complexion.

Whatever temporary stupidity was afflicting him had better go away in a hurry. He'd be giving every dabo girl vacation days before the night was out. And there was the legitimate possibility he was worrying about nothing. He needed intelligence, but he wasn't about to waltz over there and talk to Natima and Ro directly. *"Excuse me, ladies, somebody here mention my name?"* What an idiot! If they weren't laughing about him already, they'd certainly be laughing about him after that.

Quark needed a spy.

"Treir, you haven't had a chance to see if table 5 needs their drinks refreshed. I happen to know the Cardassian ambassador has a fondness for Samarian Sunsets."

"Translated: Have I heard any good gossip eavesdropping on your girlfriends?"

"You got your extra five percent. I'd say that's worth something."

Treir sighed. "Natima said something about someone never guessing that she was faking it because if she let things go any further, he'd find out that—"

Quark held up a hand to silence her. "I've heard enough, thanks. Go be the Dabo part of the Dabo-Dom-Jot special."

"I need to change first," she said. "Oh. And Councillor zh'Thane's party is up next for the holosuites. You might want to send a ten-minute warning to the group in there now. Never know if they're in a compromising position." She sauntered into the backroom.

He mulled over Treir's tidbit. His stomach tightened. He imagined every possible permutation of conversation that might lead to those comments from his former lover and the object of his present pursuit and he liked none of them. From the rear, the sounds of the cellar hatch slamming closed and storage clattering to the floor gave him one more reason to worry. *What was Treir doing back there?*

Treir emerged, a florescent pink hairpiece mounted on her head, a short spangled dress dangling beads and pearlized bells. The outfit had much in common with an exploding wedding dais.

"Um, Treir. About what you're wearing . . ." Quark began.

"They were talking about the oddest place they'd ever hid a weapon, by the way," she whispered in his ear as she pranced by.

In that moment, Quark had enough. Either that, or the whiskey had finally unbound his courage.

A Ferengi's gotta do what a Ferengi's gotta do, Quark recited in his mind, steeling himself to face Natima. The 100th Rule of Acquisition. He slid a tray off the rack, ordered up a couple of drinks and started off on what he hoped would appear to be a leisurely stroll across the floor.

"He's coming," Ro said, quietly. Because Lang's chair only half faced the bar, Ro had kept Quark under surveillance. Once they'd transcended the usual swapping of histories and small talk, the status of their dealings with Quark had come up. Ro explained her still ambiguous intentions toward him; Lang related the story of their affair. Resolving that neither woman had any reason to compete with the other, they closed the book on Quark in just under five minutes by placing a small wager on how long he would be able to endure watching them from a distance before his curiosity—or anxiety—drove him to check on them.

"He lasted longer than I thought he would," Lang said.

"You think he's built up a good head of paranoia?"

"Probably. I'll pay you after we settle up our bill."

"That's all right. Winning's enough for me."

"Ah! You enjoy the game more than the prize. I respect that." Lang grinned, raised her glass of *kanar* and clinked a toast with Ro.

"Ladies," Quark said, sliding the drink tray onto their table. "Thought I'd bring over a little theme drink I've concocted for the reception. See if you think the diplomatic corps will approve. I call it a Peace Treaty. Starts off provocative, ends on a smooth note."

"Thanks, Quark," Ro said, taking a drink from the tray and passing it to Natima before taking one for herself. Ro choked, barely avoiding spitting up. "A bit heavy on the syrup."

Thoughtfully, Natima palmed the glass, swirling the liquid around and delicately smacked her lips as if to contemplate the drink's overtones. "The sweet juxtaposes the fire of the whiskey nicely."

"Sounds like the dealings between your governments could take awhile, eh, ladies?" Quark said, bussing empty appetizer dishes onto the drink tray. "Consensus can be hard to come by."

"No, I think we've found consensus on many things," Natima said, her sparkling eyes searching out Ro's.

Taking her cue, Ro nodded in agreement. "Absolutely. I think Bajorans and Cardassians can find a lot of common ground."

"Oh. I suppose that's positive," Quark said, glancing between the women. "So . . ."

"So . . ." Natima echoed.

He stood in front of the table, tapping his foot, waiting, and clearly hoping that one of his guests would say something. Ro felt no obligation to rescue Quark. His seeming inability to string together a snappy comeback was a rare enough occurrence to be novel to her. She contented herself with surveying the crowd; playing security chief for a minute or two couldn't hurt anything. Besides, if anything was going to get out of hand tonight, she'd like advance notice. A large cluster of off-duty Starfleet personnel moved aside, giving her full view of Councillor zh'Thane accompanied by Shar's bondmates. Now was as good a time as any to update zh'Thane's party regarding her special request.

And let poor Quark off the hook.

"Quark, why don't you have a seat? I have an early shift and some business to take care of," Ro said, rising. "And put all this on my tab, would you? Ambassador, it's been a delight."

Lang raised her glass again as Ro stood up. "The pleasure was mine, Lieutenant."

"We still have our evening together, Laren?" Quark said, a bit too loudly.

Lang covered her mouth with her hand, but not before a guffaw escaped.

Ro sighed. "Once everyone's adjusted to the new security protocols and the reception is over, I'll be able to make definite plans," Ro explained, "But I think I'll be ready to put in a holosuite reservation soon." She gave Natima a little wink and headed off to meet with zh'Thane.

"Lieutenant Ro and I are exploring the possibility of a social relationship," Quark said after she'd left.

"She mentioned that you two got along pretty well," Natima said.

He watched Ro cross over to where the Andorian party—all four of them—waited for their holosuite. He'd heard rumors about some of the unique quirks of Andorian biology and was—intrigued?—by the commercial possibilities. "Hmmm. Now there's a holoprogram I'm certain would be a big hit: 'Andorian Ecstasy: Good Things Come In Fours.' Never occurred to me before now, but it might have more wide-scale appeal than just for Andorians. Few people know about Andorians and how they, you know." He grinned luridly. "Very hush-hush."

Natima rolled her eyes. "And is it possible that they tend to be a private people precisely to avoid having their intimate relationships exploited by entrepreneurial Ferengi?"

"All sentients are motivated by the need to eat and the need to reproduce. It's variety in both that keeps life interesting."

"So you see yourself as the host at a buffet table of exotic delights of all shapes and sizes?"

"Precisely."

"Quark, as much as the universe changes, you always somehow manage to stay the same." Natima shook her head.

Quark stopped smiling and found himself staring deeply into her eyes. "Another thing that hasn't changed is how much you mean to me, Natima." Quark reached over, placing his hand over hers. "Every bit of news out of Cardassia, every report, I looked for your face—your name—hoping you were safe."

"I have to confess even with everything that's happened to my people in recent years, my thoughts have often traveled back here, because I was worried about you, too. I had a feeling you'd make it."

"Takes more than a few wars to kill me off."

"I believe that."

Quark sighed. "I'm happy you're here, Natima."

She smiled, and placed her hand over his. "Me, too."

Other than when she'd first admitted them to Shar's quarters, Ro had never seen his bondmates all together. A pair might go shopping on the Promenade; from time to time she'd pass by one in the Habitat Ring, or while crossing over the various bridges to different levels of the station, but never in a group. She suspected they avoided it deliberately. Wherever they went people would talk simply because, to a person, they were striking.

The one sitting next to zh'Thane had an angular handsomeness he emphasized by wearing his hair pulled back tightly from his face. His choice of clothes—a shirt in a vivid hue of teal coupled with an ornately embroidered vest—reflected fashion sensibility Quark would appreciate. In the middle sat the bondmate Ro had met one day in the Replimat—a talkative, friendly individual, especially compared to Shar, who said little unless he was spoken to. Having explained that she was a teacher, she'd inquired about sitting in and observing the station's classrooms and Ro had forgotten she'd promised to get back to her. Ro made a mental note to add that to her task list for the morning. If she had to guess, she'd pick the Andorian who sat, just a bit a part from the other two, as the "problem" zh'Thane had come to see her about.

Unlike the congenial stockiness of the chatty one who sat beside her, she had a lean, willowy look, emphasized by her choice to wear her long white hair straight and smooth. She must have sensed Ro's scrutiny because suddenly Ro found herself facing a pair of piercing gray eyes.

"Lieutenant?" she said, her voice silvery toned.

"Umm. Yeah." Ro grabbed an empty chair from a close-by table, placed it in front of the Andorians' booth, threw a leg over and straddled it. "Yes. I apologize for interrupting your night out, but I've got good news regarding your trip."

Her eyes narrowing on Ro, the willowy one said, "Trip? What trip?"

"Thriss," zh'Thane warned.

Puzzled glances passed between the other two bondmates and Ro wondered if zh'Thane had told them about her request for an exemption. *Maybe this was a mistake and I should have handled this one-on-one with the councillor.*

Zh'Thane must have noticed their apprehension because she quickly said, "Remember we talked yesterday about the timetable for your return to Andor? I'm anxious to hear what you've learned, Lieutenant."

Warily, Thriss watched Ro, her expression flinty.

Ignoring Thriss, Ro took her cue from the senior member of the group and proceeded. "Colonel Kira paged me a short time ago with her approval for your emergency departure exemption. Everything checks out—your ship, Councillor, will be free to leave the station on an 'as needed' basis."

Confusion erupted.

"Dizhei, you discussed this with *Zhadi?*" one of the Andorians said, anxious. "I thought we'd decided to keep it to ourselves—"

"I thought after what happened this morning—"

"—believed you and Anichent were in agreement—"

Shathrissía kept silent, her eyes solemn. Ro saw her hands curl around the edge of the table, her breathing deepen.

"We can't risk—"

"—room for last-minute—"

"Wait!" Ro said, bringing her palm down on the table, a little harder than she intended. At the sound, four pairs of eyes fixed on her.

"No one said you had specific plans. Your situation isn't much different, except now you have the option of leaving on short notice without having to go through all the procedures required by a yellow-alert status." She turned to zh'Thane. "I have the codes at my office. I'll have them sent to your quarters, Councillor. Provide them to ops and you'll be allowed to depart without question."

"So you all conspired to return to Andor without talking to me about it," Thriss said softly. "When was this decided? You and Anichent have a little pillow talk, Dizhei? Or was it your idea, *Zhadi?* Trying to control us, as usual." Thriss jerked around to face zh'Thane, tipping over a mug filled with Orion ale; liquid drenched the table.

Flustered, Dizhei jumped up. Thriss sat fixed, unbending, ignoring the disturbance she'd caused.

"We hadn't decided anything without discussing it with you, Shathrissía," Anichent said. He draped an arm around her shoulder and hugged her reassuringly. "We had to make sure the proposal was feasible. All is well, *zh'yi.*"

"I am not some addle-minded child you can lie to," she snarled. Prying his arm from around her shoulder, Thriss scooted away from her bondmate. He caressed her cheek; she slapped his hand away. "Don't. Touch. Me."

Uh-oh. Looks like we might have a situation here, Ro thought. She needed to turn down the heat before it became a meltdown. "How about we take this to the holosuite? You can talk privately, work through—"

"What's this 'we'? And why are you still here?" Thriss turned on Ro, eyes blazing. "Oh I see. You're one of *zhadi's* lackeys doing her dirty work."

"Watch your impertinence in public," zh'Thane warned.

Ro shot zh'Thane a look, discouraging her from speaking further, and addressed Thriss and her bondmates. "As station security chief, I answer to Colonel Kira, not Councillor zh'Thane and certainly not you. When I suggested you take this to the holosuite, that was a polite way of asking you to resolve your disagreement elsewhere," Ro said evenly. "If you intend to use your holosuite time, I suggest you do it now. Otherwise, there's the door." Pushing her chair back from the group, Ro made it halfway to Quark and Natima's table when the sound of shattering glass caught her attention. She spun around in time to see Thriss brandishing half a broken drinking glass, the razor sharp edges within centimeters of Anichent's face. Ro started back toward the Andorians at a brisk clip. *Dammit!*

"You push and you push, but I'm not giving in this time," Thriss threatened, loud enough to be heard at the surrounding tables. "I'm not leaving the station without Shar!"

Ro watched, horrified, as Anichent grabbed at Thriss' arm, trying to wrest the makeshift weapon away from her with his free hand. She threw an elbow into his stomach; he grunted, released his grip on her wrist and toppled into her. In lifting her weapon-arm out of Anichent's way, Thriss caught her gown on a chair and her arm fell reflexively, thrusting the jagged glass edge into his shoulder. Shaking uncontrollably, Thriss gasped, stumbled backward.

Raising his hand to his wound, Anichent's face blanched gray. He teetered, tipped, his eyes rolled back into his head and his hand, smeared in dark blue, hung limply.

Dizhei screamed, bracing her weight on the table. Startled, she threw up her hands, bits of glistening glass embedded in her palm.

Ro slapped her combadge, "Security, send a team to Quark's! And alert the infirmary to expect company!" Shoving past zh'Thane and Dizhei, Ro hastily examined Anichent. He drifted in and out of consciousness, his clammy skin shone with sweat. Not being familiar with Andorian physiology, she could only guess he was in shock.

"Councillor!" Ro ordered. "Snap out of it, I need you to help him to the infirmary." Zh'Thane regained her composure, slid her arm around Anichent, and with him propped against her, helped him away from the table. Dizhei followed after zh'Thane, quaking with each step. Within minutes, medical help would arrive to tend to Anichent, but her job wasn't done yet. Ro turned to face Thriss.

Agitated, Thriss, in her blood-spattered dress, huddled against the wall, thrusting the broken glass out in front of her. Upper body hunched, she jerked toward each sudden movement in the crowd.

Her voice low and steady, Ro said, "Put down the weapon." She walked slowly, focusing her energy on capturing Thriss' attention. "Put it down and we'll talk."

"No," she whispered. "I won't."

7

Vaughn plunged his sticky fingers into the washbasin, swishing them around until the remains of the nut-syrup pastries washed away. A servant standing at his shoulder snatched the basin and replaced it the instant he finished. *And I thought Starfleet brass were pampered.* The Yrythny military chieftains, if J'Maah was representative, had a lot in common with feudal lords with their rugs and embroidered couch cushions. Vaughn had vacationed at luxury resorts whose accommodations paled in comparison to these.

"Excellent dinner, Chieftain J'Maah. I enjoyed the roasted shellfish especially," Vaughn said. The *Defiant's* replicators were good, but having a fresh-cooked meal was definitely appreciated.

Chieftain J'Maah stretched out on the floor, rubbing his full stomach with satisfaction. "Myna is a good cook. She served my House when I was growing up. I took her off Vanìmel when the promotions began. My consort consented to letting Myna come on this journey because of you, Commander Vaughn." He closed his eyes, breathed deeply and relaxed.

Vaughn wondered if this was some kind of mealtime ritual the Yrythny followed and waited to see if M'Yeoh, First Officer Meltoh and Navigator Ocah dropped to the floor. J'Maah's officers remained seated, sipping at goblets of wood wine. Vaughn followed their lead. "My best wishes to your consort, then," he said. "And my compliments to Myna."

A servant had brought J'Maah pillows for his head and feet. Another combed and braided his hair, interweaving crystal beads and ribbons as she worked. She hummed softly.

"Not the rinberry oil, Retal," J'Maah backslapped the servant's cheek. "Takes the color out of the headdress." He shook his braids, his face puckered in resentment. "Go on now, find the right one."

Vaughn was finding it increasingly difficult to stomach the scene playing out before him.

Murmuring apologies, the servant's yellow-green skin blanched; she crawled away on hands and knees. She huddled in the corner, rubbing ointment into the scrape she'd received from the chieftain's chunky rings.

Vaughn wanted to ask if she required medical assistance, when J'Maah explained, "Very loyal, that Retal. But not smart. Can't expect too much from a Wanderer."

Without a word, Retal returned to her ministrations, dabbing J'Maah's scalp with oil, her long graceful fingers deftly weaving the strands.

Vaughn watched, his chest tight. *I think I'd like to be excused from the table.*

Minister M'Yeoh materialized in the chair beside him. "Tell me Commander, how are the repairs on your ship going?" he murmured. Seated at the foot of the table, he had said little during the meal.

Turning away from his view of J'Maah's pedicure, Vaughn sipped from his wood wine. "The extra hands from the *Avaril*'s engineering staff have helped tremendously." After his concerns about the *Defiant*'s security, he'd reviewed a list of all non-Starfleet personnel allowed to access the repair bay and requested that their bioscans be entered into the security identification system. If he had Yrythny coming and going with Nog's crew, he wanted to keep track of them.

"We've received word from Luthia," J'Maah said. "Your Lieutenant Dax did an excellent job at the Assembly Chamber today."

Perhaps luck hasn't completely eluded us, Vaughn thought, relieved. *Or maybe this Other of the Yrythny is watching out for our mission.*

J'Maah burbled contentedly. "I should have asked you Vaughn, but Retal here has an excellent way with hair. You're welcome to have her attend to that—that hair on your chin even."

"Thank you for the offer," Vaughn said politely. "Another time, perhaps." Watching this slavish attention to J'Maah was setting Vaughn's teeth on edge and he hoped he'd be given leave to return to his crew shortly. Too bad Quark wasn't here—he would love all this decadence.

"As you wish," J'Maah wheezed, his barrel stomach rising and falling in a relaxed rhythm. "We have the whole way to the Consortium and the whole way back to Vanìmel."

Here comes the part where I might provoke animosity, Vaughn thought. "Chieftain, a point of clarification. The *Defiant* should be spaceworthy by the time we reach the Consortium. Once we obtain our matter load, we plan on flying back to pick up Lieutenant Dax and her team."

"Of course, of course. The needs of your crew come first. I'm sure they're anxious to get on their way," J'Maah said.

"We still hope to explore a great deal of territory before we return home."

"Whatever we can do, Commander. We're here to help." The

chieftain's breathing deepened, his body relaxed and finally his membranous lids dropped over his eyes.

The senior staff sat quietly, watching their captain's still figure for a few minutes. Finally, First Officer Meltoh whispered, "This is when we go. You first, Commander."

Hastily, Vaughn made for the exit, grateful for tinny replicated food and sleeping on the deck—without the services of a head masseuse.

"A pillow is a legitimate bet," Tenmei protested.

Julian examined her more closely and determined she was being sincere. "Fine then, I'll take a look at it, decide what it's worth."

Without sitting up, she reached back and grabbed the pillow from where it sat at the foot of her sleeping bag. "Can you put a price on a non-Starfleet issue pillow at a time like this?" she asked tossing the pillow at Bashir. "Besides, if Cassini can bet his slippers—"

"They're self-heating!" came Cassini's muffled protest. He'd tunneled into the sleeping bag two across and one down from Tenmei, having retreated there after being soundly thrashed one round back.

"—then I can bet my pillow," Tenmei concluded.

Since Nog, the commerce expert, was otherwise occupied, assigning value to crew members' bets had fallen, by default, to Julian. He preferred to play poker; running the statistical probabilities and plotting strategy was very entertaining. His crewmates, however, determined there wasn't a way to handicap him in cards and none of them enjoyed losing every single round. Either Julian dealt the cards or he watched. "Take it or leave it," Tenmei had told him.

It wasn't fair, really—he didn't consciously choose to win every contest he'd entered—he just did. During their first week into the mission, engineering sponsored a casino night in the mess. Any game that wasn't random, Julian won. After that, it became an unwritten rule that the advantage bestowed on Julian by his genetic enhancements required handicapping or elimination. No one resented his abilities, but no one would play cards with him either. In this round of poker, Julian represented the house. He sat cross-legged on the floor between Chao and Lankford and knew, from his glimpses at their cards, that they'd be joining Gordimer in the "broke" department very soon. Chao might figure out that Tenmei was bluffing—there was no way she could have better than three of a kind—but he doubted it.

When they were on the *Defiant,* the crew usually bet whatever personal items they'd brought with them that didn't exist in the replicator database. Ezri, swearing she had a sure thing, had begged him to loan her Kukalaka after she lost her last bag of *jumja* chews to Bowers. Their present resource scarcity required they be even more innovative.

Gordimer offered his sleeping spot in the darkest, least trafficked corner of the room for the night. Bashir wanted to play for that bet alone. Chao threw in a headset that emitted wave frequencies that improved REM sleep. After coming up empty, Rahim raided Leishman's candy supply, reasoning that Nog wouldn't give his engineers long enough breaks to come back to quarters and *take* a candy break. For her part, Tenmei had a Tholian silk nightshirt Chao and Lankford coveted. Bowers, who won the last hand, currently had possession of the best sleeping spot in the room, the headset, Leishman's candy and Prynn's nightshirt. If Julian didn't sign off on Tenmei's pillow, she was out of the game.

Bashir punched and hefted it, rested it in his lap, raised it to his nose to take a whiff. "Ah! Lavender. Very nice."

"Thank you, Doctor," Prynn said hopefully.

No one made any cracks about Tenmei's relationship to Vaughn earning her Julian's favoritism. Her fellow crewmates were smart enough to know they'd be talking to Julian about mending a deviated septum if they did. Squeezing Prynn's pillow, Julian had to assess its value under the present circumstances.

"Fine. The house agrees to accept Ensign Tenmei's pillow as a raise," Bashir said. "Lieutenant Bowers?"

"Fold," Bowers said with a sigh, tossing in his cards.

Tenmei chuckled contentedly and gathered up her winnings. Cassini emerged from his sleeping bag, retrieved her cards and looked at them. "Two pair? I gave up my self-heating slippers for three of a kind and I could've beaten you."

Tenmei shrugged. "Take my advice, Cassini, stick to dabo. Poker's not your game."

Before Cassini could fire off a retort, the door slid open, admitting the two Yrythny technologists who'd been helping the *Defiant* crew, Tlaral and Shavoh. "We finished our shifts and wondered if there was anything—" Shavoh began. Puzzled, he looked back and forth over the unoccupied dining area and computer station, which blocked their view of the poker game.

"Over here," Bashir called out.

Grabbing Tlaral's arm, Shavoh guided his friend to the rear of the room where the cots and sleeping bags were laid out. Both Yrythny engineers looked confused.

"You'd better have a seat before Lieutenant Nog notices you're here," Tenmei said, patting the spot on Senkowski's mattress pad next to her. Like Leishman, Senkowski wouldn't be back any time soon to use it. The redshirts and blueshirts had begun their joking predictions as to what the yellowshirts would do when Nog finally eased up. While everyone did what they could to help, Nog allowed only the nonengineers to leave at shift's end.

"We're here to help," Shavoh offered. "To work on the *Defiant*."

"Of course you are, but we've all been ordered to mix and mingle. Cultural exchanges and all that. Consider sitting for part of your duty," Tenmei said. "Right, Doctor?"

"Absolutely," Julian confirmed. "We're glad to have you, especially since I think several of our players are going to be tapped out in a minute. Are you interested in learning to play cards?"

Tlaral and Shavoh exchanged glances and Tlaral said, "You'll teach us?"

"Happy to," Tenmei said with a small smile.

Julian winced, knowing *Defiant*'s comm officer was eager to teach their "green" alien friends a thing or two about Alpha Quadrant gambling. That, and to further line her coffers.

The two Yrythny engineers cautiously eased down on the floor, trying to situate their legs comfortably. Both settled for lying on their sides and draping their legs out behind them.

"I believe it was your turn, Ensign Lankford," Julian said.

Wrinkling her nose, she shuffled and reshuffled the cards in her hand, allowed Tenmei to cut the deck, then dealt. "First bet goes to Mr. Bowers," she said after everyone anted.

"I'll open with *Burning Hearts of Qo'noS*."

Chao groaned. "The Klingon bodice ripper? I'll fold." She threw her cards into the pile.

"I take exception to the characterization of that novel as a bodice ripper, Chief," Bowers said with a wink.

"What would you call it? A face biter? I just can't believe someone finally pried it away from Nog."

"Lieutenant, Chief," Julian said, holding up a hand in the direction of each woman, "by the end of this journey, I suspect everyone on *Defiant* will have read *Burning Hearts of Qo'noS* so I'd advise you both to—Tlaral? Are you all right?"

The Yrythny technologist swayed where she sat, her lashless eyelids flickering. "I'm sorry—I feel a little unwell."

Grabbing the tricorder beside him, Julian performed a quick scan. "Obviously, I'm not well versed in Yrythny physiology, but I doubt the level of fluctuation I'm seeing in your readings is normal. Electrolytes, pulse, temperature, hormones . . ."

Tlaral tipped again, this time forward. She threw down her hands to prevent a fall. "I think I need to lie down," she whispered.

Shavoh helped Julian ease Tlaral onto her back. Prynn shoved the pillow beneath her legs, elevating her feet. Bashir ordered Bowers to retrieve his medical bag while Chao doused a cloth in water and draped it over Tlaral's forehead.

"I probably haven't eaten enough today and I've worked a double shift," Tlaral said weakly. Her eyes rolled, her lids dropped and she went limp.

Julian scanned Tlaral with his tricorder. "Prynn, help me examine her for any external injuries."

While Tenmei went to work removing the Yrythny's tunic, Bashir rechecked his tricorder readings before turning his attention to Tlaral's back. "What's this on her shoulder—a birthmark, an old injury?"

Shrugging, Shavoh covered his eyes, worried. "I don't know. She had an accident in engineering last spring, but I think she broke her foot."

"Her heart is racing—I think it's related to the hormonal surge I picked up with my tricorder."

"Wait!" Shavoh said suddenly.

"Is there something I need to know?" Julian asked.

"Check her palms, Doctor."

Tenmei lifted Tlaral's arm and turned over her hand. Her palms bore the faint imprint of a blue starburst.

Relieved, Shavoh sighed. "She's ready to go into the waters! It's her time to mate. This is her first time and I'm sure she didn't know what to expect. But she'll be fine. I'll fetch her consort. Minister M'Yeoh will be pleased." Shavoh sprang to his feet and ran out the door.

Julian dropped back on his heels as Tenmei eased Tlaral back into her tunic. "Learn something new all the time. Today it's Yry-thny fertility."

After a few minutes, Tlaral's lids flickered back, her eyes darting anxiously around the room. "What happened—I was sitting and then it all went black."

"As your colleague Shavoh put it, you're ready to go into the waters. She's gone for your consort."

She pressed her hands to her temples. "Oh. That's unexpected. I didn't think it would be for another year," she said nervously.

"Breathe a little more slowly. You might hyperventilate." Julian rubbed her shoulder, hoping it would calm her down. "The scar on your back—it's directly behind your heart and your pulse is highly irregular. Did you have an injury?"

Slowly, she relaxed, taking a proffered blanket from Prynn, tucking it up around her chin. "As a child, Doctor. I was caught in a coral tunnel near my House. Nothing to worry about."

Shavoh appeared with Minister M'Yeoh in tow. He waddled across the room and squatted down by his consort. "Thank you, Doctor," he said, taking Tlaral's hand in his.

"Congratulations are in order. You're going to be parents, I think?"

M'Yeoh didn't have time to follow up with Bashir; an announcement boomed over the comsystem, announcing the *Avaril*'s approach to the Consortium.

When Vaughn arrived on the *Avaril*'s bridge, he saw what looked like a frozen spray of brilliant white gold exploding on the viewscreen. For a moment, he questioned whether they'd actually dropped out of warp, though the warp-engine pulse had been replaced with the static hum of impulse. He looked more closely.

Geyserlike eruptions of a giant-size gas particle fountain spread slowly with spindly, chrysanthemum grace.

"Magnificent, isn't it?" Minister M'Yeoh gurgled, wiping his mouth on his sleeve.

Absorbing the spectacular vista, Vaughn simply nodded.

"Our scientists have postulated it's a ruptured singularity," M'Yeoh said.

"A white hole?" Vaughn ventured, wishing Shar were here.

"I'm afraid I'm not familiar with that term, Commander. Nevertheless, I think you'll agree it is a glory to behold by any name."

The navigational sensors were recalibrated. Chieftain J'Maah barked an order to raise shields and increase stabilizers in response to the ebb and flow of gravitational winds originating from the fountain, but not soon enough. Forceful gusts slamming into the starboard side sent the massive *Avaril* lurching and swaying. Yrythny crew and guests alike grabbed onto the closest fixed rail, chair or terminal to avoid being thrown to the floor.

"These straits before we reach the Consortium are the worst, storm-wise," J'Maah explained to Vaughn. "We'll be rocking for a few more minutes and then it's steady traveling until we dock."

The *Avaril* heaved with drunken equilibrium until she passed into a dome-shaped debris field created when matter spewing from the fountain coalesced and cooled, leaving hard, pitted asteroids behind. Nearer the fountain, hot particulate globs glowed white, gradually darkening to invisibility as the vacuum of space cooled them. It was for these nondescript space rocks that they had traveled so far, motivated by the hope of obtaining material resilient enough to manufacture femtobots.

Because the *Avaril* moved slowly, using her tractor beams to move the larger space rocks (some the size of starships) blown into the shipping lane, Vaughn had time to watch the small mining pods flitting around the debris field closest to the particle fountain. He admired the ingeniousness of the mining pods utilizing small ramscoops to gather in the cooling particle matter. As J'Maah had explained, the total matter collected by a pod on a single trip to the particle fountain was called a "load." Each Consortium member was entitled to a fixed percentage of loads. Once the member quotas were satisfied, loads became available on the open market. Tomorrow, Vaughn anticipated that one of those mining pods, now flitting about like pollinating insects, would be bringing back a load with *Defiant*'s name on it.

Full pods flew back to their launch bays in the heart of one of the larger asteroids. Rimmed with flashing lights, silver doors rised open and the pods skimmed along narrow octagonal tunnels drilled inside. Hints of the asteroid's internal structures emerged on the surface: glittering domes, needle towers, tunnelways, and massive, reinforced support struts linked to other inhabited asteroids.

One asteroid linked to another and another, and still others beyond Vaughn's sight creating a massive, asymmetrical structure resembling a complex molecular model or the frame of a geodesic dome. Here, a surface glowed with radiant lights where architects had burrowed deep into rock; there, derrick-style living space perched on the surface of an asteroid. J'Maah had shown him a Consortium map more akin to a molecular model than any city-state Vaughn had familiarity with. He had counted more than eighty-five "suites" (as inhabited asteroids were called) before J'Maah clicked to the next screen.

The *Avaril,* because of her size, would dock at a publicly held platform. Such a location facilitated better access to the Core, host to the Consortium's primary business operations, the matter collecting operation, and public facilities.

Vaughn's task was straightforward. A small Starfleet contingent would go with Minister M'Yeoh to the Member Business Offices. The necessary permits would be acquired, a trade negotiated, and once the matter load was safely ensconced in the *Defiant*'s storage bay, the *Avaril* would return to Vanìmel. Vaughn expected to see Dax's away team six days from now, even anticipating a few bumps along the way. Rare was the plan that proceeded without some complication. Consequently, he decided to hold off contacting Dax until the deal had been settled. That way, she'd have a better idea of how much time she had to work with the Yrythny assemblies. Reassurance that a critical component of the *Defiant*'s upgraded defense system had been acquired would put her mind at ease. If luck smiled on them, they might be able to establish a subspace link early enough in the evening that Julian and Ezri could exchange good nights before retiring for the day.

All in all, a workable plan, he thought, and left his observation post to set the gears in motion.

"File these," Lieutenant Dax ordered, offloading a shoulder bag and passing it to Shar as they walked down a winding streetway in one of Luthia's upscale residential districts.

Taking the bag, Shar studied his commanding officer quizzically. What exactly was it he was filing, where was he supposed to file it, and how was it, after four years at Starfleet Academy where he'd won a shelf full of awards, published several well-received articles and graduated with honors, he was filing at all? Mostly he was unsure how moving padds, tomes and isolinear chips from conference room to conference room would help resolve Yrythny civil unrest. "Yes, sir," he said neutrally. "Is there anything else you need?"

Lieutenant Dax seemed not to notice his uncertainty. She'd hardly looked at him this morning. Earlier, she'd walked past him to her desktop terminal, pulled up her daily meeting schedule, and brewed a hot seaweed tea before saying "hello." Not that her preoccupation wasn't understandable: the Yrythny committees she worked with had a tendency to change their minds almost hourly.

"Breaking down the historical precedents for establishing Wanderer rights—" she said, "—have you written the summaries yet?" Dax absently waved to an Assembly official Shar remembered meeting during yesterday's padd and data shuffling. Attended by servants and clerks, the official cocked his head in their direction, looked down at his hand, clearly wondering what Ezri meant by wiggling her hand in the air.

"They're in your database, filed under 'representation issues,' " Shar answered. "Delegate Keren signed off on them late last night. She will join us at the Aquaria."

"With Vice Chair Jeshoh following shortly after, I suppose?" Ezri said, rolling her eyes.

"Yes, sir." The morning argument between Jeshoh and Keren had become part of the daily routine. Keren would arrive with her agenda; Jeshoh would arrive with his and the two would quarrel until the next meeting. Whenever they entered the room, Shar's antennae tingled with the kinetic energy they exuded. He found them more stimulating than most of their colleagues.

Dax suddenly stopped. "Let's eat. Once the Assembly members start arriving, they'll keep us talking nonstop."

Chasing after her, Shar cut in front of a pushcart loaded with bushy, orange flora, past several apartment courtyards to a merchant window where a line of Yrythny waited for *shmshu* cheese and leaberry pastries. Ezri ordered one for each of them, using her Assembly meal card to pay the vendor. She took a few bites and crooked her finger at Shar, pointing them in the direction of a crescent-shaped bench. Between nibbles, Shar determined the time had arrived to present a suggestion to Dax.

"Lieutenant," Shar said, hoping he looked authoritative, but respectful; he strove to avoid the just-beneath-the-surface insolence that his *zhavey* accused him of when he was determined to make his point. Insincerity would not help his case with Dax. "I have a request."

Without interrupting her breakfast, she mumbled something about his continuing, put down her pastry, made a notation in her padd, and returned to her eating.

Maybe while she's distracted, she might agree without thinking too hard about it . . . "Sir, while I agree that an understanding of historical and social precedents provides context for your work with the committees, I think we're neglecting a critical area of research."

"Go on." She dabbed at the corners of her mouth.

"The Yrythny conflict is based on the supposition that the Wanderers are biologically inferior to the Houseborn," Shar struggled to keep the excitement out of his voice. "But what if the Houseborn supposition is wrong and we can prove it scientifically?"

"That the inequities between Houseborn and Wanderer biological programming are perceived, rather than actual? My guess is that it's mostly perception," Ezri agreed, throwing her legs out in front of her. "At least I haven't noticed much difference between the groups I've been working with. I think they've built a complex social culture of castes and customs based on suppositions and preconceptions, regardless of any basis in actual fact." Dax wadded up her paper refuse and held it in her fist. Looking at Shar, she smiled indulgently. "Perception is nine-tenths of reality, and in the perceptions of the Houseborn, the Wanderers are inferior. I doubt scientific proof would change that perception. Besides, sometimes even the most absurd traditions and customs evolve as a way to preserve a species or protect a planet."

Shar agreed with Ezri in principle, though he didn't say so. Over the years, he'd learned from Charivretha how the seemingly illogical customs of many worlds had legitimate roots. For example, many religious dietary codes emerged from pragmatic realities. How avoiding a forbidden food because it would make one "unholy" before the divinity sounded more meaningful than saying it was forbidden because it would make the follower hallucinate, foam at the mouth and die. Still, not all customs and codes were so well intended. Prejudice and fear still allowed for cultures to rationalize bad policy. From his own studies, Shar had discovered that the Wanderers had emerged as the artisans, architects, and scientists among the Yrythny. The Houseborn's insistence that the Wanderers "lacked proper instincts" wasn't logical in the face of such clear, measurable evidence of superior intellectual abilities. He was surprised Dax didn't raise the point herself. "In most circumstances, a species is better protected by developing a quantifiable strategy," Shar reasoned. "Such as resource management or environmental restoration."

"Since the Yrythny didn't evolve naturally, it's possible that whoever augmented Vanìmel's primordial soup intended these instincts to play out." She shrugged. "Maybe there are chromosomal mutations or weaknesses in the helices."

"Maybe there aren't," Shar argued.

"For example," Ezri went on, "what would happen if every Yrythny were allowed to reproduce? Could the planet sustain that kind of population explosion?"

"It may not," Shar conceded. "On the other hand, perhaps it can. I've seen no evidence that anyone has yet attempted to answer the question. But even if it can't, science might solve that problem, too."

Ezri sighed. "Maybe these social customs, as repulsive as they may seem to us, serve a purpose not immediately obvious to the outsider. That's why examining their history is crucial. Tracing the origins of this social order might help them course-correct. If you pull out a weed without killing the root, the weed will grow back."

"Yes, sir," Shar said. He set down his pastry, his appetite withering.

"You should know something of restrictive social customs and how they relate to physiological and biological realities from your own experiences."

Shar looked away uncomfortably. He knew that over the course of Dax's eight previous lives, knowledge about Andorians that was unknown to the majority of outsiders had entered into Dax's purview. How much knowledge and how explicit that knowledge was, he couldn't say. Shar hadn't yet probed Ezri's recollections or allowed her to probe his, but he did know Dax wasn't speaking carelessly. He considered what she had said for a moment longer before responding. "But it's my opinion, Lieutenant, after years of studying the interrelationship between sociology and physiology among my people, that it is the rigid structure of our customs that have, in part, landed my species in the predicament it now faces."

"You're saying that the Yrythny adherence to a rigid caste system might be leading them to a similar fate as the Andorians?" Lieutenant Dax said, skeptically.

"I am saying I believe we need to ask the scientific questions in addition to the historical and cultural questions." Shar knew he could prove it to her, given the chance.

Her face softened and she offered him a half-smile. "I don't disagree with you, Shar. But let's look at this realistically. To conduct a proper scientific inquiry, you'll need enough time and cooperative research subjects to create a viable statistical sampling. Otherwise, your conclusions might be specious to the Yrythny."

"Their universities must have databases—"

"We have finite time. Finagling access those databases could be difficult, especially since the decision to admit me as a mediator was hardly unanimous. Not everyone likes—or trusts—us."

"Respectfully, sir, I am not questioning your decision to pursue the angles we've worked through so far. What I am asking is whether I can tackle some of the scientific questions. I'll complete everything you assign me and pursue those issues on my own time, if you'd rather."

She paused, resting her hand against her lips as she studied him. "All right then, Ensign. I can agree to that, but if I believe you're neglecting my assignments, I'll ask you to desist."

"Yes sir." *A fair enough compromise,* he thought.

"Any word from Commander Vaughn?"

"Not since yesterday. I know he said that he expected they would reach the Consortium today, but circumstances—"

"I know, Shar." She gazed up at Luthia's clear ceiling, starlight refracting through the panels, spraying faint rainbows on volcanic rock facades adorning the surrounding buildings.

Shar knew she worried, though Vaughn hadn't given her any specific reason to be concerned during his regular check-ins. Shar might not have a lover on *Defiant* as Ezri did, but after weeks of working closely with his shipmates, he'd grown accustomed to having them around. Not a day had passed without Shar turning to ask Nog for input on what tools might be more effective in his inquiry on Yrythny genetics. Each time he gazed out Luthia's windows, he wondered how long it would be before Ensign Tenmei persuaded Commander Vaughn to let her try surfing on Vanìmel. He'd also come to know Dr. Bashir on the trip. It had become a private game for Shar to see if he could beat Bashir at anything, be it darts or data recall. So far, Shar had lost every time. The sooner *Defiant* resumed its journey, the better. On this, Shar and Ezri agreed.

At last, Ezri said, "We should go. I'm sure they'll be waiting."

She predicted rightly.

The Aquaria's excellent acoustics allowed the hollow dissonance arising from the Assembly officers milling about to be heard several streetways down from the entrance. Shar and Ezri descended a flight of coral stairs to discover that not a single empty seat remained in the amphitheater. She climbed back up the stairs where she could view the gathering.

Shar waited for Dax to indicate where she wanted him to sit, but with a minimum of five officials dogging her, he assumed she'd appreciate his taking care of himself. On the landing across from her, he noticed an open spot beside a plant bed, swollen with speckle-throat roses and vines twisting over and under small trees. There, he could listen and observe Dax and stay out of the way. Gazing through the Aquaria's transparent floors at Vanìmel's whorled cloud cover, he watched shuttlecraft streak back and forth between the planetside Houses and Luthia's ports. He was intrigued by the illusion of being able to free-fall, through the floor, into the atmosphere. He enjoyed how the Yrythny incorporated awareness of their planet into their living spaces; Luthia felt like an extension of their world, not something separate.

"On the morning agenda—" Ezri began loudly.

Reluctantly, he tore his eyes away from Vanìmel and listened—or tried to listen—to Ezri. Officers continued their discussions, ignoring her.

She cleared her throat, "We're discussing civil rights issues." A pause. The chatter continued. She linked her hands behind her back and rolled back and forth on her shoes a few times before asking loudly, "Can we please focus on the issue at hand?"

Shar looked on helplessly, knowing nothing he could say or do would make them pay attention.

Skin pockets quivering, Rashoh ringed the room, forcing his associates into chairs. Other senior officials, including Jeshoh and Keren, followed suit. Shar was reminded of his *zhavey*'s favorite plant, a leafy tree that refused to accept pruning. Trim a branch, within hours a new shoot had sprouted.

Ezri climbed atop a stool, put a finger in each side of her mouth and whistled.

Pained by the shrill tone, Shar winced, his antennae curling.

But the chattering stopped.

"You and you," she pointed at Jeshoh and Keren. "Select small groups of trusted associates because from now on I'm dealing only with representatives of each Assembly. It's the only way we'll accomplish anything. And if you want to schedule a meeting, a discussion, or a visit, you will first clear it with my assistant, Ensign ch'Thane."

His initial gratitude at regaining control over their schedule dissipated slowly as the implications of his new assignment gradually dawned on him. The Yrythny officials stampeding toward him with their demands represented minutes, hours—possibly precious days—where research would be rendered impossible. *Dax knows what she's doing, focusing our time on her chosen issues,* Shar reasoned. *After all, hadn't she been Curzon Dax, one of the most renowned diplomats in recent Federation history?* Removing a padd from his pocket, he organized petitioners in a line and patiently took down their requests for appointments.

Since his night with Keren's underground, Shar had burned with a yearning to help these people. He simply had to believe, to trust, that Dax knew the best way.

8

"You might try *shusha* herb packs for the swollen ankles," Kira said, tipping back in her chair and resting her feet on the console in front of her. "Apparently the leaves contain some chemical that helps the tissues shed any water they're retaining. Julian doesn't like them because he can't prove in his lab that they work, but most Bajoran women swear by them." She took a sip of her *raktajino* and waited for a response from the viewscreen.

Kasidy Yates, sitting in a loose lotus position on a braided rug in front of her fireplace, wrinkled her nose. *"You think those will work for a human woman?"* She yanked strands of blue yarn out of a skein and was winding them into a ball in preparation for knitting . . . something. Baby footwear, Kira supposed.

Kira shrugged. "Humans and Bajorans have enough in common that what works for us usually works for you. Give it a try. Couldn't be worse than having to stay off your feet."

"True enough," she conceded. *"You look tired, Nerys. Still haven't taken any time off, have you?"*

Dropping her feet to the ground, Kira leaned forward, resting her elbows on the desk. "I'm fine." Shrugging off Kasidy's dubious expression, she reiterated her stance. "Really. With all the VIPs around, the tempo around here's a little more crazed than usual. But I'm staying on top of it all, though I'm still working on the fine art of balance. The captain had it mastered."

"True. Ben could throw a dinner party in the middle of a crisis—

or take time to visit his land when he faced a serious decision," she said while focusing her gaze on the length of yarn she'd just pulled out. *"Sometimes he'd go out in the back where the porch is now, pull out the baseball bat, and whack some balls. Made him feel better."*

"Are you saying that taking up a hobby will better my leadership skills? Or are you guilting me into coming to Bajor?" Kira chuckled.

"You caught me." Kas smiled, allowing the yarn to roll off her lap. She looked up at Kira. *"I'd like the company. Someone who knows me for me and not merely as the Emissary's wife and mother of the Avatar. And don't forget the farmers are bringing in the katerpods over the next few weeks. You don't want to miss that!"*

Memories of dark, smoky autumn nights nudged their way into the present. Kira sighed, feeling pangs of longing for those few simple moments her people had stolen from the Occupation: walking winding farm lanes with lighted copper lanterns to ward off the inky darkness, and singing the harvest melodies, thanking the Prophets for another year of bounty, even though that bounty might be little more than a handful of katerpods.

"I know you want to visit," Kas said. *"I have your room all ready— it has a lovely view of the river. They're starting the sugaring in a few weeks. . . ."* Her voice trailed off, her tone teasing and tempting.

"All right, all right! You've convinced me." Kira held up a hand in good-natured protest. "I'll talk to my staff and see what works best into the station's schedule."

"If you're structuring your plans on the station's schedule, you'll be here about the time my child's grandchildren are born," Kasidy snorted.

. . . and that may be how long it takes for my fellow Bajorans to start speaking to me again, all things considered, Kira thought ruefully. "Work before play, Kas. You know the drill."

"Yeah, I do," Kasidy nodded. *"But that doesn't stop me from trying. We'll talk next week?"*

"Sooner if we have word from Jake. I promise."

Kasidy closed her eyes and inhaled deeply. *"And please let there be word from Jake,"* she said, invoking whatever powers the universe might use to bring him back home.

"Prophets willing, Kas," Kira said earnestly. She straightened up, slapped her thighs and smiled to lighten the mood; she wanted to end their conversation on a positive note for Kasidy's sake. "Besides, I'll want you to tell me how well the herb packs worked on those swollen ankles. Without having Julian around to tell you how it's all just a bunch of folk hokum, you don't have any excuse not to try them."

Kasidy smiled. *"Yates out."*

Before Kasidy's face winked out, Kira noted that it had started to exhibit that soft roundness characteristic of mid-pregnancy. Her hand dropped to her own belly and she ran her fingers over her flat stomach, remembering what it felt like to carry a life inside her. She wondered how Kirayoshi liked Earth, if her presence even shaded his memories.

Enough, Nerys, this is the part where you look at your endless to-do list and come up with meaningful reasons why you won't be tumbling back to your quarters until after midnight. She gave a cursory glance to a half dozen padds sitting on her desk. Ro's mostly informational report on the Ohalavaru trinkets left on her doorstep awaited her attention. In moments of morbid curiosity, she watched reports from the Bajoran news feeds, read the opinion pieces cropping up in the journals; the furor had yet to die down. She wanted desperately to believe that the late-night visit to her door was only a misguided gesture by some well-meaning individual. But in her heart she feared it was a portent of things to come . . . things she herself had set into motion by making the banned Ohalu text public.

Stop it, she told herself. *This is getting you nowhere.* Before diving into Ro's report, she decided to scroll through the list of music selections in her personal database: Charlie Parker, Dizzy Gillespie, Sarah Vaughn . . . *Hmmm. I have to remember to ask Elias if there's any relation.* She mulled over the list, figuring something among the unfamiliar titles would help her to relax. They were all Captain Sisko's choices: a gift to her some years ago on the occasion of a Terran holiday, she couldn't recall which one. The memory made her wish she'd made as much of an effort to share Benjamin's culture as he had always made to share hers.

"Computer," she said finally. "Play Sisko Jazz Compilation Number Nine, track seven: 'Yardbird.' "

A wailing alto saxophone pierced the stillness, its clear, passionate notes lulling her into passivity as she contemplated the vast canvas of stars outside her great eye of a window. *I could stand here and dream all night, except for that nagging sense of duty that never goes away. Even if I put off the reports, I still have one last bit of business that won't wait. But then what? Catch up on latest Starfleet regs. Call it a night, take a late supper in quarters.*

Or not.

She hadn't felt this restless for a long time, plagued by the feeling that she had a forgotten task. Unknown anxiety twisted her stomach. Not with anticipation so much as apprehension. *What's next? If I had a friend close by, I'd go for a walk.* A stroll along the Promenade balcony would be a perfect distraction. Maybe Kasidy was right: time for a hobby. A new sport like orbital skydiving. Plant sculpting or cultivating orchids. She could start knitting something for Kasidy's baby.

Or . . . I could figure out what the Cardassians are up to.

Now it was out there. She dared to think it. For the bulk of the day, Kira had ignored Macet's surprise visit except in the most superficial terms. Avoidance wasn't her usual method; tackling conflict head-on was more her style. Considering how she'd allocated her time these last months, Kira realized she'd spent little—if any—on Cardassian matters. Outside of keeping the supply line of humanitarian aid flowing to Cardassia as the ships came through the station, and the brief interaction she'd had with Macet during the Europani evac, Kira had pushed Cardassia far out of her train of thought. Let someone else worry about them for a change.

Hadn't she done her part, training Damar in "Resistance 101"? To her knowledge, she was the sole Bajoran hiking through Cardassia's bombed-out ruins after the Founders meted out their punishment. *What do they want from me? From us,* she amended quickly. *This wasn't personal. Whatever Macet and Lang had come for, it wasn't about Kira Nerys.* All that was required of her was to serve honorably as commander of Deep Space 9. Follow orders, make sure nothing blows up, protect the public trust, end of story. Her chapter in the Cardassian saga ended with her testimony to the Allied Tribunal negotiating the Dominion War Accords. Period.

Her stomach growled and Kira wondered if it might be time to replicate dinner. Aching muscles up and down her spine begged for attention. She ignored her discomforts. "Computer, search main library database for references to knitting with yarn."

"Two hundred ninety-two thousand, seven hundred sixty references. Narrow search parameters."

"Maybe I should just call Kas back," Kira muttered.

"Input not recognized," the computer intoned.

"Never mind. Cancel search," Kira said irritably. The computer issued a bleat of acknowledgment before falling silent. Her musings ended abruptly when, out of the corner of her eye, she saw the indicator light on her desk that signaled the arrival of a turbolift into ops. She checked the time; too early for her last appointment. Kira turned toward her office doors, looking through the windows and across ops to see who her visitor was. When she saw him, she found herself fighting down the instinct to go for her phaser.

He descended the stairs into the pit with slow, steady steps, past the situation table and toward the opposing stairs that led up to her office. She could see several of the ops crew reacting to the new arrival, looking to her for orders. In response, Kira steeled herself and touched the control on her desk that would open the office doors to admit her visitor. *No ghosts tonight. No ghosts.* She mouthed the words, intent on believing them.

He paused before stepping over the threshold. "Colonel Kira. I hope I'm not interrupting anything important."

Kira couldn't suppress the grim smile that came to her lips at the Prophets' sense of humor. "What can I do for you, Gul Macet?"

". . . and while I recognize that postwar reconstruction tends to focus, by necessity, on basic needs like potable water, adequate food supply and medical care, don't you think that expending resources on life's little luxuries serves morale?" Quark waited for Natima to agree with him, but she'd half turned away from him, peering out into the crowds. "Yoo-hoo." He cleared his throat, waved a hand in front of her face, but she brushed it aside.

"Check out what's going on across the room," she admonished him.

What could be more interesting than me? he thought. Glancing over Natima's shoulder, he saw Ro run-walking toward the Andorians' table, reach up to touch her combadge. *Something's cooking. Glass shattering! What the hell—?*

From over the din of customers, he heard a plaintive exclamation, "You push and push, but I'm not giving in this time!" and the sounds of scuffling. A chilling scream.

A hush descended on the bar. Curious onlookers left gambling and eating to get a better view, effectively blocking Quark's as they huddled around the table. Rising from his own chair, he caught the dabo boy scurrying to the bar and ducking behind the counter.

"Let her handle this, Quark," Natima warned. "She seems capable of managing far worse."

Yeah, but how many chairs and glasses will be broken in the process? Quark smiled. "I'll be right back. Don't give away my seat."

Racing across the bar, Quark pushed his way through the crowd to the front just in time to witness Ro spinning into a sidekick, her foot connecting with the Andorian's arm, sending a broken glass spinning through the air and vaporizing when it hit the floor. The Andorian retaliated, slamming her fist, full speed, into Ro's cheek. He took a few steps backward to avoid the falling bodies; the Andorian's momentum had toppled them both.

Ro planted her hands on her attacker's collarbone, shoving against her. She threw an elbow into Ro's stomach; Ro replied with a leg hooked around the Andorian's hip and a boot heel jammed into the small of her back. The Andorian jerked back with a wail and crumbled onto her knees, giving Ro a chance to untangle herself and scramble to her feet.

With split-second response, the very attractive (in Quark's opinion) Andorian sprang to her feet and lunged at Ro, who successfully sidestepped the Andorian's attack. The women circled each other.

"Stay out of what doesn't concern you!" she shouted.

"Back off!" Ro ordered. "Now!"

"Can I help anyone here? Drinks? Maybe take a few wagers, 3 to 1 odds in Lieutenant Ro's favor." Quark hastily pocketed latinum slips, hoping he remembered who bet what.

A pair of security officers arrived to assist Ro. Quark held them back until he could be assured that their involvement wouldn't compromise Ro's safety. The blood pooled on the floor beneath the table testified to Quark's fear.

The Andorian lunged and tackled Ro, pinning her flat to the floor. From her back, Ro had been unable to assume a proper offensive position, giving the Andorian time to pull back her arm for another punch. Ro swept her opponent's legs from beneath her and sent her sprawling. She had a sidearm out of her concealed holster and targeted on the Andorian before she could make a second pass.

"That's my girl," Quark said to the impressed onlookers.

"I dare you to fire," the Andorian hissed, her chest rising and falling rapidly. Crouched and tensed on her hands and knees, she resembled a Norpin falcon ready to spring on her prey.

"Don't tempt me," Ro countered. Keeping her weapon fixed on her assailant, Ro scrambled to her feet and turned to one of her deputies. "Sergeant Etana, I want this individual in restraints. If she resists, shoot her. Quark, can I get a glass of water?" She swiped the sweat off her forehead with her sleeve.

Quark dispatched a slack-jawed dabo girl to fill Ro's request. No way was he going to miss a moment of Laren in action.

"Eat. Drink. Gamble. Leave." Ro shooed away the crowds, encouraging a return to whatever form of debauchery they were indulging in. When they were satisfied she wasn't cheating them out of any action, they gradually dispersed. The dabo girl arrived with Ro's water; she downed it in one swallow. With the Andorian restrained, Ro took her by the arm and dragged her toward the door. "We're going to have a little chat in my office, Thriss."

Thriss complied, but before she left the premises, Ro turned to Quark with a wrinkled brow and opened her mouth as if she had something to say.

"Something the matter?" Quark asked.

"Only three to one in my favor?"

"I'll lay better odds next time," he promised, giving her a wicked grin. *What a woman!*

In each encounter, Macet's appearance rendered Kira momentarily dumbstruck: the resemblance was extraordinary.

His voice had the same rolling timbre, the rounded rising and falling tones and elongated diction as Dukat. Kira saw him in profile: the aquiline nose and square chin casting an exaggerated silhouette on her wall. She pushed away images of Dukat's hand curling around Meru's chin, his fingers stroking the surface of her mother's ugly facial scar. Of a blue velvet dress he had sent her to wear to a dinner party, as if she were a decorative accessory whose purpose was to bring him pleasure. Of him standing at the altar of the *pah-wraiths* on Empok Nor, seducing his followers into decadent, sensual worship. But Dukat was gone. Kasidy had confided what she'd learned from her vision of the Emissary, and Kira believed the story. She took comfort in it.

Especially now.

"I didn't anticipate meeting with you until tomorrow," she said told Macet. "I'm sorry that I wasn't able to greet the *Trager* when it docked. First Minister Shakaar has given me several assignments, including overseeing the planning of the reception—" Kira gazed over at him, standing statue still. *No ghosts . . .*

"It's the reception I've come to speak with you about." Macet strolled languidly toward her desk. "Alon Ghemor has a gift he'd like presented to Bajor on behalf of the Cardassian people. We'd expected to give it to the first minister privately, but since Minister Shakaar elected to have our first official meeting at the reception, it seems appropriate to share it there." He stopped in front of Kira's desk, hands folded before him.

He has an almost noble carriage, she thought. *And his mouth has none of Dukat's cruel twist about it.* Nonetheless, her skin crawled. Kira pursed her lips. "Ensign Beyer—one of my staff—is doing the bulk of the planning. Feel free to contact her."

"Our request is simple," he said. "We would like the opportunity to say a few words. The presentation will take fifteen to twenty minutes."

Grateful for the excuse to look anywhere else, Kira turned to her console and pulled up Beyer's files on the reception. Playing music proved to be a fortuitous choice: the energetic jazz melodies filled a potentially uncomfortable silence nicely. "Based on what I see here, I think we could manage a half hour after dessert."

Macet acknowledged her offer with a smile. "I believe Ambassador Lang will be satisfied."

"I'll make sure it's arranged. Would it be too much to ask for some idea about what we might expect?" *Ladies and gentlemen, presenting Skrain Dukat! And for his first act, he'll invite a* pah-wraith *to possess the first minister.*

"Something that I believe will set the proper tone for our visit," Macet said earnestly. "I'd rather not say more until the reception."

Kira frowned. "Let me be frank, Macet: I hate surprises."

"You'll like this one."

Steady, Nerys. This is still the man who helped us pull off the Europani evac, when he certainly didn't have to. "In that case, I'll look forward to your—surprise. Thank you for stopping in."

Macet didn't move from where he stood, lingering expectantly for a long moment. Kira straightened up. She'd be damned if she'd cower in his presence. Even raised to her full height, she had to look up at the gul to meet his gaze. His broad, thick shoulders enhanced his dominating stature. *So what.* She'd taken down opponents far more intimidating than Macet.

"There is a story going around," Macet said at length, "that you had a—how shall I put it?—a unique experience during the gateway affair. I'd be most interested in hearing about it."

Kira had to admit it took a certain amount of fearlessness to seek out, without support personnel or weapons, a former enemy in the enemy's territory. Wasn't that what the entire Cardassian delegation was doing? Still, Macet had yet to provide answers about the purpose of their mission. *Not too much trust on your part either, gul.*

"Actually, I have another appointment due to arrive at any moment," she said.

He nodded, his expression once again emotionless. "Another time, perhaps. Forgive my presumptuousness, Colonel. But please reserve a moment for me tomorrow at the reception, should duty permit." Not waiting for her to reject him again, he offered her a brusque nod of his head and promptly exited her office.

Kira watched him leave. It seemed to her as if it took forever for the turbolift to arrive. When it finally did, it was occupied.

Taran'atar stepped onto ops. From her vantage, Kira could see the cold set of his eyes. Symbolically adjusting his weapons belt, the Jem'Hadar's hand hovered over his sidearm as he strode past Macet without acknowledging him, a pointed gesture he clearly wanted the Cardassian to see. Because in seeing his hands ready to engage a weapon at the slightest provocation, the gul would know

Taran'atar was prepared to fight. *He's laying the footings for a psychological war with Macet.*

Macet responded to the Jem'Hadar with a smirk before he entered the lift. "Habitat ring," he said, and as the lift descended, he turned his smile on Kira before disappearing from view.

"You wished to see me, Colonel?" Taran'atar said as he entered her office.

Kira was still looking thoughtfully at the turbolift doors when she got down to business. "I believe there was an incident recently involving your continued shrouding aboard the station that we need to straighten out . . ."

When she reached her office, Ro pushed Thriss into a chair and immediately contacted Dr. Tarses with a request that the new Starfleet counselor stop by for a consultation. Councillor zh'Thane would have concerns about privacy, but Ro didn't give a damn. Thriss had started a bar brawl and deserved to be treated like anyone else who might have started a fight, be she common drunk or royalty.

As she began to process Thriss—taking her personal belongings and performing a general scan to assure she wasn't carrying any hidden weapons—Ro couldn't help thinking how ironic it was that trouble hadn't come from where it had been expected. They'd taken massive precautions to assure that the station would be safe from the Cardassians and that the Cardassians would be safe from the station. That Ro's biggest headaches had come from the Andorians instead of Macet's crew was predictably unpredictable.

Thriss complied completely with Ro's orders. She didn't cry, offer protestations of innocence or petulant sarcasm; she stared off at nothing. Neither did she resist being led away to the holding cell and once she was there, she immediately lay down and fell asleep. Ro wrote her incident report, ignoring the semiregular pages from Councillor zh'Thane. She told the night shift corporal to take the names of anyone—meaning zh'Thane—who wanted to talk with her. Or let them make morning appointments and she would deal with their grievances then. From her monitor, she periodically checked in on the sleeping Thriss until she was satisfied this round was over. At least until Thriss woke up and then, with any luck, Ro would be back in her quarters and the counselor could manage any outbursts. Overall, Ro had guardedly optimistic expectations, though Councillor zh'Thane might still make her life a living hell in retribution for locking up Thriss.

When the therapist arrived, Ro put aside her usual distrust of counselors and shook Lieutenant Commander Phillipa Matthias's offered hand. The counselor met her eyes directly when they exchanged names, unapologetically bypassed the usual social niceties and went straight to business. *Impressive,* Ro thought. If Matthias didn't employ the usual touchy-feely, mind game hocuspocus techniques, she might look forward to involving the counselor in more of her investigations. Ro had developed a healthy dislike for mental health professionals during her incarceration. *"Could this be latent anger against your sense of childhood abandonment?"* had been Ro's favorite query. *Excuse me? A sense of abandonment? How about wholesale repression of your people as justification for being a little pissed off!*

When Matthias asked for background information, Ro launched into the story of the bar fight and the parameters of the odd meeting with Councillor zh'Thane. Matthias halted Ro before she could get into specifics.

"Councillor zh'Thane's perspective, while illuminating, is still her perspective. Thriss deserves an unbiased evaluation. Knowing that there's some precedent for Thriss' behavior is enough to get started. You have her in a holding cell. That would be . . . ?" She gestured, inquiring at the four doors in Ro's office that led deeper into the security station.

Before Ro could reply, a dark, bearded Bajoran man, hair threaded with gray, entered from the Promenade carrying a squirming toddler—a girl—and holding a young boy's hand. Ro didn't need to ask who the children belonged to: they had the same hazel-green eyes she'd been looking into for the past few minutes.

"Sibias . . . ?" Matthias said, clearly fishing for an explanation.

She nodded toward her guest. "Lieutenant Ro, station security."

"Chon Sibias, Commander Matthias's husband, and these are our children," he said, shifting his daughter's weight from one shoulder to another. "Pleasure meeting you, Lieutenant."

Whenever Ro met a Bajoran, she peered at their earring to see if she could discern the individual's family or geographical origins.

The unique characteristics of Chon's earring intrigued her, but before she could inquire further, the chubby-fisted girl wriggled out of her father's arms and threw her arms around her mother's legs, nearly tipping her backward.

"I couldn't sleep, Mommy!" she wailed.

"The children wanted to say good night, Phillipa," Sibias offered apologetically. His wife threw a hand against the wall to maintain her balance. The boy, about eight, shuttled behind his father, peeking out from behind his legs with shy seriousness. His rumpled pajamas and mussed hair indicated he might have been roused from bed to accompany his sister on this late-night visit.

"My room is scary. There are monsters in my closet," she pouted, petulantly extending her lip.

Brushing the child's tangled dark curls out of her face, Matthias dropped to one knee and refastened a crookedly done-up nightgown. "Mireh. Your father will make sure you have a wristlight so you can check under your bed as often as you like, but you need to go back to your bed. No dropping your tooth cleaner in the replicator and pretending you can't find it. No hiding Walter in Arios's closet. Your father will say no if you ask to sleep in our room," she said over the child's head, directly to her husband. "Right, Sibias?"

He rolled his eyes in mock protest. "You say that like she's the one in charge, Phillipa."

"Isn't she?" Matthias said, arching an eyebrow.

"My father used to play the *klavion* to keep me from being afraid," Ro interjected. She crouched down beside Matthias. "Maybe your dad has something special like that he can do for you."

"Hey, you have funny wrinkles like my dad and the kids in my class," Mireh said, pointing at Ro's nose. "And like me!" She touched her finger to her own nose and began giggling.

"Mireh has never been—I've never been—around a lot of Bajorans. It's still a novelty to her," Sibias explained.

Matthias stretched an arm toward her son. "I'd like to say good night before you leave, Arios." The boy twisted his head into his shoulder, blushing. Sibias lifted him by the collar and pushed him toward his mother. She caught Arios's elbow and pulled him into her arms, feathering his forehead with kisses.

Ro stood up, giving the mother and her children some room to be affectionate. Normally such scenes of domesticity pressed all the wrong buttons with Ro. Having been orphaned young and having grown up in the resettlement camps, Ro had known little of family life, the closest thing being the time she served on the *Enterprise* and she had more or less messed that relationship up. But this family, for some reason, didn't annoy her so much. *Maybe I'm mellowing in my old age.* She stood next to Sibias, who appeared content to let his wife have some one-on-one time with their children.

"You didn't grow up on Bajor?" she asked him.

"I was an orphan in the Karnoth resettlement camp, or so the records say," he said matter-of-factly. "Smuggled off when I was Arios's age. I grew up far away from here on a Federation colony. While Phillipa is stationed here, I'm hoping to find out exactly where my family comes from." He twirled the earring chain between his thumb and forefinger, as if this piece of his heritage was at once familiar and foreign.

Ro had heard far too many stories like Sibias' during her years away from Bajor. Thousands of misplaced children were spirited away from starvation and disease only to discover as adults that they lacked cultural bearings. "Start near the Tilar Peninsula in the Hedrickspool Province. These markings," she pointed to several ridges and runes, "they're unique to an area just outside the outback."

He touched her arm, his eyes full of questions she knew he couldn't ask. "Thank you."

"If I can help . . ."

"I know. I'll stop by sometime. I'd like to talk with you."

With a reluctant sigh, Commander Matthias sent both children scurrying back to their father. "I might be all night," she warned her husband.

Sibias nodded. "I plan on attending the first service in the morning. Will you be back by then?"

"I hope so, I—" With eyes watering, Matthias pinched her lips tightly together; she swallowed a yawn with a gulp. "So tomorrow night?"

"We'll try to go out again." He kissed her. "You know how much I hate sleeping without you." They exchanged smiles and she watched as her little family departed.

"Let's go see Thriss," Matthias said, letting Ro lead her out of the office. As they walked, Ro guessed the holding area wouldn't be the most pleasant spot to work from; it was designed to accommodate prisoners and guards, not host therapy sessions. "The visuals can be transmitted into the conference room if you'd rather work in comfort."

Matthias didn't seem concerned. "All I need is a place to sit—the floor is fine. I'd like to start off with in-person observations."

They wound through a hallway and passed through another door before arriving at the holding area. The Andorian hadn't moved since Ro had last checked her; prostrate on a hard bench without a pillow or blankets, she slept with her knees curled into her stomach, her hands balled into fists. She failed to stir when they entered. "She doesn't seem to be in a talking mood," Ro pointed out pragmatically.

"Exhaustion will do that to a person," Matthias said, walking up next to the force field where she could study Thriss at closer range. She tipped her head thoughtfully, brought a hand to her chin and gnawed on her index finger. "I'm satisfied to work from here. Thriss' posture, her muscular tension, the length of her REM cycles—all can yield significant data about her state of mind." She patted an equipment bag she had thrown over her shoulder. "Besides, I have a tricorder I've engineered to my own specs that can help out." Matthias paused, scrutinizing Ro after a fashion that made Ro wonder if her secret thoughts were translatable via the number of times her eyes blinked or how often she pushed back her bangs. Counselors, even reasonable ones, made her nervous.

"Your cheek," Matthias said, addressing Ro's quizzical expression. "You might want Dr. Girani to look it over."

"Good idea." *Still more than ready to assume the worst about people's intentions. Nice going, Laren.* Ro touched her face, feeling out the size of her bruise with her fingers; she had forgotten about her own injuries. A swipe with a dermal regenerator would likely fix the bruise on her face, but there was always the chance Thriss's assault had resulted in a fracture or sprain. "Okay. Since I'm done here, go ahead and make yourself at home. The replicator's over there. If you need additional help, page the corporal on duty. Don't hesitate to contact me if the situation blows all to hell."

"Oh believe me. If it goes to hell, you'll be beamed here in your sleepwear."

Ro appreciated the new counselor's lack of faux sympathy; she hated how some counselors felt obligated to put on the "I-feel-your-pain" face. Matthias knew her job and went about doing it—without theatrics.

As Ro started for the exit, she heard Matthias move to the replicator and say, "Espresso, double and black," before she settled in to begin her observations of Thriss.

9

Down a dim tunnel, the rattling slidewalk chugged toward the Core, periodically stalling when the grinding gears jammed, only to resume with a jerk and continue forward. Vaughn hardly noticed: he might as well have been standing still. Seething sounds receded as his thoughts consumed his attention. The dregs of the Gamma Quadrant swirled around him, hefting their tankards, negotiating sales and sharing canisters of psychoactive vapors. So preoccupied was he, that when a Knesska miner's red horned lizard jumped off his master's shoulder and onto Vaughn's it took a moment to register. In the last few minutes, an inescapable sense of déjà vu had vaulted him back more years than he'd admit to.

During the summer between Vaughn's second and third years at the Academy, he and a group of friends had heard rumors of an exotic shrine on a tropical world in the Braslota system. Supposedly, drinking the water flowing through the shrine from the underground pools endowed the partaker with potent aphrodisiac powers. Lured by the promise of decadent delights, native men and women would sneak out of their homes at night and into the pilgrim camps where they would offer themselves up for seduction. While most thinking individuals would find such a legend highly suspect, Vaughn and his classmates, looking for diversion from the rigors of academia, decided a vacation was in order. They procured passage on a Rigelian shuttle, transferred to a freighter bound for Volchok Prime and met a merchant willing to drop them off.

After three days hiking through the jungle, they found the shrine, attended by a wizened humanoid of unknown extraction, drank the water, retired to their sleeping bags and awaited their prospective encounters.

Instead, Chloe came down with dysentery, Vaughn's tricorder was swiped from his backpack and everyone awoke with a profusion of deter-fly bites. The experience taught him the wisdom of the old adage: if it sounds too good to be true, it probably is.

This humiliating moment from his youth replayed in vivid detail as he listened to Minister M'Yeoh explain that for all their painstaking efforts during the last day, the desperately needed matter load eluded them. Everything M'Yeoh and Runir had said indicated that success was guaranteed; Vaughn hadn't even conceived a contingency plan. Yes, there was something to be said for enjoying the journey, as he'd learned from his encounter with the Inamuri but with each passing day, he wondered how long the mission would be permanently bogged down in this region. If there was quicksand in the Gamma Quadrant, they'd flown into it.

As he half listened to M'Yeoh's quasi-intelligible explanations about how and why the trade might have failed, Vaughn reviewed the day, from the beginning, and tried to figure out where he misstepped.

Early in the Consortium's thirty-hour day, Vaughn and Minister M'Yeoh obtained the proper permits for trading on the Exchange, the forum where loads were traded. M'Yeoh took Vaughn to meet the broker—a mild-mannered Legclian named Runir—who would represent them on the Exchange floor. Runir handled the Yrythny accounts. From the plush divans to marbled-glass light fixtures, he appeared to successfully manage the accounts of other clients as well. *Maybe this is where we fell down—all the documentation we signed off on had to be translated into Federation standard. If our translators missed cultural nuances . . .* He shook his head, knowing they had to solve this problem quickly.

"Can we resubmit our bid tomorrow?" Vaughn asked, loathing the prospect of wasting more days attempting to devise an alternative defense to the web weapons.

M'Yeoh pushed his hands up into caftan sleeves, pinching his mouth into a tight line. "I think not. We start over."

"Runir must earn profit by the word," Nog groused. "But the thing that doesn't make sense . . ." He twisted his lobe between his thumb and forefinger as his voice trailed off. When he realized Vaughn, Prynn and M'Yeoh waited for him to complete his sentence, he grinned broadly. "Never mind. It's nothing. I still say we should reuse the contract."

Vaughn recognized that look. Nog was on to something. Thankfully, his chief engineer knew when not to finish a sentence.

And Nog was right. It had been a perfectly decent contract. He had examined it with an eye to every possible deceitful angle and found nothing. Initially, Nog had been invited to join Vaughn and M'Yeoh to evaluate the metallurgical quality of available matter loads. His radiant face as he'd watched Vaughn and Runir wheeling and dealing proved that you can take a Ferengi out of commerce, but you can't take the commerce out of the Ferengi. The femtobot simulations back on the *Avaril* were all but forgotten as Nog had hung on Runir's explanations, constantly interrupting the trader with nitpicky questions: "What are the currency units?" "Who sets the exchange rates?" and the finer points of the Exchange's bartering protocols. Nog's willingness to do most of the talking had allowed Vaughn to keep his eye on M'Yeoh, look for any hint of impropriety. He hadn't forgotten the tactics employed by the Yrythny back on Luthia, or discounted the fact that the *Defiant* had been illicitly boarded within hours of the *Avaril*'s launch. Surrendering the acquisition issues to Nog served both of their causes. Even the needs of their other companion, Prynn, appeared to be met as she enjoyed every hour away from *Avaril*.

Cabin fever had started taking root when the relentless engineering repairs, disrupted routine, and being caged aboard the *Avaril* began to wear on the crew. Morale had steadily declined since leaving Luthia and he sympathized. As a goodwill gesture, Vaughn had offered the "break" as a poker bet in last night's game. Prynn rode a lucky streak to a win. *Who'd have guessed my own daughter would turn out to be a card sharp?* For the others, mini-shore leave would come after business was taken care of.

Except now it appears business won't be taken care of, he

thought. Shoulder to shoulder, aliens blocked Vaughn from being able to see how much distance separated them from the Core's Central Business District. He leaned off to the side only to have his view obstructed by clouds of chemical coolants bursting from cracked conduits.

Behind him, M'Yeoh muttered a question that Vaughn couldn't hear over the racket. "Excuse me, Minister, but would you repeat that?"

"Runir," M'Yeoh sniffed, "believes that depressed interstellar commerce has reduced the demand for the starcharts and navigational data, even though the information you offered is unparalleled in this sector. Our explorations simply haven't taken us as far as yours have."

"What I can trade, I've offered. I've nothing else," Vaughn said firmly.

"There's always something," M'Yeoh said, "If the need is desperate enough."

The slidewalk ended. They walked with the anonymous masses into the sweltering Core quad. Stalls sandwiched between kiosks and storefronts hawked spangled jewelry and *object d'art* interspersed with much less innocent contraband. Vaughn suspected the services of prostitutes and slaves were as easy to purchase as gaudy earrings. M'Yeoh led them to a booth out of the traffic flow, presumably to regroup.

Once seated, M'Yeoh twisted the sleeves of his government robe, his expression puckered; the Yrythny appeared to be legitimately miserable. Runir's failure cast aspersions on M'Yeoh's competency. Explaining to his superiors back home why the mission to the Consortium failed would be unpleasant. But Vaughn didn't give a damn whose fault it was—he just wanted it fixed.

The group scooted into the half-circle booth, the rubbery seat coverings sticking to their uniforms. A dingy globe rested in the table's center, providing minimal muddy light to see by. Nog hastily lifted his tricorder after discovering gummy residue on the table's surface. Prynn's hands stayed safely in her lap.

Vaughn shooed away a drink server; the time to unwind would come later. Time to reassert his authority—he'd followed M'Yeoh's lead long enough. "Prynn, Nog. Head back to the *Avaril*. Rerun those femtobot simulations and see if there's something we've overlooked—maybe an alternative deployment method that won't require the degree of structural integrity we're looking for. We may have to take our chances with whatever we have on hand."

Nog failed to veil a dubious expression, but accepted Vaughn's order with a nod.

His beady eyes darting from side to side, M'Yeoh hunched closer to Vaughn. "There are still some who might help you. No legal protection. Very dangerous, but you could see—"

"Belay that," Vaughn called to Nog and Prynn, then turned back to M'Yeoh. "Back up a step, Minister. Say that again." Vaughn interrupted, knowing if he didn't the minister might yammer on endlessly without reaching his intended point.

He gulped and whispered, "A shadow trader."

"You mean a freelancer. An unauthorized broker," Vaughn guessed.

Minister M'Yeoh nodded.

Now that's interesting, Vaughn thought. *"Tell me more."*

"It's a dangerous undertaking," the minister stressed. "We could be duped if we link up with the wrong one." M'Yeoh nervously scanned the crowds, presumably for hostile elements. "But they don't trade what they don't have. Find the right one, you'll have your load." Sweat drizzled off his forehead; he dabbed at it with his sleeve, his gray-brown skin took on a decidedly paler hue.

Vaughn exchanged looks with his chief engineer. He was counting on Nog's acute listening skills to pick up nuances in the business discussions that Vaughn might miss. Nog looked intrigued, but suspicious.

Turning back to M'Yeoh, Vaughn said, "If such an option ensures results, why didn't we start with a shadow trader?" Why was it that at every turn in his dealings with the Yrythny, he found that they'd conveniently omitted information? Not enough to technically be considered a lie, but certainly less than all the facts.

"A shadow trader's demands may be costly or risky," M'Yeoh squeaked. "Outlawed technology. Slaves. Illegal goods. Weapons. You made it clear what you were willing to negotiate with. Your terms would be better accepted on the Exchange."

Or you were too afraid to deal with anything but the known entities, Vaughn thought. He needed to remove M'Yeoh from the equation if he wanted to make a quick deal.

Loud, laughing revelers stumbling toward a casino careened toward their booth, drinks held high. They jumped out of their seats, missing a frothy soaking by seconds. Prynn and M'Yeoh stumbled into a cloth barrier that delineated the workspace of an odd-looking creature, sitting staring at the wall. Tools crashed; bins toppled, drizzling milky syrup on the floor gratings.

Startled by the invasion of his workspace, the creature glared glassy-eyed at Prynn, while one of his five hands scraped brownish wax off strands of hair with his fingernails. Once he'd collected a thumbnail full, he dropped it on his black tongue, smacked his lips and repeated the process. Prynn slowly backed away, but the creature hissed at her. She stopped.

Vaughn, no stranger to unusual life-forms, had never seen anything like it. A cross between a squid and a mantis might explain whatever it was. He looked to his Yrythny host for information, but M'Yeoh tiptoed around the basins and back toward the main walkway.

"Excuse me," Prynn apologized, extracting her foot from a pan of goo. "I hope I didn't ruin—"

The creature scrambled off his chair, thrusting his face as close to Prynn's as he could without pressing their lips together. Vaughn's hand inched toward his phaser . . .

"You," the creature burbled rapturously.

"Huh?" Anxiously, Prynn's eyes darted first to Vaughn, who shrugged, and then to flustered M'Yeoh whose lips flapped soundlessly.

"The one I search for. To finish my commission," the creature clapped two of its hands together. "I sit day after day, hoping to find the one I need to finish my commission and I see nothing. I sense nothing. Until you." Spittle flecked the matted hair around its mouth.

Taking a step away from him, Prynn smiled weakly. "You've mistaken me for someone else. We're not from around here."

Vaughn assumed a position at Prynn's side. "We apologize for intruding on your space. If there's something—"

"No, no!" the creature protested. "I don't want apologies. I want—that one," it said, jabbing a finger at Prynn.

With surprising courage, Minister M'Yeoh lifted up the goo-pan and sniffed the contents before dabbing a finger inside and wiping the goo on an adjoining wall. Gradually, the goo turned blood red.

Recognition registered on his face; M'Yeoh's breathing steadied. "Commander, I don't think you have reason to worry. I believe this is a sense artist."

"Yes! Yes! I have a commission," he said, throwing a canvas drape aside to reveal a three meter by two meter collage of multi-hued textures. "For the Cheka Master General. He is unhappy that I haven't finished, but you will make it complete."

"Sense artist?" Vaughn asked.

"This substance," M'Yeoh indicated the goo-bucket. "When it comes in contact with living tissue, it takes a sensory impression based on body temperature, metabolic rate, body chemistry . . ." He dipped in his hand until it was covered with goo and then re-moved it to dry in the air, fanning it carefully. The clear sticky sub-stance slowly assumed a creamy lemon tone. "Once the polymer dries," M'Yeoh peeled from the wrist, carefully easing up the now rubbery impression of his hand until it slid off readily, "this is what results. Sense artists collect a multitude of impressions and then arrange them in sculpture, hanging mobiles, wall mountings—"

"My commission for the grand foyer of the Master General's suite," the creature said proudly. "I need the last element. I have waited for weeks. And now you are here!" His grin revealed a mouth of crooked, graying nubs Vaughn assumed were teeth.

Prynn combed her fingers through her spiked hair. "We're only visitors and won't be staying long."

"Oh please oh please oh please change your mind. Oh please oh please oh please!" He threw himself prostrate before Prynn. "Only you!"

Taking Prynn by the elbow, Vaughn extracted her from the crea-ture's ardent attention to her feet. "Tell you what. If our business concludes and time allows it, we'll come back and you can take your impressions."

"Commander!" Prynn exclaimed, drawing back. Vaughn ex-pected she might throw him a punch under different circumstances.

The creature knelt penitently and while its ratty hair failed to camouflage his despondent posture, Vaughn's words mitigated his sadness somewhat. "Fazzle. Ask anywhere in the Core for Fazzle and you will find me."

As they walked off, pushing their way through the thronging

crowds clogging the Core's central district, Vaughn couldn't resist teasing his daughter, "Think of it as a new cultural odyssey: immortalizing yourself for posterity."

She smirked at him. "I'll stick to living fast, thanks."

Waiting for the lifts back to *Avaril*'s platform, Vaughn approached the minister. In a low voice, he asked about making contact with a shadow trader.

"Word of the needy spreads quickly. The Exchange is watched. When the shadow traders figure out what you have, they will find you."

"So we wait," Vaughn said.

M'Yeoh nodded.

Vaughn closed his eyes, wishing circumstances could be different. From the first moments after the *Defiant* had triggered the Cheka weapon until now, Vaughn had felt he'd been standing at the helm of a rudderless craft. At every turn, he'd been compelled to accept whatever course circumstance had selected, whether it was the not-so-subtle attempt of the Yrythny government to engage Dax as a mediator, having to turn over bartering to a broker or this latest pronouncement of M'Yeoh's. Vaughn didn't like it. He understood that part of the hunt was patiently waiting in the tall grass for your prey to stroll into your sights, but some part of him couldn't shake the feeling that he was the one doing the strolling, not the waiting.

"So how much fun are you having, Ensign ch'Thane?" Keren asked, taking a seat on the edge of Shar's desk. They were alone in the government office Lieutenant Dax's team had been provided.

"Work doesn't need to be entertaining," Shar said practically, dropping an unused data chip into a drawer.

"But your antennae . . . they're drooping. You could borrow my headpiece to cover them up and then no one would be the wiser."

"Oh." Andorian antennae often conveyed emotional states. Any hope he'd had of getting to his genetic research today had vanished when Ezri had given him his daily orders. His antennae must be betraying his down mood.

Keren examined a statue of a naked Yrythny riding a whale-size sea animal—a gift from a well-meaning Assembly member courting favor with Ezri—now residing on Shar's desk. Upon seeing this odd gift, Ensign Juarez had doubled over, convulsed with laughter. The Wanderer delegate appeared equally bemused. "Where's Lieutenant Dax?"

"I'm surprised you don't know. She went with Jeshoh and the Houseborn contingent for a planetside tour of one of the Houses." Juarez, Candlewood, and McCallum had gone with her. Shar had— meetings. Ezri apologized profusely for asking him to act in her stead, but she felt the mission needed to proceed on two fronts.

"Ah. Probably House Tin-Mal. One of Jeshoh's pet stories. I'll be interested in her conclusions."

"Tin-Mal?" Shar thought he knew the names of all the Yrythny Houses, but Tin-Mal wasn't familiar to him.

"My Houseborn brothers and sisters are excavating the bones from the House crypt in an effort to make a point. I'll have my office send over the Journals of Tin-Mal," she said. "I'm certain they aren't in the database you've been given."

"You're saying the historical and cultural data the Houseborn have been providing us is incomplete?"

Keren shrugged. "A politically sound tactic. Select the facts that prove your argument, suppress the rest."

The constant push and pull of politics had always seemed futile to Shar. It had been his observation that after the arguing and manipulation and propaganda, truth eventually won out. Dealing in postulates and suppositions and perceptions . . . what a muddle. He liked pursuing causes he could measure—and not in votes. "What do the Houseborn want Lieutenant Dax to see?"

"The ancient majesty of these castles rising out of the water, with the lava and coral walls, sea glass sparkling. It's quite seductive," Keren reached over Shar's shoulder, tapped in several access codes, bringing up a vid of an underwater seascape played on his viewscreen. "But Tin-Mal happened because both sides made mistakes and I believe she'll see through the facade put up by Jeshoh's people. She has to."

But how would that help? Shar thought. For almost a week, Shar had stayed on Luthia. He had watched Houseborn and Wanderers live in segregated neighborhoods and walk on opposite bridges. Houseborn Yrythny congregated, usually by House affiliation, for dinner and social events. Wanderers, orphans all, used separate eating and recreational facilities. How Ezri Dax could find a working solution when the Yrythny were determined to live separately, Shar couldn't imagine. Behavior patterns had been ingrained for generations. And now, with the Cheka siege, when the planet would most benefit from putting internal disputes aside, the Houseborn and Wanderers seemed to be finding more reasons than ever to distrust each other. *If only I had more time for my study,* he thought. A realist, he knew that science couldn't solve everything, but it was a solid way to start.

Keren interrupted his thoughts. "You're certainly solemn about something."

Shar flushed. "I-I—" he sighed. "I have an idea about how to approach your internal issues, but I don't have enough time or resources to make it workable."

"Go on," Keren said, resting her elbows on the desk and watching him intently.

"I've studied your DNA and to say that it's a marvel of genetics is an understatement." He'd spent hours last night, watching the computer simulate Yrythny cellular mitosis, the DNA unzipping, spiraling in a dance of base pairs lacing together to create life. "I have a . . . a hypothesis that whoever aided your evolutionary process—call it the Other if it suits you—whoever could engineer your biochemistry to the extent I've observed so far, could have forecast problems with genetic drift or mutation. Like those recessive traits that make Wanderers, Wanderers."

"And you think the answer to our problem might be in the Turn Key?"

Shar nodded. "Maybe. But access to your labs is restricted—even to Ezri—and I can't organize a statistically significant sampling in the time we've been given."

"For fear of the Cheka stealing and exploiting our results, we haven't done significant genetic research in decades. What we *have* done is barricade what data we have behind layers and layers of security." She furrowed her brow thoughtfully. "You need a large body of DNA samples to make your generalizations and forecast possible conclusions, correct?"

"Yes," Shar answered. "And because one of my specialties is cytogenetics, I'm actually uniquely qualified to undertake genetic mapping. I could process the information quickly if I had it."

"Let me look into it," Keren said. "I may be able to help." She turned on her heel to go, but suddenly spun back around. "Oh. I almost forgot the reason I came to see you. The Cheka broke through the defense perimeter again."

"That's the third time since we've been here." Beetlelike strikers had penetrated Yrythny defenses, raided the mating grounds and attacked planetside villages. The assaults happened so quickly that the military could rarely be mustered in time.

"The Cheka are getting impatient. I know at least three of the systems under their domination are revolting. To maintain the military advantage—at least as far as the numbers go—they're going to need to augment their armies, especially if they plan to continue their expansion."

"Negotiating a treaty with the Cheka isn't possible? Shar asked. "If their goal is to isolate the Turn Key in your DNA strands, why not just give them the computer models? Or cryogenically preserve cellular samples?"

"The Cheka are only satisfied with fertilized, viable eggs that they can experiment on as they develop. They do surgery. Augmentations. They monitor when certain genes are activated in the course of maturing so they can develop their own chromosomal map."

"Successful research sometimes requires unorthodox methodology," Shar conceded, guessing that while the Cheka approach might not be ethical by Federation standards, the moral codes governing Cheka society might view experimentation on sentients differently.

Filmy eyelids lifting abruptly, she gaped at him. "You're thinking reasonably. That's your first mistake. The Cheka aren't reasonable."

Shar believed the Yrythny perceived the Cheka as evil, but civil war was an evil of a different kind—a reality that loomed larger each time they violated the perimeter, for every ship that a web weapon destroyed. "Still. The Cheka blockade is exacerbating the discord among the Yrythny. Is there no compromise to be reached?"

"I have something to show you," Keren had crossed to the door before Shar could turn off and secure his terminal.

"I have a meeting," Shar protested, knowing every postponed item carved precious minutes from his research.

"On my authority, consider it canceled," she said.

"But—"

"Please, Thirishar," Keren said. "This is more important."

How the message arrived on Vaughn's workstation aboard the *Avaril,* the commander never learned. He had intended on sending a recorded greeting to Dax on subspace, updating her as to the latest stumbling block when he noticed a blinking yellow light. Touching the button affiliated with the light had launched an audio-message. M'Yeoh had been right: a shadow trader had found them. The trader had designated a time and place for a meeting where they would discuss terms. Vaughn was to come alone.

So he stood, as instructed, in the hall outside the Cheka suite, wondering if he was supposed to knock.

On the other side of the door, the shadow trader, a Cheka named L'Gon, waited. If he had been truthful, he owned the load that would solve Vaughn's (and thus the *Defiant's*) problem. Vaughn's concern was that while he technically honored L'Gon's request and came alone, L'Gon was under no obligation to do the same. In fact, Vaughn believed that the Cheka Master General, several platoons of soldiers and whatever entourage a Master General traveled with would also be inside, but not a single operative representing his crew's interests. If there was any other way to get this job done. . . .

Two hours ago, he'd sat in the repair bay with Nog, Bashir and several of the engineering staff, watching computer simulations of Nog's proposed *Defiant* defense system. Every alloy Nog had synthesized failed. Most of the femtobots were destroyed as soon as they were deployed beneath the shield envelope. The femtobot defense would have to be scrapped unless a solution could be devised. Attempting to leave this region without protection against the Cheka weapon wasn't an acceptable risk as far as Vaughn was concerned. Yrythny intelligence had persuaded him that they would be facing additional Cheka weapon deployments indefinitely. *With time, we could find an alternative, but next to this raw material we need to make Nog's scheme work, time is the commodity we lack the most.* Vaughn had resigned himself to dealing with L'Gon.

The irony of transacting with the Cheka in order to combat their own weapon didn't escape him, and he took some satisfaction in the poetic justice of it, but another part of him resented having to pay the neighborhood bully for protection against the bully himself.

When M'Yeoh learned of the deal with L'Gon he'd offered a squadron of J'Maah's soldiers as backup, reminding Vaughn once again of the double-dealing ways of some shadow traders. The gesture had been appreciated, but Vaughn questioned the judgment of putting armed Yrythny within striking distance of the Cheka suite. Though the Consortium was politically neutral territory, legal declarations meant little in the face of heated emotions.

But Vaughn wasn't a fool. Knowing M'Yeoh's estimation of the danger was probably accurate—and having learned that Nog had succeeded in, among other things, restoring *Defiant*'s transporters—Vaughn put Bowers and Nog at his back. *Defiant*'s tactical officer would accompany him as far as the suite. (Certainly L'Gon wouldn't consider that a violation of their agreement.) His job was to stay in the corridor, prepared to contact Nog for an emergency beam-out, should Vaughn fail to emerge at the designated time. Bowers treated the task like something out of the old Western vids he loved so much: he would be the gun-toting deputy while Vaughn was the sheriff heading in to negotiate with the criminals. Vaughn appreciated Sam's enthusiasm, but cautioned him against scratching the proverbial "itchy trigger finger."

The door slid open at Vaughn's approach, and he stepped into the darkly lit lobby, clicking on the alarm on his tricorder's chrono. In half an hour, without word from him, Bowers would send the signal to Nog, and Vaughn would be transported back to the *Defiant*. *And how hot is it in here? If I'd known I was walking into a sauna . . .* He dabbed at his forehead with his sleeve. When his eyes adjusted to the lack of lighting, he realized a robot had arrived to serve as his escort.

"You are expected," the robot squawked. "Follow."

Vaughn complied, still not sure if he was walking toward *Defiant*'s salvation, or his own doom.

Funny how childhood memories color present expectations, Ezri thought, *literally.* She stood at the fore railing of the great hydrofoil, watching the rise and fall of teal waves garnished in white foam, still surprised that oceans could be any color but purple. She might have been raised around the mines on New Sydney, but extended family on Trill brought her regularly to the homeworld and its violet seas. The first time she'd walked across the Golden Gate Bridge during her Academy days, her eyes seldom lifted to the shimmering cables suspending the bridge above the bay, but focused instead on the dark gray-blue waters, all the while wondering why they were blue. On this world, blue waters would have been too staid; teal waters better suited this stirred-up planet.

The view of Vanìmel from Luthia's observation decks and windows captured a portrait of a warm, sleepy moss-green world, with white clouds sedately churning through the atmosphere. Descending through the clouds and close in on the surface, Ezri expected a dewy spring day and primeval forest; plants unfurling tender stalks and limbs to the sun's soft tickle, waters lapping at the seashores with a puppy's harmless eagerness.

Instead, hurricane force winds forced a bumpy detour away from a storm-sieged landing pad, swerving in and out of the lava-belching volcanoes that dominated the northern continent until finally, the shuttle skidded onto the flat top of a dormant volcano. She questioned the dormant part, seeing as steam oozed out of the cracked ground, the rotten-egg stench of methane permeated the air and she *swore* she'd felt the earth beneath them trembling. Ashen landscapes extended in every direction as far as the eye could see, the terrain devoid of flora and fauna. None of the Yrythny seemed worried. Vanìmel was a geologically volatile world whose rapid plate tectonic shifts had more in common with a game of checkers than a reluctant, long-simmering buildup that resisted release. As a counselor, Ezri had known those who nursed grudges, simmering privately until some provocation unleashed suppressed torrents of anger, and those who lived daily from eruption to eruption. Vanìmel appeared to be the latter type.

A swift land shuttle delivered them to the port city of Malinal where they boarded the hydrofoil that took them out to sea. By her calculations, they had been traveling for several hours, past kilometer after kilometer of water farms and quaint aquaculture villages mounted on stilts. Village residents tended the plants and animals being cultivated in surrounding waters, or served as lookouts, protecting the spawning grounds nestled along the continental shorelines. Once, the hydrofoil paused at the request of three marine patrol boats. Uniformed naval personnel talked in hushed tones with the hydrofoil captain—Ezri gathered they had been traveling on the border of a military training reservation and the officers wanted to examine the travel logs for security reasons. Later, one of the Yrythny representatives explained that a Cheka spy craft had been detected making several attempts at shoreline penetration; the military wanted to make certain their enemies weren't gaining access to secure areas with Yrythny assistance. Otherwise, the journey had been uneventful, almost leisurely. Had the circumstances been less formal, Ezri would have been tempted to throw on some sunlenses and sunscreen, sprawl on a deck chair and make shore leave out of it. She had a feeling her hosts might not like that too much, though she wasn't sure exactly what it was they would have preferred instead.

From the start, the Upper Assembly committee had been vague about what they wanted her to see, plying her with exquisitely prepared food, offering her comfortable seating, and breathtaking views from the hydrofoil's observation deck. *Schmoozing,* as the humans called it, was expected in this line of work. In the course of his years serving the Federation, Curzon had been offered latinum, liquor and the company of beautiful women (he'd taken them up on that offer); a little gourmet finery didn't phase Ezri. She liked the pampering. All the fuss hadn't totally distracted her—she hoped. Several times already she'd found her mind wandering through the last time she'd done this—right before Risa, when the Federation Council . . . *Scratch that. The last time Curzon had done this.* But did it really matter who did what? She was Dax. Curzon was part of Dax, and allowing some of his harmless vices to creep into her own behavior couldn't be all bad. Besides, she'd already learned a lot during this trip, even if it hadn't been synthehol in that last carafe of wine. Dax had a good head for liquor, having drunk more than her fair share of unsavory types under the table . . . Had that been Curzon, too? Or had it been Jadzia? Ezri shook her head, hoping the cool sea spray might sharpen her senses and make her forget her argument with Julian over these very issues.

Unbidden, she remembered a similar conversation she'd had with Dr. Renhol of the Symbiosis Commission during the Europani evacuation—how she'd confronted Ezri with her recent tendency to slip into her past-host personae, blurring the lines between present and past. And it wasn't like the weeks and months after joining either, where she'd wake up uncertain as to her sex. More like she didn't feel inclined to reign in Dax's various personalities. Maybe when she got back to the Alpha Quadrant, she'd return to Trill for her *zhian'tara*. She could only imagine what it would be like to meet these people she so enjoyed being. Ezri snorted. *Who am I now, standing here looking out over this ocean? One thing's certain, Lela would be more on task than I am.* She could hear Lela's firm, focused voice. *"Time to buckle down, Lieutenant. Start putting the pieces together so you can do the job you were left here to do."* Recommitting herself to the task at hand, Ezri considered what she'd learned.

What struck her most, as she considered the day's observations, was how lacking in arable land this planet was. It was astonishing that the population had proliferated as well as it had, considering. Yes, Vanìmel had five primary continental masses and hosts of island chains. Faults, toxic levels of minerals leeching into the watersheds from constantly shifting land plates, and geological instability (such as the volcanoes) made utilizing the planet tricky for sentients like the Yrythny, whose life cycles required both land and water. The degree to which they'd adapted the oceans for their use was a tribute to their cleverness. Yet at some point, Vanìmel's capacity to sustain life would be maximized.

Adding more modules to Luthia or farming more square kilometers of the oceans would work, but not indefinitely. During their first year, Yrythny hatchlings required thousands of kilometers of open seas. Confined spaces inhibited their maturing processes. Consuming ocean acreage to feed a growing population would only bring another level of complications.

Ezri had caught her first glimpse of "newborn" Yrythny about an hour before, when a school of hatchlings swimming close to the surface had been pointed out to her by Jeshoh. Longer tails and the undifferentiated limbs indicated these hatchlings had been in the water only for a short time. He'd explained that during the first year, hatchling respiratory systems gradually matured beyond utilizing gills to extract oxygen from the water, to lungs requiring gaseous oxygen. By the time they came ashore as younglings (as Yrythny in their first five years out of the water were called), the Yrythny were dependent on the atmosphere. Vanìmel's geography made it difficult. Even with the aquaculture villages, Luthia, and other communities built over the water, dry surfaces were difficult to come by. Maybe she'd been correct in her hypothesis, that indeed, caste customs, especially those related to reproduction, had arisen out of a fragile planet's needs.

When she noticed the hydrofoil slowing down, she turned to one of her Yrythny escorts for an explanation. He had said simply, "Force field ahead," and left it at that. Ezri guessed that they might be entering a section of the military reservation. McCallum, Candlewood and Juarez, her companions on this trip, emerged from the lower decks to see what had stopped the hydrofoil. Together, they walked over to the port bow. From there, they had a clear view of multistory towers extending out of the water at kilometer intervals directly in front of them. Signal lights on the top of each tower flashed orange. The lights continued blinking for a moment longer, dimmed, and began flashing blue. The hydrofoil moved forward, between two of the towers, across the waters beyond.

A representative Ezri knew as Lesh approached the four Starfleet officers and indicated that she wanted them to follow her. Ezri found she needed to jog to keep up with Lesh's bowlegged amble. Thankfully, Lesh was impossible to lose in a crowd, her distinctive mottled brown-yellow striping running from her forehead, beneath her headpiece and down her neck, setting her apart from the others. Color and striping, she knew, unlike the distinctive ridges of the Klingon crest, were not necessarily indicative of an Yrythny's House affiliation. The real test of a returning hatchling's identity was the distinctive chemical taste of its skin. Hatchlings with the "wrong" taste were raised in the Houses they came to, but as servants.

A Wanderer, clearing dirty plates off deck tables, had coloring similar to Lesh's and Ezri wondered, not for the first time, how it would feel if you knew where you were supposed to belong, but were unable to do anything about it. *"Can't you simply send the lost younglings home? If a youngling from House Fnoral swims ashore to House Soid, why not send the lost one back to Fnoral?"* she'd asked.

Jeshoh had looked at her like she'd sprouted another head. *"Because if they can't find their way home in the first place, there's something wrong. Isn't it compassionate that the Houses take in one that's not their own instead of casting it back out to sea or killing it?"* he'd answered. *"A thousand years ago that's what the*

Houses used to do: club to death any hatchling that wasn't theirs. We've come quite a distance from those days, Lieutenant."

As she watched the servant Yrythny scrape food scraps into the recycler, she wondered if the distance they'd come was as far as Jeshoh believed it to be.

Keren offered no explanations as to their destination. They passed the university, the health sciences center and the Aquaria before arriving in a nearly abandoned cluster of offices; none bore signage. Even the nondescript foyer—beige chairs, pale green carpets and white urns overflowing with flowers—provided little hint as to what the facilities' purpose might be. A flecked-skinned Yrythny female floated across the floor to greet them. Clasping Keren by the elbows, she said, "Come in, come in, Delegate. So pleased to see you. Your presence blesses us."

"Mresen." Keren nodded graciously, interlinking her arms with those of her hostess. She indicated Shar. "My companion, Ensign Thirishar ch'Thane."

Shar proffered the traditional greeting to Mresen. Her bejeweled skirt and the multicolored braids streaming to her waist marked Mresen as a high-ranking Houseborn. *Rarely do Houseborn—even Keren's colleagues—treat Wanderers so politely,* Shar thought, puzzled. A glance at Keren informed him that she expected his surprised reaction.

"A beverage perhaps? Take a seat where you're comfortable—" Mresen fluttered to an armoire, removed a serving tray from a cupboard. A click of her tongue brought a gaunt but more elaborately dressed Yrythny bearing baskets of braided seed crackers and pollen spread. Mresen poured coriander-scented water into the finger basins when Keren halted her.

"Ensign ch'Thane has come to visit our lost ones," Keren said, gnawing on a cracker.

Mresen clicked her tongue against her teeth, the skin drooping off her jaw jiggling apologetically. "Of course. You know where to take him." She reached for Keren's arm again. "Thank you, Delegate. For honoring us."

"The honor is mine," Keren replied, bowing.

When they'd left Mresen, Shar wasted no time in questioning Keren. "She's Houseborn."

"She is. House Soid, in fact. Her aide is House Yclen."

"And yet—"

"There are some aspects of Yrythny life even Houseborn and Wanderer agree on. Here we are—" A door hissed opened onto an arboretum, bordered on all sides by water gushing over fish ladders. They hiked up a carpeted ramp to where two rows of invalid chairs, suspended in the air before the floor-to-ceiling windows, provided their inhabitants an unobstructed view of Vanìmel. Where benches might be, Shar saw biobeds and in each, Shar discerned Yrythny patients. Medical attendants shuffled around efficiently, carrying trays with medication and nutritional supplements. Keren searched the residents' faces, honing in on one specifically.

"Witan!" she exclaimed, brushing her cheek against the ailing Yrythny's scaly scalp. Squatting down beside him, she checked out the view. "Are there storms in the archipelago today?"

The gnarled figure, prone in bed, twisted toward Keren's voice and garbled unintelligibly. The loose patient robes failed to hide the twisted vertebrae, the stump where an arm should have been. Witan's legs splayed limply on the mattress. Around the room, Shar saw Yrythny in similar physical states in every bed and chair. A few had smooth indentions where eyes should have been. Some lacked legs or arms. Others were attached to biobeds by sensors and life-support mechanisms. He understood that Yrythny technology hadn't yet attained Federation sophistication, but he was curious as to why little had been done to surgically correct the maladies these individuals faced. A VISOR transmitting sensory data to an optic nerve could provide sight. Biosynthetic prostheses could replace deformed bones. Even a vocal synthesizer properly implanted could allow a mute, bedridden patient to communicate. *Perhaps we might share some of our medical knowledge with these people, help them ease the suffering of their disabled,* Shar thought.

He followed Keren to the bedsides of several patients. The medical attendants—some Houseborn, some Wanderers—recognized Keren and offered her respectful greetings. Keren had personal words for every patient they encountered, all of whom suffered from different maladies. Whatever commonality brought the patients here was not readily evident in their symptoms. In Shar's Starfleet experience and in following Thriss around the medical wards on Betazed, he'd found that patients were usually organized by diagnosis. He suspected that Keren's agenda was the unifying thread here.

In a private moment, Shar asked at last, "What selected facts are you presenting me to prove your point, Delegate?"

"These are Yrythny rescued from Cheka research labs. All of them have undergone genetic tampering. The oldest residents were subjected to environmental research—like having limbs amputated or having their legs surgically fused together."

A wave of nausea squeezed his stomach; his antennae tensed. Although he'd been spared much frontline participation in the Dominion War, he'd seen enough of its horrors that he'd had to learn to cope with them: death, illness, destruction. Defending one's people or way of life, whether Federation, Klingon, Yrythny or Cheka, necessitated a degree of ugliness. But this . . .

Speaking softly, her voice coarse, Keren continued, "A few have been castoffs that we found by accident. That group over there"— she pointed to a number of patients suffering from orthopedic maladies— "was discovered left for dead in a damaged ship the Cheka had abandoned. Environmental systems had essentially collapsed. When we rescued them . . ." She inhaled deeply, sat silent for a long moment. She turned to Shar, her eyes glistening. "We can't negotiate," Keren said softly.

And finally, Shar thought he understood.

10

Lieutenant Commander Matthias rocked back and forth in her boots while she waited for the turbolift—in part, because her feet hurt. Never mind the progress of the last three hundred years, military bureaucracy was still incapable of designing comfortable footwear. Sore feet aside, falling asleep while standing was a real possibility considering how she'd worked through the night, managing only a few hours of sleep after she'd completed her chart notes around noon. Excited after a successful day at school, Arios had barged into her room and roused her from a satisfying dream of hiking across Vulcan's Forge. She'd hoped to rest a bit before the reception, but Lieutenant Ro paged her, requesting an in-person consultation before Thriss could be released from custody. Work waited for no one and mental health rarely conformed to a convenient schedule. Shathrissía zh'Cheen wasn't an easy case, though the patient wasn't necessarily the problem.

Ro's immovability in the face of family pressure impressed her. Councillor zh'Thane, after being told that her political standing had no sway in station security policy, had gone to Admiral Akaar. He too, had contacted Ro and she repeated her assertion that Thriss would remain in custody until she was assured that there would be no further disruptive incidents. Nudging the process along, Akaar stopped by Phillipa's office with a request that she deliver her evaluation promptly, thus "assuring that the time of all involved parties be spent on the Federation's business and not on personal issues." Apparently, years of pushing her agendas through committee had forced zh'Thane to develop not only the interpersonal finesse to grease the political process, but mastery in the art of being an exquisite pain in the ass when circumstances required it. *I suppose becoming a Federation councillor involves learning how to get your own way,* she thought, hoping that she was never required to do more than brief zh'Thane.

To prep for the consult, she'd spent the last hour combing the Federation database for any information pertinent to Andorian psychology, going so far as to contact her mentor/professor back home on Centauri. The case wasn't as simple as pronouncing a diagnosis and offering appropriate treatment. Thriss had been schooled by her culture to repress her personal concerns in favor of the collective needs of her betrothed partners. Trying to weed out what issues were endemic to Thriss versus what issues belonged to Thriss by way of her bondmates proved challenging. The longer she worked, however, the clearer it became that she didn't have time to study for her meeting with Lieutenant Ro, feed the children, read them a chapter from *The Adventures of Lin Marna and the Grint Hound Challenge* and prepare to attend the evening's diplomatic reception for the Cardassians.

To placate her neglected spouse, she'd brought a formal dress, secure in the packet tucked beneath her arm (side-by-side with her dress whites), ostensibly to change into after her meeting. "Just ask them, Phil," he'd wheedled. "I'm sure this one time they won't object to you wearing a beautiful gown instead of that stodgy old dress uniform." Phillipa imagined that line of reasoning wouldn't work on Admiral Akaar. Nevertheless she carried both garments with her—the uniform for the reception; the dress for Sibias, *after* the reception.

Where's that damn turbolift? She continued to run through her mental checklist: the babysitter was supposedly on her way (once her botany final ended); Sibias, using a tricorder, had persuaded Mireh that nothing more serious than a hairbrush lurked beneath her bed; Arios had made a good start on his science project. On the frivolous front, she'd made an appointment with a stylist who had a booth on the Promenade, hoping he'd be inspired to do more with her hair than the ponytail she typically defaulted to. Tonight, she was slated to meet her new commanding officer and she wanted to make a good impression, though she doubted Colonel Kira was the type to care much about hairstyle.

Phillipa had met her share of fascinating people while warping around the quadrant studying xenoanthropology, but no luminaries in the colonel's league. News coming from DS9 usually had focused on Captain Sisko but it had been Kira's exploits that intrigued her. In the weeks immediately following the end of the war, she recalled watching the colonel's tribunal testimony over the newsfeeds, trying to fathom how one crossed the gulf between Bajoran resistance fighter and consultant to the Cardassian resistance. She studied Kira's body language, her vocal modulations, and her facial expressions, concluding only that if there were a more focused, intently devout person in the quadrant, Phillipa hadn't heard of them. *Now I'm about to serve under her command,* she remembered thinking. She'd wanted to get every detail right.

I just hope my dress uniform still fits, she thought, trying to remember if she'd worn it since Mireh was born. *Not much need for dress whites while doing posttraumatic stress counseling in a war zone. Maybe Ro will let me change in the security office . . .* Focused on planning for the hours ahead, she missed hearing the approaching footsteps.

"Lieutenant Commander Matthias?"

Phillipa spun on her heel to see that Colonel Kira, striking in her dress uniform, had joined her. *And me completely preoccupied and frazzled.* "Yes, sir." She snapped her ankles together and tried not to stare too obviously at the colonel. Even if she hadn't already known what Kira looked like, she would have recognized her from the absence of her earring. To her knowledge, Kira was the only Bajoran officer on the station who didn't wear one: even Ro wore hers, albeit on the "wrong" side.

"At ease," Kira said with a smile. "When I saw you waiting here, I thought I'd introduce myself more informally than tonight's reception may allow. I'm just sorry we haven't met sooner. As you probably know, circumstances have been a bit more chaotic than normal."

The turbolift finally arrived and both women stepped in, Phillipa requesting the Promenade; Kira said nothing, apparently headed for the same destination.

"I don't mind at all," Phillipa said. "I appreciate being able to stay busy. My patients so far have proven to be—challenging."

"From what I understand, Shathrissía zh'Cheen comes with her own set of issues," Kira said. "I'm sure you've had your hands full—though I was hoping for your sake that she'd sleep it off. Have we seen the end of her outbursts, or can we expect them for the duration of her stay?"

Ro's report must be pretty comprehensive, Phillipa thought, wondering when Kira would have had the time to concern herself with one visitor. Her confident tone in speaking of Thriss was also surprising considering she hadn't shared her notes with anyone, including Lieutenant Ro. Maybe Councillor zh'Thane had been hounding Kira with her own version of Thriss' problems. Or the colonel might be drawing conclusions based on Phillipa's appearance.

Staying focused, all night, through Thriss's flare-ups of temper and her long, stony silences required Phillipa to stay physically sharp for extended periods. She'd managed, but not without paying the price. Untreated bloodshot eyes hinted at sleeplessness and she'd acquired a stiff walk from six hours sitting in a standard-issue, hard-bottomed chair. Since Kira had shown up, Phillipa had periodically rolled her shoulders to loosen them; her neck muscles remained sore, even after Sibias' massage. Kira wasn't stupid—she knew physical exhaustion when she saw it and could logically conclude it was the result of a night spent battling Thriss. Still, Phillipa, feeling protective of Thriss, wouldn't share information with Kira without cause. It was an old trick: pretend you know something in the hopes that the person who really knows will talk.

"While I respect your interest, I'm not at liberty to discuss specific patients, Colonel," she said politely. "Patient confidentiality."

Kira threaded her arms across her chest and stepped closer to Phillipa. Her expression, were it not so serious, could be read as humoring. "Regulations permit me to supersede all confidentialities—clerical, medical and therapeutical. You know that I could request your chart notes and you'd be obligated to produce them. Instead, can we agree that you'll share what's relevant to station security?"

Without ever raising her voice or moving into Phillipa's personal space, Kira had deftly established her authority. *Excellently done, Colonel. I can be reasonable—but on my terms.* "Patient information relevant to station security will not be shared with family members, however well intentioned those relatives might be," Phillipa said, quickly adding, "Just so we're clear on that, sir."

Kira laughed. "I'm not spying for Thriss' family, though based on the number of people hassling you about it, I could see why you'd think I might be. You think this emergency exit permit Councillor zh'Thane asked for is justified?"

"Councillor zh'Thane has cause to be concerned. This is a trying time for Thriss. Going home to familiar surroundings could be critical to her well-being, especially if something unexpected happens to Ensign ch'Thane." While Thriss hadn't been willing to talk about why she launched herself at Ro, by dawn, Phillipa had learned Thirishar ch'Thane's history by heart.

"Does the station have a reason to be concerned?" Kira asked.

"Thriss isn't a threat to the station or anyone presently residing here."

"And to herself?"

Phillipa contemplated how to answer, mulling through the long night's events. At one point, she'd seriously considered calling in Dr. Tarses for a neuropsychiatric consult, wondering if psychoactive medication or neurological mapping techniques would benefit Thriss. *For some, depression meant too much sleep or blue moods. For others, it took a more violent turn. For Thriss, it's probably a bit of both.* "Thriss is impulsive, volatile and passionate. Those traits, individually, are problematic. Combined with depression, they can be deadly. Her bondmates can offer her a measure of emotional stability that might mitigate any motive she might have to hurt herself. She wants desperately to please them. In fact, one of her biggest worries last night was how what she'd done at Quark's would reflect on Anichent and Dizhei. With their support, I can help her."

Silently, Kira considered her. Meeting her gaze directly, Phillipa didn't shy away from the colonel—whatever it was that she was measuring. She had nothing to hide.

The turbolift stopped with a soft thud and the door admitting them to the Promenade opened. Not sure that she had been dismissed, Phillipa walked beside the colonel who moved at a brisk clip through change-of-shift crowds milling about.

Finally, Kira stopped and smiled. "Ro was right about you. Keep me apprised of any developments with Thriss."

"Yes, sir."

Phillipa waited for Kira to disappear beyond the curve of the Promenade before she heading for the security office. *So that's what a legend looks like,* she thought admiringly. *Your reputation hardly does you justice, Colonel.*

And that's saying something, she amended mentally.

"Have you ever been in love?"

Positioned within a meter of the force field, Ro blinked her eyes a few times, and mentally replayed Thriss's question. Thinking that perhaps she hadn't heard Thriss correctly, Ro asked that she repeat it.

"Have you been in love?" Thriss said, enunciating her words loudly, assuring that Ro couldn't misunderstand her. As she strolled the length of the holding cell, she never broke eye contact with Ro.

Though the question's frankness startled Ro, she refused to be the one to lose the staring contest. "That's not relevant to the issue at hand."

Thriss tossed her hair. "If you knew exactly how relevant that question was, we wouldn't be having this conversation. I've answered your questions. Humor the crazy Andorian. Answer mine."

Combing her romantic history for anecdotes that might satisfy

Thriss appealed to Ro about as much as eating an oversized bowl of gree worm consommé. She wasn't so obtuse that she didn't get the gist of Thriss' line of questioning. After all, the primary reason Ro was carrying on a pointless discussion with an uncooperative Andorian (instead of hiding out at a dark balcony table in Quark's, pretending she didn't have a party to go to) was that Shar had left his lovesick bondmate for a mission into the Gamma Quadrant. Ro Laren was many things, clueless not being one of them.

"I've been involved in relationships. I understand how complex they can be."

She stopped pacing and studied Ro. "You never have been in love. I can see it in your face. No wonder. . . ." Her voice trailed off. "I'm sad for you."

"Don't be," Ro snorted derisively.

"You've never connected with another person out of more than primal urge, loneliness or social obligation. That's sad."

Ro gritted her teeth. "My choices, my life—have no bearing on whether you get out of here."

Thriss turned toward Ro, the smooth folds of her pale green tunic rippling as she walked. The cool cell lighting illuminated her white blond hair; the long wisps wreathed her face like a halo. "What you're missing is the interconnectedness between individuals that transcends biology or emotion. It's about redefining your life because another exists. You breathe because they do."

Thriss's voice, low and musical, had a mesmerizing quality that, when combined with her unabashedly romantic words, simultaneously enchanted and embarrassed Ro. All this ethereal sentimentality made her queasy. Commander Matthias better arrive pretty damn quick to rescue her or she would, she would—Ro didn't know what she would do, but it wouldn't make Councillor zh'Thane happy. Still, minus the dramatics, Ro understood Thriss' passion when framed in the context of what she'd been willing to sacrifice for the Bajorans.

Ro allowed an uncomfortably long silence to elapse before she addressed her prisoner; she wanted to control the tempo of their conversation and silence was an effective tool in accomplishing that. "I understand those emotions. I also know how incredibly dangerous they are." Her chest tightened at a flash of memory—

Picard, seated across a barroom table, his hand on her cheek, his voice in her ear telling her in no uncertain terms that she would not betray Starfleet for the Maquis.

"I'm not a risk, Lieutenant." Thriss balled her fists and planted them on her hips. "You got caught in something that started between me and my bondmates before we even came to the bar. What happened at Quark's won't happen again."

"Damn straight it won't." Promises rarely persuaded Ro. "Because if it does, even Councillor zh'Thane wouldn't be able to prevent your deportation."

Thriss and Ro stood, face-to-face, separated by less than a meter. Ro searched for the rage she'd witnessed in the bar, but failed to find it. Yes, Thriss appeared to be penitent—for the moment—but what about later when zh'Thane said the wrong thing or loneliness got the better of her. What then?

"Will anything satisfy you?" she pleaded. "Can't you believe that the knowledge that I hurt Anichent has almost destroyed me? I won't hurt anyone again. I promise to control my temper—to behave myself in public. And if I break my promises, I'll surrender willingly to your custody and allow myself to be returned to Andor. Would that be enough?"

"If I thought that you kept your promises."

"Might I state, for the record, that I believe you're safe in releasing her, Lieutenant."

Two heads swiveled toward the new presence. How long Commander Matthias had been standing in the rear of the room listening to their conversation, neither could guess. *I must have been pretty focused to miss the door opening.* Ro, for her purposes, hoped the counselor had heard the unsettling conversation Thriss had initiated believing it was proof plenty that Thriss was a bit unbalanced. But Matthias's perfectly neutral face failed to yield even the smallest clue of what she might or might not have learned. Matthias's opacity contrasted sharply with Thriss's transparency: when the counselor spoke, Thriss's shoulders relaxed and she inhaled like a swimmer rising to the surface to take a swallow of air. For the first time during this latest conversation, her antennae stopped twitching nervously.

"Go ahead. Disable the force field," Matthias said.

What? Ro failed to understand what it was Matthias was trying to accomplish by releasing Thriss. She looked questioningly at the counselor who nodded, as if to say all was well.

When the barrier fizzled off, the counselor stepped into the cell. Thriss remained fixed in the spot she'd been in when Matthias appeared. *So far, so good,* thought Ro.

Moving to Thriss's side, Matthias talked in hushed tones; Ro couldn't make out much that was said until the counselor informed Thriss that she could leave the holding cell. The Andorian left first, compliantly, following Ro to the main office with Matthias picking up the rear.

Matthias waited for all to be seated and comfortable, before addressing Ro. "Thriss understands that if there is any hint of a problem, if her bondmates or Councillor zh'Thane have concerns about her behavior or if situations arise that require security's attention, she will be returned to your custody. From tomorrow forward, she will have daily appointments with me until such time that I feel we've resolved the issues that prompted the outburst at Quark's. Are these terms agreeable to both of you?"

Thriss and Ro exchanged wary looks before Ro answered affirmatively; Thriss' eyes dropped to her lap and her antennae curled slightly down. But she, too, nodded in agreement.

"I took the liberty of contacting Dizhei, Lieutenant Ro. She should be here soon."

"How, how—" Thriss began haltingly "—is Anichent?"

Matthias touched Thriss's knee, saying gently, "Dr. Tarses released him to his quarters early this morning. He'll be fine. He'd be coming along with Dizhei, but he's still physically drained."

Silent tears dripped down Thriss' face. "I have to fix it—make it up to him somehow. I am horrible to have become that carried away . . ." Hunching over, she buried her face in her hands.

Ro looked out through the clear door and saw Dizhei entering the Promenade from the Habitat Ring bridge. Thriss twisted her dress fabric between her fingers and tapped her foot. "Can I have some juice?" She hiccuped.

While Ro went to the replicator, Matthias leaned forward, resting a hand on Thriss' chair. "I talked with them. They're fine and they love you," she said softly. "Thriss?"

"And I love them, but . . ."

Before she could finish, Dizehi entered, greeting them in polite tones but her excellent manners failed to hide her tensed antennae and tight-lipped smile. Since the previous evening, her skin had paled markedly.

Ro handed the juice to Thriss who gulped it eagerly; she seemed relieved to have something new to do with her hands. "Thriss agreed to the terms we set forth for her release," Ro said to Dizhei. "She's free to leave with you, if she chooses. Or she can leave here when it suits her." Thriss deserved the right to decide whether she went with her bondmates; Ro wondered if some of Thriss' frustration stemmed from her relationships with them, though neither Thriss nor Matthias had mentioned problems within the bondgroup.

Thriss looked between Dizhei who, given her longing gazes and quivering antennae, might gather Thriss into her arms any moment, and Commander Matthias who offered encouraging smiles. Scooting back deeper into the chair, she took another swallow of juice.

"If you'd like to move into the anteroom, you could talk with a bit more privacy than you have here," Ro said. She touched her combadge. "Ro to Sergeant Etana. Please make the interrogation room available to the guests I'll be sending into your office within the next few minutes."

"Zh'yi?" Dizhei whispered.

Thriss turned abruptly, looked up at her bondmate and searched her face for answers to some unspoken question.

"Sh'za," Thriss said, rising from the bench. Dizhei was at her side, pulling her into a hug before she could take more than a step. A flurry of embraces, concerned glances and excited exchanges followed. Standing apart from Dizhei and Thriss's emotional displays, Matthias gently ushered them toward the adjoining room; the two touched constantly until the door closed behind them.

Grateful that they had left, Ro exhaled loudly. "I have a few questions, Counselor."

Matthias shrugged. "Ask away."

"How do we know Thriss won't be back here by tonight?"

"Typically, we're bound by expectation." Matthias placed her palms together contemplatively. "Since Thriss defines herself by others' expectations, I wanted to make sure she knew we believed she was capable of meeting ours. I wanted her to know she has our trust, that we believed she could succeed."

"Is she really going to be okay?" Ro asked, recalling Thriss's longing as she talked about love and emotion and her life.

"She's not going to hit you again, if that's what worries you."

. . . *Have you ever been in love?* That question defined Thriss for Ro. "No, what I mean is, can she make it until Shar comes home?"

The counselor sighed. "If I were laying odds at Quark's, I'd say better than even that two months from now, she'll be on her way to Andor, with Shar, for the *shelthreth*. Once it's taken care of, the worst of Thriss' obstacles will be overcome."

Whatever it takes. She deserves a reward for her fidelity. Though satisfied with Matthias's answers, Ro wanted to make certain Thriss was comfortable with how her situation had been resolved. "Could you stay around, you know, just in case Thriss has any concerns, or if her bondmates decide they'd rather not have her at home?"

"I expected that I would," she paused. "I have a favor to ask."

"Sure." Matthias had proved to have very few demands so Ro was willing to accommodate her in whatever way she could.

"Is there somewhere around here that I could change my clothes for the reception?" she said sheepishly.

Ro laughed, causing Matthias to blush. "You're going? I'd heard it wasn't mandatory for Starfleet personnel." Would that First Minister Shakaar was as flexible as Admiral Akaar on social matters. Shakaar wanted to be impressive, prove that Bajor wasn't the backward, orphan child of the Alpha Quadrant anymore, that she deserved to be included in the first worlds of the Federation.

"I don't *have* to go. I like to dance," she explained. "I take it if you had a choice—"

"I'd be at the gym. Or the Replimat. Or scrubbing plasma conduits. Anything but a party with dozens of dignitaries and high-ranking political figures." Ro shuddered, picturing herself monopolizing the quietest corner of the buffet table. "At least I'm on duty. Maybe I'll get lucky and voles will invade the duct system, giving me an excuse to leave."

Matthias laughed.

Ro gestured back toward the holding cells. "You're welcome to use the head next to the guard's station to change. I probably should be getting ready myself. Let me know—"

"—If there are any problems with Thriss. I will."

"Thank you, Commander."

"Thank you, Lieutenant. See you tonight?"

"I'll be the one eating the dip," Ro said, hoping that Quark would supply at least one dish that wasn't pus yellow, alive, or raw. The prospect of spending three hours in a large crowd was trying enough without having to go hungry.

Matthias pursed her lips thoughtfully, her expression entirely innocent. "I can ask Sibias to take you for a spin on the dance floor. He's very light on his feet—"

"Don't make me issue an order, Commander," Ro warned, mock seriously. "You need to treat your station security chief with a certain deference."

"Yes *sir*," Phillipa said.

As she exited, Ro glimpsed Matthias's cheeky salute. *Maybe there's hope yet for me with Starfleet if this is the kind of officer they're growing these days.* An optimism she hadn't felt in a long time suffused her. *I might actually survive the reception,* she thought. *Or not. Wouldn't want to become too optimistic . . .*

Cynics who thought Alpha Quadrant sentients could never peacefully stand side by side on any matter had never seen the stirring sight that met Kira's eyes when she entered the formal reception room in the office station's Upper Core, a few levels below the Promenade. Sirsy and Ensign Beyer had outdone themselves.

Festooning one broad side of the great elliptical room were vividly colored flags and banners representing the Dominion War allies and non-Federation worlds like Ferenginar. The Bajoran flag had an honored position at the front of the room, standing a half meter taller than the other flags on the right side; the Cardassian flag stood exactly opposite the Bajoran flag on the left. The United Federation of Planets flag stood even with Bajor's and Cardassia's flags in the room's center. Vivid colors and symbols representing thousands of years all brought together in one place on this optimistic occasion—Kira thought she finally understood why Shakaar had been so adamant about having a celebration.

Quark's staff had already brought down the cold appetizers and set up the heating units for the hot dishes that Kira assumed would be arriving shortly. Platters of pulpy melons, *q'lavas,* Palamarian sea urchins and finger-size vegetables sat beside baskets overflowing with *mapa* bread and whole Tammeron grain rolls. The bar had been fully stocked with *languor* and *kanar* for the Cardassians; and a selection ranging from Bajoran springwine, *tranya,* Saurian brandy and tulaberry wine to Vulcan port and Terran Cognac had been provided for everyone else. A service turbolift hidden behind a curtain opened, admitting half a dozen servers carrying containers that billowed steam clouds. The smells of rich broths and spices permeated the air.

Everything appeared to be coming together as planned.

Kira walked along the tables, checking the place cards by the layout displayed on her padd. . . . *Ambassador Gandres, Andar Fal, Hiziki Gard . . . that takes care of the Trill delegation. Now to the Romulan attaché*—carefully situated far away from his Klingon counterpart on the other side of the room, Kira noted with relief—*the representatives from the Bajoran Commerce Ministry and the Vedek Assembly; Captain Mello and her executive, Commander Montenegro, from the* U.S.S. Gryphon. Thankfully, Beyer and Sirsy's collective attention to detail resulted in perfect execution of tasks such as this one. Though Kira knew it was too late to make dramatic changes in how the room was configured, she still second-guessed the decision to put all the VIPs in one place instead of dispersing them throughout the room. She didn't want to appear elitist, but a more egalitarian approach would have required stricter security measures and social protocols, neither of which she had time for.

Important guests would eat at long, rectangular banquet tables placed in two L-shapes mirroring each other; all tables faced the center of the room so every honored guest would be visible to every other honored guest. Additional invitees would be seated at smaller, more intimate circular tables behind the main tables. Seating decisions had been preassigned based on rank, delegation, and organizational and planetary affiliation. Since Kira had received the guest list, Beyer had learned of several old grudges still being nursed and a few badly ended romantic relationships that required a reassessment of some of those assignments, but for the most part, this was a group that knew how to behave themselves.

At Sirsy's insistence, Kira sat between Admiral Akaar and the Bajoran government's delegation. "A bridge between who we are and who we will be!" she'd enthused. Kira didn't buy the symbolism. As station commander, she held a highly visible position, but this night—this reception—wasn't about her. It was about Bajor and Cardassia's tentative steps toward dealing with each other as equals. She didn't want to distract from the task at hand on any level and she accepted that, to many Bajorans, she was a distraction.

She already knew that Shakaar had tapped Second Minister Asarem to deal with any Cardassian business that might follow the reception, while he, as first minister, would remain focused on the Federation talks. Though they'd met before, Kira knew Asarem mostly by reputation: a sharp negotiator who had campaigned for her present job by taking a hard line on all things Cardassian. Her party's role in Shakaar's coalition had been to represent the views of older, Occupation-era Bajorans who still favored a hawkish stance; Kira had heard gossip that Asarem had privately protested Kira's role in helping Damar's resistance during the Dominion War. Asarem felt that, regardless of the strategic value of undermining the Dominion's stranglehold on the Cardassian military, a Bajoran national such as Kira shouldn't serve the Cardassians in an advisory role: should complications arise, it would be too easy to blame Bajor or make accusations that escalated the existing bad blood between the two worlds.

Kira hadn't seen Gul Macet since he'd visited ops. She assumed he'd been assisting Ambassador Lang. Since Macet had requested time on the program, Kira had contemplated—and worried about—what he or Lang might have planned. *It's probably nothing worse than a proclamation from Alon Ghemor or a plaque commemorating this "historic occasion."* But no matter how she tried to reassure herself, Kira remained uneasy. Cardassians irritated her.

No, she amended her last thought. *Macet especially irritates me.*

From out in the corridor, Kira heard the low buzz of chatter from the first group of guests to arrive. Shakaar's enthusiastic voice rose above the noise. Seeing that the first minister would be serving as the gathering's host, Kira was glad he had arrived before the others; she had no desire to play host, covering for his absence with small talk. Because Sirsy accompanied Shakaar's party and she knew how the evening was to go forward, Kira could disappear until her presence was required. The room might be ready, but she still had a few items on her list before she could say she was finished. She discreetly moved to a position by the curtained turbolift and touched her combadge. "Kira to Ensign Beyer."

"Go ahead, Colonel."

"Report to the reception hall, Ensign. Guests are arriving and I don't have a clue what to do with them," she whispered, hoping she could go unnoticed for a few minutes longer.

"On my way, sir. I was helping Quark solve a replicator problem—"

"Nerys! What are you doing hiding behind there?"

She startled and took a sideways step to peer beyond the curtain. Shakaar stood directly in front of her, arms outstretched, with an exuberant grin on his face. So much for going unnoticed.

"Get out here," Shakaar continued jovially. "I have people you need to meet. Come socialize! This is your night, too—this is Bajor's night!"

Propelling her toward the group, he steered her past Sirsy and in the direction of a handsome black woman that Kira recognized from the newsfeeds.

"Second Minister Asarem, you remember Colonel Kira, your Militia contact here on the station? I know you two have met, but this is the first time you've worked together. Kira also plays a mean game of springball should you be in the mood."

Minister Asarem nodded politely; Kira reciprocated.

Kira surveyed the guests, checking to see if there was anyone else she needed to greet, if any old friends had come calling. Behind Shakaar, a prylar she recognized as being a protégé of Yevir chatted amiably with one of the trade ministers. He must have sensed he was being observed because he looked up to see Kira and frowned; his eyes instantly shifted to a spot directly over Kira's shoulder before physically turning his back to her.

When Yevir had first passed down his judgment, Kira believed she would gradually desensitize to the Attainder's consequences. As one of the faithful, she understood her peers' behavior and couldn't fault them for following the edicts of their religious leaders. But each cold encounter still smarted and this last one had a sharper sting considering present circumstances.

Here in this room were former enemies, people representing repressive or violent cultures, those espousing primitive traditions and backward belief systems, and yet all worked to overlook what divided them and focus instead on their commonalities. And Bajor, pious, spiritual Bajor, couldn't let go of punitive measures against one of their own for one night. This was supposed to be a reception celebrating Bajoran progressivism!

To Yevir's credit, the Attainder was working. Being the conspicuous outcast in almost every room she walked into assured that she would never forget what she'd done, never stop atoning for her mistake and wasn't that, in part, what it was supposed to accomplish?

At least Yevir himself isn't here to add insult to injury, she reflected. He'd been on the original guest list, much to her consternation, but had been forced to bow out, citing some "Assembly business" that apparently superceded an official state function. Kira found herself wondering if the "Assembly business" was related to schism rumors Kasidy had told her about.

She felt Shakaar's hand on her elbow again as he directed her toward the back of the room where the newest group of guests to join the reception stood: the half-dozen Cardassians.

"I haven't met Gul Macet or Ambassador Lang, yet, Nerys," Shakaar said cheerily. "I'd appreciate it if you introduced us."

And the evening just gets better and better, she thought, putting on her most polite expression as she prepared to face the evening ahead.

With the servers dispatched to clear the tables, Ro decided to take a break from her scintillating dinner companions (a doddering member of the Alonis delegation, and the governor of one of the Klingon-controlled Cardassian protectorates) and went in search of Quark. As she crossed the room, she spotted Kira chatting with Shakaar and the Cardassian delegation, the colonel somehow managing to look far more at ease within this gathering of luminaries than Ro imagined she would. Ro's eyes panned the room as she went on, pausing to note Hiziki Gard, seated a few tables away, looking in her direction. The Trill ambassador's aide—and her counterpart in Federation security—smiled pleasantly and raised his glass to her. Ro nodded back, accepting the compliment graciously: *Nice work,* he was saying.

She wound her way through clusters of servers milling around in the side rooms, diligently recycling used glasses and plates while replicating condiments and flatware in preparation for the next round. Quark's bellows were better than sensors or tricorders when it came to tracking him down. The employees grew progressively more anxious the closer she came to where he was working.

"Vulcan port is served by request only! It's too expensive! Push the Gamzian wine—we have that by the crate load. So help me, Frool, I'm deducting that port from your wages. Now get to work!"

The chastised waiter skulked by Ro, who had been waiting in the doorway.

Quark finally noticed her. "Oh. Hello, Laren. How's it going out there? Everyone talking about how wonderful I am? The artful presentation and the balanced diversity of my menu? Who needs the bar—I'll have jobs lined up until the end of the century when this is over." He scanned the crates piled up around him, making notes on a padd about what he'd used from each before closing it up and shoving it off to the side. Later, he'd send employees up to take each container back to whichever cargo bay he was using these days to stash his legal goods.

"If you say so," she answered. "As long as it isn't field rations, I'm happy." Ro knew all Quark's black market and embargoed items had been stowed away in cargo bays 16, 43 and 51. She was saving that knowledge for the day when she needed to motivate Quark to help her on official business. In the meantime, she knew that everything he thought he'd hidden from her was more innocuous than dangerous. Well, *mostly* innocuous.

Quark removed a meter-high stack of plates from a shelf and placed them on a cart. "Broik! Take these to Shakaar's table." He continued his inventory as he resumed speaking to Ro. "You're staying for dessert, right? You *have* to stay for dessert—it's Spican flaming melon."

"You know, I meant to ask you about that. Are you using actual flame gems for the effect?"

"Just three in each dish," Quark said absently. "I assume everybody will know not to eat them. Except maybe the Klingons." He stopped his inventory abruptly and looked at her. "You aren't gonna tell me they're toxic, are you?"

"No, that isn't what I—"

"Because the last thing I need is some extended family member of Chancellor Martok winding up facedown in the melon."

"Relax, Quark. No one's going to die tonight from eating your food . . . strange as it is to hear myself saying that." Ro hurried on before Quark could retort. "To answer your original question, though, I'm stuck here for the duration." She hopped up to take a seat on the edge of a table. "The colonel's pretty uptight about whatever Lang and Macet have planned."

"I don't know why she's worried. Natima's about as honest as they come—I always liked her in spite of that."

"You have any clue what she might be up to?"

"You're asking me? I thought you two were best friends these days. Doing each other's hair and having sleepovers."

"Quark—"

"All I meant is that you have better access than I do under the present circumstances. What did you come out here for, anyway? You miss me?"

"Don't flatter yourself. I came by to tell you I decided what we're doing for our evening in the holosuite." She slid off the table and started back toward the reception hall.

"Oh? And what might that be?" he pursued her doggedly through the maze of tables and chairs.

"I think I'd rather surprise you."

"Surprise? Is this a 'you're under arrest for tapping the comlinks to the habitat ring' kind of surprise, or is it a 'I'm not wearing anything underneath this raincoat' kind of surprise?"

She stopped and turned around to face him, stopping his mouth with her index finger. "I swear, Quark, you say one more word and this little experiment is over. 2100 hours. In two days. Holosuite one. Assuming you aren't on my last nerve by then." Quark opened his mouth to speak. "Not a word," Ro said, cutting him off.

Quark's mouth snapped shut. He smiled genially and nodded to her before retreating into the side rooms.

Ro wondered not for the first time since she agreed to see Quark socially whether such an agreement was a monumental error in judgment. Regardless, she'd said she'd give it a try and she felt obligated to keep her word. And it wasn't like she wasn't getting anything out of the deal. Quark liked her for herself, taking her on face value. And he didn't have any expectations except to have a good time (she wanted that, too) and good company. Whether there was any potential for something more than friendship had yet to be seen—actually going on a date with him would go a long way in establishing whether they were hopelessly incompatible.

Empty plates were coming off the tables when Shakaar stood and moved to the front of the room, holding a full glass of spring-wine. He tapped the goblet, calling for his guests' attention.

Shakaar might have protested his unsuitability for politics when the idea of running for first minister was first suggested to him, but he'd certainly grown into his leadership role in the years since. With hundreds of eyes focused on him, he radiated a serene confidence that Kira admired. In that moment, she found it easy to forgive the ongoing strangeness between them because he was so good at what he did. She was grateful it was him, and not anyone else, who was navigating Bajor through these confusing times.

"Our visitors, the Cardassians, have requested a moment of our time tonight and we are honored to hear from them. It's my understanding that our visitors hope to invite us to embark on a journey with them. And while we Bajorans have traveled with the Cardassians before, we must have courage to explore new territory. I don't anticipate this will be an easy journey, but this time, we have another companion to offer us aid and support: the Federation." He placed his glass down on a buffet table, freeing up his hands to applaud. Everyone in the room followed suit. "So let us move forward bravely, always mindful of what brought us to where we are now but always hopeful of where we can someday be. I raise a toast to the hope of new friendship!"

Over two hundred voices joined to proclaim Shakaar's toast and Kira, her own glass raised, gazed out over the room, filled to capacity with peoples of every species and political stripe, unified. To her immediate left, she saw towering Admiral Akaar leaning down to speak with Ambassador Lang, a mere slip beside him, and beyond her, Macet, nodding his head in apparent agreement with whatever Akaar was saying. The Andorians—Dizhei, Thriss, and zh'Thane, the councillor a portrait of elegance with her upswept white hair—earnestly conversing with the Romulan attaché and Captain Mello. Across the room stood Minister Asarem beside Klingon Governor Krodu, listening intently to the very animated Trill Ambassador Gandres.

Only the Federation could have done this: brought together, in friendship, former enemies and associates of disparate political stripes. *What the Federation does best,* she thought with a wry smile, pleased that someday, Bajor would be part of facilitating this process.

A young Cardassian, presumably an aide, pushed a portable holoprojector into the center of the room. Kira was suddenly jarred back to anxious expectation. There was a lot of present that needed to be lived through before that idealistic future came into being.

Lang assumed the spot where Shakaar had stood only moments ago. The crowd hushed.

"Because I believe First Minister Shakaar articulated very eloquently the task at hand, I wish to offer, on behalf of Alon Ghemor and the people of Cardassia, a token to christen this journey. A symbol of hope that personifies not only the terrible beauty of where we have been, but a vision for the future." She nodded to her aide and the lights dimmed.

Kira directed her gaze to the center of room and waited. The hologram flickered into focus.

Of the many possibilities she had imagined, what followed was not one of them.

Jeshoh treaded water while patiently waiting for Ezri to adjust her gear. Activating the lens datafeed proved challenging with her dexterity hampered by the gloves she wore, but she had it working properly after the third try. The goggle viewscreen was a neat feature. Instead of Jeshoh providing her with a running narrative, she had only to press a button on her wristlet to take a sensor reading. Within seconds, the data would be displayed on the lower quarter of her goggle lenses. At that point, she could request further clarification. She double-checked her suit temperature, made certain the rebreather's oxygen ratios were comfortable, and then indicated she was ready to explore the ocean. While most of the committee—and Dax's crew—went one way, Jeshoh pointed Ezri in the opposite direction.

No one had told her what they were visiting or why. Ezri assumed that she would learn as she swam. Dax stirred inside her not long into her dive. Since her joining, Ezri noticed she responded more intently to liquid environments, from the glub-glub of air bubbles rising to the surface and the feel of water caressing her body to the swish of sea grasses swaying with the currents. And that was odd. Ezri paused, studied the environment more intently and realized it was devoid of any plant life. She initiated several scans, discovering that outside their dive party, only microbial life existed within sensor range. Not even algae or barnacles grew on the empty shells scattered on the sea floor. An ocean not teeming with life didn't seem possible, especially on this world. Jeshoh noticed her falling behind and swam back to check on her.

"Is something wrong?" he said over the comlink.

Ezri shook her head visibly. "What's wrong here? Where are the fish? The seaweed?"

Jeshoh pressed a series of buttons on his own wristlet, pointed it in the direction of Ezri's and transmitted data to her.

Ezri read the chemical analysis scrolling across her goggle lens. "The levels of nitrogen in here are toxic. What—?"

Nudging his head in the direction of dark, shadowy mounds, Jeshoh swam off, with Ezri following behind. She kept expecting to tangle her feet in a kelp bed or encounter a school of fish; the eerie lifelessness made her nervous. The sound of her own breathing sounded foreign and in the vast, empty plain rolling out as far as she could see, she felt vulnerable, exposed. Increasing the tempo of her kicks, she propelled nearer to Jeshoh.

Growing closer, Ezri recognized that the mounds weren't the coral or rock formations she'd supposed; as her eyes adjusted to the goggles, she discerned several carved archways, one partially collapsed, a lump became a fallen dome and so forth until she realized she saw the remains of a city. All the way out here? Corroded skeletons—hundreds of Yrythny—lay beneath fallen walls and wedged in window frames. Swimming from ruin to ruin, the sights varied only minimally. Such destruction characterized worlds less evolved than this, usually those fumbling toward warp in the fossil and nuclear fuel stages. What happened here? A nuclear blast? She activated her sensors, and while waiting for the results to appear, Ezri asked Jeshoh to explain what she was seeing.

"You're looking at the remains of House Tin-Mal, a social experiment of four hundred years ago," Jeshoh said. *"You see, Lieutenant, we're not the narrow-minded elitists you might think we are. In fact, in the case of Tin-Mal, my ancestors were very progressive."*

"This was a Wanderer city, wasn't it?"

Jeshoh retrieved a platter-size chunk of wall, carved with Yrythny pictographs and passed it to Ezri. Brushing off the sand, Ezri traced the story with her gloved fingertip, imagining that by so doing the tale was being written in her mind.

"Your translator program will confirm this, but this segment explains how House Tin-Mal rose from the sea off the Fès reef, glorious in its spires and towers, a testament to how wrong the Houseborn were to repress our brethren. They grew in numbers. Built more platforms. Advanced aquaculture."

Among the litter on the sea floor, Ezri deciphered the rusted outlines of machine gears, tools, weapons and primitive energy chambers. Of course she couldn't be certain, but the design exhibited the same original flair she'd seen in Luthia. The Wanderers didn't seem content to make something work when it could work with panache. She had to admire their creativity, though she knew their boldness likely resulted in the disaster crumbling all around her. "They did this to themselves, didn't they?" she asked, more to affirm her suspicions than to learn something new.

"Carelessness. Arrogance. Stupidity. Pick one. For all their intellectual capacity, the Wanderers decided their energy system wasn't adequate so they began augmenting the existing infrastructure with incompatible technologies. There was an accident, an explosion and everything for a thousand kilometers was contaminated and destroyed. How many hatchlings died, the fish and plant life, the reef itself? None of it survived. Now, almost half a millennium later, the waters are still recovering."

His mournful tone touched Ezri and she wished she could offer him consolation. During the time she'd worked with Jeshoh, his love for his planet informed his every word and action. She knew he believed in pressing forward, taking Vanìmel into a new era. For all his efforts, however, the consequences of the past reverberated through generations. How well Dax understood that truism! Wisps of memories—especially Lenara and Worf—drifted back for a wistful moment. And Dax was reminded that by constantly revisiting the past, one could easily be shackled to it. Time passed, circumstances and technology changed. As horrific as the Tin-Mal experiment was, Vanìmel had moved on, as had the Yrythny. Maybe the time to rethink this chapter in the past had arrived.

Though she had no doubt that Jeshoh spoke from knowledge and conviction, she had lived far too many lives to accept only one perspective on any situation. Expect a child to do an adult's task, the task will be done as a child would do it, not as an adult. Ezri suspected the Wanderers had been set loose here with all the exuberance and idealism of youth, but with no practical experience. House Tin-Mal was doomed to fail before the first archway had been built. How to say this to Jeshoh? Audrid had always had a way of phrasing things just right. What words would she use? Ezri allowed Audrid's steady nurturing nature to suffuse her before speaking again. "While the outcome speaks for itself, I can't help but wonder if these Wanderers had been raised with the same opportunities and experiences as the Houseborn, would the outcome would have been different? Couldn't they be taught how to be proper caretakers?"

"And in the course of teaching, how many more mistakes would they make? How many mistakes could Vanìmel's fragile ecology withstand?" he argued. *"I accept that Houseborn history is not without its ugliness. Pollution, destruction, squandering resources. And how we treated the Wanderers? I am ashamed by my ancestors' ignorance. But now they have representation, education—everything they need to lead long, fulfilled lives. Is it so hard to understand why we don't permit them to breed and pass on their weaknesses?"*

Thick silence fell between them as Ezri searched for the right words, the only sound, faint echoes from far above them, of water curling up into frail crests, crashing into weak whispers.

* * *

So far, so good.

L'Gon waited for Vaughn in a cramped vestibule located down the hall from the main door. The dark paneling and orange-tinted lighting made it hard for Vaughn to see much. Squinting, he saw the brushed fold of floor-to-ceiling velvet draping, a plate bearing food scraps—greasy bones and skins sitting in a pool of bloody juices—and in the rear was L'Gon, clinging to a silken web. Vaughn's misshapen face mirrored in the burnished surface of his eyes. The Cheka deigned to rise, instead gesturing with one of his slender legs for Vaughn to take a seat on a backless stool sitting beside his couch. The robot offered beverages, brought a bowl of fried cartilage to snack on.

L'Gon didn't waste any time dancing around his payment demands. As soon as the robot delivered Vaughn's drink, the Cheka listed them.

Because the Cheka's vibrating metallic voice took some getting used to, Vaughn asked his host to repeat his request. *Doubt I heard L'Gon correctly, hundred-year-old ears and all,* he thought cynically.

"We want your cloaking technology." With pincers affixed to the end of a leg, he clipped a fine filament suspending an amorphous chrysalis from the ceiling. L'Gon squirted sticky brown liquid into the sack, waited a moment, and then slurped up the liquefied contents through a tubule. Carelessly, he chucked it aside, biomatter dripping off his fangs onto the fine hairs growing around his spinnerets.

Vaughn's face betrayed nothing. How the Cheka had come by his knowledge of *Defiant*'s cloak, didn't matter at the moment. What did matter was that Vaughn treat the revelation as nothing unexpected. "I'm afraid that's impossible."

"We don't require the device itself," L'gon went on, "just the engineering specifications and any parts we might find difficult to reproduce. In return, the matter load you require can be delivered immediately."

Vaughn dropped his glass on a drink tray and stood up. "Thank you for your hospitality. I'll let myself out." He'd taken only a few steps when L'Gon stopped him with a question.

"You do understand how this process works? I have something you want, you have something I want. We negotiate."

"I've made clear what I was prepared to offer in exchange for the matter load. So by all means, please let me know if you change your mind." Vaughn turned back for one last look, though L'Gon's hard-shelled thorax made reading body language impossible.

With silk thread extending from his abdomen, L'Gon lassoed fried cartilage from the tray, dousing it in gooey enzymes before lifting it to his mouth.

For a moment, Vaughn waited, watching L'Gon for a sign that he was interested in further negotiations, but saw no indication the Cheka wanted anything but lunch. "I'll let myself out." He left without another word, even to the android chasing stiffly down the corridor after him.

When the Cheka suite doors locked behind him, Vaughn checked his chronometer. Less than ten minutes. He'd always been a man who knew what he wanted—why waste time tilting at windmills? Bowers looked disappointed when he saw the commander emerge unscathed, having looked forward to a showdown at the O.K. Corral. Vaughn slapped him on the back, assuring him that he was fairly certain the bad guys hadn't yet left town and that he still might get his chance.

Not wanting to risk an encounter with any of L'Gon's henchmen who might be lurking in the Core, Vaughn called Nog and requested a beam-out.

How the hell did he know about the cloaking device? The question ran round and round in Vaughn's mind. Few of *Defiant's* crew had left the *Avaril* since they'd arrived at the Consortium and knowing them as he did, Vaughn believed all to be the soul of discretion. Once again his mind was pulled back to their first day on the journey here. *Someone is watching us. The question is, who?*

By his calculations, Shar and Keren had been hiking along the cliffs for almost an hour. Whether they'd made any progress was another issue entirely: every time the trail turned, Shar expected to look down and discover they'd reached the top. Instead, he faced trudging through yet another stretch of rocks and mud, sending pebbles skittering through the grasses with every step. Rainstorms had brought down weathered branches, gravel and debris from the above hillside onto the footpath. One way, Shar would have to scramble up a collapsing slope; the other required secure footing on water-slick lava rock. His muddy uniform testified to how much success he'd had the last time he'd gone off the path. How he wished they were traversing the wonderfully flat stretch of black beach below. He'd happily walk from here to where the beach vanished into the horizon if it meant he left the mud behind.

It hadn't looked this difficult when he'd agreed to hike in lieu of using transporters. He enjoyed hiking—having grown up in Andor's western hill country, he spent a good deal of his youth scrambling up and down the slopes around Threlfar Province. But the terrain hadn't been anywhere near as treacherous as this.

Before they left Luthia, Keren had shown Shar a regional map of the Hebshu Peninsula, one of Vanìmel's few land-based farming provinces. The two-dimensional version of the peninsula showed the trail as leading from the landing strip, cutting switchbacks across the steep mountain foothills, curving sharply near the summit, and dropping into the valley gap where they would make a swift descent into the peninsula's chief agricultural region. Simple enough. For a nimble-footed *tathrac,* perhaps.

"I have the remote transporters activated, Keren," Shar panted. "We could use them."

Keren spun around and walked backward, never making a misstep. "Consider this part of your research. Firsthand understanding of the environmental conditions." Laughing, she turned and skipped up the trail.

"And the farmers and herders have to bring their goods down this track to ship them?" Shar called. He couldn't fathom any vehicle successfully navigating these ruts.

Keren, deftly picking her way around mud puddles in the path, laughed. "Our transporters don't have the range yours do and weather conditions aren't always ideal—atmospheric interference and all that. When the volcanoes go off there's further interference—"

"And the most valuable resources you're transporting are dairy products and animal hair, correct?" Food made sense. The value of the hair puzzled him, but Thriss had always accused him of being obtuse about fashion.

"Excuse me, Thirishar ch'Thane, you of many locks, could it be that the quantity of hair on your head impairs your brain function? Why do you think hair is such a status symbol among my people? If it were easy to come by, why would it be so prized?" She tossed her long braids to make her point.

"I apologize. Questions of commerce are lost on me. My friend Nog has a much better grasp of such subtleties than I do." Drained, Shar paused and leaned back against a boulder. "I'm sorry, but I'm not used to this gravity—or the thin air at this elevation."

Keren backtracked and joined him. She closed her eyes, threw back her head and soaked in the sunlight. "It's always lovely after a storm. The skies are so brilliantly green they almost hurt to look at. And the smoke-wisps of clouds . . . I love it here."

Ocean breezes blew steadily, tossing his hair, chilling his antennae. He, too, turned his face toward the sun, seeking warmth. "So why not live planetside?"

"Choices for Wanderers are sorely limited. I could have learned aquaculture or raised livestock. I could have tried to work my way up the ranks of the serving staff in a House or tried to find a noble lady to be my patron. None of those things appealed to me. As soon as I came of age, I left the House where I was raised and went to school on Luthia."

"But you chose your life's work. You didn't have someone standing over you telling you what you could and could not do." Shar cringed inwardly, remembering the series of arguments he'd had with Charivretha about going to the Academy before the *shelthreth*. Dizhei and her put-out sighs, Thriss pretending that she hadn't been crying, Anichent spending longer hours in the observatory. Pleasing any one of them was difficult; pleasing all four was impossible.

"I want you to see something, Thirishar." Throwing her cloak to the side, she untied her blouse cord and pushed the fabric down her arm, revealing her bare shoulder. She turned her back to Shar so he could have a clear view. Above her protruding shoulder blade, her gray-brown skin was rough with three scars each outlined in black dye. "When I was five years out of the water, they strapped me, facedown, on a board and burned those markings into my back with a surgical laser. To make sure the meaning was clear, they injected black dye into the scars. Every Wanderer female is so branded. It's the Houseborn way of assuring that we are marked, set apart. That way, Houseborn males have no excuse. They can't take a fertile Wanderer female as a consort and be deceived." Keren pulled her blouse back over her shoulder and replaced her cloak.

"You see, Shar, my choices about what I can do with my life are

199

limited. Could I ever do what you're doing? Explore the universe? Travel far from my homeworld and find a different life somewhere else? Unlikely. Even here, I can't take a consort. Not really, anyway." She pointed out a moss-covered monolith in the distance, rising out of the surf, residual morning fogs not yet fully burned off. "Close by those rock formations is an entrance to a series of grottos. They're only accessible by sea—and half the year, they're submerged when the glacial runoff from the Pyoyong River comes from the mountains, but for centuries, Wanderers have used those caverns as spawning grounds."

"I thought that—"

"Yes, Wanderer males are sterilized as younglings, but Wanderer females can't be sterilized without sustaining permanent physiological damage. Too many Houseborn females want us as servants to risk killing us off. We're *compassionately* force-fed hormones from our youth, supposedly preventing our reproductive systems from maturing. But the supplements don't always work, like in my case, and so we submit ourselves to injections once we reach adulthood. But there are those of my sisters who don't comply with the law and sneak away to mate with Houseborn males."

"That's not legal, either," Shar observed. "The taboos for crossing castes are as old as your recorded history."

"True. Houseborn males breaking the law are executed. Some pairs, however, are willing to take the risk. They can't have an official union so they take a chance and share the one thing they can."

Shar exhaled deeply. "This I understand."

"What do you mean?" Keren asked.

"The lengths your sisters take to be with the one they love. The one they choose to love. How trying it must be for you." He flashed to a memory of his own Time of Knowing, when he received the identities of his bondmates, how terrifying and exhilarating it was to find out who he would be bonded to. What if it was someone he hated? Or someone dull-witted and stupid? In hindsight, his youthful fears seemed simplistic.

"Ah! Ensign ch'Thane has a consort waiting for him back in the Alpha Quadrant," Keren teased. "Tell me about it while we walk." She dragged him to his feet and they resumed walking up the hillside.

"It's a long story. Something we don't usually talk about outside our species."

"But you seem to come from such an open society," Keren said.

"True, but even my people are unique within the Federation. Our physiology, our rigid social customs dictate that we keep to ourselves those issues relating to family life."

"I've heard Ensign Juarez use the word 'family,' is that like a House?"

"A smaller unit-where adults nurture young who are usually related to them. Because most humanoids where I come from carry their offspring within them until they are ready to live semi-independently, the identities of the parents are rarely in question. Such children can't properly develop apart from their parents, un like Yrythny."

"It would be as if I returned from my year in the water to live with the consorts who laid me," Keren clarified.

"Yes. Exactly," Shar said, thinking for a brief moment that being raised in a large group—like the Yrythny younglings were—might be easier than being tied to a parent. Pleasing his *zhavey* was complicated, but he couldn't imagine living his life without her.

"What about your family, Thirishar?" Keren prodded gently.

From his first night on Luthia, Keren had openly shared her life with him. The underground. Her career. Shar's sense of fair play dictated that he ought to reciprocate. After all, wasn't he prying into the most intimate threads holding their society together? He took a deep breath. "On my world, we don't have 'pairs,' we have quads. I have three bondmates."

"Three?" Keren looked surprised.

"Shathrissía, Thavanichent, and Vindizhei," he said, seeing their faces flash before him as he said their names. "You have two sex chromosomes. Andorians have four sex chromosomes—we have four genders. It's challenging for most two-sex species to delineate the physiological differences between us, so we accept being called 'he' and 'she' rather than try to explain why those pronouns are an oversimplification."

"What *are* you supposed to be called?"

Shar smiled and rapidly reeled off a series of Andorii words, enjoying the confused expression on Keren's face as he said them.

"Do you mind if I think of you as 'he'? Like Jeshoh is a 'he.' " Keren asked sincerely, "I don't mean any offense by it."

"I've spent so many years away from Andor that I rarely think about it anymore. Sometimes, I even think of myself as 'he.' "

"I don't know what's harder—not having any parents—as we Yrythny—or having four."

Shar agreed, but felt that was a discussion for another time. "Among my kind, producing offspring isn't as simple as a female laying eggs and a male fertilizing them, as it is with your people."

Keren considered him thoughtfully. "I can imagine. Tell me about it. We have a long way to go."

They had cleared another stretch of trail as they walked; Shar admitted to himself that talking had made the hike go faster. *Why not?* "In recent times, my people endured a horrific biological holocaust, resulting in wide-scale chromosomal mutations. More *zhaveys* miscarried; more offspring were born with trisomy or hexsomy complications. In short, reproduction became much more difficult, when it was learned that the window of an individual's fertility had narrowed to a scant five years.

"Our scientists initiated a comprehensive gene-mapping project. Every family's genetic history was decoded, recorded and added to a database. The scientists' intention was to track genetic drift, to note when mutations occurred and to repair what abnormalities they could."

"I see why the Other's Turn Key is so fascinating to you," she said.

Shar nodded. "It might be that the genetic engineering that allowed the Yrythny to successfully evolve might also be applied to shoring up Andorian chromosomal problems."

Keren latched onto this idea of gene mapping, peppering Shar with questions. The more he talked to Keren, the more he hoped that this trip would help him locate the information he needed to help the Yrythny. Intuitively, he knew he'd find their answers written into the elegant helices of deoxyribonucleic acid, though gene mapping hadn't readily yielded any solutions for his people. He explained this to Keren.

"In spite of science's efforts to prevent or correct genetic disorders," Shar went on, "our reproductive problems persisted; population numbers continued slipping.

"Another approach was taken: instead of trying to genetically engineer a way out of the problem, scientists used the database to match mates with the highest likelihood of success. When I was born, my genetic profile was matched with those of three compatible bondmates."

Incredulous, Keren clicked her tongue against her teeth. "You didn't choose your consorts?"

Shar shook his head. "And once the matches are made, our focus is on providing a stable homelife for a child, placing the child in a community where he can grow up naturally with his bondmates. Without knowing I was bound to them, I'd worked side by side with my bondmates in school—since I was two and three years old."

"For all the trouble your people went to, I hope it worked."

If only you knew how complicated that statement was, Shar thought, recalling years of classwork, all-night study sessions, papers and days on end of lab work, focused on just that question. But Keren didn't need to know how the answer to her question had shaped his life. This time was about her world—not his. "Our population stabilized for a time, but in recent generations, new genetic ailments appeared. Weaknesses in certain chromosomal segments left us vulnerable to a host of maladies; these new mutations proved elusive to identify and fix. Bondmate matching has becoming merely a stopgap measure."

"And so . . ." the sober expression on Keren's face revealed that she expected what Shar would say next.

"Barring a permanent solution, we face extinction." *Why is it easier to say these things to Keren, a stranger, and not Nog or any of my other Starfleet colleagues?* It felt good to say the words aloud, especially since he usually checked every word he said, being careful to shield his people from outsider curiosity. Not once had Keren made a face or snickered; Shar couldn't say the same for several of his Academy roommates.

The unique dynamics of Andorian sexuality meant the most intimate parts of their lives could easily be misunderstood or exploited. In truth, Andorian familial structures demanded a far more conservative approach to sexuality than most humanoids employed. Shar had been amazed by the number of partners humanoids "tried on" before finding the right fit. Because his gender identity wasn't easily quantifiable to those enmeshed in cultures that defined reproductive relationships by twos, it had been easier to rebuff interest expressed by his peers, either as a potential romantic partner or in his unusual physiology, than try to explain himself. Modesty was a natural outgrowth of his culture. Keren seemed to understand that.

The telling of his story lasted the duration of the hike and they arrived at Valley Gap about the time he'd finished. Finding a relatively dry spot in a hollowed-out tree root, they broke for lunch; Shar ate another ration bar, Keren brought bread and fruit. Sunshine broke through the towering evergreen forest canopy, dappling the scrub brush and carpet of fallen leaves in light and shade. Occasional wind gusts rustled the highest boughs sending dried needles and flaking bark scattering to the ground.

Keren turned to Shar, studying him. "Just so I understand what we've been talking about for the last hour, your life is oriented around creating a new life with your bondmates? Having offspring?"

"It's supposed to be. Every choice was made to better facilitate my contribution to creating a child."

"Supposed to be?"

"I have rather . . . radical ideas about how to help my people."

"Why doesn't that surprise me?" She offered a toothy grin. "But surely such sentiments aren't unique among your kind? Many must feel as you do."

"Feeling as I do and acting on those feelings are very different things. I want to be brave enough to ask every question." *'But the answers are at home, with the* shelthreth,*'* Zhavey had said. And risk losing an unprecedented opportunity? He recalled a story about a pharmacologist seeking a treatment for the *nezti* flu. Months in the lab yielded nothing. To clear his head, he'd taken a vacation. And while on that vacation, he discovered a rare plant that made the difference in developing a cure. To Shar, life was about countless intuitive choices, and listening to his inner voice had guided him surely. Choosing between *Defiant's* mission and the *shelthreth* was choosing between two correct choices. Shar had followed his intuition here, to Vanìmel. He now had to trust that in time he would find the answers.

"I can only imagine your claustrophobia," Keren said.

"When I was younger, the stories my *zhavey* told me were moralistic parables and fables, praising the virtues of living for the needs of the Whole over the needs of the individual," Shar said, walking beside Keren. "My life's purpose is to live for the Whole. And yet, I believe that as an individual I can still make a contribution to the Whole."

"In this area, Shar, we aren't that different," Keren said finally. "I've never known anything but a collective life. Now I want to know something else. I want to choose my own destiny. What I wonder, though, is why you haven't done what your people want? Go home, start a family—and then once those obligations are met, you're free."

"Because no matter where I might go, I'd still be bound. My child's life, my bondmates—the only way I can have the life that I choose"—*maybe a life with Thriss,* he amended mentally—"is if I help solve the problems facing my people."

"I see," Keren said. She pointed out the road ahead. "We're only a short way from the valley now."

From the gap, the whole valley panorama spread out like patchwork; neatly groomed fields, rows of vegetables, farm buildings in miniature, herds of *shmshu* grazing. A ribbon of water snaked through the land, reflecting silver in the noon sun.

"I think, Ensign ch'Thane, that the Other did bring you," Keren said, quirking a half-smile."

Shar didn't feel compelled to respond, though his antennae vibrated inexplicably with an excitement. *There are answers here,* he thought.

Through an archway of densely foliated tree branches overhanging the road, Shar and Keren began their descent.

One advantage in dealing with Ferengi was their sense of pragmatism. Whatever was needed to do the deal was accepted without question. Nog hadn't so much as creased his forehead when Vaughn had interrupted a trying diagnostic with a request for a private conference off the *Avaril.* He'd delegated the remaining tasks to Permenter and Leishman, and followed Vaughn down to the Core.

In a dark corner of the crowded casino, Vaughn waited for the server to fill his drink order before raising a finger to indicate that he wanted Nog to refrain from speaking. Taking out his tricorder, Vaughn surreptitiously ran a scan across the booth and table before relaxing. He pulled a chip-size device from a hidden fold in his jacket, pressed a button that started a light flashing and placed it between them on the bench.

"A signal-jamming device?" Nog guessed.

Vaughn nodded. "I couldn't find any indication that there are listening or visual sensors in here, but if you've got good tech—"

"You won't be able to detect them," Nog finished for him.

"Right. This is a little something Starfleet Intelligence uses sometimes to annoy the Tal Shiar." Vaughn accepted the drinks and a basket of snacks from the server, paid her with currency that M'Yeoh had provided them and turned back to Nog.

"Before I forget," Nog said, "I wanted to tell you I sent our report to Colonel Kira this morning. It's about three days late, but she'll understand why when she reads it."

"Good work. And Ensign ch'Thane's letter?"

"Piggybacked it on the transmission. Ops will be able to extract it, no problem."

"Nice to cross one thing off our list, considering how many items still remain." Vaughn sipped his drink.

"I take it your meeting with L'Gon didn't go well?"

Vaughn scanned the crowd—the dancers strutting down a catwalk, anonymous faces hunched over drinks and games of chance. Through loud chatter of the cooling system gears and the music, he doubted their conversation could be eavesdropped on, but he still wanted to be cautious. "He wanted the cloaking device."

Nog's eyes widened. "He didn't! We've had *Defiant* under surveillance since the first day. No unauthorized personnel have been in or out of the bay without my sensors recording it."

"Then we need to start looking at the authorized personnel," Vaughn said, "because someone is leaking information to the Cheka and I want to know who. What about the Yrythny engineers?"

"Why would they deal with the Cheka?" Nog picked through the appetizer basket, arranging the geometric-shaped crackers in patterns on the table. "I thought something was up the day we went to the Exchange."

"How so?" Vaughn sipped off his wine spritzer.

"I listened very carefully to Runir's explanations. Even did some independent reading on the subject to cover the subtleties."

Vaughn laughed.

"I'm a Ferengi!" Nog reminded him unnecessarily. "It's my moral obligation to take any and all opportunities that further the advancement of commerce. I paid close attention to what happened on the Exchange and from what I could tell, our bid was successful."

Vaughn allowed the meaning of Nog's suspicions to sink in. "You think our load went to L'Gon just so he could deal with us for the cloaking device?"

"Probably. Maybe whoever wants the cloak was willing to share it with L'Gon and his fellow Cheka if L'Gon was willing to front the deal."

Vaughn considered Nog's hypothesis. "It fits. We have to stay one step in front of whoever it is. How long before the *Defiant* can fly?"

"Without the femtobot defense? Not more than a day or two."

"I'll let the Yrythny leadership know we'll be leaving the day after tomorrow."

"But sir, I have serious concerns about trying to leave this region without a defense against the web weapons."

"I'm sure you do. But we may have to take our chances."

Nog paused, pushed crackers around with his index finger, and pursed his lips together.

"Lieutenant?"

Dropping his eyes guiltily, Nog said, "Why not deal with L'Gon? If I can prove he has what he says he has, I say we get the load from him and be on our way."

"Out of the question." Vaughn frowned, willing Nog to meet his eyes.

"We're in a bad place, Commander."

Who am I seeing? he thought, studying the Ferengi for evidence of artifice. *The Starfleet officer striving to protect his crew or the Ferengi willing to deal no matter what?* Through the pulsing red neon, Vaughn watched a scuffle over a prostitute break out across the casino. Law enforcement rushed in through the back door, hauling off a group of inebriated miners in restraints. "You might say that, Lieutenant," he said, polishing off his drink. Throwing some of M'Yeoh's currency on the table for a tip, he waved Nog in the direction of the door.

Ezri pulled herself up the rungs of the ladder and heaved through the hatch onto the bottommost deck of the hydrofoil. She craved a hot steamy drink—maybe a Tarkellian tea because she was missing Julian—but first a shower. The wetsuit had been comfortable enough, but she still felt chilled from the water. She eagerly peeled the clammy thing off and went hunting for her boots when she noticed—

A pair of armed soldiers guarded each entrance to the room. All the Yrythny who had accompanied her on her underwater journey to Tin-Mal knelt silently, hands at their sides. Candlewood, Juarez, and McCallum, all pale and with wet hair dripping into their eyes, stood next to Jeshoh.

"What's going on?" Ezri said finally, since no one seemed eager to provide her with an explanation.

"There's been an attack on an aquaculture village," a soldier said gruffly. "Explosives were set off by a signal from this vessel— shortly after another transmission was sent here from your workstation on Luthia. Everyone on this vessel is to submit to questioning."

"Surely you don't think that I know anything about this. My people and I have been away from my office all day." Then it hit her. *Shar.* Ezri touched her combadge. "Dax to ch'Thane."

No answer.

"There's a logical explanation for this, I assure you," she said. She tapped her combadge again, repeating the call and still, nothing. *Dammit, Shar, where are you . . . ?*

Kira heard the gasps, the whispered questions and sensed waves of confusion spreading through the crowd, but the tears pooling in her eyes blurred her view. Her breath caught in her throat with each ragged intake. Closing her eyes, she allowed silent tears to wash down her cheeks, grateful for how the dimmed lighting obscured her face. Her intently focused seatmates gave no indication they noticed her struggle; her emotional shock could pass without comment, and for that she was grateful. She needed to feel this alone.

From the center of the room, the hologram, a deceptively lifelike child-woman shifted in her chair, her gaze directed at the unseen person capturing her image in photons and force fields. She dipped her head and laughed shyly. "My name is Tora Ziyal and I'm an artist," she said, trying to sound confident. "Or I'd like to be. My teachers—they say I'm promising. That's why they asked me to make this introductory holovid so that they can have something to present to the art council when they petition to have me included in the upcoming new talent exhibit at the Cardassia Institute of Art." She paused, squeezed up her shoulders, unable to repress her excitement. "I still can't believe they think I'm good enough!"

Kira had held up the drawing, impressed by the combination of simple forms executed with confident, elegant lines; the composition was thoughtful and expressive. Peering at Ziyal over the drawing notebook, she saw a young woman, anxious to please, and smiled. "These are lovely! Such serenity. You can really see Vedek Topek's influence in the texture of the shading over here," she pointed out the variegated, monochromatic tones of the rocks, "and in the geometric choices over here."

Ziyal had clasped her hands together with childish glee. "I'm so happy you like them. Do you think my father will like them?" she had asked.

"I'm certain he's very proud of you." Kira had hoped Ziyal didn't notice her smile tightening or her eyes glassing over at the mention of Dukat. Whatever her feelings for Dukat, Kira felt nothing but genuine affection for Ziyal. That Dukat was Ziyal's father was a curse of luck and genetics. The ability to sire a child and be a father weren't always mutually inclusive. She wondered, not for the first time, how such a monster could have helped create so lovely a soul.

"I wish I could say that there's some deep meaning I was trying to impart from my work." The hologram Ziyal shrugged. "I don't know that *I* know what each piece means, but if I talk about what I was thinking and feeling when I created them, perhaps it might help the committee discover whatever it is in my art that pleases my teachers. I just draw what I feel and somehow, it just comes out as art."

Wide-eyed, Ziyal had gazed lovingly between Kira and Dukat, relishing being between the two people she adored most. "It's a chance to show that Bajorans and Cardassians look at the universe the same way," she had explained to them. "That's what I want to do with my work: bring people together." The passion imbued in her guileless words broke Kira's heart.

Dukat had stood by, playing the proud parent, having convinced himself that he deserved credit for Ziyal's sweet sincerity. Kira had quelled her disgust for Ziyal's sake. Her loathing for Dukat needed to be kept from his daughter. Insulated from his crimes, Ziyal could continue to see him as her heroic rescuer; she deserved to see her father that way because that was how daughters were supposed to see their fathers. Kira understood that in her naïve fashion Ziyal believed she could bring Cardassia and Bajor together in her own world by casting Kira in the maternal role opposite her father. How could she comprehend what she hoped for? She had stood there, with Ziyal as the apex of their triangle, and hated Dukat for encouraging Ziyal's misplaced optimism. He had gone along with his child, allegedly being supportive, but in reality he was exploiting Ziyal to perpetuate some sick fantasy.

Kira shuddered, remembering. In light of what she now knew about her mother and Dukat, she understood that after a fashion, in another lifetime or reality, she and Ziyal could have been sisters. *Damn you, Dukat.*

Out of the corner of her eye, she saw Gul Macet, eyes trained on her. She swiped at her tears with her fist and fixed her gaze forward, pretending she didn't feel Macet's eyes drilling into the back of her head. She didn't know how much of her history Macet was aware of, but she wasn't about to give him any reason to go nosing around.

Holo-Ziyal rested her chin in her hand. "I think some of the reason why I draw—or paint—is because I'm looking for ways to make sense of my life. See, I don't entirely belong to either part of my heritage," she said, her voice cracking. The hologram swallowed, bit her lower lip and sighed. As Ziyal smoothed her skirt, twitched nervously—whatever business she could distract her hands with while she struggled to push down her emotions—the guests sat in awkward silence, uncomfortable voyeurs of her pain.

Kira watched her friend's shoulders shake. Trembling, she fought the illogical impulse to rush to her side and cradle the girl in her arms.

Kira had threaded her fingers through Ziyal's cold ones, searching for any sign that the life force, the pagh *she cherished, lingered. No vedek attended the body and where was the family to remove the Tora earring that by rights, Ziyal should have worn? The only family she had, her father, was in no condition to mourn. He rocked back and forth in his prison cell, prattling on about buying her a new dress or taking her home to visit, seemingly unaware of her death. To Dukat, she remained alive and Kira knew, after a fashion, she was, but where? What happens to the* pagh *of a child that no one will claim?*

Holding Ziyal's hand, feeling the warmth dissipate from her fingers, Kira refused to accept the notion that whatever energy it was that made Ziyal the vibrant, creative person she was had died with her. That all had been lost and that none of her lived on.

And now Kira sat in this place, predominantly surrounded by strangers, and knew, of a certainty, she hadn't been wrong. Something of Ziyal yet lived.

"I remember looking up into her face and wanting to have my mother's smooth skin. It looked so clean!" Ziyal whispered. "When I was very little, I tried scrubbing my face with the harshest cleaner, believing that I could wash this gray, this tint, from my skin. My mother had to mend all these scratches I'd given myself. Then she cried."

Covertly, Kira glanced at those sitting in front of and beside her; eyes glistened and sober faces abounded, stonelike with melancholy. She felt some satisfaction. *Finally, the grieving! And who cares if these are strangers. Ziyal deserved this!*

"And the relief I felt when I saw people who looked more like me—like my father." She gnawed her lip absently, contemplating what she would say next. "But I don't think I looked enough like him to please his people either. In my art, it was all me. In my world—where I was every shade of gray—life made sense. I hope it can mean something to someone else, though who, I don't know."

The projection paused and the lights raised. Ambassador Lang, serene, assumed a place in the room's center, the flags of many worlds hovering above her. Shoulders squared, she turned her gaze over the room's perimeter; she spoke without notes. "In a less enlightened time, with the vision of Bajor's *kai* and the political wisdom of Vedek Antos Bareil, Bajor and Cardassia negotiated a peace treaty. Alas, we were unprepared to honor our promises," she said, her voice tinged with regret. "We have a new opportunity in this postwar era to prove that we can be an honorable people. It's for this purpose I've come to Deep Space 9—to seek a meaningful, lasting peace between our worlds."

Deafening stillness overtook the stunned crowd. Kira knew everyone in the room, save perhaps the Cardassians, questioned the veracity of their understanding of Lang's words. She blinked back her own surprise. *Lang wants to normalize relations with Bajor. She's here, asking that Bajor recognize Cardassia as a co-equal partner in this corner of the quadrant. Can it happen?*

Lang continued. "But we understand why both the Federation and the people of Bajor might be skeptical. The leader of our provisional government, Alon Ghemor, believes we needed to offer a token of goodwill, to make a gesture that would both symbolize our hopes, and set the tone of our new relationship."

A dozen Cardassians filed in from the side doors. Each carried a large, flat, draped object, all in various geometric shapes. They lined up behind Lang, and waited, perfectly still. Kira tingled expectantly, knowing better than anyone in the room what was about to be unveiled.

Lang walked down their line and one by one, removed the coverings, revealing framed and mounted drawings. Some exhibited abstract qualities offering no discernable subject but rather studies of color and line; others were monochromatic pencil and ink still-life drawings of native Bajoran flora. A notable exception was a cubist study, all in gray tints and shades that showed the discernable profiles of two faces, welded together at the picture's center. But even the "face" painting and the unique personalities of the other pieces were unified by a consistent tone.

In a gallery covered wall to wall with a hundred artists' work, Kira would have recognized these pieces. Was this, then, where Ziyal's pagh now resided?

Waiting for the buzz of comments to simmer down, Lang resumed speaking. "The final days of the war destroyed many of Cardassia's monuments and historical treasures. Thankfully, the underground archives of the Cardassia Institute of Art in the capitol city survived the worst of the attacks. The head of our government devoted some resources to finding what could be salvaged from the Institute in the hopes that any surviving artwork might reignite a sense of Cardassian identity—that my people could heal not only their bodies, but their minds. Holocaust, by definition, goes far beyond physical parameters, something my people have now learned.

"During our search, we discovered an archive in which the work of Tora Ziyal, daughter of Tora Naprem, a Bajoran woman, and Skrain Dukat of the Cardassian military, had survived. You see its contents here—her introductory holovid, her art portfolio. Understandably, it struck a chord with those seeking a different sort of healing—those who feel that the gaping wounds between Bajor and Cardassia must be healed before either of our peoples can move forward, Bajor into the Federation and Cardassia into wholeness."

Shakaar leaped to his feet with applause. Less speedily, Minister Asarem joined him with the entire Bajoran delegation following suit. Kira scanned their faces, noting some discomfort but recognizing their reluctance to appear to be questioning Shakaar's enthusiasm. Kira stood, though in her heart she stood for Ziyal. Gradually, other members of the audience continued the ovation, the Starfleet personnel being the first to stand behind Bajor's gesture, with the Federation diplomats following almost immediately.

Smiling, Lang raised both of her hands and brought palms downward, asking for her audience to be seated. She continued speaking. "Symbolically, Ziyal embodies both the horrors of the Cardassian Occupation of Bajor, how women were taken from their homes and made to serve the military as concubines, and the possible glories that can come from a true alliance of our peoples. Our worlds *can* come together and create something beautiful. We see this in Ziyal's art.

"As a token of goodwill and a symbol of hope for the future, the people of Cardassia are giving a collection of Tora Ziyal's artwork to the people of Bajor to serve as memorial honoring the past, but recognizing the potential future we might find if we can find a way to see past our differences."

Another round of applause erupted, even louder than before. By now, the back walls were lined with Quark's servers and on-duty Militia and Starfleet personnel, crammed into every corner not filled with chairs, banquet tables, or bodies. Cheers rang over the steady clatter of applause. Lang nodded humbly, threading a trembling arm through her aide's proffered elbow.

Admiral Akaar nudged Kira, urging her out of her chair. She staggered up, her energy spent on emotion; she leaned against the table for support. The towering admiral bent down and asked her to accompany him to see Ambassador Lang. Kira followed, barely able to keep up with the admiral's strides that were nearly twice the length of hers. Standing in the circle around Lang, Kira fervently hoped she blended in; she had no desire to detract from Shakaar's moment.

The first minister had taken the ambassador's hand between his and had engaged her in an earnest conversation while Second Minister Asarem stood by. Kira recognized the fire in Shakaar's face. *He's really excited about this.* Standing less than a meter behind the admiral, Kira listened to the hopeful words being exchanged. When the conversation returned to Ziyal, she strained to hear Lang's comments.

"Ziyal's art, which embodies the traditions of both sides of her heritage," she said, "is proof that we can be harmonious. We can find common ground. This dream she had—of belonging to both her people—can be realized by us."

"Inspiring, Ambassador," Admiral Akaar said, shaking her hand again. "I must confess to being quite moved by your presentation. I hope this does indeed set in motion a new era of understanding."

Lang nodded graciously, thanking Akaar. Then she turned her gaze on Kira. "Ah, Colonel. I was hoping we would speak after the presentation." she said. "Were you pleased?"

" 'Pleased' isn't the first word that comes to mind, Ambassador, but I'll echo the Admiral's sentiments: I was very moved," Kira replied. "May I say that you're the perfect choice for this job. Good luck."

"First Minister Shakaar and I were just discussing beginning formal negotiations as quickly as possible. He has designated Minister Asarem to be Bajor's representative. But I was hoping you also would sit in on some of the talks, Colonel. That would be acceptable by you, First Minister, wouldn't it? Assuming it doesn't interfere with the colonel's command duties?"

A look passed between Shakaar and Asarem, and for a fleeting moment, Kira sensed disapproval from the first minister. While she knew she wasn't on the current list of Shakaar's favorites, she couldn't understand what would bother him about having her present during the talks. None of the others in the group appeared cognizant that anything passed between Asarem and Shakaar. *Maybe I'm just imagining things . . .*

Shakaar wrapped an arm around Kira's shoulder. "First thing tomorrow, Colonel Kira will need to locate an appropriate spot to house the Ziyal exhibit. I'm anxious to make it available to the station population for viewing immediately." He smiled down at Kira, who wondered what the hell he was doing with an arm around her in public. Leaving aside the fact that they were once romantically involved, it wasn't professional—and showing public approval of Kira wouldn't help push through his political agenda.

A waiter carrying a tray full of springwine passed behind her, giving her an inconspicuous way to maneuver away from Shakaar. "We're going to display the artwork here?" Kira was a little surprised. It seemed more appropriate to exhibit it at the Chamber of Ministers or the Museum of Bajoran History and Art in Dakhor.

"For the time being, until we can package it in such a way that it can travel all over Bajor for all of our people to experience. I think there are enough individuals on the station who remember Ziyal that it's particularly appropriate that it start out here. I'm certain you'll do a wonderful job." Shakaar carried on, seemingly oblivious that Kira had extricated herself from his embrace.

"However I can be of service," Kira replied, taking a sip from her goblet. With Shakaar's enthusiasm directed at preparing for the exhibit, she hoped the time had arrived when she could slip away before he demanded that she moonlight as the curator. Maybe one of these days he'd recognize that being a starbase commander was a full-time job! The reception had gone well, but she wanted to go back to worrying about malfunctioning docking clamps and temperamental Cardassian computers. "If you all don't mind, I'd like to check in at ops. Duty calls and all that." She stepped back, deposited her wine glass on a table and moved to leave when Lang stopped her.

"When you're finished arranging for the exhibit, I look forward to your visiting the talks. I think you could offer them a unique perspective," she said.

Before Kira could respond, Asarem, who had remained on the periphery of the conversation, stepped forward. "May I ask why you feel that way, Ambassador? Why you see Colonel Kira as being different from the rest of us? She's Bajoran. A former resistance fighter even." Asarem hadn't exactly thrown down the gauntlet, but she had offered Lang her first direct challenge, the opening move in a game of strategy.

Kira had almost wormed her way out of the group when Shakaar grabbed her by the elbow and steered her back into the circle, presumably to hear Lang's answer and provide any necessary clarification. *Damn. So much for getting out of here in a timely fashion . . .*

"Because Colonel Kira is a living witness to atrocities inflicted on my people, as well as her own," Lang answered, countering Asarem's pawn by moving out her own.

The conspicuous position Kira had been avoiding all evening finally found her; Admiral Akaar, Minister Asarem and Shakaar watched her, waiting for her response. *Wait a minute, I'm not one of the players here—I'm not even the referee. What I think—what I feel—has absolutely no bearing on this situation.*

And while Lang technically spoke the truth, Kira sensed that the ambassador's perceptions of the facts contrasted strongly with the second minister's perceptions of the same facts. She couldn't read Asarem, however: the minister's relaxed countenance betrayed nothing but impartiality. "I think you're overstating my understanding of the circumstances, Ambassador Lang," Kira said. "I'm only one person with one opinion."

Admiral Akaar's solemn face broke into a genial smile. "Among humans there is a saying that 'No man is an island, entire of itself.' Rather, every individual is a piece of the whole. I take that to mean that we do not have the luxury of thinking that our opinions—our actions—as individuals do not matter."

"I understand what you're saying, sir, but I hardly think that it's fair to give my opinion that kind of weight, under the circumstances. I'm not—I *can't*—speak for Bajor. That task has been assigned to Second Minister Asarem." Kira deftly forfeited her turn in whatever game Asarem had instigated. She had no desire to launch a political career and she wasn't about to be maneuvered into starting one. "Now if you'll excuse me, Admiral, Minister Shakaar, Minister Asarem, Ambassador Lang, I have a station to run."

Bowing out of the circle, she walked briskly away, her steps slowing when she discovered that Macet stood, like a sentinel, beside the exit. He smiled at her approach, which only got under her skin. Macet's persistent, unwanted attention was like having an itchy rash you couldn't scratch; except that, in this case, she wanted to scratch it with her fists.

"Gul Macet," she said with a nod.

"Colonel. It appears another evening has passed without us finding a moment to talk."

"That does, indeed, appear to be the case. We'll have to address that situation very soon."

"I'll hold you to that, Colonel. I anticipate being on the station for some time."

"I expect you will be. Now if you don't mind—"

"Of course." He unfolded his arm in a "after you" gesture, directing Kira toward the door.

Once she was safely beyond the reception room, beyond Macet's eyeshot, she threw back her head and tensed her whole body. If it wasn't Shakaar and his endless list of menial tasks or Lang wanting to use Kira as a buffer between her and Asarem, it was Macet, looking for a new friend. "Arrghh!" she growled, throwing a punch into the air.

Quark poked his head out of the doorway where he had been working. "You seem a little stressed there, Colonel."

"What?" she snapped.

"You should let off some steam," he said congenially. "Couple of hours in a holosuite. *Buff Beach Boys of Risa.* You might feel better. I'll even give you a discount."

"You're being serious."

"As a citizen of the community, I'm looking out for our best interests. A happy commander makes for a happy station."

Kira narrowed her eyes. "And you signed up to be morale officer . . . when?"

"Well—"

"I should take advice from the used spaceship salesman who probably put personal profit before the well-being of his nephew's best friend?" Kira wrapped her fists in his lapels. "I don't think so."

"What? Colonel, you can't really think I'd ever do anything to hurt Jake," he stammered. "You saw Nog's report on the shuttle I sold him—"

"Yes, I saw it. And lucky you, everything he found cleared you of any culpability for Jake's disappearance. But I'm more interested in what he may *not* have found."

"Really, Colonel, I was only trying to help your mood just now—"

"Twisting your ears off would help my mood. Are you volunteering? No? Then shut the hell up!" Shoving him out of her way, Kira stormed past him toward the turbolift, then stopped. "One more thing, Quark. If I ever find out that what happened to Jake was the result of your negligence, there won't be a hole deep enough or dark enough for you to hide in. Are we clear?"

Quark frowned. "Crystal, Colonel," he said quietly.

Following Thriss's release from station security, Dizhei was relieved to see her rhythms return to normal. She seemed to enjoy the reception, though she was moved to tears by the message left by the late artist. The following day she ate meals with Dizhei and Anichent, something she'd stopped doing in recent weeks. She sent out several applications for available medical residencies and she was sleeping regular hours—not too much or too little.

Always an early riser, Dizhei awoke the morning of the second day after the reception to find that Thriss, too, was up, eating breakfast before an appointment with Counselor Matthias. *Oh, please let us be through the worst of it,* Dizhei thought. For the first time since they'd left Andor, she felt buoyed by hope.

Her cheery mood must have hastened their pace because they arrived in the station's hub well before Thriss's appointment. Since she hadn't had a chance for quality time alone with Thriss since before the arrest, Dizhei guided her away from the flow of pedestrian traffic and into a mostly deserted corridor, used primarily for service access, with the hope that they could talk.

"Are you sure you're going to be okay?" Dizhei asked, squeezing Thriss's hands tightly. "I can postpone my observations until later. The classrooms aren't going anywhere."

Thriss shook her head. "I'll be fine. After my appointment with the counselor I'm going to do a little shopping. I saw a new variation of *kal-toh* on display that day we ate at the Replimat. I think Anichent would like it—he can play it solo since neither you nor I are very good at chess. And I want him to know how much I regret hurting him."

After looking both ways in the hallway to assure that they were, indeed, alone, Dizhei sighed and leaned into her bondmate's shoulder. "He knows, *zh'yi*. Despite the strife between us since we left Andor, he loves you deeply. And I think I've helped him see that you love him as well."

"I do! I'm sorry you feel that you're always caught between us. You manage your worries about Thirishar far better than we do—it becomes easy to take out our frustrations on each other, especially when Anichent's always certain that he's right," Thriss said, with good humor. She leaned back against the wall. "Remember that day in sh'Dasath's class when Anichent insisted that he knew better than sh'Dasath how to prove that theorem? Never mind that sh'Dasath had published papers on it. Anichent gets these ideas in his head . . ."

"I'd say between Shar, you and Anichent, it's a miracle we find consensus on anything," Dizhei said, taking Thriss by the hand. The feel of Thriss's elegant fingers against her wrist soothed her worries more than words possibly could.

Suddenly Thriss turned to Dizhei, concern written on her face. "You do know that I don't love Anichent any differently than I love you."

"But you *do* love Shar differently."

Twisting a straying lock of hair between her fingers, Thriss blushed dark blue. *"Sh'za—"*

"It's fine that you do, Shathríssía. I understand," Dizhei reassured her. "Maybe it would be more truthful to say that I respect your feelings." Or she hoped she did. She didn't like what she perceived to be between Shar and Thriss because it existed outside the bond, but she tried to comprehend it because she couldn't combat something she didn't understand. Keeping the bond strong meant she had to work with what she'd been given, like it or not, because the bond was first. *Always.*

From the time she was little, Dizhei relished that she was the most rare of her species: all Andorian offspring originated from her gender. Her unique maternal role suited her own career inclinations toward taking care of and teaching children. The entire focus of who she was—of what she believed she should be—was this deeply felt longing she had to be a parent, to be a part of a bond and create a life. At an early age, she came to understand the significance of her gender identity; all her priorities, all her desires fell into line behind that role. If anything, she envied Thriss's role as the *zhavey*. Their child would begin with Dizhei, but it was Thriss who would carry their offspring and give birth. Dizhei was continually astounded at how casually Thriss treated the privilege of carrying their child. What could possibly be a greater honor! Certainly not medical school or reputation. So many of their classmates had admired Thriss' vibrant personality, her zeal for new experiences and how quick she was to question the dictates passed down by the Elders. Dizhei never found Thriss's nonconformity as romantic as their peers did.

Since the day Thriss had been bonded to her, Dizhei had watched her *zh'yi*'s moods—her passions—dictate her life path. Not a commitment to principles. And for some years now, Thriss's passions had centered on Shar; everything else was secondary. Even having a child seemed to be a means for Thriss to bind Shar closer to her instead of her life purpose.

The more she witnessed the consequences of Thriss and Shar's decision to violate their bondgroup covenant, the more she recognized the Elders' wisdom in establishing the boundaries of the *shelthreth*. Intimate acts belonged in a group context. Dizhei felt the longings, but as Thriss proved, the consequences for yielding could be dire; she refused to take the risk. Without proper guidance, Thriss might forfeit her responsibilities as *zhavey* to follow Shar. Should that happen, Dizhei was prepared to do what she always had: fix whatever had broken.

Nuzzling Dizhei's neck, Thriss sighed, bringing Dizhei back into the moment. She drew Thriss into her arms and held her close. *I hope I'm wrong, zh'yi. I hope I'm wrong about many things.*

"There's nothing to understand, *sh'za*. I love you and Anichent the same as I love Shar," Thriss said finally.

Dizhei pulled back, curled her hand around her bondmate's cheek and considered the beloved and familiar face. Thriss's words belied Dizhei's own time-distant images of Shar, dappled in long shadows, pretending that everything was as it always was, though his darkened eyes said differently. She closed her eyes, relishing Thriss' warmth and drawing comfort from her embrace. But as much as she might long to indulge Thriss's romantic notions, Dizhei knew those notions threatened their greater purpose. She extracted herself from their embrace and took Thriss by both hands. "Don't lie to me, *zh'yi.*"

"I don't know what you're—" Thriss protested, halfheartedly.

"Don't. Lie. To. Me," Dizhei reiterated. "We're betrothed. I sense these things. I've always known. Anichent knows, too, though he doesn't want to admit it. We both know you and Shar shared *tezha.*"

Thriss flinched. "We didn't do anything wrong. We belong to each other. You and I—we could share the same." Thriss reached up to Dizhei's face.

Dizhei pushed Thriss's hand away. "It was a mistake. A serious one. But it's done." Even as Thriss confessed, envy twisted inside Dizhei, threatening to taint her with bitterness. She would not, she could not, allow herself to become the source of conflict. *I will not condone—I will not give you permission to believe that what you've done is acceptable when it could still destroy everything we've worked for.* Oh, how she wanted to shake the selfishness out of Thriss! To make her understand that she didn't have the luxury of destroying herself without destroying Dizhei, too.

Even now, all these years later, Dizhei vividly felt each moment of the first day Shar and Thriss had violated the bondgroup covenant. The panic of the night before, when Thriss and Shar had been missing, hadn't yet subsided. Shar claimed he'd been performing research for his environmental studies class; Thriss had gone off to find him and they had spent the night away from the compound after becoming lost. Both her bondmates claimed that nothing forbidden had passed between them and Dizhei believed them. Especially Shar, who had barely contained his frustration with Thriss.

For hours, Dizhei had waited for Shar to return from his disciplinary conference, but he never appeared. She had checked with Anichent, *Zhadi,* and the school before discovering Thriss was gone. How long had she stood in the corridor, waiting for Thriss to come with her to dinner—the wait felt endless. When Thriss finally showed up, she had been so overcome, both physically and emotionally, that she could hardly move. Collapsed on her bed, Thriss drifted between sleep and delirious consciousness while Dizhei, numbed with jealousy, worry and fear, sat beside her, uncertain what to do next. Tell Charivretha? Tell Thriss's *zhavey?* The Elders? She worried that if she did tell, it would ruin everything. That the Elders would punish Thriss and Shar, and perhaps put in jeopardy everything Dizhei lived for.

She kept Thriss's secret. But she had never fully trusted Thriss since.

"You must hate us for what we did . . ." Thriss's voice trailed off.

"I could never hate you," Dizhei said, she hoped convincingly. A maintenance worker emerged from a supply closet. He nodded a polite greeting. Dizhei waited until he'd passed before saying, "We can't talk here."

Guiding Thriss farther away from the corridor, Dizhei found a darkly lit nook offering them greater privacy. "You know I'm not my *zhavey's* only *shei,*" Dizhei continued in a husky whisper. "Having had two siblings go before me, I saw some of what goes on after the *shelthreth.* I think I understand better than Anichent. He sees things narrowly. He sees our obligations as being precise, exact—not negotiable. Anything that he perceives as undercutting our greater purpose pains him."

"Which is why he wasn't happy when Shar took this assignment so quickly after the war. Instead of coming back to Andor," Thriss observed.

Dizhei nodded. "And why he's never been happy with the risk you and Shar took."

"Has he always known? I mean, like you?"

"Anichent probably knew on some intuitive level, but he didn't know, in fact, until Shar left for the Gamma Quadrant and I told him."

"Is that why he's been more angry with me than usual?"

Dizhei nodded.

"I'm so sorry, *sh'za.*" Thriss leaned forward and brushed her lips on Dizhei's forehead. "Believe me when I tell you that I want what's best, too. I can't wait to become a *zhavey,* but I don't think I'll be very good unless I have lots of help from you."

Dizhei knew that Thriss meant well; she didn't want to hurt anyone. If Dizhei could believe Thriss, their lives would be considerably simpler. But Dizhei had spent too many years following behind her, mending whatever Thriss had carelessly broken, to accept her bondmate's word. She thought about pursuing the conversation further but after taking note of the time decided they needed to move on. A quick hug would have to suffice.

With a gentle, but firm hand on the small of Thriss' back, Dizhei steered her toward Matthias's office. Keeping Thriss focused on most pressing concerns had always been her role and Dizhei anticipated it would take her soft-glove discipline to assure that they all ended up back on Andor as soon as possible.

Word of the proposed exhibit spread quickly through the station community. Daily, dozens of private petitions filled Kira's message queue before lunch, variations on requests that the art be placed as far away from/as close to, their quarters/place of business/place of worship as possible. As she considered the list of spaces available for the Ziyal exhibit, Kira concluded that no option would please everyone. A curator from the Bajoran Museum in Ashalla would be arriving tomorrow, but Kira, who had the final decision, planned to consult with the expert before making a public announcement. At least that way, she would share the blame.

As much buzz as was floating around the station regarding the exhibit, the peace talks figured even more prominently in conversation. Kira's curiosity was piqued—she hoped to find the time to drop by and see the delegations in action—but snarls in the implementation of yellow alert protocols often required her personal attention. On the surface, those who saw Deep Space 9 as a spaceport understood the importance of increased security, but the pragmatic reality of changing plans, rescheduling deliveries, changing course or having cargo inspected inconvenienced more than a few ship captains. People tended to be very accommodating—as long as they didn't need to do the accommodating. Until her day-to-day duties became less laborious, Kira had to be satisfied with ops gossip if she wanted to stay updated on the battle of wills between Lang and Asarem.

Because the talks weren't public, the only record of the goings-on came from individuals who had been in attendance. Eavesdropping on two Militia corporals, Kira learned that the first few days of talks had accomplished little. She hadn't expected that the gulf separating Cardassia and Bajor would be bridged overnight, but she thought that Asarem would at least take a step. Find consensus on something, like come to an agreement about when to come to an agreement! From what she could gather, Lang's methodically planned agenda outlined discussions on issues ranging from sharing medical technology to assuring the rights of Bajoran nationals while on Cardassia. Asarem's approach had been to nitpick every detail and definition Lang raised.

The days allegedly played out thus: Lang would explain Cardassia's concerns, what their position was on the issue and where they wanted input from Bajor. She would then look to Minister Asarem to elucidate the Bajoran response. So far, the breadth of Asarem's commentary consisted of variations on: "That sounds reasonable. I'll take it under consideration. What else would you like to discuss?" That Asarem was listening was positive; that she wasn't engaged in dialogue was puzzling. During her days in the Chamber of Ministers, she'd had a reputation as a tenacious debater and orator. To sit in a chair, hands folded in front of her, watching impassively—didn't sound like Asarem. It was distinctly possible that the minister's approach wasn't being fairly represented.

This, Kira knew, having based her suppositions on snippets of second-hand accounts, was a situation she planned on remedying as soon as possible. Because she anticipated being busy with the curator in the morning, she planned on dropping in at the end of her shift. As seemed to be the case every day, a situation arose that prevented her doing as she'd planned. Irregular Core readings troubled the engineering staff and they requested she remain in ops, should an emergency decision be required. Since the Core transplant, the engineering crews had been especially vigilant, always on the lookout for the one item they might have overlooked; Kira appreciated their thoroughness. When the diagnostics concluded, the acting chief engineer was satisfied, allowing Kira to escape. Though the hour was late, it wouldn't be unprecedented for the delegations to still be working.

Rounding one of the last corners before the conference room, Kira encountered the retinal scanner and voice imprint unit Ro had felt so strongly about installing. Lang had repeatedly reassured them that such precautions weren't necessary; she felt as safe as she could under the circumstances. Though safety was a concern, Kira knew Ro's primary motive in installing a checkpoint wasn't to protect the diplomats. She reasoned that if someone wanted to assassinate a member of either delegation, they'd have easier access from a location other than the conference rooms. No, Ro intended to monitor who went in and out of the conference rooms at all hours, should questions arise. Those authorized to pass had been approved by Lang, Shakaar and Kira. No one else needed access. Unauthorized personnel attempting to maneuver past the checkpoint would be stopped and interrogated.

On her way down the hall, she passed by a cleaning team—a couple of Bajorans she recognized as having worked in the Habitat Ring public areas—but otherwise, the sector was utterly silent, save the sound of her footfalls.

The talks must be over for the day, she thought, disappointed. Kira resolved to return first thing in the morning, when an odd scent attracted her attention. Ozone. Burnt synthetic materials—not organic. Maybe one of the nearby labs had a waste disposal problem, sending the aroma wafting through the air ducts. She resisted the impulse to call for an environmental systems diagnostic, choosing to investigate the situation herself. Scorch permeated the air the closer she came to the conference room. Wondering if a replicator was malfunctioning inside, she deactivated the door lock, grateful when a billow of smoke didn't greet her.

Her eyes took a moment to adjust to the dimmed lighting. When they did, she scanned the room for evidence of anything amiss and saw that most everything seemed to be in place . . .

. . . Save the silver, green, and sand-colored Cardassian flag draped over one of the chairs, stripped from the pole behind it, scarred with angry, carbonized wounds. The gleaming edge of a knife blade glinted in the starlight, stabbed through the heart of the chair.

Cursing, she stepped back into the foyer, instinctively touching her combadge. "Kira to security. We have a situation on level 10, section 65, conference room 4. I want a team up here *now.*"

13

Shar tingled with anticipation. He had never believed in fate or luck, but if this day turned out the way he hoped, he might be persuaded to change his mind.

Two hours before, Shar and Keren had entered the farm country of the Hebshu Peninsula. Carved out by a glacier millions of years ago, the region suffered from none of the geological dangers afflicting most of the continental masses; the closest active volcano was hundreds of kilometers away and there hadn't been an earthquake recorded in centuries. The peninsula enjoyed mild winters, rich soil and a long growing season. It was also one of the rare spots on Vanìmel (or Luthia for that matter) where Wanderers and Houseborn lived side by side on their farms. Mingling herds and sharing farm equipment wasn't unheard of. Keren had explained that because most Yrythny didn't consider living off the land a natural inclination, the Yrythny who ended up choosing to live here were nonconformists. Farming and ranching attracted a quirky, independent breed that followed their own rules, refusing to adhere to any but the barest caste frameworks.

Since they'd met on his first day in Luthia, Shar learned that Keren rarely acted without an ulterior motive. The trip to Hebshu proved to be consistent with her pattern, though he suspected where she was taking him concerned his research. They'd wandered down the lanes, chatting with the locals as they encountered them.

They'd eaten a basket full of berries offered to them by a group of younglings combing the forest for the tangy treasures, and Shar had his first real encounter with Yrythny children. Like most children, they were inquisitive, and spent a great deal of time studying Shar, touching his skin and hair, climbing him as they grew bolder, and laughing delightedly when he made his antennae move.

Not long after that, Shar encountered his first *shmshu,* the primary suppliers of the hairpieces most Yrythny wore to indicate rank and caste position. Different breeds of *shmshu* provided hair in varying qualities. Shar had stood by a fence, watching as Yrythny carefully combed out their coats, waving over the animals from head to toe with a handheld version of a sonic shower. As diverting as the domesticated animals had been, Shar was ready to move on. They'd been walking for more than an hour when Keren finally explained why she'd brought him here. And when she did, Shar concurred that it was well worth skipping the meetings he was to supposed to have attended.

Hidden here in Hebshu were the most comprehensive records of Wanderer genetics on Vanìmel. For obvious reasons, genetic research was tightly controlled and kept secret. Hebshu's rural, out-of-the-way personality made it easy to conceal equipment and files without attracting government attention. Most of the research was performed during the winter months when the ground lay fallow and the *shmshu* grazed in the fields instead of in the hills. Repairing equipment, reading and indoor pursuits grew tiresome. Intellectually rigorous scientific inquiry kept minds sharp and hands busy. From generation to generation, the equipment and records were passed down, with Kremoroh being one of the newest custodians.

Kremoroh descended the cellar steps first. He activated the light panel, inviting Shar and Keren to join him.

Shar's initial disparaging thoughts quickly dissipated when he considered how much painstaking work it must have taken for these scientists to labor with antiquated equipment, limited time and few resources. Most of what he saw crammed into corners and spilling out of boxes would have been current in the Federation two hundred years ago. Still, he couldn't help smiling, imagining these tall, gawky farmers hunched over cellular scanners, squeezing into these small underground labs, customarily used for off-season vegetable storage.

Taking a seat by one of the filing cabinets, Shar pulled open a drawer where he discovered dozens of neatly labeled, clear-lidded containers filled with data chips. Another drawer revealed identical contents. "Your records?" he asked.

Kremoroh nodded. "Those go back hundreds of years. Every Wanderer who finds their way to Hebshu ends up being mapped."

"Mapped?" Shar asked, wanting to make sure he understood the usage.

"Gene maps."

A miniature, cruder version of what existed in the Andorian genome database. Shar couldn't help but be impressed. With very little training—and no assistance—they'd tackled a sophisticated area of study. Looking around him, he imagined how these scientists had made do with ill-fitting parts and poor tools with which to assemble them. Everything in the room had been designed and built using whatever technology was available. Shar admired their creativity.

"The original idea was that we were going to figure out how to identify what House the Wanderers were supposed to be from and prove to the high-thinking Houseborn that the Wanderers weren't really wandering," Kremoroh explained. "Storms, water temperature, predators—any number of things could set a hatchling off course."

A variation on what I said to Dax, just yesterday. When this thought occurred to Shar, he looked over at Keren who sat, smiling serenely. *She knew what she was doing bringing me here, this is all part of her plan. After years of watching the machinations of the Federation Council, you'd think I'd be a little less trusting.* Shar turned to Kremoroh. "Since you're still here and Keren is still in the Lower Assembly, I take it you haven't been able to draw any meaningful conclusions."

"First, we had to figure out what part of which chromosomes did what. Without Luthia's computer power or the right splicers and scanners, it's been hit and miss about what techniques work, and avoiding contamination. What I'd do for a decent computer!"

They need more than tools . . . The nucleus of an idea formed in Shar's mind, but he needed a bit more information to assure it was feasible before he could propose it out loud. "And as a comparison group? The Houseborn?"

"The other major problem. Not many Houseborn want to be part of a Wanderer genetic study. We can compare our DNA with our own kind, but we don't have the same basis of comparison for the Houseborn. We have a smattering from those Houseborn who've lived here on the peninsula, but not enough to draw conclusions."

Surveying the room, Shar realized some of the filing cabinets stood two and three deep, with drawer after drawer filled with variations on data chip storage. These farmer/scientists appeared to have accumulated thousands of different samples. "This is your main storage facility, I take it?"

"No. We have labs like this scattered all around here. Makes it easier to go unnoticed."

"Have you put all these into an aggregate database?" Shar said, hoping.

"In fact, that was last winter's project."

Keren perked up. "Is it possible—"

"The *Sagan*. It has the computing power—"

"And the Houseborn samples?"

"Medical records? Or we could take some ourselves from their drinking glasses—"

"Tonight! At dinner!" She jumped off her chair, clapping her hands.

Kremoroh scratched his head. "Excuse me? But I think I've missed something."

"You'd better come up with a new project for next winter, because I have a feeling that what Thirishar accomplishes with your data could change things—for all of us!" Keren beamed.

The cumulative datafiles were stored several farms over—a quick stop as they set out to return to the *Sagan*. Keren carried the bulk of the chips in her pack. Shar wanted to make the best use of his time so he planned on working as they walked, relying on Keren to prevent him from stumbling into trees. He reached for his tricorder, planning on formulating a few basic equations as he tried to frame the parameters of the statistical sampling.

"Ensign ch'Thane!"

Shar turned, and saw Kremoroh moving toward them from the farm. He had a youngling with him. And not just any youngling, Shar saw, but one of the ones he'd encountered earlier, who had shared berries with him and Keren. "Is something wrong?" he asked as Kremoroh caught up with them.

Kremoroh nudged the youngling forward. "Do it," he said sternly.

The youngling looked unhappy, but at Kremoroh's urging stretched out his arm, holding up Shar's combadge.

Shar's eyes widened. He accepted the combadge with a sincere word of thanks. "Where did you find it?"

"Tell him," Kremoroh told the youngling.

"I took it while we were playing with you," the child admitted. "I'm sorry."

"I accept your apology," Shar said kindly. *Idiot!* he chastised himself. *How could you not realize it was missing?*

"My apologies as well, Ensign ch'Thane," Kremoroh said. "Oh, and I feel I should tell you: a voice was coming from the device earlier; that was how I became aware that Cosho here had it. Whoever it was sounded angry, but it's since stopped."

Oh, no . . . "Thank you, Kremoroh. I'm very grateful to you." Kremoroh and the youngling departed, and with Keren looking on in concern, Shar steeled himself and pressed his combadge. "Ch'Thane to Dax."

"Shar, where the hell are you? Why haven't you answered until now?"

"I apologize, Lieutenant. I had a bit of a mishap involving my combadge—"

"Where are you?" Dax repeated.

Shar swallowed, recalling that he hadn't explicitly asked for Lieutenant Dax's permission to come planetside. "I'm with Delegate Keren, sir," he said evasively.

"But where? Someone appropriated the computer terminal in our office and used it to send an illegal communication to the surface. That wouldn't happen to have been you?"

"No sir. Actually, I'm here, planetside. On the Hebshu Peninsula. Part of my fact-finding, Lieutenant."

"I assume you have the Sagan *with you?"*

"Yes, sir."

"Get airborne immediately and lock onto my signal. I want you to fly over my position and be prepared to pick up the away team."

"Understood, sir. I'm on my way." Shar swore and established contact with *Sagan's* onboard computer. "Ch'Thane to *Sagan,* two to beam back on this signal. Energize."

* * *

"He's just not being reasonable!" Nog growled. Frustrated, he threw the padd down on the floor. He fisted his hands and kicked the broken tablet aside.

Rahim, Gordimer and M'Nok, who were sharing ration packs from *Defiant,* stopped talking when the padd skidded across the floor and crashed into M'Nok's shoes. Huddled in the corner, Shavoh, Tlaral and Ensign Senkowski halted their review of conduit repair specs when Nog spoke. The three engineers exchanged concerned glances. One by one, every person in the room looked up from what they'd been doing to see what might have prompted Nog's uncharacteristic entrance.

Realizing he had the room's attention, Nog scooted off to sit on his sleeping bag, dropping down cross-legged, making a deliberate point of sitting with his back to the group.

Chief Chao's fork, loaded with pasta primavera, paused midway between mouth and pack. "Excuse me, sir?" she said. "Is everything all right?"

Though he felt Chao's placid gaze on him, Nog kept his back turned. "Commander Vaughn! He isn't taking the threat of the Cheka weapon seriously enough. He wants to leave without a working defense against the web weapon! And we just don't have the resources or the manpower to handle repairs like this again, especially if we're stranded in the middle of nowhere."

Mikaela Leishman, the shift commander in Nog's absence, went over to talk to Nog; the two Yrythny engineers joined her. She squatted down to his eye level. "Lieutenant, is there something we should know before we return to *Defiant?*"

Throwing his head back, Nog laughed, a bitter sound that startled everyone within hearing. "Something you should know? How about we're killing ourselves trying to put the *Defiant* back together but our ever-dutiful CO refuses to let me have the tools I need to ensure our safety."

"I don't think you should be talking that way—" Leishman paused when Nog glared at her. "Sir?"

"We didn't get the load, Mikaela," Nog spat. "No load, no metal. No metal, no femtobots. No femtobots, we're ripe to be picked off like a *targ* running from a Klingon blood hunt."

"Commander Vaughn isn't one to make a decision like that

lightly," Chao reasoned, twirling her pasta with her fork. "He wouldn't leave us virtually defenseless if he didn't think it was the only way. He must have an another plan."

"But there was a way to make this plan work, Chief," Nog said, scrambling to his feet and stalking over to Chao. "That's what's so pointless about all this! If he'd given the Cheka trader what he wanted, we'd be starting to manufacture the femtobots next shift."

"Do I dare ask what he wanted?" Senkowski said.

"The cloak. The Cheka wanted the cloaking device."

A few pairs of Starfleet eyebrows shot up, but Tlaral gasped. "You can't give it to them! We'd never be able to defend ourselves if they could cloak their ships!"

"Or worse, their weapons platforms," Shavoh added.

"Practically speaking, Lieutenant," Chao said, "the commander can't give technology like that away. It's not Federation property, just a loan from the Romulan Empire. Besides that, what about Prime Directive issues? Cloaking tech would radically impact the balance of power in this region. I'm with the commander on this one. Sorry."

"Me, too," Senkowski added, returning to study conduit repair specs.

Permenter rolled over on her stomach and looked up at Nog with sorrowful eyes. "I know I've been complaining as much as anyone, but I'd rather play by the rules. You want some candy? A little chocolate might make you feel better." She held out the bag to him.

Nog slapped it away, got up, and stormed out of the room, growling, "This attitude is gonna get us all killed."

The aquaculture village burned.

Collapsing into the ocean from their derricks, the flaming houses and outbuildings outshone the setting sun. Filtered through the acrid smoke, the last rays of light burned brilliant fuschia and tangerine; descending darkness gradually defeated the day. Greasy, rainbow chemicals glazed the sea's surface as unrecycled wastes spilled into the water. Dead fish and sea life bobbed along with rising and falling waves.

Ezri stood on the observation deck, Jeshoh beside her, gazing out over the waters, trying to avoid looking behind her where the Yrythny military had lined up all the Wanderer servants working on the hydrofoil and prepared to interrogate them. Despite their claim that her workstation had been utilized to carry out the terrorist act, the soldiers seemed less interested in talking to the *Defiant* people than in rounding up every Wanderer on board. She couldn't bear to watch. Even with her back turned to them, blocking out the soldiers' shouted accusations and servants' protestations of innocence proved difficult. Ezri understood the troops had a job to do, and she knew that maybe one among those servants might have a connection to the attacks, but certainly not all. Why did so many people have to suffer?

Squinting out over the heaving sea, she hoped the dark objects floating in the water were broken pieces from buildings and not bodies. Another explosion burst after flames greedily ate through the planking outside the fuel cell supply. She vaguely understood the village layout, noting that another fuel cell supply was at risk. Not a problem if the villagers had been evacuated, but she still saw figures leaping from dock to dock, carrying younglings in arms or in backpacks. *Where are their evacuation craft? Surely there must be flying transports or marine vessels on their way.* She slammed her fists into the deck railing, frustrated. *There has to be something I can do to help.*

"I need a magnification device, Jeshoh," Ezri snapped.

He clicked open a supply station, and produced a boxy monocular device.

Taking readings off Ezri's optical nerve, the lense sensors fed information to its computer, sending the mechanism humming and whirring into focus.

After first surveying the shoreline where the lights of House-Minaral blinked, Ezri shifted her focus to the waters, subsequently taking in the entire 360-degree view around the hydrofoil. Nothing. She saw nothing resembling a watercraft heading in their direction. Turning her attention to the burning village, she studied the surface of each dock and platform, then dropped the lense. Ezri stopped counting at twenty, no thirty—too many—Yrythny, clinging to the pylons, structures collapsing all around, desperately trying to avoid falling into the convulsing waters.

"Your people are out there!" Ezri cried, throwing aside the magnifier. "We have to help them—"

"Shhh," Jeshoh admonished her. "We need to keep to ourselves until the commandant gives us permission to—"

"If you think I'm going to stand here and watch innocents die while that commandant throws his weight around, you haven't learned much about me during the last week." Ezri shot off across the deck, igniting commotion among the soldiers.

"Hey you! Stop!" a patrol leader shouted, running after her.

Smiling politely, Ezri waved to acknowledge that she'd heard the soldier's order. She dropped over the side, taking the ladder to the lowest deck, having some vague recollection of seeing the lifeboats and emergency equipment being stashed near where they'd changed for their dive trip. Dax lived by her own ethical compass; she'd be damned before she dawdled around, watching the military blowhards feeding already overinflated egos while people were dying. These Yrythny wanted her; she didn't ask to be their savior and they needed to remember that involving her in their civil conflict was *their* idea. Dax was a package deal—take all or none—but nothing in between.

Just as she'd started to go below, Jeshoh charged across the deck after her. He skipped rungs down the ladder to help him catch up, but she still beat him by a minute. She kept the exterior door propped open, but as soon as Jeshoh's feet touched the deck Ezri pulled him inside, closed the portal behind him and locked it. The clamor of boots clattering down the ladder outside didn't bother her in the slightest.

"I don't think the commandant wants you to leave—" he panted, bent over, trying to catch his breath.

With only a door between her and a squad of angry Yrythny, Ezri yanked off the doorpad cover, removed two circuit chips and snapped them in half. Two other doors led out of the room and deeper into the ship, but she figured it would be a few minutes at least before the soldiers made it down that way.

"What are you doing?" he said, incredulous. "They're going to be furious. They'll blow the door open."

"This is still a ship of state. You think the Assembly Chair would appreciate his hand-picked mediator being hunted like a common criminal?"

"You looked guilty when you ran."

"Let's not kid ourselves, Jeshoh. Your troops have already decided the Wanderers are guilty—they're not focusing on me or my crew. Well, I'm not about to lounge around, sipping wood wine when your people need our help. It's not like we don't have the resources." She walked down the hallway, examining each and every locker she found. If she had to dive into the water and swim over to those villagers with the lifejackets, she would. Let them try to stop her.

"There's a criminal investigation underway here, Lieutenant," Jeshoh said. "You heard the commandant. To the best of the military's ability to trace, the explosives that destroyed the village weren't triggered on site, but remotely, from someone on this ship, right after another signal was sent here from your office. You're right: they don't actually suspect your or your people, Lieutenant, but they do believe you may be able to help them identify the real terrorists."

"Why? Because only Wanderers commit crimes?" Dax mocked. She scanned the pictographs identifying the contents of each locker. *Rations, rope, water purification, emergency communications . . . ah! Here it is.* She opened the cabinet identified as storing the life preservers and removed the packs inside. An adjoining cabinet had the same contents. She repeated the process, tossing the packs to Jeshoh, who dropped them on the floor in protest. Ezri promptly scooped them up, slung them over her other shoulder and moved on to the next locker. "Is this knee-jerk assumption of Wanderer guilt the reason we aren't running a rescue mission?"

"In part," Jeshoh said reluctantly.

"What the hell does that mean?"

"The aquaculture villages are staffed with Wanderers," he said bitterly. "I've seen it before. When terrorist attacks take out Wanderers, the military is slow to rescue or help the victims. Partly because high body count bolsters military propaganda. The Wanderers are evil, dangerous and so forth." Jeshoh hesitated.

Ezri refused to let him off. "And?"

"And because they believe they shouldn't save the terrorists from the consequences of their actions. Their attacks hurt fellow Wanderers, let them take the blame for the casualties."

"That's despicable!" she said.

"Would you believe me if I told you I agreed?"

Looking deeply into Jeshoh's eyes, Ezri probed his sincerity. Physically, he towered over her; she knew if he truly wanted to stop her, he could probably overpower her with little trouble. He made no such move. Instead he willingly subjected himself to her scrutiny.

"Help me then," she said softly.

Knocks became kicks and kicks produced dents as the soldiers continued pounding on the outer portal.

Jeshoh nodded and reached over to free the packs of life preservers from Ezri's shoulder. "There are four rescue boats on the next level up. The door on the left is a back way. If we hurry, the soldiers may not realize our goals before it's too late."

The other door opened and Ensign Juarez peeked out, followed by four Houseborn assembly members, with Candlewood and Mc-Callum bringing up the rear. Juarez sighed with relief when he saw Jeshoh and Ezri.

Good timing, Ezri thought.

"Everything all right, Lieutenant?" Juarez queried, stepping out cautiously.

Ezri filled him in on the proposed rescue mission. "I don't think the troops will be happy about it, but I don't really care. Still have your medkit? Good, you're gonna need it. Grab those as well," Ezri said, indicating some Yrythny medical supplies near the nurse. Ezri stuffed emergency blankets into her pack and threw assorted items at McCallum and Candlewood. Whether the Yrythny adapted well to water or not, the sun was dropping, and so would the water temperature. Shock would make survivors more vulnerable to hypothermia.

Jeshoh, who had been huddling with the other Yrythny, said, "They are willing to pilot the other rescue craft. I can persuade any other committee members remaining below decks to hold off the commandant and his men until we get the lifeboats into the water."

Ezri nodded in approval. "Looks like we have ourselves a rescue team."

The whir of computer circuits, the thrum of impulse engines and the patterns of blinking lights had a tempo Shar found comforting. From time to time, when his head spun with worries and have-to's, Shar found refuge in working a spacecraft. Performing routine physical tasks helped him wrestle down the mounting anxieties that sometimes beset him. Most of the time, a spacecraft followed predictable patterns. Shar enjoyed the orderliness of it all, finding it comforting when the world around him refused to conform. His peace would dissipate shortly.

Though the Tin-Mal quarantine zone was in the opposite hemisphere, once Shar had locked in the navigational data and checked weather conditions (storms directly to the east of Ezri's location), the *Sagan's* ETA was only twenty minutes. A massive force field surrounding Tin-Mal combined with the curve of the planet made it impossible for Shar to transport Ezri to the *Sagan* from where they launched. Rather than track along the surface, Shar launched *Sagan* out of the atmosphere and into an arc that would take them to Dax in minutes instead of hours.

Few words passed between him and Keren; he was grateful for the quiet. He had a feeling he'd be in a siege of words from Lieutenant Dax soon enough.

A signal from his console alerted him that *Sagan* was approaching Ezri's location.

"*Sagan* to Lieutenant Dax. We are within transporter range."

The comm system crackled with static. "*Stand by,* Sagan. *Prepare to beam up wounded Yrythny.*" Shar blinked. *Sagan* was a decent-size shuttlecraft, but Dax had to know the ship couldn't handle too many casualties.

"Coming through the cloud deck a hundred kilometers out, sir. I'll have you on visual in five, four, three, two—on screen." The companel monitor on Shar's console lit up, but billowing smoke in the twilight obscured the view. "Computer, increase magnification and activate beacons." Shar swept the ocean with spotlights, finally finding small dark figures on a dock. He thought he could see Ezri waving. Several midsize marine shuttles loaded with Yrythny were skimming away from the disaster site. "Keren, inside the starboard passenger bench are emergency medical kits. Please retrieve them." *What had happened down there?*

Clouds of fine ash hung on the wind. Coughing, Ezri raised her uniform sleeve, dank with smoke and Yrythny blood, to her mouth. She pillowed the head of a wounded Yrythny on her lap; he'd stopped moving a few minutes ago and she hoped the *Sagan* hadn't come too late to save him. Ensign Juarez had done what he could to stabilize his vitals, but the chemical burns to his lungs might have irreparably comprised his respiratory system. Waves heaved against the pier; the rotted wood platform groaned in response, swaying ever so slightly. Ezri envisioned the whole structure giving way, collapsing into the sea like most of the aquaculture village.

Her entire body, stiff with cold, ached. Over the last hour, she'd drawn on physical strength she didn't know she had. At one point, Jeshoh had tied a line around her waist and sent her over the side to help a Yrythny with a broken arm into one of the rescue boats. Dangling in the air, she was tossed by the wind like a ball on a pendulum. She remembered digging injured people out from under collapsed cottages, putting out fires and helping Juarez transfuse Yrythny blood. Even with the lifeboats, Ezri knew many Yrythny that had survived the attack had perished in the water. She couldn't think about her losses right now. She needed to assume command of the *Sagan,* deliver casualties to the proper medical facilities and figure out how to prevent her diplomatic mission from collapsing under the weight of suspicion.

When the shuttle spotlights finally appeared, the wait between transports felt unending, though she knew only seconds transpired between the time Jeshoh, Juarez and the five remaining wounded were beamed aboard. Her turn came. She blinked—it seemed once—and saw familiar environs, the shuttle's interior; Jeshoh huddled with Keren, Shar had left the *Sagan* on autopilot while he helped Juarez.

"It's gonna be a tight fit, everyone, so hold on to whatever's bolted down. Ensign ch'Thane, with me." Soot-smudged and soaked, Ezri settled in front of the conn, ordering Shar into the co-pilot's seat.

He complied without comment.

He'd damn well better follow orders without question, she thought. "Prepare to return to Luthia," she said hoarsely and cleared her throat.

"Lieutenant, I'm sure I can manage if you want to go back and have a medical check."

"You've managed quite enough for one day, Ensign," Ezri snapped. *I need tea, a hot bath and,* with a sigh she thought, *Julian.*

* * *

"Tell Fazzle he's getting what he wanted," Prynn said, trying to stay pleasant. The brutish guard posted outside the Cheka suite had no response. She shuddered when she thought about Fazzle touching her. *I don't care how badly we need those codes, I am not sleeping with anyone to get them. Lieutenant Dax or Doctor Bashir should be doing this. They seem like the types who really get off on the "let's pretend" stuff.*

"Can you tell Fazzle I'm here?" she said, forcing a toothy grin. *This crew is going to owe me . . .*

The guard raised his wrist to his mouth and whispered something unintelligible into his comm unit. A moment later, the doors opened.

"I can go in?" Prynn said.

Before the guard could answer, a familiar howling echoed from within the suite. She peered around the guard to see inside. On two hands and knees, Fazzle ambled down the hall toward Prynn, squealing, "Oh yes oh yes oh yes oh yes," as he approached.

Prynn gulped. *How did I get into this?* When her father approached her about a "special assignment," Prynn thought maybe he would ask her to take the *Defiant* for a shakedown before setting a course back to Vanìmel. Subjecting herself to Fazzle's artistic whims? Not even on the list of possibilities. If that weird creature said or did anything untoward, Prynn would demand unlimited shore leave. It was only fair.

"Come, come," Fazzle said, waving her in with one of his free arms. "My masterpiece is this way."

She strolled down the hallway, subtly checking out whatever could be seen through the open doors. One of these rooms had to have a computer interface. She didn't need the main computer itself, just a computer terminal. Her instructions were simple: find an interface, not in use, attach the encryption decoder/transmitter, known in Starfleet parlance as "the worm," and get out. Not in a way that would make the Cheka suspicious, but swiftly enough that should her gadget be discovered, she might escape without having a link drawn between her and the transmitter. A hostage was the last thing her father needed right now. After passing more than a dozen doors and not glimpsing anything remotely resembling a computer, Prynn started to despair, worrying about what she might have to do in order to find a computer. Fazzle had stopped; she knew his work-space was close by—she was quickly running out of options.

"Hurry, hurry!" he squawked, patting the floor beside him. "Sit here. Quickly."

As she approached, she began formulating several backup plans and then—there. She grinned. Over there. Beneath his tarp. Right in the middle of his artwork. The crazy creature had built his entire piece around a computer terminal. She could see from the wiring and sensors integrated into the various "sense peelings" that he intended this sculpture to be animated with lights or movement.

Prynn dropped down on the floor beside Fazzle and looked at him, but not "at" him. Over his shoulder, she had an excellent view of the computer. "What do you need me to do?" she said sweetly.

Lucky, lucky me, she thought. The terminal was active, the viewscreen displaying a root menu offering options ranging from data retrieval to food replication. *I've got me a live one!*

"Off!" Fazzle said, cocking his head.

"Excuse me?"

"Off." Fazzle pawed at her uniform.

Ugh. It just gets better and better, she thought, stripping off her jacket and turtleneck. Thankfully, the Cheka kept the room tempera-tures high; sitting around shirtless wouldn't be unbearably cold. *Now how to get at that computer,* she mused. *I can pretend to trip and when I stumble forward, I'll just—*"Yikes!" she shrieked. "What *is* that!"

Fazzle brushed the sense-artist goo on her shoulders. "Hold out your arms," he ordered, demonstrating by holding two of his arms straight out to the side. "Like this." Prynn complied warily, but cringed when he started in on her neck, down her back, down her front—and as it dried, it itched. Prynn started making her mental list of all the places she would inform her father she would vacation when she made it back to the Alpha Quadrant. *Ewwwwww this is so disgusting!*

Shar stood at attention in front of Ezri's desk, eyes fixed on the wall behind her. In a way, Ezri was grateful that he avoided eye contact. She could say what she needed to without feeling like it was personal. The present situation was about authority—hers—and regulations. And while Shar didn't blatantly disobey the letter of her orders, he rationalized his way into believing that flaunting the spirit of them was acceptable.

"While I understand your intentions were honorable, Ensign, your timing was poor. And you should have contacted me with Delegate Keren's proposal."

"Yes, sir."

"Lieutenant McCallum, working with the Yrythny authorities, has been unable to uncover who used this workstation to send the "go" signal to the hydrofoil. Fortunately, no one on our team is under suspicion."

"I assure you, Lieutenant, I took all necessary precautions before I left."

"I believe you, but in hindsight, there were other precautions that ought to have been taken." Of all the problems caused by Shar leaving Luthia, this was the worst. Yes, he'd left the offices secure and the terminals locked down, but he hadn't made provisions for covering his station. There wasn't a Starfleet officer anywhere in Luthia at the time the offices had been broken into and the signal sent. Lieutenant Candlewood, their computer specialist, had performed every diagnostic he knew and had come up with nothing.

Shar stayed silent, standing stone-still, his face composed. Even his antennae remained curiously unexpressive.

His mind must be elsewhere, Ezri thought, leaning back in her chair. She sighed. "Was it worth it, Ensign?"

"Permission to speak freely, sir."

Ezri sat for a long moment, wondering if she was capable of responding fairly to anything that he said, whether her frustration with him had abated enough that she could listen without reacting. The day's events had taxed her energy. She'd been placating angry Yrythny officials for hours; her rescue mission to the aquaculture village hadn't exactly endeared her to the military. On the other hand, she was curious to know what incited a usually compliant officer to recklessness. Finally, she shrugged. "Of course."

"I brought enough data back from the peninsula to conduct a statistically significant study of Yrythny DNA."

"What?" Now this was news. She leaned forward to listen more closely.

"The farmers on the peninsula have been collecting and mapping

Wanderer DNA for several centuries. They wanted to use it to match Wanderers with their proper Houses. That way, they wouldn't have to be Wanderers any longer."

Promising idea. "Go on," she urged.

"But I think we can use this data to model Yrythny chromosomal architecture," he said. "To see if there's any genetic basis for the caste system."

"Those models will only work if you have the Houseborn samples to compare them to."

"We don't have them, but we can get them," he said pragmatically.

"That's pretty optimistic of you, Shar. Do you honestly think the Houseborn will cooperate willingly with your study?"

"No," Shar conceded. "But we can obtain the samples surreptitiously through Wanderer domestic laborers. I realize I haven't mentioned this before, sir, but Delegate Keren took me to a meeting of the Wanderer underground, and through her connections there—"

"Hold it," Dax said, standing. "Keren is connected to the underground?" The terrorists. Those responsible for planting the explosives in the village. The ramifications of Keren being the head of the Wanderer Assembly and working in the underground were staggering. All the negotiations, all their strategies, plans and schedules—she could be feeding confidential proposals to the underground. The agitators could have gained access to her office through Keren, if she had the security clearance. Ezri swore under her breath. *Has Shar been lying to me? He had to know getting mixed up in this would come back to haunt him later. Please let me be able to trust you, Shar.*

He met her eyes. "Yes sir, she is."

"And why haven't you come forward with this until now?" she asked. Shar hesitated a second too long and Ezri shouted, *"I asked you a question, Ensign!"*

Shar flinched. "I should have, sir. I knew I was wrong to go, but my curiosity got the better of me. Afterward I convinced myself that if I pretended it never happened, it would never come up. I was foolish. I'm sorry, sir."

"Yes, I'm sure you are," Ezri said, watching him closely. "You're certainly full of surprises this evening, Ensign." *How the hell do I salvage this?* "Tell me, from your observations of the underground, can Delegate Keren represent the Wanderer side fairly if she has any ties to those terrorists?"

"Respectfully, sir, to call them terrorists is an overgeneralization," Shar protested. "They're ordinary people who have been pushed to the verge of breaking. Not everyone affiliated with the underground endorses violence. Most of the agitators are looking for peaceful solutions."

"The fact remains that you've consorted surreptitiously with a political leader who may have been involved in the destruction of the aquaculture village, and dozens of casualties. And you still haven't answered my question. What can you say to convince me that Keren can be trusted?"

"Nothing, I suspect. But are you convinced that the Houseborn didn't blow those villages simply to persuade you that the Wanderers can't be trusted? Has anyone given you evidence that proves unequivocally that the underground is to blame?"

Ezri tried to ignore his insinuation that the day's events had been staged to influence her opinion, and remained focused on Shar. "The planetside incident is, more or less, an internal matter. What isn't in contention is that you acted in bad faith with respect to your commanding officer. You betrayed my trust, Shar."

"If you want to discipline me for going with Delegate Keren to the agitator meeting, I won't protest," he said. "But we can't ignore the potential significance of this scientific research. What we discover could transform their lives—"

"That's enough, Ensign."

"Please don't punish the Yrythny for my error in judgment," he whispered.

Was that the real question, then? Ezri wasn't a fool: If the research Shar proposed bore fruit, it had the potential to redefine the Yrythny identity, to find out, once and for all, whether there was any biological basis for the caste system. On the other hand, the Assembly had requested that she help mediate a resolution to their internal conflict—to find a way to help these people live together in peace. They hadn't asked her to conduct scientific research that would change the paradigm they'd built their society on. But truth was truth. If new truths forced the changes required to live in peace, their mission would be successful.

She looked at Shar, frustrated by the fact that she knew his intentions had been honorable. During the war, she recalled, even Benjamin had been willing to forgive her theft and loss of a runabout—not to mention subsequent capture by the Dominion—because not only had she managed to rescue Worf, she'd also returned with the knowledge that Damar sought the Federation's help against the Dominion. That information became the turning point of the war.

Sometimes, she knew, the only difference between poor judgment and a calculated risk was the outcome. In Shar's case, the jury was still out. But she couldn't ignore what he'd learned through his actions.

"You can conduct your research," she said finally, "but you can't use the underground to collect Houseborn data. If the Houseborn in the Upper Assembly agree to provide you with DNA samples, I'll authorize you to proceed. On your own time."

Dubious, he furrowed his brow. "Sir, I thought we agreed that the Houseborn will never willingly provide—"

"You think that any research performed with secretly obtained samples can be taken seriously?" Dax shouted. She'd spent enough of her 358 years as a scientist that she knew the rules of that game. "You'll be accused of using doctored samples. If you want your results to be legitimate, you have to start conducting *yourself* legitimately." Ezri could see from Shar's reaction that she was finally getting through to him.

"May I ask for official cooperation during our meetings tomorrow?"

"Yes. I'll present your proposal. If it's rejected, that'll be the end of it. Understood, Ensign?"

"Yes, sir."

Before she let him return to his quarters, she wanted to address—and bring to an end—the ongoing situation where Shar picked what rules he wanted to keep. "And Shar, I am repeating and reinstating Commander Vaughn's original order: you're not to have unauthorized contact with the Yrythny. In the course of your work, I know you'll deal with them, but you aren't to be sneaking out to underground meetings or taking trips planetside without first clearing it with me. And I want reports of any interaction you have with Delegate Keren. Until I feel more comfortable with her status, we need to assume she's hostile to our goals. Is that understood?"

Shar nodded. "I'm supposed to meet with her later so she can give me the datafiles on the Wanderer genome. In all the confusion of the rescue, she mistakenly kept them when we dropped her off."

"Fine. And Ensign? I don't need an answer to this question, but I think you'd be wise to think about it."

"Sir?"

"Having a desire to answer the Yrythny's request for help is, by itself, an honorable motive for what you're doing, but is it possible that there's a deeper reason?" she said gently. "Maybe a personal one? Because the risks you're taking are extraordinary. I think whatever you believe you stand to gain from taking these risks ought to be worth the price."

Ezri waited for him to raise his eyes from the floor and for a moment their gazes tangled. Shar rarely unveiled his emotions in any circumstance, but she caught a glimpse of a ferocious intensity that might have frightened her, had she been his enemy. "Dismissed," she said. And when he had vanished into the corridor, she collapsed into her chair, feeling grateful to be alone.

14

His uncanny knack for bringing out the absolute worst in Kira notwithstanding, Quark ought to have been rewarded for his triumph at the reception. His heroic efforts had impressed all the guests. Sentients of every stripe, rank and affiliation continued to rave about the exquisite presentation, the excellent food and the unparalleled service. He'd assumed that going out with Laren would be the sauce on the slugsteak. The capstone of this exceptional week.

Quark pulled the brightly printed blanket tighter around his shoulders, hoping to stave off the chilly night breezes. But being wet made warmth difficult to come by. It wasn't like he didn't understand wet; growing up on Ferenginar meant he understood every nuance and permutation of wet. Perpetual wetness had a consistency that one could reasonably acclimate to. When wet was juxtaposed with dry, an uncomfortable state known as "cold" followed.

Quark *hated* cold.

Would he ever feel his ears again, was the question. He had spent a late afternoon hurtling across the water from crest to crest, white foam spitting around his feet, clinging to a skimpy sail and balanced on a board even Nog would find small, only to lose sensation in his lobes. No female was worth this.

Never mind that, in the aftermath of that ordeal, staying warm necessitated wrapping himself in a blanket, because he'd stupidly refused Laren's offer to modify the program just to make him more comfortable. What kind of an idiot was his infatuation with her turning him into? He should have at least let her delete the targ-size salmon that kept smacking against the rudder of his windsurfing board. Vile creatures. What kind of animal willingly takes the path of most resistance and swims *upstream* to spawn? Clearly those monsters with fins had compromised survival instinct because any sensible creature would have hailed a hovercraft and called it good.

Like me with Laren. Always swimming upstream because I can't seem to help myself.

Crouched down beside the flickering pile of sticks Ro seemed to think qualified as a fire, she placed a spit loaded with bird carcasses over the coals. She dabbed sauce into the meat's crevices; dripping off the sides into the heat, it sizzled and smoked sending up clouds of ash. "Dinner should be ready in a half hour or so. I added a little kick to the fire in the holoprogramming," she said by way of explanation. "Temperature's a little hotter than it would be in real life."

Sounded better than waiting for that primitive stick heap to make the replicated bird edible, Quark thought ruefully. "Can't wait. I'm sure it'll be delicious," he said aloud.

Leaving the birds to roast, Ro circled behind the logs surrounding the fire pit to her backpack, which was filled with all the things one allegedly needed to survive in the outdoors. She rifled around

246

inside, removing a wristlight, what looked like a wicked permutation of a knife, another fire starter, several field ration bars, an ax,
and two long sticks with handles at the ends. "Aha. Here we are,"
she pulled out a clear container filled with dark, roundish objects.

Hoping she'd answer "tube grubs," Quark asked, "And those
would be . . . ?"

"Chestnuts," she answered, dumping them into a metal foil
pouch and securing the opening. "Roasted like this, they're really
good."

He sighed. If he was lucky, she'd thrown a couple of Slug-O-
Colas in that backpack so he could wash down the charcoal-cov-
ered bird with something palatable.

"The windsurfing wasn't that bad," Ro said, tossing the foil
pouch into the flames. She took a pair of tongs, fished coals from
the graying embers and placed them on top of the chestnuts.

"No, not at all. . . . If plunging headfirst into water is your idea
of fun. I'm thinking next time we ought to pull out Worf's old *Road
to Kal'hyaH* program and really have a party," Quark groused.
Even his wilderness sojourn with Sisko and the boys a few years
back hadn't made him *this* uncomfortable, not even after they'd
been captured by the Jem'Hadar. Of course, single-handedly dragging a wounded, belligerent Odo up the side of mountain on the
freezing surface of a class-L planet had proven, once and for all,
that Ferengi were made of sterner stuff than most people gave them
credit for, but that didn't mean he relished such experiences, unlike
some people he could name . . .

Ro snorted indelicately. "Oh please. The Columbia rarely dips
below 10 Celsius this time of year and you fell in because you kept
letting go of the sail handle." She retrieved a log from a woodpile
she'd gathered earlier. "Besides, you had a wetsuit on. You should
have been warm enough. I thought Ferengi were used to water."

"Damp, swampy, steady warm drizzle? Yes. Ice bath? No. It's
the difference between wet and drowned." Shivering, he pulled the
blanket tighter around him. "Not that I'm complaining or anything," he added hastily.

"You? Of course not," Ro said, clearly fighting down a smile.
Placing the log on a large, flat tree stump, Laren raised an ax over
her head and brought it down with a *thwack*. She gathered up the

smaller pieces and fed them into the fire. Greedy fingers of flames gratefully accepted her offering.

"So," she said, tipping back on her haunches. Scooting through the dirt, she settled against the weatherbeaten log, leaning back to rest her neck. She continued shifting and adjusting until she'd fitted the curve of her neck with the curve of the log. Her gaze went up at the moonless spring night. Pines jutted up all around them, their straight, prickle-covered branches aimed at the sky, threatening to puncture the smooth night canopy. Only intermittent wind gusts swayed the trees from their rigid posture.

"So . . ." he answered, knowing he'd surrender half ownership in the bar to Treir if she'd only page him with an emergency.

"Not like this matters, but I spent the last week before I started the Academy here. I've been to more exotic places since then, but I always feel awed when I come here. Millions of years of the land submitting to the relentless waters. And it's like the water knew that if all the dirt and rock exterior was swept away, the planet's soul would be exposed and all could see how majestic that soul was."

Quark blinked. "I never took you for a poet, Laren."

"All Bajorans are poets, Quark. Don't you know that by now? We were poets when your kind were leaving slime trails through the mud of Ferenginar," she teased.

"Sure you were, but was there any profit in your poetry?"

Ro threw a pinecone at him.

"So what's next?" he said, imagining what recreational torture she might have conceived for round two.

"Ah. Now that's a multilayered question."

"Because—"

"Because if you're asking what's next tonight, I'd answer dinner, coffee, and maybe a night hike. There's a watering hole not far from here frequented by the local wildlife—deer and raccoons. A family of beavers dammed up a water trickle and it became a pond," she explained, scratching lines in the peaty soil with a stick. "But if you're asking what's next after today, or after next week, or next month after Bajor joins the Federation? Honestly. I don't know."

Quark said nothing. He knew that he and Ro were feeling the same sense of uncertainty about the future, both believing they'd have no place in the coming new order. For Quark, the prospect of starting over in some other galactic backwater didn't have the same allure it once did during his youth. He suspected that was even more true for Laren.

"You know . . . after my second fall from Starfleet, I started to believe the reason I had so much trouble playing by its rules was that I kept finding causes that seemed more important than my career. First Garon II, then the Maquis . . ." She sighed, sprawling out so she could study the night sky. "I never meant to turn against Starfleet—a lot of who I am I owe to what I learned serving the Federation alongside good people. Both times, I eventually found myself faced with a choice. Both times, I followed my conscience. And both times, it ended in disaster."

"So what are you saying?" Quark asked. "You think you made the wrong choices? Maybe you did, maybe you didn't. But that isn't really the issue."

"It isn't?"

"No. The problem with Starfleet is, its fundamental principles are flawed."

Ro raised a sardonic eyebrow. "Oh, I can't wait to hear where *this* is going."

Quark sighed, realizing he was joining the salmon again. "While it's all well and good to want everyone to be happy, the reality is that making sure every world has food, medicine and education doesn't guarantee happiness. As much as the Federation tries to fix what ails the quadrant—and hell, sounds like they're starting to preach their good news to the Gamma and Delta quadrants, too—their way of doing things doesn't work for everyone. Because no matter how hard they try, or how honorable their intentions, equality is a bogus ideal and you can never make everyone be 'good' the way they define it."

Even in the dark, Quark could sense Ro's dubious expression. He refused to give up without at least attempting to prove his point, so he continued, "You're one to believe in scientific principles. What's the law of thermodynamics that says that for every action there's an equal and opposite reaction? Or what about the one that matter moves from a state of order to disorder? Either way, no matter where you look, nothing and nobody stays the same. You can't have the good guys without the bad ones, and as quickly as you transform the fortunes of one backwater world, another one will be blown to hell. The Federation forgets that as quickly as you fix one problem, another one crops up. Starfleet flits about in their pretty starships, trying to make everyone happy and it's mostly an exercise in futility. Is that what you want from your life Laren? Chasing a dream that can never be realized?"

Through dancing flames, Ro studied Quark pensively for a moment. Finally, she asked, "What's better in life than dreams?"

"Results," Quark spat. "You sail the Great River, you throw in your nets, you bring in your catch. I measure my successes by the latinum in my vault. Quantifiable, measurable results."

"Latinum can't love you."

"Latinum can't hurt you either," Quark retorted sharply.

Ro sought Quark's eyes, scrutinizing him closely. "You're bothered about something. What?"

Commander Matthias's words about Ferengi being easy to read came back to him. He pulled the blanket up over his ears. "I don't know what you're talking about."

Suddenly, Ro was sitting next to him, yanking the blanket back down. "Come on. You can tell me willingly or I can coerce it from you. Remember I interrogate people for a living."

For once, bondage fantasies didn't enter Quark's mind. Instead, he considered what good it would serve if he talked about his feelings. He supposed if he wanted Ro to trust him, this was the moment to prove it. "Okay. Fine. I'm a little preoccupied with the Jake situation."

"What about it?" She looked confused.

"Kira pretty much laid the whole thing at my feet the other night. And even though I know the ship I sold him was fine, I keep asking myself, 'Am I responsible?' " *There, I said it. I might have sent a trusting young man to his death by trying to make a profit off him. And not that much profit at that.* He braced himself for Ro's response.

She chuckled.

"Oh, that's sensitive of you, Laren.

"Quark, I've had some of Starfleet's best engineers review Nog's inspection. They all concur: there was nothing to suggest there was anything structurally or systemically wrong with the ship you sold Jake. And Kira knows that."

Quark shook his head. "You weren't there—"

"No," Ro agreed. "But I'd been watching her most of the evening, and even though she did a fine job of masking it, I could tell her emotions were coming to a boil. My guess is she lashed out at you for reasons that had nothing to do with Jake, or you."

"You mean she put me through that abuse for nothing?"

Ro smiled, shook her head and rested her arm next to his. "I suppose that depends on your point of view. Probably did her a world of good to blow off some steam. And as a direct result, I just got to see your conscience working. It's a sweet conscience, Quark. You should let it out more often."

"It would ruin me," Quark said weakly, suddenly realizing he was no longer cold.

"Yeah, it might," Ro agreed, a small smile playing on her lips. "But I think you could stand a little ruining."

"Devil woman."

"Troll."

"Kira to Lieutenant Ro."

Quark closed his eyes and buried his head in his hands. *There's just no justice . . .*

Ro shrugged apologetically and touched her combadge. "Go ahead, Colonel."

"I need you on level ten. Section 65, conference room four."

"The Cardassians." Instantly, Ro was on her feet, brushing dirt off her clothes. "I'll be right there. Ro out." She turned to Quark. "Sorry, but duty calls. Computer, end program."

Earth's Pacific Northwest forest dissolved instantly, leaving Quark sitting on the hard holosuite floor, still wrapped in a blanket. Ro hollered her regrets for the abbreviated evening as she exited the room. He waved back absently, but remained seated on the floor for some time, trying to recapture the moment that the colonel had thoughtlessly extinguished.

From the beginning, Ro knew that putting Cardassians and Bajorans together on Deep Space 9 would be akin to a Rakantha typhoon. It might start off slow, but once the air masses collided, the tidal waves would start. *The first tidal wave came ashore tonight,* she thought, hoping this would be a sprinkle as opposed to a downpour. She had expected the storm front before now, but who was she to complain about a few extra days of quiet?

Traversing back corridors, an engineering turbolift, and not bothering to strip off her wetsuit, Ro reached the conference room in a matter of minutes. Kira, to avoid contaminating the crime scene, waited in the anteroom with Sergeant Shul, who ran security's delta shift. Two corporals stood posted outside the conference room doors.

Being prepared for the worst, Ro was initially grateful she wasn't dealing with a murder. On another level, the careful staging of what she saw inside the conference room was almost as chilling. Whoever, whatever did this, might well be capable of murder. She suspected the sick mind she now contended with would be vain enough to show off a few more times before blood was shed, giving Ro time to smoke out the culprit.

Ro performed a cursory inventory, looking for obvious clues, but didn't observe anything incongruent; even in the dimmed lights, she could see the conference room had been divvied up by delegation and individual, with each spot at the table corresponding to an identifying nameplate, indicating who sat in what chair. The Bajoran team lined one side of the table, with Minister Asarem seated in the center of her group; the Cardassian team lined the other, Ambassador Lang being seated in the spot directly across from Minister Asarem. Nothing unusual rested on the table either: neat collections of padds, writing styluses, maps and several legal tomes, etched with Bajoran pictographs. All the items appeared to be consistent with the work underway.

Whoever defaced the flag had used a natural flame of some sort, Ro guessed; the singed fabric edges had too much fraying to have been caused by a precision laser instrument such as an engineering drill or a surgical scalpel. And a beam weapon would have set off an alarm. The lines burned over the crest of the Cardassian Union followed an artful pattern, likely an Old Bajoran rune, though Ro wasn't sure which one. She looked over at Kira, who appeared to be studying the same insignia.

"I think it means 'war.' From one of the religious texts, I believe," Kira said.

After a tricorder scan of the flag proved inconclusive, Ro ordered Shul to comb every centimeter, every wall, keypad and hallway for evidence. No one was to touch anything. She didn't even allow Kira to sit until she'd scanned the chair for hair and fiber samples. Taking a seat beside Kira, Ro had her recite the sequence of events leading up to the discovery of the violated conference room. Unfortunately, Kira's experiences didn't cast any light on who might be responsible for the vandalism. The cleaning personnel Kira had run into as she entered had already been found and questioned by Shul. They claimed not to have seen or heard anything unusual.

"Whoever did this is playing mind games with the Cardassians," Kira concluded. "Now that I think about it, even the rune has layered meaning. It comes out of the *Book of Victory* from the First Republic. A rallying symbol. A symbol of righteous indignation that warriors would paint on their foreheads in the blood of their fallen comrades. Whoever did this wanted the message to have the narrowest of interpretations."

"But it was done quietly, in a clandestine fashion where the public won't see or find out about it. Quite an effort for such a small audience," Ro observed. "No chance of a rally when the propaganda warfare is invisible."

"I've reviewed the checkpoint logs. No one has been in or out of this area that hasn't been cleared through channels," Kira said, puzzled. "Is it possible someone transported this flag in?"

"The flag, maybe, but the knife through the chair more or less indicates that our vandal was in the room. The stabbing angle, the irregular entry. Maybe the vandal transported in and out from one of the docked ships. I'll check our transporter logs and request the logs of every ship in the vicinity." Ro repeatedly ran her eyes over the chair, the flag, the knife, hoping that she'd find a new piece of information.

"Will you brief Ambassador Lang?"

Ro nodded. "I'll give her all the forensic analyses as well. There's always the outside possibility that someone within her group did this. Kind of a reverse psychology approach from a Cardassian who wants to prevent the talks from succeeding." She had witnessed firsthand the reluctance among Macet's men to turn in their weapons. If the lack of progress in the talks had frustrated any one of them, Ro could envision a Cardassian sending a symbolic warning. The rune could have been pulled out of the station database. Hardly classified material.

"I'll sit in on the talks tomorrow," Kira said finally. "Ambassador Lang needs to know that she has our official support. If the culprit is on either side, it might not hurt to observe the parties involved."

Letting whoever it was know that they were being watched might not be a bad idea either, Ro thought. "Recommend we place a gag order on all Militia and diplomatic personnel. This incident shouldn't be reported anywhere outside the highest-ranking officials and those it impacts directly. From now on, information is on a need-to-know basis. We don't want to encourage our terrorist by providing publicity."

Kira nodded her approval. "You classify the report and briefings. I'll notify Admiral Akaar and the first minister."

Imagining how ratcheting up the tension on the station with rumor would complicate security matters, Ro hoped that senior staff would understand this wasn't an order to be second-guessed. If she discovered any in her purview that violated her declared policy, strict disciplinary measures would be taken. She felt grateful she had a commanding officer that put the interests of the job first, one who wasn't jostling for political influence or courting popularity. She walked Kira to the door. The colonel paused, resting a hand on the door frame. Since they had dispensed with business, Ro guessed what Kira might still have on her mind.

"I take it you were in the holosuite when I paged you," she asked, with a bemused half-smile.

"Windsurfing," she affirmed. "With Quark."

"And he—"

"Hated it."

"Are you two—" Kira began, then cut herself off. "On second thought, belay that. I don't want to know." The colonel shook her head as she left the conference room.

Walking the room's perimeter, Ro mapped out an investigation strategy in her head and then sent her deputies back to the office to retrieve the equipment they'd need. While she waited, she sat down in a chair across the table from the vandalized one, rested her elbows on the table, threaded her fingers together, meditationlike, and reexamined the room.

The calculated neatness felt especially wrong. Passion crimes tended to be messy. Ro hypothesized that the criminal had gone to his or her quarters, desecrated the flag, returned here to drape the flag over Lang's chair and then, as an afterthought, driven the knife into the chair, making certain the vehemence of the sentiment was unquestioned. Pathological anger, anger so vivid and vicious that it motivated one to lash out rarely exhibited this kind of control. Not a padd out of place. Chairs tucked neatly against the table. All was in order. Her eyes traced the inscription on the nameplate marking the chair where she sat: "Asarem Wadeen, Second Minister, Bajor" in standard script. In an instant, Ro realized that she sat on the cusp of an investigation that required she scrutinize the most powerful individuals currently in this sector: the list of those with access to this conference room read like a list of who's who in postwar politics. Any one of the people sitting at this table might have a motive.

She toyed with the nameplate. *Even you, second minister.*

Only two hours into alpha shift and Kira felt like she'd never gone off duty. Dealing with last night's attack on the conference room continued into morning. She might have slept for a few hours, but she couldn't remember if there had been a pillow involved. Making an executive decision on the exhibit, she left orders to have Ziyal's art moved into its new home where the curator could spend the day arranging and rearranging it. *Time to take Lang up on her offer—and take a welcome break from ops at that.*

Sliding into the second row of chairs behind Sirsy and a handful of Federation observers, Kira's seat placed her within eye-line of Lang and the Cardassian delegation. With every clattering stylus or chair scraping the floor, Lang jerked abruptly or lost her chain of thought. *Damn, I knew the attack impacted her more than she let on.* The ambassador had received Ro's report with consummate professionalism, but the knowledge that she had an enemy making overt threats against her had to be disquieting. As she watched the proceedings, Kira brainstormed for more secure, alternate locations, on or off Deep Space 9, where the talks could be held.

When she changed to a new set of notes, Lang's eyes registered Kira's arrival and her mouth curved into a barely perceptible smile. She continued, however, with a seamless reading of her text.

". . . and to continue humanitarian medical assistance until such time as Cardassia's medical infrastructure has been reestablished and is strong enough to manage the needs of its people. Furthermore—"

"Excuse me, Ambassdor Lang," Asarem interrupted, raising a hand. "But I'm not certain that aid on the scale you're proposing is agreeable to our side."

Lang sighed, bit her upper lip and paused, clearly trying to hold her tongue. "This isn't a new proposal. These are the levels agreed to in the postwar Accords by the Romulans, the Klingons—"

"I'm aware of who signed the Accords, Ambassador. But that doesn't change Bajor's position that maintaining such levels of aid, indefinitely, is undesirable." Asarem leaned back in her chair and rested her hands in her lap. Though Kira couldn't see her facial expressions, she sensed Asarem felt comfortable in the lay of the battlefield. How she eased into the chair back, loosely crossing her legs and relaxing her shoulders said that she controlled the field. The burden was on Lang to flank her.

Kira recalled an experience with Shakaar when their cell awaited the arrival of a Cardassian weapons shipment they planned on stealing since their own supplies were running low. Though they had been outnumbered five to one, Shakaar remained in good humor. When asked why, he answered simply, "Because we hold the hills." Watching Asarem, Kira couldn't help but think that the second minister believed she held the hills. And why not? Her delegation hadn't been threatened. *At least Asarem won't be susceptible to any Cardassian double-talk.* She felt reassured that Bajor had an excellent steward. *So why am I having a hard time trusting her?*

Earlier, the task of briefing the Bajoran delegation had fallen to Kira. Asarem made sympathetic noises when she heard of the surreptitious threat against the Cardassians. Her immediate concern had been for Ambassador Lang's safety and she asked what measures she personally needed to take to circumvent any future attacks. Nothing in Asarem's manner suggested insincerity. Her untainted political record served as proof that she was an honorable public servant. *Maybe that's my problem,* Kira mused. *I don't believe in perfection—there's something in Asarem's manner that's so polished, it feels scripted. Still, if I agree with her positions, what's my problem here?* A marked increase in the volume in the room startled her back into paying attention.

"You want to maintain our high infant mortality rate?" Lang said, unable to blunt the shrill edge in her voice. "The numbers succumbing to the Calebrian plague? What we're receiving now barely addresses those needs!" Her aide, the one Kira recognized as a former student, placed a reassuring hand on her teacher's arm, but Lang shoved it off.

Asarem shrugged. "No need to raise your voice, Ambassador. I'm merely pointing out a previously overlooked complication in providing your people with virtually unlimited medical supplies. When taken individually, crates of biomimetic gels and isomiotic hypos have legitimate applications. In combination with other agents, Cardassia could conceivably manufacture biogenic weapons," she said, her tone mild.

What? Startled, Kira sat forward in her chair, waiting to hear what would be said next.

The phrase "biogenic weapons" triggered a low hum of hushed exchanges from spectators in every corner of the room. Asarem must feel very secure in her position to make such audacious suggestions. Given the same evidence, Kira wouldn't have drawn those conclusions. Even in these days of quantum torpedoes and orbital weapons platforms, an unseen enemy terrified populations more effectively than any particle beams or warships ever could. *Why is it that we default to the presumption that we're safe simply because we can't perceive, with our senses, any immediate danger?*

Clenching her hands around the arms of her chair, Lang's eyes narrowed to dark slits, incredulity etched on her face. Kira felt the room collectively holding its breath in anticipation of the Cardassian ambassador's response. She scrutinized Asarem for a long moment, allowing extraneous murmuring to die down. Uncomfortable silence swelled until Lang spoke. "I accept that you hold us in little esteem. But what kind of soulless ghoul would I be to come here, begging for help, if it were my intent to divert desperately needed medical supplies to manufacture weapons? What possible motive would we have?" Her soft-spoken tone belied her incisive words.

Heart pounding in her throat, Kira willed Asarem to show mercy, to rise above forcing Lang to flay herself in order to prove good faith. *If we fail to show compassion when compassion is called for,*

*we succumb to the same cruelty exhibited by our oppressors during
the Occupation.* She held her breath.

"Reestablishing military supremacy. Blackmailing Bajor. There
are a host of logical reasons that aren't unprecedented," Asarem
said, sounding like she could reel off another long list of potential
Cardassian black deeds if asked to. "Besides, what reason would
you have to elucidate your government's true intentions here and
now when you know Bajor and the Federation would never agree
to assist in any sort of rearmament?" She paused, waiting for the
meaning of her words to sink in. "And it's possible the Ghemor
government could be using you: why would they tell you what their
true intentions are if feeding you sympathetic stories about children and helpless pregnant women helps them accomplish their
long-term objectives?"

Kira felt sick. *This isn't negotiation: this is retribution.*

Inhaling deeply, Lang gritted her teeth. "To this point, Minister,
Bajor has been extremely generous in helping us rebuild a social
services infrastructure that provides pediatric hospital facilities,
vaccinations and basic preventative health care."

"And we will continue to be generous," Asarem said reasonably.
"But I believe imposing some restrictions or implementing time
limits on the type and amount of aid we continue to provide is not
unreasonable, given the probability that Cardassia, at some point,
might divert that aid for militaristic purposes."

Kira noted, with concern, the panicked expressions on the Cardassians seated beside Lang. And it wasn't the fear of being caught
engaged in treachery, it was the fear of those watching hope flicker
and die. All eyes looked to their leader for guidance.

Shadows, new since her triumph at the reception, darkened
Lang's lower eyelids; her shoulders hunched slightly with fatigue.
She leaned over the table, putting her in closer physical proximity
to Asarem. "With all due respect, Minister, a week before I left, I
spent five days helping deliver supplies to our medical facilities,"
Lang began, "and I have to ask, when was the last time you held a
child in your arms dying from the curable Fostassa virus?"

Lang's words scraped Kira raw; a flood of memories poured
over her, stinging like saltwater.

In the hours following the final assault on Cardassia, she and

Garak walked the decimated streets, picking their way around twisted metal from collapsed buildings, chunks of stone and broken glass. Acrid smoke hung like thick fog: the breath of destruction. Weak cries attracted Garak's attention, leading him to a dirty-faced little boy in shredded clothes, huddled against a toppled pillar. The child rocked back and forth, crooning a discordant song, to a floppy-limbed doll he hugged against his chest. When the boy failed to acknowledge either Garak or Kira's approach, Garak waved a hand in front of the boy's eyes, quickly ascertaining the child had been blinded. He had instantly scooped the boy into his arms, the child clinging to him, wrapping his gaunt legs around Garak's waist. Garak passed the doll off to Kira. She reflexively hugged the cold thing against her, knowing the boy would want his toy back until, horrified, she discovered the true nature of what she held. Mustering all her self-control, she avoided recoiling and tossing the baby's corpse away; instead, she waited until she found a small indentation in the ground, probably a bomb crater, where she could show the dead proper reverence.

And now she wondered if Lang had been there, that black night on Cardassia.

The Cardassians had paid exorbitantly for their arrogance. Regardless of what had been done to her—to Bajor—at their hands, Kira failed to see how extracting further payment would be justified. *I wouldn't take up the lash if it were handed to me.* The realization stunned her. Kira sought Natima's eyes, hoping she would find comfort in the knowledge that a former enemy understood, but Asarem's chair suddenly shoved back. Kira steeled herself for the minister's response.

Asarem stood up with deliberate slowness, her body vibrating with sinewy tension. Squaring her shoulders, she faced Lang, still posed offensively. "The last time a child died from Fostassa virus in my presence?" she said, her voice glacial. "Eight years ago. Just as the Cardassian Occupation of Bajor ended."

Lang froze.

Brittle quiet chilled all present.

"Ambassador, Minister," came Gul Macet's quiet appeal. Seated at Lang's elbow, he had thrown a cautionary arm in front of his superior. "I believe this is an appropriate juncture to call a recess. Our delegation will review the numbers your staff has provided us and after we've eaten, we'll meet back here to see where we can reconcile our differences."

Now composed, Asarem said softly, "Based on the substance of the talks to date, it's my judgment that we take an indeterminate recess until such time as both delegations are better prepared to delineate definitive parameters on the items we've discussed." With a visible tremor in her hand, she passed off a padd to an aide and turned piercing eyes on Macet. "When we both know how flexible our respective governments can be in negotiating specific points, I believe we'll accomplish more."

"You mean, when Cardassia is willing to do whatever Bajor demands?" Lang said cynically.

"Natima," Macet cautioned without looking away from Asarem. "By indeterminate recess, do you mean the rest of the day?"

"I mean as long as it takes," she said. Asarem cleaned up her workspace without comment as her aides packed up any extraneous supplies. Support staff for both sides studiously avoided contact with the opposition.

Shaking, Lang collapsed into her chair until Macet coaxed her outside, ostensibly for lunch. Her aides, some looking glum, others angry, followed close behind.

The Cardassians and Bajorans exited through opposite doors. Kira waited until all but Minister Asarem had left before she rose from her chair. *I'll be complicit in this injustice if I don't speak up.*

"Minister, might I have a word?"

Asarem arched an eyebrow. "Colonel Kira. I presume you want to share your enlightened perspective."

"I don't know what you mean by enlightened, but any reasonable person would be concerned about what just happened here." Whatever she had done to alienate the second minister, Kira wished she understood so she could apologize.

"You think I'm being unfair to the Cardassians?" she asked sourly.

Be rational, Nerys. Don't lose your temper, Kira admonished herself. "Lang is asking for medical supplies, not quantum torpedoes. She's not even requesting raw materials that could more easily be diverted to develop weaponry." From her own experience, she knew that crude weapons spewing shrapnel or obliterating infrastructure were just as effective as the sophisticated weaponry Asarem seemed to believe the Cardassians were interested in building. "What's unreasonable about wanting plasma replicators and surgical equipment? How does traking a hard line, making it difficult to save Cardassian lives, benefit Bajor?"

"Your attitude surprises me, Colonel," Asarem said pointedly. "You of all people should appreciate the need to do whatever is necessary to ensure that Cardassia is never again in a position to harm Bajor, or anyone else." The minister turned back to packing her briefcase. "Perhaps the reports of your patriotism are exaggerated."

I don't have to take this! I'm not the enemy. Kira resisted the urge to snipe at Asarem. "Last time I checked, I was wearing the uniform of the Bajoran Militia, Minister. I do have some experience relevant to this situation." Kira tried smoothing her sharp tone, but knew her impatience seeped through.

Asarem paused, cast a glance at Kira's bare ear. "Last time I checked, faithful Bajorans follow the counsel of the Vedek Assembly."

Kira's eyes narrowed. Biting back a dozen thorny responses, she pushed forward on the critical issues. "Have you even been to Cardassia since the war?"

"No," Asarem said. "I haven't."

"Then how can you compare what you know of Bajor with what Cardassia is going through? What right do you have to dismiss Ambassador Lang the way you did just now?"

"The rights given me by the people of Bajor who elected me to serve them."

"And the people of Bajor elected you to be their avenging angel? To single-handedly make the Cardassians pay for fifty years of wrongdoing?"

Asarem slammed her case on the table. "I decided to hear you out because as the commander of Deep Space 9 you're owed a measure of input. But I'm done." Walking briskly, she left the conference room; Kira maintained her pursuit. She locked onto Asarem and refused to let her escape until she'd said her piece; her conscience wouldn't allow her to walk away.

Addressing Asarem's back, Kira persisted with her argument. "We may have been thrown out of our homes, seen horrible starvation and disease, but our shrines are still standing and after thinking the Celestial Temple was lost to us forever, the Prophets brought us the Emissary and we became stronger. The prophecies tell us that we will be stronger yet. For all the horrors inflicted on us by the Cardassians, half our population wasn't executed and millions of our children haven't died since with flesh melting off their bodies due to radiation sickness. We didn't emerge from the Occupation drowning in our own dead." Kira jumped directly into Minister Asarem's path, blocking her from moving any farther. "Where is your compassion, Minister?"

Cold fury burning, Asarem's voice shook. "With the generations of dead and brutalized Bajorans who committed no crime save being born Bajoran. The Cardassians allied with the Dominion. They brought destruction on themselves. Now get out of my way before I call First Minister Shakaar and inform him that we need to reconsider your position as commander of this station."

For a long moment, Kira stood rooted to the spot, staring defiantly at Asarem, daring her to make good on her threats before finally stepping aside and allowing her to pass. She watched Asarem disappear down the corridor. *I hope the air is pure enough for you there on the moral high ground, Minister.*

How dare Asarem talk to her like she had some vastly enlightened understanding of collaboration and innocent Bajorans dying that Kira didn't have! She knew. She had lived it; the Occupation had set the stage—had framed her decisions—for her entire life. But at some point, Kira had to stop defining her life by her losses and if that meant accepting friendship with Cardassia, then she damn well would! Breathing deeply, she closed her eyes, mouthing a prayer for peace, hoping consolation would come from faith. As much as duty pressed on her mind, Kira knew she had to sort out all the confusing threads unraveling in her mind.

Did I just leap to the defense of the Cardassians? Prophets help me, what am I doing?

First order of business upon retiring to her quarters was changing into civilian clothes, but the usually comfortable, well-worn fabric irritated her skin; the sleeves and neck felt tight and confining, like she'd accidentally put on another's clothes. She gave up on eating when her replicated hasperat tasted like spicy sawdust. Her mind dulled whenever she attempted any routine task; she found herself in a stupor, wondering what it was she had started but now couldn't recall. The staticlike quiet pressed on her.

Opening the cupboard that housed the few small remains of her religious life—a few candles, incense, an icon—she removed her earring from a shelf and draped it over her palm, feeling the cold metal links, the weight of the silver. She encapsulated the earring in her fist, gripping it until she felt its edges digging into her skin. One by one, as if in a trance, she lit the candles.

With hands outstretched and eyes closed, Kira prayed.

She interspersed recitations of every prayer she'd memorized since childhood with blunt, almost impatient pleas for the clarity that had thus far eluded her. Time drizzled away—maybe hours—and Kira remained standing. She would stand until she dropped or until her prayers were answered.

At last, her hands fell to her sides and she knew what was required. She considered her earring with longing one last time before she reverently replaced it on the shelf, blowing out the candles and locking the cabinet door.

Gul Macet scrolled through one of several intelligence files he'd brought with him from Cardassia. While he hadn't always approved of Central Command's tactics, he wasn't above sifting their refuse if it aided Cardassia's cause. A good strategist never discounted information on the basis of how it was collected or who had done the collecting.

Before him on the table, Kira Nerys' official Singha Internment Camp record lay open, accompanied by the annual ID holos taken until she left the camp to join the resistance. He thumbed through the screens, finding nothing new—nor did he expect to. *I thought we had her this afternoon,* he thought, recalling the conflict playing across her face. He knew she'd been in the capitol city the night of the attacks. Something haunted in her eyes told Macet he shared that in common with the young Bajoran.

The door chimed. Expecting that Natima had returned to take him up on his offer of a late meal, he ordered the computer to admit his guest. *We'll have to make a plan for tomorrow—Asarem will make us fight for the privilege to return to the table.* "Natima, did you have any luck contacting Sirsy?" he asked without looking up from Kira's file.

Silence.

Usually, Natima's gown swished as she walked; he hadn't yet heard footsteps. *Perhaps young Vlar has brought me dinner.* He twisted away from his studies to see what awaited him.

"Gul Macet," Kira Nerys began, "I wondered if you might be interested in taking a walk?"

15

"She did it!" Bowers exclaimed. "The worm is transmitting. It'll only take me a minute to search their system and see if I can find the codes to claim that matter load."

"Timer set," Julian said. "We have three minutes before the Cheka system security starts their sweep of the computer. Ensign Tenmei's lock shows green." With a transporter lock on Prynn, Bashir tracked her location from the sciences station. She hadn't moved for ten minutes, but her vitals remained normal, other than indicating agitation.

"Status of Chief Chao?" Vaughn asked.

Bashir rechecked his display and reported, "Also in position."

Now comes the fun part, Vaughn thought. *Waiting.* He paced the *Defiant*'s bridge slowly, keeping his head clear, focusing on the next step in their plan. "We can't get overconfident, Sam. Breaking into the Cheka system isn't enough. If we can't locate the codes, we'll be right back where we started without the materials Nog needs for the defense system." And there was the little matter of making sure Prynn had enough time to escape the suite before security linked the computer penetration with her presence. She had been insistent about avoiding a beam-out while she was with Fazzle, wanting to avoid drawing any unnecessary attention. Once she attached the "worm" to the terminal, she'd initiate her exit strategy.

Hunched over tactical, Sam attacked the incoming data with the determination of a grint hound on the tail of a razorback. He tapped through screen after screen, filtering data, running language decryption algorithms and using the *Defiant*'s computing power to run a separate search, narrowing the amount of information he had to plow through.

"Two minutes," Julian announced. "So when's part 'b' of our plan supposed to play out?"

Vaughn checked the time, "Shortly. Where are we at, Sam?"

"The computer is searching the Cheka's trade records"—he paused, grinning—"hey, this is interesting. You think an up-to-date map of where the Cheka weapons are deployed in this sector would be helpful?"

"The codes wouldn't be as critical, then," Julian said. "Simplify our lives considerably."

"Only data for this sector, I'm afraid," Sam said. "We'd still need the femtobot defense, but it would buy us time to test and deploy it."

"Download it," Vaughn ordered. "And any other strategic or military information that might help us navigate our way out of here."

"Yes, sir." Sam continued hunting through the data.

Vaughn rested a hand on the back of Sam's chair and watched. He struggled to believe that such a politically powerful species could manage with such crudely constructed databases. *But that's what happens, I suppose, when you're too lazy to innovate or organize for yourself.*

"Gordimer to Commander Vaughn. We have a situation."

"Go ahead, Ensign."

"Yrythny security caught Lieutenant Nog making an unauthorized attempt to leave the Avaril. *He had classified Starfleet technology downloaded into his tricorder. Specs for* Defiant's *cloaking device."*

Stunned, everyone on the bridge turned to look at Vaughn. "Stay focused, people," he said sternly. "Ensign Gordimer, keep Lieutenant Nog in protective custody until I get there, and secure the tricorder. Vaughn out."

"One minute," Bashir announced.

"Okay, sweetheart, talk to me," Sam coaxed his console. "Wait . . . here we are. I'm gonna grab it all and we'll sort through it later."

"Just do it," Vaughn urged. "Doctor, go ahead and signal Prynn that we're clear." Before she left, Bashir had fitted her auditory canal with a tiny receiver that allowed her to hear signals, but not send them. Concerned about activating any sensors in the Cheka suite's security net, Vaughn insisted on radio silence until the computer break-in succeeded or failed.

"Done, sir," Julian said. "No indication that she's left Fazzle's work area. Thirty seconds."

"Almost got it—" Sam said.

Based on the percentage of information that Sam had captured, Vaughn could see that the data transfer would take more time than was safely left. Prynn needed to leave. Soon. Worry sent his heart racing. "Status of Ensign Tenmei, Doctor?"

"Still no movement, sir. Fifteen seconds."

"Prepare for emergency beam-out," Vaughn ordered.

"I'd advise against that, sir. She's in the heart of the Cheka suite. A sudden beam-out would—wait. She's moving."

Vaughn sighed, watching the blinking dot on Bashir's screen progress down the hall.

"Ten seconds."

Come on Prynn, get out of there. Keep moving . . .

"Five."

With only a few meters to go, the blinking dot paused.

"Time's up," Bashir announced.

Sam turned toward Vaughn, "I'll have the end of this file shortly, but an internal computer sweep is underway. Depending on their sweep sequence, it might be two seconds or twenty minutes before they find us."

"I want her out of there, Julian," Vaughn demanded.

"I'll grab her as soon as she makes it out of the main entrance."

"Cheka sensors nabbed us, sir," Sam said. "But the data transfer is complete. I'm shutting down the link . . . now. Link severed."

The blinking dot on Bashir's screen moved quickly, streaking down the hallway and out the front door.

"Initiating transport," Bashir said. Then he added with a smile, "She should be downstairs, Commander."

Vaughn exhaled with relief. *Thankfully, L.J. isn't around with his fifty reasons why having your daughter under your command is a bad idea.*

"I've isolated the codes, sir," Bowers announced. "Transmitting to Chief Chao . . ."

Moments later, the bridge doors opened, admitting Prynn. She marched onto the bridge, wearing her regulation tank top, but with her uniform jacket tied around her waist. Bashir's eyes widened when he saw the scaly purple blotches covering most of her exposed skin.

"Someone better produce some damn rash spray in the next twenty seconds or I'm resigning my commission!" she announced, jamming her fists into her waist.

Bashir and Vaughn exchanged glances before bursting into relieved laughter.

"What?" Prynn demanded.

"Nothing, Ensign," Vaughn said. And, throwing protocol out the airlock, he walked over to her and placed a soft kiss on her forehead. "Good work. The doctor will take care of you while I take care of Lieutenant Nog. Sam, advise me when Chao is back aboard."

Shar exited Ezri's office, only to discover Keren waiting in the outside corridor. Hundreds of Yrythny coming from the day shift or going to the night shift streamed past, making it easy for Shar to pretend he didn't see her. Without any acknowledgment, he headed in the direction of the guest quarters, knowing she'd be chasing after him anyway.

"Thirishar!"

"If I talk to you, I have to report it to Lieutenant Dax, so don't say anything you don't want repeated," he said as he walked rapidly away.

"They've sent armed squads into the Old Quarter, Thirishar," she said, her voice tinged in fear.

"What?" He paused, waiting for her to catch up.

"The Assembly. Looking for those responsible for the attacks. They've gone into the Old Quarter with weapons," she said breathlessly.

Keren was panicked, and Shar sympathized, but hadn't her own kind landed themselves in this mess? "Can you blame them for wanting to prevent further attacks?"

"I don't know that the underground is responsible for them," she confessed, averting her eyes.

"What do you mean?" Shar demanded.

Grabbing Shar by the sleeve, she pulled him into a dark, deserted side corridor. She peered down the hallway in each direction, before leaning in close, speaking directly in Shar's ear. "A schism has formed in the underground leadership. Some believe that the only way we're ever going to help our people is by force. Waging a war of fear might pressure the government into conceding. The rest of us, me included, believe that we should take up arms only if negotiations don't work."

"Keren, what do you want want from me?" he hissed. "It isn't as if I have troops that can defend the Old Quarter. Even if I rounded up all my colleagues, it wouldn't be appropriate for us to play a role in an internal standoff."

"I'm not asking you to, but your research has become more urgent. You have to press forward as quickly as possible."

"And I plan to go to work as soon as I can."

"That's the problem. The data files, they're hidden in my apartment. If I go back there, I won't be able to leave again—perhaps indefinitely."

"Keren, you're not listening!" Shar pleaded. "I've been ordered not to spend unauthorized time with you. If the lieutenant finds out that I've disobeyed her orders, I'll spend the rest of this mission in the brig. You need to send them by messenger."

"You have to believe me. The casualties in the village will be miniscule compared to what will happen if the Old Quarter is provoked into riots."

More deaths. More delays. More shadowy choices. *Damn it, I've been given a direct order and if Ezri checked up on me and found me missing. . . .* Maybe he could talk to Lieutenant Dax and see if she had any ideas. But there was always the chance she'd refuse to involve Starfleet. Should that happen, Shar wouldn't have a choice of whether to retrieve his data. He needed a little more time. "I can't come immediately."

"In a little while, then. I'll come to your quarters with clothing like I did the first time." She clutched each of his arms in her hands.

"Give me half an hour. I'll meet you in the courtyard. But this has to be the end of it." He had serious reservations about going through with this, but in the end, his personal commitment to the

pursuit of scientific truth won out. That . . . and his wish not to
have Keren come to harm.

Without a word, Keren turned on her heel and left, Shar watching as she walked away. *This whole situation is about to ignite,* he
thought. *Both sides are so busy taking revenge that the truth is slipping between the cracks. This has to end.* Marching back to his
quarters, he wondered whether he'd have time for his project before civil war erupted. *I'm going to make this work,* he vowed. And
maybe there was a better way to help Keren . . .

Upon entering his quarters, Shar went immediately to the computer terminal, calling up the Luthia root menu. *The military here
doesn't do anything without making a big show of it . . . there has
to be an announcement or a policy statement about the troops
going into the Old Quarter.* There. Shar tapped in the commands,
captured the page and saved it to his personal files. Then, he
browsed until he found a public mail outlet on Luthia's main system and forwarded it to the terminal in Dax's quarters:

> LUTHIA: *Pending a conclusion to the criminal investigation
> into the attacks on the Coral Sea Bay aquaculture village,
> the Old Quarter will be under martial law. All residents will
> be required to submit to police searches, on demand and
> without resistance, or risk arrest. Force will be used as nec-
> essary. Any information leading to the arrest or capture of
> those responsible for the attacks will be rewarded.*

Hopefully Ezri would read between the lines and take action.
Shar sent the message, clicked off his terminal and waited for
Keren to arrive.

"I apologize for any inconvenience caused by Lieutenant Nog's
action. Thank you for detaining him for us. I'll have Ensign
Gordimer escort him to our brig," Vaughn said to Chieftain J'Maah
and the other Yrythny staffers standing around, horrified by this latest development. The Yrythny had offered to meet Vaughn aboard
Defiant, but not wanting to burden his hosts, he told them he would
come to the *Avaril* to take Nog from their custody.

Vaughn nodded his head at Gordimer, who stood beside Nog.

Gordimer grasped Nog's arm, but Nog jerked away, sending a sour expression in Vaughn's direction. Gordimer gripped Nog's arm harder this time, refusing to be dislodged by the Ferengi's thrashing about.

"Sir? The item Lieutenant Nog was carrying?" Gordimer said, tipping his head toward the chair where Nog's tricorder sat.

"I'll take care of it. Make sure Lieutenant Nog is safely ensconced on the *Defiant* until his disciplinary hearing."

Nog glared at Vaughn as Gordimer nudged him forward. The whole pathetic display was embarrassing. Placing Nog under arrest was bad enough, but having it play out in public was humiliating, especially when it had been Nog's Yrythny technologist friends who turned him in. When he'd arrived on the *Avaril*'s bridge, he discovered the entire senior staff and Minister M'Yeoh were in attendance. *The more the merrier,* Vaughn thought.

Shoving Nog into the inship transport car, Gordimer ordered the door closed and the car shot off, winding its way down the dozens of decks to the bay housing the *Defiant.* After the junior officers had left, J'Maah turned to Vaughn. "When you told me the *Defiant* was repaired and ready to return to Vanìmel, I'd so hoped we'd have enough time for proper good-byes. I'm sorry our last day together had to end on such a tragic note, Commander."

"As am I, Chieftain. But the sooner I can reunite my crew and resume our mission, the better for all of us," Vaughn replied, "As you can see from Lieutenant Nog, the stress has taken a toll. I'll now retrieve the rest of my crew from their accommodations, and we'll prepare to depart."

J'Maah clasped Vaughn by the elbows. "Farewell, Commander."

"Farewell to you, Chieftain." Holding the tricorder tightly in one hand, he started back toward the bay, relieved to have finished playing this act of the drama.

Within minutes, he'd arrived back at his crew's makeshift quarters. Off-duty personnel pounced on him the minute he walked in the door, asking questions, expressing worries and concerns about how to proceed. Vaughn held up his hands to quiet them.

"One thing at a time. First, the Yrythny caught Lieutenant Nog attempting to abscond with the specs for *Defiant*'s cloaking device." Gasps went up; a hum of curious murmurs emitted from each segment of the group. Vaughn shushed them again. When they were quiet, he continued, "Apparently, he believed he could negotiate a deal with the shadow trader for the matter load behind my back. He has been relieved of duty and will remain in custody until we've returned to Vanìmel."

Brow furrowed with worry, Ensign Permenter called out, "Sir, who will be overseeing engineering?"

"The *Defiant* hasn't had a shakedown yet, there might be problems," echoed Leishman, Nog's designated shift chief.

"Ensigns Senkowski and Leishman will co-manage the *Defiant*'s engineering department until other arrangements are made," Vaughn said. "The *Defiant* will leave for Vanìmel at 2130 hours. Please prep your gear and wait for any further instructions from Lieutenant Bowers. Once we've cleared Consortium space, a staff meeting in the mess hall is planned for 2200. Attendance is mandatory. Ensigns Leishman and Senkowski, you're with me. That'll be all."

Confusion and concern persisted among the crew; Vaughn wished he could alleviate their fears, but he knew they would have answers soon enough. Leishman and Senkowski followed him out. He would take them to the *Defiant,* pass over the material load, and put them to work on the final phase of the femtobot defense. Until a short while ago, Vaughn had worried that they'd end up launching without the defense system. But as he was leaving *Defiant* to deal with the Nog situation, Bowers had contacted him to confirm that Chao successfully procured the materials from the mining office, using the codes taken from the Cheka. Vaughn had finally relaxed. If Leishman and Senkowski asked where the load came from, Vaughn would tell them, honestly, that they discovered that a matter load belonging to them had been illegally transferred to another buyer. Nog's assumption had been correct: Runir's negotiations on the Exchange had been successful but their codes had been routed to the Cheka. Prynn's covert operation was merely to reclaim what was rightfully Starfleet's. No point in saying "stolen," an inflammatory word indicating criminal behavior, when the phrase "returned to its rightful owner" better fit the situation.

One concern still nagged at Vaughn. All their detective work had failed to yield the identity of who might be undercutting their efforts at the Consortium. If their luck held, the bait he'd left behind might yet be taken and Vaughn would have his first solid night's sleep since encountering the Yrythny.

Ezri almost missed the blinking light on her console.

She had returned to her quarters, immediately undressed and showered, but still feeling wound up, decided to sit and read by the courtyard fountain, hoping the distraction would help her unwind. As she unlocked her courtyard door, the reflection of the blinking light on the glass caught her eyes. *Maybe it's a message from Vaughn.* By her calculations, the *Defiant* should be starting home within the day. Opening the message file, she puzzled for a moment over the contents.

The sender, anonymous—though Ezri suspected one close to the talks had been responsible—felt the matter urgent enough to request her attention tonight. Her first perusal of the contents didn't yield the implied meaning immediately; before completing the second pass through, she'd roused Assembly Chair Rashoh from sleep, and demanded that he meet her in her office; or, she would be at his apartment within the hour. What the hell did these fools think they were doing reacting with military force? Any kind of consensus she'd built—or could build—would be shattered if the patrols went into the Old Quarter to implement a crackdown.

The fools! Never pick a fight with a wounded animal. And like it or not, hundreds of Wanderer dead numbered among the day's casualties. Who was responsible for those deaths didn't matter one iota right now. *My guess is the Wanderers believe the attack was a set up to give the military an excuse to search their properties and make arrests. The Houseborn are poised to give the underground a pantheon of martyrs if they don't keep their tempers in check.* The more she considered what the night might bring, the more worried—and angry—she became.

Flattened against the wall, Shar watched, waiting for the "all clear" signal from Keren. His hand rested on his phaser, but so far, he hadn't drawn it once.

Word of the imminent crackdown had spread quickly. All public places in the Old Quarter had been abandoned in favor of private dwellings. The desolate plazas hosted empty merchandise carts and litter, but not much else. Even the halls, normally jammed body to body with Yrythny, were bare as far as the eye could see. The swift evacuation made Shar and Keren's task difficult. Lacking crowds to hide in, they crept along walls, using shadows for camouflage. They avoided main thoroughfares, choosing alleys and the back-doors of businesses instead.

Keren waved him across the alley. Avoiding patches of moon-light, Shar chose an irregular path, pausing behind a bin, dropping to his knees and crawling beneath a fence before dashing across a slip of open space. Upon reaching her, Shar followed Keren closely up a narrow set of stairs. At the top, where the stairs ended, she sound-lessly pulled herself up and over a balcony railing. Shar joined her a minute later and they sat, catching their breath for a long moment.

"We need to be careful entering my apartment. There's a chance that enforcers have been sent ahead to take me into custody," she whispered.

"Why would they do that? What have you done?" At this point, Shar wasn't even sure she'd tell him the full truth if he asked. There was so much subterfuge surrounding Keren's life, Shar wondered how she kept track of what was real.

"Because it's an easy way for them to make a statement, and be-cause I don't keep my politics a secret. If they want to harass civil-ians, they'll want me far away where no one can hear me."

"I'll go in first," Shar volunteered. He unholstered his phaser, double-checked that it was set to stun, and eased up to his knees. Looking out over the edge of the balcony, he saw that the alleyway behind remained empty. He climbed all the way to his feet and moved toward Keren's quarters a step at a time. As he drew closer, he noticed her window was open, curtains fluttering. He twisted back to check with Keren, whispering, "Is it supposed to be open?"

Keren shook her head.

Replacing his phaser on his hip, Shar took out his tricorder. A quick scan revealed at least one Yrythny inside, hiding in the dark. He put his tricorder away, pausing to focus his senses on any dis-cernable energy. *Curious,* he thought, his antennae twitching. *The energy is charged—intense—but not angry, not so much fearful ei-ther. More like . . . worried?*

Shar braced himself on the window ledge and pushed off to get the leverage he needed to throw his leg over. Straddling the frame,

Shar shifted to a sitting position and soundlessly dropped to the floor. Gradually, his eyes adjusted to the dark; surveying the cramped quarters, Shar saw no evidence of a break-in. He considered taking another tricorder reading, but he froze where he stood when he heard the intruder shuffle around in the next room.

In a flash, a hooded figure streaked toward the apartment door. Shar lunged to block his escape. A plant-filled urn tripped him, sending him careening over the top of the couch.

The hooded figure unlatched the door, throwing it open, admitting the bright lights of the inner compound. Shar winced, squinting enough to see Keren's intruder pause, also blinded. Untangling himself from the clutter, Shar lurched for the door, grabbing onto a wrist. He pulled back, dragging the intruder back into the apartment. The intruder brought his forearm and elbow down, the hard blow breaking Shar's grip. Clutching at the knobby Yrythny fingers proved futile; the intruder eluded him, escaping into the hall. Shar staggered outside, realizing whoever it was had vanished.

Keren came in from the balcony and turned on the lights. She immediately went to a floor tile in one corner of the room and pried it open, revealing a secret compartment. "The datachips are still here," she said with relief. "Are you all right?"

Shar sat down on the couch. "Whoever it was seemed more interested in escaping than in hurting me," he said, dropping his head into his hands and rubbing his eyes.

"Did you get a good look at him?"

Shar shook his head. "But I did notice something. There was a mark on his hand. I don't think I've seen it before."

Eyes wide, Keren sat down beside Shar, draping her arm over the top of the couch and tucking her legs up beneath her. "Describe it."

"A blue starburst pattern over the palm. A tattoo?"

Keren considered Shar soberly, her lips pressed tightly. She had something to say, he waited—and then the moment passed.

"Let me check the alert status before you leave," she said. "I'm surprised we haven't heard anything by now." She left Shar sitting on the couch, nursing his bruised arm, while she checked her terminal. "This is odd. The alert has been changed. Martial law is still in effect, but patrols—unarmed—won't be coming in until morning. Questioning is voluntary. That's unprecedented."

My turn for secrets. Thank you, Ezri. "The danger seems to have passed. I should be heading back to my quarters."

"Thank you," Keren said simply.

Accepting the proferred datachips finished the business between them. They took reluctant leave of each other, Shar knowing that Keren, too, understood that their unusual relationship would end here.

Careful to avoid being seen, he moved swiftly through the Old Quarter. He encountered few Yrythny until he reached the outer neighborhood. As the modules transitioned from the antiquated crude technology to the newer, modern systems, crowds increased. Where he could, Shar looked at the palms of those walking by. Once, he thought he might have seen the mark and he followed the Yrythny for almost a kilometer past his own turnoff before losing him in the crowd. *Maybe I'm imagining things,* he thought. *Darkness can deceive the eye.* Becoming conscious of his own exhaustion, he made his way back to his quarters.

He didn't drift immediately off to sleep. Lying on his back, Shar held his hands in front of him. With a finger, he traced the shape of the mark on his own palm, over and over.

With a satisfied grin, Bowers looked up from his station. *"U.S.S. Defiant* ready to go, sir."

Vaughn turned in his chair to face forward. "Conn, prepare for launch."

"Gladly, sir," Tenmei answered, hands dancing over her console. *"Avaril,* this is the Federation *Starship Defiant* requesting departure clearance."

"Defiant, this is Avaril. *Bay doors opening. You are cleared to depart. Safe travels."*

Like great teeth-lined jaws, the doors groaned open, and Prynn eased the starship through, into open space. "We've cleared the *Avaril,* Captain."

Cheers exploded from every station; Vaughn savored the moment. "Follow Consortium shipping lane to grid number 8-5-1 delta, Ensign Tenmei."

"Yes, sir."

Until the femtobot defense was on-line, Vaughn anticipated taking advantage of the nonaggression treaty that protected the Consortium shipping lane. The Cheka wouldn't touch them through those sectors unless they wanted to forfeit all their matter rights.

"Leishman to bridge. We're good to go in engineering."

"Good work, engineering. Ensign Tenmei, when we've cleared the particle fountain perimeter, lay in a course for Vanìmel, warp five." Vaughn breathed deeply. Tonight, he would sleep. First, he would read—maybe that Klingon romance novel he'd won in the poker game. He would drink a steaming mug of mulled cider and then he would sleep.

"Gordimer to Commander Vaughn. Lieutenant Nog is missing!"

Vaughn smiled. He'd discreetly released Nog to his quarters 45 minutes ago. The chief engineer had been quite convincing in his traitor role. A career in holoacting surely awaited him should he ever find Starfleet not to his liking. Once underway to Vanìmel, Vaughn had intended to explain the ruse to the entire crew. "Nothing to worry about, Ensign. Lieutenant Nog has been released to quarters."

"Begging your pardon sir, but I checked the brig logs and I already know you used your codes to release Nog. I assumed you'd decided he'd be safe confined to quarters, so I didn't question it. But on my last pass through the ship, I stopped by Nog's quarters to see how he was doing and the lieutenant wasn't there."

"Computer, locate Lieutenant Nog," Vaughn ordered.

"Lieutenant Nog is not aboard the Defiant."

Once again, every eye on the bridge focused on Vaughn.

"Well, *that* wasn't part of the plan," he said through his teeth. Taking a deep breath, Vaughn clasped his hands together and raised them to his lips. So much for sleeping. "Ensign Tenmei, when we reach the end of the shipping lane, find an asteroid and park the *Defiant* behind it. Ensign Cassini, sweep the Consortium for any Starfleet homing beacons."

He had an answer within seconds. "I'm picking up a low-frequency homing device coming from Consortium grid 4–7–5. It's the *Avaril*, sir."

Not surprising. Not surprising in the least. "Address intership."

"Intership open," Bowers acknowledged.

"Attention all hands, this is Commander Vaughn. Lieutenant Nog has been abducted and is being held on the Yrythny ship *Avaril.* Our return to Vanìmel will be postponed until he is safely returned to us. Strategy and possible solutions will be discussed at the crew meeting scheduled at 2200 in the mess hall. Vaughn out."

"Sir," Cassini said, "Why would Chieftain J'Maah take Lieutenant Nog?"

"I don't think it's Chieftain J'Maah, Ensign. In fact, I'd bet Chieftain J'Maah doesn't know Nog's aboard the *Avaril* and that whoever has taken him has him well hidden."

"Any clues as to who it is?" Bowers asked.

"We'll probably find that out about the same time J'Maah does." He wasn't sure who exactly was responsible, but he hoped the bogus cloak specs he'd deliberately left aboard *Avaril* would unmask the perpetrator. Apparently Vaughn and Nog's sleight of hand had been too convincing— or not convincing enough—because Nog was snatched along with the tech, possibly because giving the Cheka an engineer familiar with the technology would sweeten whatever deal was being made.

Time to dip into my bag of tricks and see what we can come up with. Getting Nog off the *Avaril* before the Yrythny ship pulled a disappearing act of its own might require more than magic.

Any doubts the Assembly might have had about Ezri's fitness to be a mediator vanished after her swift, decisive intervention averted violence in the Old Quarter. During their midnight meeting, she persuaded Rashoh to see the folly of offensive action when the Wanderer population was already inflamed. The Assembly leadership's astonishment at her prescient understanding endowed her with a certain degree of clout. All she'd done was spell out logical consequences, where both Houseborn and Wanderer leadership lacked the emotional or intellectual distance to find reason themselves.

She wasn't about to admit that had it not been for the anonymous message, she would have gone to bed without a second thought. No need to needlessly confuse the outcome. In the following days, a grateful Assembly Chair Rashoh readily agreed, on behalf of the Upper Assembly, to provide DNA samples to Shar for his genetic experiments. Rashoh's reasoning had been that Shar would put to rest, once and for all, any doubt of the Houseborn's superiority. Whether Shar would finish his research in a timely fashion was debatable, but he could always transmit the results to Vanìmel when and if he drew any substantive conclusions.

In Ezri's eyes, her diplomatic victory vindicated her methodology. There had been a few moments along the way when she doubted her own competence, worrying that the Yrythny conflict would only be settled through war. Even Shar's insistence that a scientific solution should supersede diplomatic initiatives caused her to waver in her commitment to see the talks through. In hindsight, thanks to Dax's cumuluative wisdom, she'd instinctively known the best course from the start.

With Shar analyzing Yrythny DNA and word from Vaughn indicating that the *Defiant* was three days out from Vanìmel, Ezri recognized she'd reached a place where she needed to pull all her fact-finding, interviews and analyses together. The Assembly expected, and deserved, a proposal and they would have one.

She didn't have the luxury of waiting for Shar, who might or might not have concrete results before Vaughn returned. The underground might launch another attack. Yrythny life didn't stand to change much before Dax left.

Returning to her quarters, Ezri stood on her head to think. She considered her knowns. The most reasonable among the Houseborn, Jeshoh for example, still had legitimate, significant doubts about the Wanderers' capacity for self-regulation, and House Tin-Mal was proof enough to him. From her own experience on Vanìmel, Ezri wasn't convinced the planet could sustain unlimited Yrythny proliferation. If the Wanderers were allowed to reproduce, both sides would have to impose limitations on reproduction unless the sustainability questions could be suitably resolved. The Wanderers, justifiably, wanted to be held as equals, to escape servile lives, to take consorts and mate as other Yrythny did—and they were prepared to use violence to secure those rights if the Houseborn didn't agree to their demands.

Ezri didn't need blood rushing to her head to conclude that she didn't see a way that these two castes could continue to coexist on the planet unless one side or the other was willing to divvy up the ring city, the oceans and the arable land. Partition it all. Nothing in Vanìmel's history or her knowledge of either side led her to believe that the Yrythny would accept this as a solution.

Dropping her feet back to the floor, Ezri slowly stood up, trying to avoid the lightheadedness that often followed a headstand. Padds and datachips covered her couch. She picked through the pile, searching for inspiration, passing over histories, legislative calendars until her hand hovered over starcharts for the surrounding sectors. Hadn't Vaughn's last message said that they'd figured out how to make Nog's femtobot defense work? Once the Yrythny had that technology and could use it to defend themselves, her solution would be much more hopeful than it currently seemed. It wasn't a glamorous solution or an original one, but it had the benefit of successful precedents.

She touched her combadge. "Dax to Candlewood."

"Go ahead."

"Bring me anything in the *Sagan*'s database on Earth's 16th through 18th century colonial movements."

"Will do. Anything else?"

Ezri plopped into a chair and threw her feet out in front of her. The triannual Yrythny Homecoming was scheduled to begin the day after tomorrow. Three times a year, Houseborn Yrythny returned to their House of origin to go into the waters with their consort and lay eggs. A good time to announce her proposed treaty. "Yes. Please set up a meeting with Assembly Chair Rashoh. Tell him I think I've got something he'll want to hear."

Sitting down at the terminal, Ezri forced herself to work on the draft proposal. Her hands hung in the air; mentally, she drew a blank as she tried to coax out the language. *At least I have something to offer. Throw in a few Dax flourishes and they'll be pleased. I'm sure of it. Of course they will. Why wouldn't they? It's not like they have any ideas of their own and this is a solid solution.*

Her hands remained suspended over the terminal keys.

Nothing else has been proposed. What are you waiting for, Dax? Go for it.

Drawing from the initial draft of the Khitomer Accords, Dax composed the opening of the Yrythny Compromise, all the while unable to ignore the nagging feeling that she ought to wait. But didn't she know everything she needed to know by now? She'd lived longer than all of them put together.

Under cloak, *Defiant* shadowed *Avaril*.

The Yrythny ship hadn't strayed too far from the Consortium

shipping lanes to Vanìmel. Once Nog had been rescued the *Defiant* wouldn't have far to go to reunite with the away team, though Vaughn hadn't been able to contact Ezri and update her as to their latest dilemma. To avoid detection by the *Avaril*, the *Defiant* had remained under cloak and maintained communications silence.

Having left Bowers, Prynn, and Senkowski manning the bridge, Vaughn went to the mess hall to meet with the rest of the crew for the strategy session. The bridge team would attend via the ship's comsystem. Part of Vaughn's agenda for the meeting was to buoy morale. Nog's kidnapping had been a blow. Every crewman wanted to help, but no one knew how. By bringing everyone together, Vaughn hoped to make his team feel like they could make contributions to solving the problem.

By the time Vaughn arrived, five minutes early, the crew had already assembled. *Eager to go to work. Excellent.* "Let's start with what we know. Ensign Leishman, your report," Vaughn said.

"Wherever Nog is being held, there's some kind of transport-inhibiting field in place. We can't beam him off. If he's moved, we might be able to grab him, unless the inhibitor is something on his person. But in order even to make the attempt we'd be risking exposure."

"The *Avaril*'s offensive weaponry and maneuverability are limited," Gordimer interjected. "If we decloak and fix phasers or torpedoes on them, they might give up Lieutenant Nog without a fight."

Shaking his head, Julian countered, "We could be in an indefinite standoff, waiting for one side or the other to blink. If Nog's kidnapping has been done without J'Maah's knowledge, who's to say the kidnapper won't escape with Nog while we're arguing with J'Maah. Or worse, kill him."

"J'Maah might not be involved at all. This could be a conspiracy in his ranks," Vaughn said. "With members of his crew going against orders, the *Avaril* and her 1,800 crewmembers could be in serious danger."

Bowers' voice suddenly rang out. *"Captain. We've picked up something new on long-range sensors. You're going to want to see this."*

"What is it, Sam?"

"Judging from the biosignatures I'm picking up . . . I think it's a Cheka warship, sir," Bowers said.

"Show me," Vaughn ordered.

On the viewer of the mess hall companel, blade-winged starship appeared. Not as large as the *Avaril,* but definitely more powerful, if its energy output readings were any indication. In a fight, the *Defiant* might be the underdog.

"Sensors show the Cheka vessel is following a trajectory that'll have it intercepting the Avaril *five hours out from Vanìmel at current speed."*

So is she planning on poaching the Avaril? *Or is she meeting up with them?* Vaughn mulled over both possibilities, looking for clues as to which one was most likely. He kept returning to the fact that whoever had sabotaged the deal on the Exchange had used the Cheka as a go-between. The Yrythny cut a deal with the Cheka. *What the Cheka want is clear—the cloaking device. But what the Yrythny want—that they'd be desperate enough to deal with the devil on . . .*

An idea struck him. "Sam, keep track of the Cheka's progress. Let me know if it changes course. See if you can listen in on their communications. If they're in contact with anyone, I want to know who. And I want details about that ship. Life-forms, energy sources, propulsion, tactical systems, everything."

"I'm on it," Bowers replied.

Vaughn turned back to his crew. With all eyes fixed on him, Vaughn clasped his hands behind his back and announced, "I think I've figured out how to get Nog back."

16

Oh, to see the look on Vedek Yevir's face when he learns I went walking with Gul Macet! Kira thought, amused by the shocked expression on Prylar Kanton's face as they passed him. Kira knew that being seen publicly with Macet would have only minimal impact on her reputation. Those who knew her well would see her as being fair-minded; those who were wary of her would have another item to add to their arsenal of reasons why she wasn't trustworthy. A public walk also assured that she could honestly answer any who might express concerns about a potential conflict of interest: if she had something to hide, she wouldn't be talking about it in public.

And Kira wasn't fool enough to believe this impacted only her. There were those in Macet's company who would have reservations about the gul talking with a Bajoran. They both needed protection from accusations that might arise from either camp.

Hoping to minimize civilian contact, Kira elected to take a route that took them over the habitat ring bridges and up to the Promenade balcony. At this hour, minimal foot traffic meant fewer encounters with curious onlookers, but the constant security presence in the area assured reliable witnesses to whatever passed between them.

At first they walked in silence, searching for a comfortable rhythm, neither of them certain where one began a conversation like the one they needed to have. About the time they approached the Promenade balcony, Kira finally decided she felt safe to begin.

"I realize I haven't been very hospitable since you arrived. I apologize," she began, clasping her hands together behind her back.

Gul Macet smiled, his face softened by amusement. "It's not all that surprising, Colonel, that you find my presence disturbing, as do your fellow Bajorans. I'm not troubled by it."

"Good," she said, nodding her head with relief. "I'm glad that you don't hold our prejudices against us." They rounded the final corner before moving into the main walkway. Only a handful of people milled around the balcony at this hour: lovers cuddled on a bench, dismissing the awe-inspiring expanse of space out the windows for the wonders in each other's eyes; intoxicated revelers stumbling out of Quark's, lighter in pocket and spirit; and Ro's security people, watching it all.

"My likeness to Dukat isn't exactly positive for either of our peoples," Macet acknowledged. "For everyone who celebrated him as a hero, there were many of us who saw his egocentricity as an obstacle that prevented him from serving Cardassia's best interests. He didn't want power for the good he could do, he wanted power for the good it would do him. There's a distinction there that I think you Bajorans saw before my people did. Our loss."

"Indeed." Kira nodded an acknowledgment to a security officer keeping watch at the top of the spiral staircase. If Kira's companion startled him, his alert gaze offered no evidence of it.

As she and Macet strolled along the Promenade balcony, the exquisite irony of the situation didn't escape Kira. Had it been only days ago when she sat alone in her office, wishing for a friend to walk with? She had envisioned that she and her companion would walk this very stretch she presently stood on. And here she was, standing beside someone she could hardly call a friend, knowing that she was exactly where she was supposed to be, with the person she was supposed to be with.

Her thoughts were broken when Macet said abruptly, "And now that we've reestablished why you feel awkward in my presence . . ."

Kira wondered if she wore her ambivalence on her face. "Gul Macet—" she began, feeling compelled to explain.

". . . I think we can move on to more pressing matters. The talks."

Out of the corner of her eye, Kira noticed the not-so-subtle pointing and gawking that had begun below as worshipers from evening services flooded the Promenade. An idea occurred to her. "I think we'll accomplish more if we find a quiet place to sit down."

"Your office?" he suggested.

"I have another idea."

Within minutes, Kira had admitted herself and Macet to the Ziyal exhibit, on display within the walls of Garak's old tailor shop. And indeed, the tailor shop, vacant and dark since the end of the war, had been transformed into a gallery.

The curator from the Bajoran Ministry of Art, one who had known Ziyal, designed the exhibit. Recessed lighting had already been installed, canvases stretched, and several holoprojectors installed to display representations of works lost in the war. The curator had used blue- and red-tinted spotlights to bring added drama to Ziyal's stark, jagged charcoal lines, to illuminate the multilayered oil paint dabs, roughened by bold brush strokes. She had drawn from both sides of her heritage to create thematically challenging pieces: some of her paintings dripped with the violent blood-reds and slate gray tones of war, while others conveyed the serenity of spirituality through water and nature. Kira wondered how Garak, with whom Ziyal had somehow forged a special connection during her time on the station, would feel when he learned to what purpose his old space was now being put. She thought he would approve.

After a fashion, Ziyal symbolized a trying time for those station residents who lived through the Dominion War Occupation, reminding some of Dukat, others of Vedek Yassim's suicide. For others, Ziyal recalled a darker era, an era when Bajoran women were slaves to Cardassian soldiers. Because Kira loved Ziyal, she didn't want her memory dishonored in any fashion. On Bajor, where fewer individuals had personal associations with her, people would be more inclined to find hope and insight from her story than to resent it.

Public access to the exhibit wouldn't begin for a couple of days; if casual talk between staff working in ops represented a cross sampling of the station's opinions, the admission lines would be long. All those who had been privileged to see Lang's presentation at the reception had openly conveyed their enthusiasm for the Ziyal project.

With the ever-vigilant presence of Militia security hovering outside, Kira and Macet strolled around the various artworks, making simplistic comments about the personalities of the pieces and saying little else until they gravitated to the center of the gallery, where the curator had placed a bench. Macet sat down, facing a floor-to-ceiling canvas—an abstract cubist-style oil painting entitled *Gallitep*—and threw his legs out in front of him. In counterpoint, Kira sat beside, but apart from Macet, facing the opposite wall where a more modest, pencil drawing—warm chalks on black paper—called *Mother* hung. Pale blue lights, the room's sole illumination, shrouded Ziyal's artwork—as well as its two viewers.

"Have the talks always been as contentious as they were today?" Kira asked, still dismayed by the stubborn posturing she'd observed.

"Minister Asarem has always been eloquent," Macet answered, "but her pleasant manners fail to mask the rigid, almost provocative positions she's taken."

Kira shook her head, allowing her eyes to meander over the pale colors puddled on the canvas in front of her. "I had no idea how stuck both of the delegations were," she said. "I sincerely believed that our people could find at least a place to start, but it doesn't appear that either side can agree on even that. If you can't find consensus on humanitarian issues, I don't know how much hope we can hold out for normalized relations."

"This, I believe, is where you come in, Colonel," Macet said gently. "You need to be our intermediary."

"Me?" Kira said. Keeping her back to Macet, she walked over to a painting that hadn't been hung yet. Crouching down, she tried losing herself in an analysis of the geometric forms, but Macet's absurd suggestion intruded on her thoughts. Asarem had hardly been subtle in hiding her dislike for Kira; Shakaar didn't mind using her as a social liaison with the Cardassians, but had reservations about her assuming a larger role, if she'd correctly read his behavior at the reception. Admiral Akaar didn't have a say, yet—this was still a matter between the Bajoran and Cardassian governments, not the Federation. Macet must be delusional. "What exactly do you see me doing?"

"You are the one to put the talks on a successful path," Macet explained. "Even with your own people, you've handled more difficult scenarios."

"I don't know who you've been talking to, Gul Macet, but obviously you have outdated notions about how much my opinion matters around here. Maybe once upon a time . . . Right now, I serve in a quasi-military but primarily administrative capacity. The replicator in your quarters isn't working? Call me. I have an in with the acting engineering chief. Anything requiring politicking, influence peddling or persuasion? I'm more or less useless."

He chuckled. "I'm beginning to see why, at least on some level, you and Gul Dukat were fated to hate each other. As much as he saw the universe circumnavigating him, you're just the opposite."

Kira stiffened. "Don't make the mistake of thinking I didn't have better reasons to hate him, Macet."

"My apologies, Colonel. I only meant that you seem unexpectedly—humble—for someone of your accomplishments. I noticed this at the reception. How can you not appreciate your own magnitude, even among the formidable figures assembled on Deep Space 9 right now?"

"I don't think you understand what an Attainder means among my people."

"Actually I do. Quite well. I spent this afternoon reading up on it. After Vedek Nolan told me what to look for," Macet said. "I accept that your present status imposes a separation of sorts between you and your people, but that doesn't negate who you are."

Kira stood up and turned to face him, arms folded, only to find that Macet was no longer studying the oil painting, but watching Kira intently. "What exactly do *you* know about who I am?"

"Of all the people on the station, you have the unique position as one who has earned the respect of Bajorans, Cardassians, the Federation, even the Romulans and the Klingons," Macet explained patiently. "You've worn the uniforms of both the Bajoran Militia and Starfleet. And you've succeeded Captain Sisko as commander of one of the most critical outposts in the Alpha Quadrant. Now a Starfleet officer serves as *your* second in command. To my knowledge, it's unprecedented."

Kira studied Macet, looking for proof that he might be lulling her into letting her guard down. "All these things are true, but you're neglecting to mention that each one of these items predated my being declared persona non grata." Kira had her own version of the truth to offer. "I retain command of this station because Shakaar can't risk looking provincial while he's trying to win the favor of Councillor zh'Thane and Admiral Akaar. Dismiss me and he has to explain to the Federation why a perfectly qualified officer is dismissed on religious grounds unrelated to command duties. Those who I count as my friends in Starfleet are either in the Gamma Quadrant, on Earth, or with the Prophets. And I'm fairly certain that Minister Asarem would like nothing more than to shove me out the nearest airlock."

Macet tossed his head back and laughed heartily. "You sound not unlike the precocious, brilliant student whose cleverness has left him working off demerits after school, never mind that you're graduating first in your class."

"You're overstating my influence in the circles of power," Kira said.

"And you are obviously not the best judge of your capabilities. I'm sure most would see you as a true daughter of the Prophets," Macet pronounced solemnly.

"You have a helluva a lot of nerve talking about what makes a true daughter of the Prophets," she said sharply, refusing to be bought off by Macet's lofty rhetoric. "If anyone thinks that the resemblances between you and Dukat end at appearance, make sure they're informed otherwise. Flattery won't negate the reality of my situation."

Macet met her gaze. "It isn't flattery, it's truth. And it's why Ambassador Lang, and I, speaking on her behalf, are asking you to use your influence to help us broker peace."

"I thought we'd established my lack of influence." Kira rubbed her forehead, wondering how awful her headache would be by the time she and Macet stopped arguing in circles.

"You are the only one who truly understands all sides in this, as your remarks to Minister Asarem proved today."

"You overheard?"

"You weren't exactly keeping your voices down, Colonel."

Damn. If Macet heard, who else might have eavesdropped on her conversation with Asarem? For a moment, Kira worried about the vandal who had targeted the Cardassian delegation, hoping her outburst eluded that pair of ears. Her words might be interpreted as being too supportive of the Cardassians, and she didn't want to further stoke the anger that had defaced the flag. She knew then that she needed to do what she could to hasten this process along. "What exactly is it that you expect me to do?" she said at last.

"Appeal to First Minister Shakaar. Ask him to intercede."

Kira shook her head. "You don't know what you're asking."

Macet suddenly stood up. "You've seen for yourself what's happening. Minister Asarem isn't interested in negotiating peace. She wants revenge."

"But how do I know that what happened today is typical of the talks?" Kira argued, remembering what passed between all the involved parties.

"Review the transcripts. Interview me, Lang, any member of our delegation. And I'm sure if you asked, you could talk to the Bajoran delegation as well. Weigh the evidence," Macet urged. "If you review the proceedings and find that all parties acted reasonably or that our party acted in bad faith, then I'd invite you to act on your conscience or walk away. But if you find that the facts support my contentions, will you go to First Minister Shakaar and plead our case?"

Kira rolled Macet's request around in her mind, looking for any possible loopholes or places that might ultimately damage the precarious situation between Bajor and Cardassia further; she found none. "I'll see what I think after I review the information."

"Isn't it accurate to say that true followers of the Prophets believe that all things may be done through their instrumentality?" he asked.

"If it's right for Bajor."

"And if brokering peace between our peoples is right for Bajor, do you not have faith that the Prophets will light your path?"

Kira met his direct gaze, seeing integrity in his eyes that Dukat had never feigned successfully. "If you know me as well as you claim to, you know the answer to that question."

"I'm counting on it," Macet said quietly.

That the security post inside the exhibit had been vacated without her being informed struck Kira as odd. She understood that the exhibit was to be guarded around the clock. The deserted Promenade pulsed with taut stillness, a tension that squeezed out all the sound. Without thought to Macet, she walked as if in a dream toward the front door, when the silence ruptured—an angry cacophony of screams and crashes, of breaking bodies and shattering glass.

A tangle of humanoid bodies was spilling out of Quark's, many clutching random objects from the bar as makeshift weapons. She saw a group of Cardassians wielding table legs like clubs at charging Bajorans brandishing bottles and chairs. An abandoned cart loaded with incense, crystals, and candles toppled over, spilling wares onto the floor; a pair of combatants skidded to a halt, falling flat on their backs before their fists could make contact. Bar stools sailed through the air. Scents of spilled liquors and hoppy Terran ale permeated the air.

Kira touched her combadge. "Kira to Ro."

"I know Colonel. Quark contacted me. I'm on my way." Ro sounded breathless; she must be running from her quarters. *"I'm closing the Promenade to everyone except security and medical personnel, and yourself, until we get the situation under control. All my off-duty people have been summoned and I've alerted the infirmary—but even so, this sounds pretty bad."*

"Actually, it's worse. I suggest you hurry, Lieutenant. Kira out." With her phaser drawn, Kira charged onto the west platform. She estimated the number of brawlers higher than sixty. She turned to Macet to ask for his assistance in putting down the tumult, but realized, too late, he'd already raced into the crowd and was prying his men off whoever their opponents might be. She quickly lost track of him in the sea of constantly heaving bodies. Hoping that any security officers present might help defuse the fray, she saw, to her anger, the unmistakable colors of the Militia swirling in the mix of Cardassian gray. *Our own people are part of this . . . !*

Kira scanned the room with her eyes, seeking a position from which to disrupt the melee in the quickest, surest way possible. She saw arms, bloody uniforms, limbs twisted at grotesque angles, and was wondering where the hell the medics were when she spotted Dr. Tarses. Simon had begun treating an injured Cardassian when he was suddenly accosted by an enraged Bajoran. The man started beating Simon until Sergeant Shul appeared from somewhere, yanked him off the doctor, and put him in restraints. For his part, Tarses went back to caring for his patient, ignoring the bruises that were already darkening his face.

Crouched down, out of sight between the gym and the jeweler's, she waited for the strategic moment, phaser pointed at the ceiling, finger on the trigger. . . .

Shielding himself with a tray, Quark bellowed demands for order, utterly ignored by anyone who heard him. Kira watched as he pushed anyone still inside the bar—anyone who even looked dangerous—out onto the Promenade. When he appeared satisfied that only his staff remained (and Morn, peering out at the chaos from behind the dubious safety of the bar), Quark activated a force field to prevent the brawlers from returning to further damage his establishment.

Macet was having mixed success in stopping his men; he'd break up one quarrel only to be drawn into another. Suddenly Kira saw an enraged Klingon, wielding a *d'k tahg,* charging Macet after the gul had forced the Cardassian that the Klingon had been fighting to retire.

Kira pivoted out, spraying a round of warning shots at the walls behind the Klingon. Startled, the Klingon turned to face his new assailant, only to be tackled by Macet. Keeping a knee wedged between the Klingon's shoulder blades, Macet waved appreciatively to Kira.

Several brawlers had paused and ducked when the metallic sound of phaser fire rang out; some dove to the floor, but one particularly determined pair continued trying to kill each other until Kira stunned them both. They dropped, grunting. Kira kicked them out of her way.

"This is Colonel Kira!" she shouted. "Any and all Bajoran nationals are to stand down immediately or face criminal charges!" Several Bajorans paused, midpunch, to look toward Kira's voice, but many ignored her demands.

Another round of phaser fire whizzed from the balcony above and everyone looked to see Ro standing over them all, phaser held out in front of her, and flanked by a dozen armed security officers. "The next person to flinch gets more than a warning shot!" Ro shouted.

As if daring Ro to make good on her threat, a man Kira recognized as an off-duty Militia engineer charged a Cardassian who had just allowed a badly beaten Bajoran to fall to the deck, unconscious. Another well-targeted shot from Kira's phaser brought the engineer down instantly. A wave of compliance flowed through the crowd as fists fell, neck holds were released and all matter of objects being used to pummel clattered to the ground.

Ro nodded appreciatively at her commanding officer, then began deploying her people into the crowd below, keeping her weapon trained. "Everyone remains where they are," she cautioned. "No one moves until you're given permission to move." The security chief found the man Kira had wounded and, hauling him up by his good arm, led him off to sit in front of the shrine as medics swarmed from the infirmary.

Macet appeared at Kira's side. "Colonel. I apologize for the behavior of my crew."

Kira shook her head. "We don't know who started this."

"It doesn't matter who started this," Macet said sharply. "My men were wrong to have been fighting. They will be appropriately punished, I assure you, and will submit to any interrogations Lieutenant Ro might require."

"Interrogation is a very strong word," Kira said, picking her way through collapsed, bruised and beaten revelers toward the west platform.

Macet walked alongside Kira, paralyzing with a cold glare whoever among his men dared look at him. "If interrogation is required
to assure my people's compliance you have my blessing to do
whatever you need to do."

"Thank you. I'm sure Lieutenant Ro will appreciate your cooperation." As she walked, Kira began making mental calculations
about how much damage had been done, what the cost would be,
who would pay, and whether they would even be able to reopen the
Promenade before morning. Irritated by the pointlessness of such
wanton destruction, she gritted her teeth. *When will we ever learn?*

Out of the corner of her eye, Kira saw Dr. Girani and four nurses
rushing out of a turbolift to join their colleagues already tending
the wounded. Several of the medics appeared to have been roused
from their beds: Lieutenant Chagall, usually a stickler for regulation, wore shorts and his Academy T-shirt; and Ensign Mancuso
had thrown on a flowered bathrobe. Kira allowed herself to relax a
bit: at least the wounded could be attended to properly.

"Considering the numbers involved, I hope that you don't have
any objections to my securing Cardassian prisoners in the brig on
my ship," Macet said. "Lieutenant Ro can post her own squad of
security guards, of course, but I suspect your facilities will be over-
taxed if she has to detain my men as well."

Kira paused to look over at Macet. *He's trying as hard as the rest
of us.* "I'll inform Lieutenant Ro. Let's get to work."

After Ro delegated the investigatory assignments, she went to interview Quark. Kira made herself useful helping out both the security and medical teams. Amazing how a threatening glare from the
CO helped induce a belligerent Militia member to cooperate, or how
an extra pair of hands, regardless of rank, were appreciated. Case in
point: a massive, but unconscious Cardassian had collapsed on top
of his groaning crewmate. With Kira taking the shoulders and a security officer taking the legs, they heaved him off, leaving the for-
merly pinned crewmate available for Macet to take into custody.

How could this have happened? Kira wondered, nauseated by
the smells of sweat and blood. A hand touched her shoulder and she
turned to see Counselor Matthias and Thriss standing behind her.

Matthias, like Ro and some of the others, looked like she'd tumbled out of bed. Unlike Lieutenant Ro, who had been striding around barefoot, Phillipa had managed to slide her feet into a pair of fuzzy pink slippers. Gratefully, Thriss wore sensible, nondescript civilian clothes.

"Ummm, Colonel," Matthias started in a gravelly voice before interrupting herself with a yawn. "I only have Starfleet's field medicine certification, but when I heard the emergency call go out over the com, I knew you'd need extra hands. I'm here to help."

"Thank you, Commander. And Thriss has joined you because . . . ?"

Commander Matthias rubbed her eyes with the heels of her hands. "Thriss trained as a medic through level three. Preparing for med school, in fact." Phillipa yawned again. "She worked with the civilian population on Betazed after the emancipation. Situations like these are all in a day's work for her."

"I spent two months working in hospitals in the capitol city," Thriss said, thrusting out her medkit for Kira to inspect. She appeared to have the right tools, but Kira had reservations.

At Kira's skeptical look, Matthias added, "I'm confident that Thriss can handle anything Dr. Girani would assign her. Allowing her to help out could be mutually beneficial."

"Report to Dr. Girani, then," Kira instructed them both. "And thank you."

Matthias lingered behind for a moment, waiting for Thriss to be out of earshot. "Colonel, I'll stay close by. If I sense that she needs to leave, I'll escort her back to her quarters."

"Thriss does seem more—alert—maybe cheerful?" Kira observed.

"She expects to hear from Ensign ch'Thane when the next batch of communiqués comes from the *Defiant*. She loves him—misses him. Hearing from him reassures her," Matthias explained. She yawned again and trailed off after Thriss.

Kira appreciated Matthias's efforts: the only way they'd survive the current craziness was to be vigilant in looking out for each other. *No matter the planet of origin, parentage, past misdeeds or present challenges—we have to assume that our success or failures come by every individual's choice.* She considered the work being done before her, the cooperation of diverse organizations and species in helping these stupid fools who probably deserved their misery.

A Cardassian sporting a bruise on his forehead the size of a *jumja* fruit moaned somewhere to her left. She dropped to a knee, clicked the tricorder off her utility belt and scanned his skull, looking for evidence of a concussion. Jerking away from her, the soldier stared up at her, fear and distrust in his eyes, his body rigid.

"You're going to be fine," Kira said, reassuringly. "I'll find you something that will take care of the pain."

Ro made her way around the debris until she reached the keypad access port to Quark's bar. An alphanumeric combination overrode Quark's lock and the door obediently opened. Nonchalantly, she strolled into the bar, nodding a hello to Morn, who sat nursing a mug.

What a mess.

Shattered goblets and snifters, malodorous cheeses and seafood sauces smeared into the upholstery, wadded-up napkins, overturned *tongo* wheels, and more than a dozen broken wine bottles drizzling fermented fruit juice onto the floor. Navigating this in bare feet was akin to picking her way through a minefield. There had to be something . . . an idea occurred to her.

"Hey, Treir! You around here somewhere?" Ro called, craning her neck, trying to catch a glimpse of what other surprises might yet await her.

Quark popped up from behind the bar. "Not even a 'hello, Quark, I was worried about you?' We had a regular Core breach in here tonight and you're not the slightest bit concerned." He clicked his tongue. "You and Treir don't have something going on that I don't know about, do you?" he said, a shade too casually.

"Shut up, Quark. I need shoes."

"Now that you mention it, your wardrobe is on the skimpy side tonight. I'm sure I've got something in the storeroom. Back in a flash." Disappearing into the rear, he materialized a moment later, a pair of spangly, sparkly-blue high heels dangling from his ring and pinky fingers.

Ro resisted her impulse to force him to contort his feet into those podiatric nightmares. "Be serious," she snorted.

"You have such pedestrian taste, Laren." He pulled a pair of flat sandals from behind his back and plopped them onto the counter. "Better?"

Taking a seat on a bar stool, Ro hoisted one foot onto her knee and into a shoe and then repeated the process with the other foot. "You wanna tell me what happened here tonight?" she said, sweeping aside ground-up matza-stick crumbs with her elbow. She needed a space to work.

"Ask five different people who started it, you'll get five different answers," Quark said solemnly. He took a bar towel and brushed refuse into a dustpan, whose contents promptly went into the replicator. "All I know for certain is that it was Bajorans and Cardassians failing to work and play well with each other. Like it takes a quantum physicist to understand that the bad blood between your people and the Cardassians is destined to lead to disaster."

Ro placed a padd on the cleared spot on the bar and began to take notes. "Other than your astute, upbeat analysis of Bajoran/Cardassian relations, any specific things you might remember—you know, clues that might help us toss some hotheads in the brig—assign some accountability?"

"Not offhand, no. But speaking of accountability, who's going to pay for this disaster? Because there's no way that this is my fault." Quark threw open his arms, indicating the expanse of his establishment. "And the lost revenues! We're not going to be cleaned up in time for alpha shift. This is an outrage. I demand to speak to Colonel Kira and Gul Macet!" Continuing to prattle on, Quark walked from one end of the room to the other, interspersing diatribes with his cleanup efforts. He tried to impress upon Ro the gravity of every scratched chair and crumb-covered table.

Ro massaged her ridges with the tips of her fingers. *High noise, low signal,* she thought, hoping he might deign to throw in a few useful facts between his explanation of thread counts and his assertion that he'd never known a Cardassian to complain about *kanar* just past the "use by" date. Not surprisingly, he unequivocally denied any culpability for Cardassians put in sour moods after partaking of bad liquor.

A couple of hours later, Kira believed they were on the downside of arrests, medical treatments and cleanup. The Promenade wouldn't be ready by the start of the business day, and morning Temple services would also be cancelled. Still awaiting her was the unpleasant task of rousing Shakaar with the update of the night's goings-on. He wouldn't be pleased.

Starting toward ops, she glimpsed Macet on the opposite platform, herding the last of his shackled men toward a turbolift. She stopped to watch him, presuming that he likely felt the same exhaustion she did. He must have sensed her because he stopped to meet her gaze. Their eyes linked only long enough for a mutual understanding to pass between them. Turning away, he barked orders to those assisting him and disappeared from her sight.

When she was satisfied he was gone, Kira said quietly, "You can deshroud now."

Taran'atar shimmered into visibility beside her. "Colonel?"

"Maintaining surveillance on Gul Macet will no longer be necessary," Kira said, still staring after the departed Cardassian.

"I concur," the Jem'Hadar said. "Will there be anything else?"

Kira considered the question. "What do you think of him?" she asked finally.

Taran'atar hesitated. "He isn't what I expected."

Kira nodded. "I know exactly what you mean."

17

Water-light reflected in lazy loops on the rust sandstone walls, disrupted by stones skimming the surface. Rippling rings emerged as the rock fell to the streambed with a hollow plop, a prelude to the storm rumbling in the distance. The air crackled, anticipating release.

Crouched low to the ground, Shar scooped up a handful of gravel and rocks, sifting it through his fingers, fishing out the smooth flat stones, tossing aside the dross. He skipped one across the stream and another, losing himself in the rhythm of the mindless task.

"The rules of conduct are not negotiable," the headmaster had

explained patiently in a tone he'd use for an idiot. "You are not an exception."

He skipped another stone.

Her antennae rigid with barely contained fury, zhavey *had bellowed, "Tezha is reserved for the* shelthreth! *Don't tempt fate, Thirishar!" He'd protested his innocence, but she refused his explanations.*

He scratched through the damp sand for another stone, willing away their chastisements. Gradually, the voices of zhavey *and the headmaster twisted and twined into the low moans of the growing wind. A gust shaved dry needles off spindly conifers, flipped dry leaves onto their backs. Shar pulled his tunic closer to him to stave off the chill. He shivered.*

And then he sensed her.

Without hearing her bare feet sending pebbles skittering up the path or seeing the sheen of perspiration damp on her arms and face, he knew she stood behind him, watching. She always watched him and he hated her for it. He could be standing across the hallway or tucked in a window seat reading and her eyes would always find him. When he felt her closeness, his throat tightened as the air became unbearably dry.

"What are you doing here?" he said disdainfully, willing his thudding heart to steady. He refused to look at her. Attention would only encourage her. She'd been impossible yesterday, following him out into the hills, an act that had led to them both ending up in the headmaster's office to receive official notations on their records.

"That's a fine hello, Thirishar," she sniffed, tossing her hair.

That hair of hers, *Shar thought, annoyed.* That ridiculous fine, straight hair, soft like spun silk thread when she brushed against him . . . *"If I'd wanted you here, I would have invited you. Of course, that didn't stop you yesterday when you invited yourself along on my research trip. I neglected to thank you for that, by the way. I've been given a failing grade on the project."*

"Rules say you aren't supposed to go alone." She circled closer.

He picked through the dirt. "Rules say you're not supposed to go alone with a bondmate."

"You would have ended up half-frozen if I hadn't been there."

"If you hadn't been there, I might not have gotten lost!"

"And to think I came up here to apologize!"

Shar snorted. "Your apologies won't help me pass environmental studies." Reluctantly, he tore his eyes from the ground and looked at her, radiant in the bruised, colored half-light, gauzy skirt flapping in the wind. She granted him only a momentary glance of her gray eyes.

"Fine then." Thriss threaded her arms across her chest and jumped up onto a boulder sitting beside the spring. She began crossing to the opposite side, jumping sprightly from rock to rock with balletic grace. Her shimmering hair, blown by the wind, strayed across her face and she threw back her head, gazing up at the darkening sky. She closed her eyes, slightly arching her back and threw open her arms, embracing the imminent storm.

Shar watched the gentle rise and fall of her breathing. He swallowed hard and looked away.

A shadow crossed over. A violent clap of thunder announced the storm. Raindrops pelted the earth, sending up clouds of pink dust from the pathway. The stony metallic scent of rain on hot canyon rock drenched the air.

Thriss laughed, cupping her palms to capture the rain.

"Get down from there!" Shar ordered.

"Why should I?"

"Because you'll be soaked, that's why and I refuse to accept the blame when you come down with a raging case of zhem!" Sloshing across the stream, he tamped down the impulse to yell. A loss of control would only exacerbate this situation. He refused to yield the upper hand to petulant Thriss because that was precisely what she wanted. Reaching for her wrists, he encircled them with his thumb and forefinger. He tugged gently; she might be equal to him in height, but he was stronger than she.

Refusing to budge, she said, "You come up here." Her eyes danced playfully.

"Thriss—!" he warned loudly, his voice muted by the rain's plip-plop chatter.

"I think you'll find the view is quite lovely from here."

He followed her gaze to the billowing dark clouds, backlit by flashes of lightning. A stray bolt leapt out, igniting dry scrub grow-

ing in canyon rock crevices. Flames greedily devoured the parched wood, leaving behind steaming, charred carcasses.

The flash sent the nerves of his antennae tingling almost painfully. Exasperated, Shar yanked her down. Thriss lost her footing on the algae-covered rock and she slipped forward, sending them both tumbling into the water.

Bracing herself over him, Thriss sputtered, pushing sodden tendrils out of her face. She narrowed her eyes. "You always have to have your way."

"We wouldn't be here—I wouldn't be here—if you knew how to stay out of my life!"

"Your life?" Throwing back her head, she laughed grimly. "Fine. I'll go." She struggled to her feet, trying to untangle her limbs from her sopping clothes as she walked. A misplaced foot caught on her hem and she tripped, landing facedown in the shallow spring. Weakly, she pushed up on her elbows.

"Thriss!" Shar scrambled over to her side. Ignoring her halfhearted protests, he hooked her by the arm and eased her to her feet. She stiffened at his touch, jerking away as soon as they reached the bank. Shar's fears for her well-being persisted until he was satisfied that she sustained only scratches and bruises from her fall. He exhaled raggedly.

Assuming she would resist his help, Shar threw an immovable arm around her waist, guiding her inside the cavern where he'd left his pack. Thriss perched on a rock while he searched for a survival blanket or dry clothing. Teeth chattering, she crossed her arms over her chest, hunched her shoulders and shivered for warmth. Shar dropped down beside her and tended her wounds.

"You shouldn't have come up here," he said at last.

"I'm sorry," she whispered.

As he mended her scrapes, her shivering evolved into trembling. A sob escaped her throat; Shar knew that she wept often. "Come here," he said, drawing her onto his lap, wrapping her in his arms and pulling her tight against him. He rested his cheek in her hair and rubbed her back. Murmured words from an unknown place inside him settled her. Gradually, her ragged sobs ceased; she hiccupped a few times and then rested her face against his chest with a sigh. Her antennae brushed a ticklish spot beneath his chin.

He didn't feel like laughing.

He became sensitized to her hands resting on the small of his back, the way she curved into him, molding her body against his. Taking her chin in his hand, he tipped her face up. For as long as he had memories, she was in them. Difficult, childish, lanky . . . sweet-smelling like challom *flowers, hair gossamer soft and her eyes—her stormy eyes swallowed him. Exploring the velvet hollows of her throat with his fingertips, he felt her pulse quicken as he traced the edge of her collarbone with his thumb. He stared.*

Thriss held Shar's look, loosened the tie on her blouse, pushed back the wet, clinging fabric, pulling it down to puddle around her waist. He reached for her and hesitated, knowing her apparition would dissolve with his touch as it always did in his dreams. Until she placed his hand on her chest and he felt the warmth of her skin against his palm. Startled by her realness, he pulled away, wincing upon losing his connection with her.

I need her. He received this revelation with the same faith that allowed him to understand the revolution of planets and the nature of light. I need her.

He fumbled with his tunic. With shaking fingers, Thriss, too, clutched at his clothing, but her clumsiness matched his own. Pressing foreheads together they shared an awkward laugh. Hands linked, they yanked his tunic over his head and tossed it on the ground.

They pressed close, antennae touching, stroking, until trembling cascaded over them. He nestled her back against his chest, embedding each delicate vertebra into his skin; his hands settled on the slope of her hips, caressed the curve, and stroked the small of her back. She reached her arms behind her, drawing his face into her neck, knotting her fingers in his locks. All that he had been taught and warned about dissolved into languid twilight. She had been given to him, and he to her. And he accepted at last what elemental thing had been between them since their memories began.

A chime started Shar awake. His eyes opened and he found himself sitting in front off the main console of the *Sagan*. At last check, it had been close to dawn; now, it was four hours later. The vaguest sense that he was forgetting something lingered in the back of his mind.

"Model complete," the ship's computer intoned. *"Image available upon request."*

"Display," Shar ordered. Maybe seeing the model would help jar his memory about which of the three or four data files he'd been working on before he fell asleep. Sleeping was counterproductive, especially when his vivid dreams left him wondering what reality he was in.

I wonder if the others ever suspected. It isn't like I wear a visible mark, he thought. Recollections of intimacies shared with Thriss often dredged up guilt. Though he'd never regretted the choice to initiate *tezha,* he knew Anichent and Dizhei would be hurt by their choice to go outside the bond. Not only because it was forbidden but also because their choice implied infidelity to the bond as a whole. Over the last six years, Shar had gradually recognized that he would eventually face consequences for breaking the covenant. Anichent would feel betrayed. Dizhei would fear for the stability of the bond. But Shar was confident they could surmount these obstacles. *I've maintained strong, healthy relationships with all my bondmates,* Shar reasoned. *I love them all and I anticipate sharing my life with them for many years to come.*

He considered this latest holographic model of Yrythny DNA. Since his trip to the peninsula, Shar had worked, day and night, processing the data by utilizing the Andorian gene-mapping strategies he was familiar with to develop models. Thankfully, he had enough Wanderer data to track the subtle nuances of their genetic drift. Houseborn information was spottier. The samples from the Assembly and those the Hebshu farmers had managed to collect from their Houseborn colleagues provided Shar enough reference points from the past with which to compare current data.

Identifying primary gene functions had been his first priority. Once the chromosomal architecture had been adequately mapped, Shar began tracking mutations and the consequences of those mutations. The computer had spent the night comparing Wanderer samples, synthesizing generalizations about where mutations occurred and what consequences resulted. If there proved to be a pattern, Shar would project future drift and see what conclusions could be drawn.

"Computer, display results from Yrythny data analysis ch'Thane Beta four."

So far, the results hadn't yielded many surprises. In the genes governing intelligence, both Wanderer and Houseborn Yrythny had equal potential. Similar results cropped up in areas of physical strength and health. More distinctions existed on the Houseborn side between Houses. *What am I not seeing?* Shar thought, frustrated. *There's something right here in front of me and I'm not seeing it.*

"Shar?" Lieutenant Dax said, climbing through the entry hatch.

His nagging sense of forgetting vanished when he remembered the imminent trip planetside for Homecoming. "Yes, Lieutenant. I'm here."

"We missed you at breakfast," Dax said, clicking open a locker and tossing a shoulder bag inside.

"We?"

"We, Ensign." Keren entered behind Dax, with Vice Chair Jeshoh bringing up the rear.

"Oh. I didn't realize we'd have company, Lieutenant."

"Keren and Jeshoh did chair the committees I worked with. It's only fitting that they come as co-presenters. Besides, Jeshoh is House Perian's favorite son. We're VIPs when we travel with him." Dax slid into the seat beside Shar. "How's the research coming?"

Shar hesitated. He didn't want to reveal any strategy Ezri might be still trying to protect.

"Speak freely, Ensign," Dax said, evidently surmising his reservations "I doubt your study will change much at this point."

Unfortunately, she's right, Shar thought regretfully. "On the face of things, the data indicate that the Yrythny, generally, don't have a lot to differentiate them. Statistically significant variations exist within the body of Houseborn data and the body of Wanderer data, but not between Houseborn and Wanderer."

"See, Jeshoh, I told you that I was your equal," Keren teased.

"You can say it, but I don't believe it," Jeshoh retorted.

"What's next?" Ezri asked, thumbing through Shar's results on her own viewscreen.

"Projecting the long-term genetic drift. Mapping the likely mutations and the probable outcome of those mutations. I expect to complete the analysis by tonight."

"Excellent. Keep me posted." Dax leaned close enough to Shar that only he could hear her. "I know you had a lot invested in this project, and you've done superior work. Don't beat yourself up about not finishing in time. The Assembly is happy with the compromise I proposed. I think we've succeeded in helping the Yrythny."

Eyes straight ahead, Shar said politely, "As you say, sir."

Dax turned to the passengers in the aft seats. "Strapped in?"

Keren and Jeshoh answered affirmatively.

"All right, then. Ensign, prepare for launch."

"Yes, sir," Shar acknowledged. "Luthia launch control, this is shuttle *Sagan* requesting clearance for takeoff."

"Shuttle Sagan, *you are clear for launch."*

For Shar, knowing he was going to Vanìmel for the last time felt bittersweet. Vaughn and the *Defiant* would return tomorrow, prepared to resume their explorations. Dax's assurances aside, he berated himself for failing to accomplish his personal goals. He ought to be satisfied with the away team's work; they'd all played a role in Ezri's diplomatic efforts. Her proposed compromise was logical, if not particularly original. If the committees' response indicated how the Yrythny, as a whole, would respond, her ideas would be well received. But he could have done more. *I should have done more,* Shar thought. *After all we've been through, this can't be all.*

In the days since they left the Consortium, all crewmen had worked on their designated pieces of Vaughn's plan and now, they waited. Experience had taught Vaughn not to be impatient. All hell would break loose soon enough. In the last hour, the finer points of the femtobot defense had been finalized. Though engineering wasn't his forte, he found Leishman's report fascinating, including the successful synthesis of a particle fountain metal with a Federation alloy.

Excitedly, Rahim called from his station, "I've got them, Captain."

Vaughn looked up from the padd he'd been studying. "Let's hear it."

The bridge officer hurriedly tapped in a few commands. "Compensating for radiant interference, audio feed—"

"—when the shuttle with our payment leaves the Avaril, *it will also carry the alien's chief technologist, Nog. You'll need him to translate the specifications into a working device."*

"This is from the *Avaril?"* Vaughn asked.

Rahim nodded.

Vaughn knew from time with J'Maah that the subspace channel hosting the transmission wasn't a usual Yrythny frequency. *So we are dealing with a conspirator. J'Maah will be a sitting duck.*

"What are we supposed to do with him?" a metallic Cheka voice reverberated through the bridge.

"Once he's built the cloak, you can do with him as you please. It's of no consequence to us."

"Can we identify the vocal patterns?" Vaughn asked. If he could figure out who the traitor was, he might be able to send a covert communiqué to J'Maah before the deal went down.

Rahim apologized. "No, sir. I've already had to modify the audio to work with our decryption algorithms."

A small price to pay for confirmation, he thought.

The channel clicked off, but Vaughn had gained a clear visual of how the pieces would move across the chessboard. He touched his combadge. "Vaughn to Permenter."

"Go ahead."

"Have you ever heard of a noisemaker, Ensign? The tactical variety?"

He could hear her hesitation.

"I'll be right down. I have another project for you. Vaughn out. Sam, you have the bridge."

Bowers looked up from his console. "Noisemaker, sir?"

Vaughn paused at the door. "If this plays out the way I think it will, the *Avaril* will be completely vulnerable when the Yrythny conspirators initiate the trade with the Cheka. We have to make it as hard as possible for them to attack the *Avaril*—or at least improve the odds. I've had quite enough of playing by their rules." Vaughn knew he spoke for every member of the crew. *Time to blow the lid off this con game.*

Sidestepping a group of servants carrying large bins overloaded with fish, Shar ducked beneath an awning and waited for them to pass. He fingered the padd in his pocket, longing for a minute to sit down and review his research data. He'd downloaded the rudiments of his study to carry with him, anticipating that the evening's official schedule would allow him plenty of work time. Besides Ezri, most of the major government players were slated to speak; if they resembled most officials, they would have lengthy, repetitive and self-aggrandizing rhetoric to propagate. Considering he more or less knew what would be said, he felt no guilt about using the time more effectively.

As he approached the end of the walkway, Shar realized he was lost. He had taken a left turn at the Fountain Triad, passed by the servants' quarters and circled back along the north boardwalk to the plaza. Keren had instructed him to meet her near the entrance to the Colonnade, the facility hosting the evening festivities. Instead, Shar arrived at the end of his walk facing a black sea wall marking the narrow alleyway running behind the resident's wing. From what he'd seen of House Perian, little if any logic had gone into the design. The original House had been built three thousand years ago— the plaza had been at the center. Three millennia had allowed time for the natives to add on the accoutrements of modern life from a marina to a shuttleport to aquaculture outbuildings. Over the course of the afternoon, Shar had seen most of Perian but had yet to retrace his steps. He turned around, looked up to see if Keren might be descending one of the outer staircases or if he could recognize any landmarks. A cluster of Yrythny emerged from the alleyway; Shar approached them. "Excuse me, but I'm looking for the Colonnade."

The tallest in the group, an Yrythny who reminded Shar of Jeshoh, laughed heartily. "You're all turned about, stranger. We're headed there ourselves. You're welcome to walk with us."

"Thank you," Shar said, hoping this group was headed directly for the Colonnade and not eventually to the Colonnade by way of the café, the apartments or the docks. He followed alongside, seeking to regain his bearings. After walking a short distance, Shar recognized a familiar landmark and relaxed. "I'm Thirishar, by the way," he introduced himself. "But most call me Shar."

"I'm Nensoh, these are my friends Dernah and Spetsoh. I assumed from the look of you that you're part of the alien delegation from Luthia. Your hair is astonishing."

Shar had discovered his hair inordinately fascinated the Yrythny. "Do you live here?" Shar wracked his brain for other questions one asked when making polite conversation. He doubted the finer points of chromosomal architecture would interest this trio.

"Only during the summer. To help with the farming. During the winter, I serve on a starship," Nensoh explained. "I'm home because my consort and I will go into the water. Here we are."

The group emerged onto the open square, crowded with Yrythny waiting for admission to the Colonnade. Shar split off from his Yrythny escorts, knowing if he followed them into the throng, he'd never find Keren. "Thank you, Nensoh!" Shar yelled over the cacophonous crowd. He waved farewell.

Puckering his face strangely, Nensoh raised his hand, mimicking the unfamiliar gesture.

And then Shar saw it. The starburst mark.

"Wait!" he called, running after Nensoh.

Nensoh paused when he saw Shar coming toward them. "Shar?"

"The mark on your hand. I've seen it before."

Nensoh shrugged. "It's not unusual. It appears on the palm of a fertile Yrythny as they enter their reproductive period. My guess is, were you to check the palms of all of these Yrythny, most would bear the mark."

Shar nodded absently, his mind racing through questions. The night in Keren's apartment haunted him. In subsequent discussions with Keren, he'd asked about the mark, but she shrugged off his concerns, believing Shar had scared off the invader and thus any potential threat. At least the mark's commonness made it less likely that Keren was protecting a specific individual. Still . . .

"Thirishar! Over here!"

Seeking Keren's faint voice, he narrowed her location to the fringes of the plaza. He squinted, discerning that she had climbed up onto a bench, enabling him to see her over the tall Yrythny. Fixing his bearings on her location, he wormed his way in and out of the tight, packed-in crowds, relieved to emerge from the claustrophobic gathering. Before he could greet her, she jumped down and said, "We can't stay. There's an emergency."

"What is it?" He followed her away from the plaza, jogging toward the seaside path.

"Jeshoh contacted me. The Perian authorities believe the mating grounds are being raided. They'll be launching the patrols as soon as they can, but all the visitors have blocked the harbor with their watercraft."

Damn. Without hesitation, Shar tapped his combadge. "Ch'Thane to Dax. We have an emergency."

With the first moon hidden behind clouds and the second still rising over the mountains, there was little natural illumination as the *Sagan,* once again carrying Shar, Dax, Keren and Jeshoh, came within visual range of their targets.

"Increase resolution," Ezri ordered.

Shar tapped in a few commands, sharpening the visual sensors' acuity by compensating for the diminished light.

Within the small screen on Shar's console, three hovercraft skimmed in and out of the reed patches of the mating grounds while another paused in the very thick of the sea grasses. Shar zoomed in on a cloaked figure leaning over the railing, plunging a long pole, with a net attached at the end, into the water. Beside him, another cloaked figure thrust the nose of a long tube into the reeds, pumping a handle mounted on the end.

"Clever," Jeshoh muttered. "I'll wager they're spraying the reeds with tetracoxiclan to melt the adhesive seal between the reeds and the egg sacks."

"Second one follows behind with the net and scoops them out of the water," Keren said, finishing his thought. "But who among us would steal fertilized eggs?" She frowned, disgusted.

"Computer, identify life-forms in Vanìmel sector zero-four-seven," Ezri said.

"Eighteen Yrythny life-forms in grid zero-four-seven."

Imagining the anguish his own people endured while trying to procreate successfully, Shar was struck by how having an abundance of offspring shifted one's paradigm. Wondering about the reasons behind such a choice, he asked, "Why would Yrythny want to strip eggs from the mating ground?"

"Why would Yrythny blow up an aquaculture village?" Keren countered. "It's a mind game. With House Perian hosting the Compromise announcement, the eyes of Luthia and Vanìmel are focused on this hemisphere tonight. Stage it well and they'll have the attention of every Yrythny."

"Not if I have anything to say about it," Dax said firmly. She turned to Shar. "Options, Ensign?"

He'd been mulling over how to immobilize the raiders since they'd arrived. "It seems simple enough. The Perian authorities will be arriving here within the hour. In the meantime, we immobilize the hovercraft, secure the eggs in our custody and hold the criminals for the proper authorities."

Ezri nodded her approval. "Disable their engines with phasers. Make it impossible for them to move anywhere. They're far enough from shore that they can't swim to land. We'll beam-out the eggs. Proceed, Ensign."

"Aye, sir," Shar said. "Targeting phasers."

The cloaked figures on the first hovercraft scrambled for cover from the phaser fire, waving their arms to clear away the smoke churning out of the rear of the craft. Sensors indicated phasers had destroyed the engine and caused a minor water leak. But the authorities would arrive before the hovercraft sank.

Shar repeated the process, disabling both remaining hovercraft within minutes of each other. The fourth one, trying to avoid its companions' fate, led them on a brief chase; the hovercraft was no match for a Starfleet shuttle.

Circling the area in the *Sagan,* Shar double-checked sensors to make certain that no other raider craft had entered the area. Save the official vessel coming from Perian, the seas were clear.

"What about the eggs?" Jeshoh asked finally.

"We'll beam them out now," Ezri said.

Shar's scans revealed that only one vessel had successfully stripped eggs out of the mating grounds. Ezri beamed out the small storage crates and went with Keren to the rear of the shuttle to secure and properly store their cargo. Allowing viable eggs to be damaged now would be unconscionable.

Programming an elliptical trajectory around the mating grounds, Shar switched the navigating systems to auto and focused on keeping track of the criminals trapped on the hovercraft. Making a meaningful contribution to the final leg of their away mission satisfied him deeply. He hadn't wanted to admit it to Lieutenant Dax, but he did feel like his research efforts had been for naught. While rescuing fertilized Yrythny eggs from unscrupulous raiders didn't equate with making a scientific discovery that might have changed the planet's destiny, he would savor his small victory.

From around a peninsula jutting into the bay, a Perian hovership churned into the mating ground. Shar dispatched a directional flare, pointing the authorities to where the disabled hovercraft bobbed in the water.

"Shuttlecraft *Sagan* to the Perian authorities. There are four unauthorized hovercraft in the area. Transmitting locations of craft to you now. We have secured the harvested eggs and will be returning them to House Perian."

"Acknowledged, Sagan. *We have received your transmission. See you back home."*

Shar tapped Perian's coordinates into the navigation panel when Jeshoh touched his arm. "What can I do—" his voice trailed off at the sight of an Yrythny sidearm trained on his head. Jeshoh held the weapon flush against his chest, obscuring it from Dax and Keren's view. From the rear of the shuttle, Shar heard the women rearranging equipment to accommodate the eggs. They talked quietly between themselves.

"These crates belong to an acquaintance of mine," Jeshoh whispered. "We're going to deliver them. I'll provide you with coordinates. Once we clear Vanìmel's gravity well, you will set course as I direct and go to warp. We're running late, so please don't pull any tricks to provoke me into shooting you or Lieutenant Dax."

Locking out his adrenaline surge, Shar nodded. *Where does Jeshoh fit into the puzzle? I've never sensed hostility from him. He's Houseborn, what could he possibly want? Unless . . .* He wanted one answer before surrendering to Jeshoh's control. "Show me your hand."

Jeshoh smiled, raised his left arm to the square, palm forward.

The blue starburst.

"It was you in Keren's apartment that night," Shar whispered. "That's why she wasn't concerned afterward. Why would you be there . . . unless . . ." Wide-eyed, Shar stared at Jeshoh, his antennae tense with understanding.

"I went there to protect her, as I always have," he said wistfully. "We've chosen each other as consorts. Didn't she tell you that we were raised together? She swam ashore at House Perian."

"I assumed you met at the Assembly." Shar recalled the many hours he'd worked side by side with Keren and Jeshoh over the past week, their easy familiarity, their gentle ribbing. All of it fit together now.

"We can work together and no one looks askance if we're alone. But even that has become risky." Jeshoh sighed. "Our last hope was your people."

"My work's not done yet," Shar tried persuading him. "We still might have a chance. I can go back to Perian, work through the night—"

"We're out of chances. Time to leave," he said, resolutely.

Ezri called from the back, "Why are we gaining altitude? The ceremony starts in twenty minutes and I'm not sure how long these eggs can remain viable out of the water."

Uncertain as to what action Jeshoh would take, Shar said nothing as he entered the coordinates the Vice Chair whispered to him.

"Is there a problem, Ensign?" Ezri said at last.

Jeshoh and Shar exchanged looks. Shar kept silent.

The locks on the crate lids clicked from the rear of the shuttle. Shar heard Keren's light footsteps as she walked back to her seat. Ezri followed after. He sensed Keren pause and he willed her to take her seat. But she waited and Shar felt her studying him from behind.

"That worried, Ensign?" she said, her gruff voice laden with emotion.

Involuntarily, Shar raised a hand to his crown, realizing his antennae had become taut. She approached, her footfalls slow.

"Shar, what's going on?"

Shar sensed Ezri's irritation; heard her press past Keren, felt her step between him and Jeshoh. Her hands dropped to her sides. The lieutenant took a deep, steadying breath and she stood rigid.

Keren's hand curled over the top of Jeshoh's chair, her fingers trembling. "You have a weapon, Jeshoh."

Jesoh said nothing.

"I've never known you to carry a weapon, and yet you have that sidearm pointed at Shar."

"I'm defending something, Keren. I'm defending our right to have a life together."

She became visibly pale, shaking as she tried to maintain her control, even as her words became choked with sobs. "You were at the meeting—you agreed with me that the radicals' plan could destroy everything we've worked for. Please tell me you didn't join them, Jeshoh!"

Jeshoh turned his sidearm on Ezri; her eyes darted between Shar and Jeshoh. "You," he pointed at Ezri, "You take my seat."

She complied.

"If you do this, Jeshoh, we could lose it all. Nothing has to change. We can continue our struggle honorably," Keren pleaded.

"That's where you're wrong, my love. Without change, we have no future."

"Where are you taking us?" Ezri asked.

The shuttle had cleared the atmosphere. Cold starry space awaited outside the viewport.

"You'll find out soon enough," was Jeshoh's reply, and once again he turned his weapon on Shar. "Prepare to go to warp."

As Vaughn anticipated, the Cheka warship maintained a direct intercept course with the *Avaril,* a fact that satisfied him; he enjoyed a predictable adversary. True to Bowers's original estimate, the Cheka warship would intercept *Avaril's* meeting tonight, five hours out from Vanìmel. *"Meeting" is probably the wrong word,* Vaughn thought. *More like an "ambush."* The *Defiant* would level the playing field. He conceded there was a slim chance that the Yrythny leadership had masterminded Nog's kidnapping, but his gut told him Chieftain J'Maah would be caught unawares when the Cheka finally showed up. Bowers continued to monitor communications from both the *Avaril* and the Cheka warship, hoping that additional information would be revealed.

Meanwhile, the crew of the *Defiant* worked; no one had any desire to leave much to chance.

For the full shift before the showdown, every crewmember perfected his or her roles. Vaughn had walked about, first observing Chief Chao's transporter simulations, moving along to Prynn who studied the lay of the sector the *Defiant* would be flying through. Together, they visited the database for ideas to make evasive maneuvers more effective. On the bridge, Bowers analyzed every snippet of data the sensors revealed about the Cheka warship to devise their strategy. Lankford, one of their conn officers, upgraded the *Defiant's* navigational database with the starcharts purloined from the Cheka with, among other things, web weapon locations. Vaughn admired the crew's single-minded intensity.

Foremost among the single-minded was engineering. Nog's team had been assigned the most critical tasks. Ensigns Permenter, Senkowski and Leishman had hid out in a lab, working with surprising focus considering their long hours over the past twelve days. Or maybe their dedication wasn't surprising: they worked on behalf of their beloved chief.

Permenter had quickly taken to the idea of a noisemaker, once Vaughn had explained the twentieth- and twenty-first-century tactic.

"So when an aircraft or a submarine was targeted with a missile, a noisemaker was released, tricking the missile into fixing on the noisemaker instead of the intended target?" she had reasoned.

"Exactly," Vaughn had answered, pleased that she'd readily caught on to the idea.

"In this case, we want the *Avaril*'s shuttle to be the noisemaker," she had chewed her fingernails absently. "Trying to trick the Cheka into thinking that they're seeing two *Avarils*. Mess with their sensors. Possibly project a false visual."

"Again correct. Can you do it?"

She had nodded. "Yes . . . But you realize the real *Avaril* could still be attacked."

"In a situation like this, I'll take fifty-fifty odds over a hundred percent any day."

"Good point, sir," Permenter had agreed. "I'll get right on it."

Vaughn had smiled as he left engineering. *Whether we rescue Nog—whether the* Avaril *survives—may come down to how good they are at their jobs. They'll want to make him proud.*

Vaughn continued surveying the ship, stem to stern; he wasn't looking for anything specific, more like feeling his way around, renewing his acquaintance with an old friend. When the battle began, he needed to know who he was in the trenches with, to trust her without hesitation. Should the Cheka ship suddenly attack or if the *Avaril* proved to be a foe, Vaughn was prepared to go on the offensive. *Defiant* needed to be prepared for whatever she faced, for good or ill.

Quiet pervaded; all crewmembers soberly focused. If Vaughn was right, they had one chance at rescuing Nog. One chance. No one wanted to be the reason they lost another friend. Roness's loss over the Vahni homeworld was still fresh in their hearts and minds.

Having finished his review of the lower decks, Vaughn circled by transporter bay 1 where Chao rechecked the system, and then on to the bridge. He replicated a cup of *raktajino,* took his place in the captain's chair, and waited with the rest of them.

Because Shar had programmed the coordinates into the flight controls, Jeshoh rotated Ezri and Shar between piloting duties, anticipating that frazzled nerves might "accidentally" send them off course. Ezri had lost track of the number of hours they'd been flying, but she knew that dawn on Vanìmel was imminent.

When Ezri exchanged places with Shar, he immediately buried his attention in his padds. She couldn't fathom what he'd be working on at a time like this—or how he could focus. *If only I had access to weapons! I'm an excellent shot and could take Jeshoh down in nothing flat.* At the outset, she'd agreed to travel and work unarmed. Personal phasers were locked up in one of the shuttle's aft storage lockers. With little else to do, she eavesdropped on the interplay between the two Yrythny. Ezri wondered why she hadn't pegged them as lovers. Maybe her sense about such things was backfiring on her. She kept her eyes on her console, listening as Jeshoh tried, once more, to lure Keren into a conversation.

"Sending the Wanderers away to colonies won't solve our problem," he argued. "We still can't be together. Isn't that why we joined the underground? To find a way we can be together?"

"Orchestrating terrorist attacks on aquaculture villages won't solve our problems either," she hissed. "Nor will trading eggs to the Cheka for weapons to use against the Houseborn. When the Cheka steal our offspring, you're outraged. But now you sacrifice our young to our enemies?"

"We've sought to change our world since we were younglings. We vowed to do whatever was necessary, to make whatever sacrifice was required. This is the required sacrifice, Keren. These eggs aren't ours. They belong to those who deny us our chance to have offspring. We owe them nothing."

"This trade offers no hope for my people. Or for us," Keren said. Ezri listened as the argument volleyed back and forth, until

Keren refused to respond to Jeshoh's pleas. If only she'd anticipated this, she might have been able to work something into the treaty about the Houseborn-Wanderer taboos. *Dangerous relationships were a Dax specialty,* she thought wryly. Hadn't she been willing to accept the consequence of reassociation to be with Lenara? The torrid, consuming kind of love—that kind of passion—prompted the most irrational behavior.

"Lieutenant," Shar whispered. "I think I've got it."

Dax turned and saw Shar's antennae trembling with excitement. *The boy will never be a poker player.* "You've got what, Shar?"

"A preliminary genetic answer. But it will only help these two if Jeshoh can be convinced to forgo the trade."

"Pass it over," she ordered, taking the padd from Shar. Only a little of Jadzia's scientific training had been in genetics, but she knew enough to interpret Shar's data. He was absolutely correct: these findings were nothing short of astonishing.

Extrapolating the future path of genetic drift for both the Wanderers and the Houseborn, Shar's models predicted that selective mutations in Wanderer DNA indicated that they, not the Houseborn, were the next step in Yrythny evolution. The creativity and cleverness that made them innovative artists and engineers coupled with their ability to adapt to the environment insured long-term survival.

On the other side, lacking the resilience of the Wanderers (and because of heavy interbreeding), Houseborn DNA would weaken over time, bringing on problems not unlike those now facing the Andorians. Over the generations, the Houseborn would become vulnerable to chromosomal maladies that would spell their end as a species.

The solution, ironically, was that intermating among Houseborn and Wanderers would create the genetic diversity the Yrythny species needed to survive. If present taboos and traditions continued—Wanderer sterilization, the Houseborn narrowing of the gene pool, Wanderer females not being allowed to reproduce—the Yrythny would spiral toward exinction. In fact, a reasonable conclusion was that the "Wanderer traits" were appearing precisely in order to assure the Yrythny's survival as a species.

"This is incredible, Shar," Ezri whispered.

Shar nodded his head, appearing very pleased.

A sensor went off on Ezri's board. *Sagan* was rapidly approaching two much larger vessels. One seemed to be the *Avaril.* The other—

"The Cheka," Keren moaned.

"You have to tell them," Shar whispered to Ezri.

"Tell us what?" Jeshoh said.

"Shar's research," Ezri said, holding up the padd. "This is the answer you've been looking for." *Please let this be enough to put a stop to this insanity.*

"Not offworld colonization, Lieutenant?" Jeshoh said, cynically, walking toward Ezri. "What about the magnificent compromise you negotiated with such skill among my fellow Assemblymen? Peace at last for Vanìmel! All the Wanderers have to do is leave."

"It's colonization, not exile!" Ezri insisted. "There are many cultures in my part of the galaxy where those unhappy with the status quo start over again somewhere else. Earth, Vulcan—" She stopped herself, knowing the names would be meaningless to Jeshoh. "The point is that colonization has often been the most viable solution to the kind of dilemma facing the Yrythny, and it's *always* been a better option than genocide."

"Are you trying to convince me or yourself, Lieutenant?" Jeshoh asked. "If the former, then how is it that you now believe the answers we've been looking for are on that little device?"

Ezri sighed and shut her eyes. "Because even though colonization is a better option than genocide, *this* is a better option than colonization." Keying the padd to display the text in Yrythny, Ezri passed the padd to Jeshoh.

He perused the results, paging through each section of Shar's research until he reached the end. Tossing the padd on the deck, he laughed. "You expect me to believe this? Days of discussions and analyses come up empty. But in our darkest hour, you hand me research that purports to offer me the very thing Keren and I have been fighting for? It's a hoax. It has to be."

Ezri bit her lip. "The lateness of the research is partially my fault. I wasn't as supportive as I should have been in helping Ensign ch'Thane pursue his study."

"So you say now, Lieutenant," Jeshoh said.

"Persuade him, Ezri," Shar urged.

"I appreciate your efforts, Shar," Jeshoh said with a sigh. "Your heart is well aligned, but the Cheka are going to get their eggs, the blockade will end, the underground will receive arms, and the fight between the Houseborn and the Wanderers will finally be a fair one. Proceed to the rendezvous point." He walked back to his seat, still tightly gripping the sidearm.

As the senior officer, Ezri knew devising a plan fell to her. She considered Shar and Jeshoh, who embodied the extremes of reason and emotion, and puzzled over this impasse. In lieu of a phaser, she could pull out a few Klingon martial arts moves that had worked on a belligerent drunk. Startle Jeshoh. Throw him off his game. But that was Jadzia. Tobin had done that thing with the transporter to defeat a Romulan. Clever enough, but Jeshoh would be dead. She had no desire to kill anyone unless she had no other choice. Torias would do some daredevil flying to throw off his enemy, but then Shar or Keren might be hurt. And . . . Emony . . .

Stop it.

Her head hurt. She massaged her neck against the headrest, wishing away the voices in her mind. Clamoring for attention, the voices talked over one another; she couldn't think straight through the noise.

"Ezri, you're a counselor," Shar whispered anxiously. "Talk him out of it."

She stared at Shar.

Through many lives, Dax had averted crises with clever talk, brilliant (occasionally crazy) technological twists, raw nerve, un-hesitating bravery and a few well-placed punches. Of these tools, none were Ezri's, save maybe the bravery. Ezri alone had studied the workings of the mind and it was Ezri who needed to fix this. *Not Curzon. Not Lela. Not Jadzia. Ezri.*

Licking her lips, she took a deep, controlled breath, willing her respirations to steady her. Ezri rolled her head back and forth, stretching her muscles. A class she'd taken on crisis negotiations—what was the procedure? Build a rapport between perpetrator and negotiator. Focus on the perpetrator's needs. The time she'd spent with Jeshoh gave her a powerful advantage. Responsibility, loyalty and integrity motivated him. Appeal to those traits. She rose from her seat, resting one hand on each chair.

"Jeshoh, I know you're concerned about reaching the rendezvous on time, but maybe we should take a moment, settle down. Eat? We missed dinner at Perian. The hour is late. I know I'm sleepy. Aren't you a little hungry?"

He turned to Keren, "Are you hungry? Lieutenant Dax could bring you food."

"Thirsty," she conceded. "Something to drink."

He's more concerned about her needs than his own. That's where I have leverage. "Keren, water? Fruit juice?"

"Water is fine," she said.

"Shar, take conn, would you?" Ezri said, and went to replicate Keren's drink. Handing it to her, she said, "You look tired, Keren. Take the copilot's chair." She paused. "If that's all right with you, Jeshoh."

He nodded. A tenderness suffused Jeshoh's face as he watched Keren move to the front.

Assuming Keren's seat, Ezri asked Jeshoh, "Are you sure I can't get you anything?"

"Just make sure Ensign ch'Thane takes us to the rendezvous." He refused her attempts to engage him.

Ezri leaned over, speaking so only Jeshoh could hear her. "Keren's exhausted. This day has taken a toll on her."

"We'll be done soon enough."

Now to induce doubt about the viability of his choice. "I wouldn't count on that. You and I have both been in negotiation situations. They can drag on and on." Ezri shrugged, stole a glance at Jeshoh who seemed to be listening. She continued, "Your contact could back out at the last minute—the Cheka could change their minds about the deal and demand higher payment. And then there's the question of how to get back to Vanìmel without the defense forces on Luthia coming after you. We could be on the run for a while."

"We can handle it," he said stubbornly. Distracted, he twirled the weapon around his fingers.

"But if you're on the run, you won't be able to bring the Cheka weapons back to the underground."

Jeshoh hesitated. "We'll find a way."

"And Keren? She doesn't deserve to never be able to return to Vanìmel."

"We would be free. Together."

"Until when? Until my commander and the *Defiant* catches up with you? Until the *Sagan* flies into a Cheka web weapon and you're cooked? And then there's the Yrythny military who will hunt you down."

"When we're done, I'll leave you and Shar somewhere. Your commander can find you."

Ezri watched Keren, flaccid and pale, in the front seat, her chin propped on her hands, her shoulders slumped. *He had to see what his actions were costing her.* Believing she'd found a wedge to pry open Jeshoh's defenses, Ezri resolved to persist. "Oh, I know I'll be fine. And so will Shar, but what about Keren? Look what this situation is doing to her. It's a lot of stress. Especially since I know she's coming into her fertile cycle soon."

"There will be other seasons. If all goes according to plan, next year Keren and I will be able to go into the water together, without hiding."

"If you live that long," Ezri muttered.

"What?"

"Nothing." She considered the flight controls, trying to figure out how much time she had to devise an alternative plan. If she couldn't convince him to give up his scheme willingly, she would use force. At their present course and speed, she guessed they had 10 minutes before circumstances required she act decisively.

"Say it," Jeshoh persisted.

He's listening, at least. I need to keep talking. "The odds are against Keren surviving this adventure you're taking her on. The *Sagan* can't travel indefinitely without refueling. And without energy, life support will dwindle, and the replicators won't work. Then there's the problem of living on the run. The fugitive lifestyle is hard and for you to choose it for her. . . . But I'm certain you'll find a way to make it work." She shrugged and offered him a wan smile.

He fixed his attention on Ezri for a long moment. She remained composed under his scrutiny, saying nothing further.

Without a response, he vacated his seat and approached Shar, though he kept his weapon trained on Ezri. "Shar, a shuttle will launch from the *Avaril.* When the shuttle crosses over from the

Avaril to the Cheka warship, my contact will instruct us where to transport the eggs."

He's still planning on carrying out the trade, but he doesn't sound quite as confident as he did at the start. Ezri still needed to know how the exchange was supposed to happen. If needs be, at the last minute, she would risk changing courses. "I'm curious—are you going aboard the Cheka ship, Jeshoh?" she said smoothly. "Or are you supposed to transport the eggs to them and they in turn will transport the weapons to you? Or is there another ship that's taking the weapons?"

Jeshoh appeared legitimately startled by Ezri's question. "I—I—I don't know. I was supposed to receive my instructions when I arrived."

"I'm not trying to tell you what to do, but open-ended deals usually end badly. Too much room for a double-cross."

"That won't happen."

"Yeah. But you don't know for sure. Think about Keren, Jeshoh. We should transport her to the *Avaril*. At least she'd have a better chance of getting out of this alive."

Twisting to consider his lover, Jeshoh's weapon hand bobbled. Ezri thought she might be able to wrest it from him, but if she failed, he wouldn't listen to anything else she said. She elected to be patient; the *Sagan's* cause was better served if she hung back, waited, and watched.

"Shuttlebay doors on *Avaril* are opening," Shar announced.

But not for long. Either Jeshoh would choose or she would.

18

Other than the few naps that interspersed her reading, Kira worked through dawn and into the morning hours, both watching the Promenade cleanup efforts proceed from monitors in ops and reading the negotiation transcripts. Considering the edginess suffusing the station, she was thankful she had an office where she could sequester herself with a desk full of work. The Promenade merchants had contacted her every half hour, wanting updates, complaining about broken merchandise or malfunctioning equipment. Several vedeks had protested in person, resenting the cancellation of shrine services. Parents, spouses, children and lovers affiliated with anyone involved in the fight worried about the well-being of their loved ones. Kira could say, conclusively, that the only people unquestionably happy today were Thriss, whose capable assistance had prompted Dr. Girani to ask if she'd accept regular shift assignments in the infirmary for the duration of her stay, and the children, for whom school had been cancelled.

Reports to Akaar and the first minister had gone as well as she could have hoped. While Akaar had focused on the long-term, probable outcomes following such an outpouring of hostility, Shakaar saw the night's disturbance more like a field commander would see any turn of luck that went against his forces, be it bad weather, inaccurate intelligence or unforeseen cunning on the part of the enemy. He went into counterattack mode, immediately strategizing as to how Bajor would hurdle this latest obstacle. His predictable unhappiness increased when he heard the number of Militia personnel involved in the fight. A Militia Internal Affairs officer was ordered to report to Deep Space 9 to review the individual cases. The officer would mete out whatever disciplinary actions were called for, saving Kira from the detestable task. Now that it was approaching noon, she was due to brief Shakaar, in person.

While waiting in the antechamber to his office, Kira made distracting small talk with Sirsy. She had spent the last hour trying to formulate the best way to present what she'd concluded from her night's reading—that Macet's concerns were founded in fact, not supposition. Almost from the start, Asarem's approach had been to block rather than negotiate; she refused to budge on any point, even those already conceded in the postwar Accords.

As soon as Minister Kren exited, Kira ventured in to see Shakaar. With his usual energy, he bounded about his office, loading up a travel bag that lay open on his desk. Monitors running newsfeeds from Bajor and adjoining systems flashed breaking reports on screens lining the walls. From appearances, Shakaar kept continual tabs on many situations.

"Nerys!" he said with a smile. "Come in, come in."

"You're leaving the station?" Kira wondered if the Promenade brawl, combined with the vandalized conference room, had led his advisers to recommend that he return to Bajor until the station situation stabilized. An attack on Shakaar's staff or offices—even worse, an assassination attempt—would send any peace efforts spiraling into a quagmire, possibly even derailing the transition into the Federation. *He would hate having to run from a fight,* Kira thought, remembering how eagerly he plunged into the unknown, dealing with whatever challenges lurked ahead without fear for his own well-being.

"Yes and no. The Federation meetings are in recess, and I've decided to use the opportunity to accept Captain Mello's invitation to tour the *Gryphon* during one of its patrols of the system." He removed several items from his desk—a book, a plain metal case, several isolinear rods—and placed them neatly into his travel bag before he started searching the office for something else. "I expect to return to the station the day after tomorrow."

"Sounds like fun," Kira said, wondering what it was he couldn't find and whether she should help him look. She perused the items scattered over his desk, trying to imagine what a commander-in-chief took along for a visit to inspect the troops, but saw nothing she considered important.

"Anything new from Lieutenant Ro's investigation?" He asked, his voice muffled as he ducked under his desk.

Opening and closing desk drawers, throwing opening cabinets and shuffling through padds, Shakaar never stopped moving. Kira felt dizzy watching him. "It appears the toxic combination of gambling, liquor and rivalry exploded at Quark's. We haven't been able to ascertain who threw the first punch, but it seems that after the initial taunts, it was only a matter of friends coming to the aid of friends. Everything escalated from there. No fatalities, thankfully, but at least two dozen serious injuries." She held out to him the padd she'd brought with her. "You'll find Ro and Dr. Girani's complete reports here. We're keeping all pertinent information out of the main data core until both sides can agree what details are relevant to the station population. Everyone is anxious, sir, as you might imagine."

Shakaar accepted the padd, but didn't look at it. "Understandably. And without any sign of tensions abating soon. You know, Nerys, I was thinking . . ."

"Sir?"

"We've both been working hard. We could use a break. How about joining me at the holosuites for a round of hang gliding off the Cliffs of Bole when I get back from the *Gryphon?*"

Kira snorted indelicately. "I think you've forgotten how much I dislike holosuite adventures, First Minister. I'll have to pass, but thanks for the invitation."

"Nerys, please. We're alone in my office—it's just us. You can call me Edon." He held up the padd Kira had given him and quickly scrolled through the contents. "So Quark agreed to the settlement proposed by Gul Macet and my office?"

"He groused about the *yarmok* sauce he lost, but Ro knew he'd been stashing it in a cargo bay for the last six months, so he can't claim it as one of last night's losses." She owed Ro for acting as the intermediary between Quark and her office. If she'd had to deal with Quark's whining on top of everything else today, she might have been here informing Shakaar of another homicide on the station.

Shakaar tossed the padd into his travel bag. "Sounds like you have everything under control, then."

"I hope so, sir," Kira said. She remained standing, fixed in front of his desk, uncertain as to how to transition into the next topic, especially since Shakaar appeared to be done with her. For all her desire to remain uninvolved in the politics surrounding her, she knew the time had come for her, as commander of the station, to voice her concerns about a process that impacted them all. "Minister?" she said at last.

"Yes?" his said, his tone and expression obscure.

Once upon a time, she would have been able to read him. How she lamented the gradual erosion of trust between them! In the past, she could have—would have—come to Shakaar with anything, spoken plainly and known that she wouldn't have been misunderstood. Now, she had no idea what to expect from him. Kira took a deep breath. "While I was waiting for reports to come in over the last eight hours, I took the liberty of reading the transcripts of the negotiations between Ambassador Lang and Minister Asarem."

He didn't appear surprised or concerned. "Haven't yet had the chance myself. How's it going?"

At last, an opening! "I'm glad you asked that, sir."

"Edon, Nerys," he said with a smile.

"Edon," Kira repeated. "To be blunt, I think Minister Asarem's approach is unreasonable."

He looked at her blankly. "You have a basis for that conclusion?"

"I've reviewed the transcripts of the meetings, and it seems very clear to me that the second minister is obstructing the initiatives you began when the war ended, to have Bajor spearhead and coordinate the Cardassian relief efforts."

"How so?"

"Those initiatives were designed to be progressive," Kira reminded him. "We're supposed to be helping Cardassia not just survive the next five years, but get back to being a self-sufficient civilization under its new democratic regime. But everything Asarem is doing seems designed to keep Cardassia crippled and dependent on outside aid indefinitely. I think she's made this personal."

Shakaar's eyebrows went up. "That's a strong accusation, Colonel. What made you look into this?"

The time of reckoning is here, Nerys. Kira made sure Shakaar was looking directly into her eyes before she answered. She needed him to see that she told the truth, that she had no hidden agenda. "Gul Macet asked me to review the transcripts."

"Nerys—"

"I wouldn't be here if I didn't think his concerns had merit."

"To do this right, you shouldn't go around—"

"Old grudges are getting in the way of our delegation's doing its job. The Federation, with cause, could delay our petition again if they think we're not prepared to be forthright in our dealings."

Shakaar frowned. "You haven't taken this to Akaar—"

"Of course not!" she said, indignant at his suggestion.

"Because if you had, Colonel, I'd be questioning your loyalty."

Kira took a deep, steadying breath before answering. "I came to *you* because I've been implementing your initiatives toward Cardassia for the last six months—initiatives I believe in—and I'm seeing the original intent of those initiatives being compromised." She locked eyes with Shakaar. "And more to the point, I came out of my own sense of right and wrong. And what Asarem is doing is *wrong.*"

They lingered in uncomfortable silence until Shakaar at last said, "You're right and I apologize for overreacting. It's just that knowing who your friends and enemies are these days is harder than ever."

No one knows that better than me, Kira thought. *So which are you, Edon?*

Shakaar, however, seemed to feel that they'd resolved their disagreement; he smiled pleasantly. "Send the meeting transcripts to Sirsy for my database. I'll look into the matter personally."

Relief washed over Kira. "Thank you, sir."

"No need for that. I realize what you must think of Minister Asarem, but you have to know she's an absolute patriot. Her love for Bajor is as deep as yours. While she may seem harsh and inflexible, she stands on equal footing with you in terms of her loyalty. Separating her personal views on the Cardassian questions from the need for political expediency has always been a struggle for her. I think you two are more alike than you know."

Kira winced involuntarily at the comparison, thinking of the rigid, inflexible politician she had observed, what was it, only yesterday? It felt like an eternity ago. *Maybe once I was like Asarem. Maybe it's true if you still think of me as I once was. Now, I don't think you know me.* Edon would never see the subtle distinctions. "I'll go, then. If there's nothing else . . . ?"

Shakaar waved her out the door, and as he had said, Minister Asarem had arrived for her meeting. An unspoken greeting passed between the women. Kira hoped that in the future, likely after the talks had wrapped up, she could get to know Asarem as the well-intentioned woman Kira knew she must be. Until then, politeness would have to suffice.

Later in the day, when word came from Macet that Minister Asarem's office had proposed resuming talks the following morning, Kira exulted. To celebrate, she left ops early, planning on rewarding herself with an hour at the spa for a mineral soak. It pleased her to walk through the Promenade, now bustling with normal activity. Particularly gratifying was seeing the long lines waiting for admission to the grand opening of the Ziyal exhibit. For the first time since the Cardassians' arrival, Kira felt hopeful.

Once she arrived back in her quarters, she opened up her next day's schedule and cleared out a block of time where she could sit in on the talks. Not so she could gloat, or take credit for helping to break through a seemingly insurmountable barrier. Kira wanted to be there so she could one day tell her grandchildren about how she witnessed the day when Cardassia and Bajor began forging a fragile peace.

As a man of action, waiting was never Quark's strength. Under circumstances such as these, he failed to understand why he, Chairman of the Promenade Merchants' Association, wouldn't be given due deference, VIP admission, a priority position. One of the downfalls of Federation philosophy that Bajor was so hot on embracing was the misguided notion that social status should, for the most part, be irrelevant. Otherwise, he'd be at the front of the line instead of waiting with all the other plebeians to see the exhibit.

And who decided *not* to charge admission? Talk about a missed opportunity. Maybe he could come up with a promotional tie-in for the bar. *Hmmmmm . . .*

On the plus side, the longer he waited, the more time he had to spend with Laren. She wasn't in a terribly talkative mood tonight, not like he could blame her after breaking up a midnight riot and subsequently having little or no sleep. She seemed content to watch the people in line instead of gazing at him. He needed to fix that.

"Um, Laren?"

"Yeah, Quark?"

"Thanks again for getting everything paid for. There was no way I was going to ask Rom to float me a loan while I argued with the colonel." Gratitude, real or feigned, tended to grease the conversational wheels.

"It didn't take much convincing. I think part of her regrets the way she treated you that night at the reception. But paying the repair bills for the fracas is as close to an apology as you're likely to get."

Quark held up his hands. "I'm not complaining. As nonapologies go, I could do worse."

"Expecting coverage for the *yarmok* sauce was pushing it, though."

"A Ferengi can try. The 10th Rule of Acquisition: *Greed is eter-*

nal. I wouldn't be me without it." He grinned amiably. "So you got me the latinum. You have any pull with making this line move?"

"You complain about waiting again, I'm going home."

"Right, right," Quark said quickly. No need to make his tired and cranky companion more tired and cranky.

The line trudged forward a few steps, brushing against the line ropes as another group was admitted to the exhibit. A pile of program cards outlining the exhibit's contents sat in a stack. Ro removed one and began reading while they walked.

When they stopped again, Ro turned to Quark and studied him thoughtfully. "You knew Ziyal, didn't you? Who was she?"

In his mind, Quark conjured up a picture of the wide-eyed child-woman. He wasn't one to be sentimental about much—life and death happened in the course of business—but Ziyal had a genuine sweetness that couldn't help but touch you. "She was a good kid. Really. Good isn't generally a word I use to describe Cardassians—ruthless, cold, predatory, devious—all qualities I can appreciate, to be sure—but good? Except Natima, and you already know she's amazing. But, Ziyal. She was special. Never could figure out how a bastard like Dukat popped off a kid like her." Quark *tsked* as he thought of the former prefect.

"What do you remember most?" Ro asked.

"She called me 'Sir' or 'Quark,' instead of 'Hey you, Ferengi,' like most Cardassians. She'd sit on her stool, talking with Jake or the colonel—even drink root beer with him—and they'd yammer on about holovids and games and such." Had it only been a few years since she died? It felt like another lifetime when all of them had been together on the station . . . Jadzia, Odo, Rom, Leeta, O'Brien, Captain Sisko, Jake, and . . . Quark stopped. No, Ziyal had her weakness. "The only thing she did that didn't make much sense was falling for Garak. If Ziyal was good, Garak was just wrong. You could never really trust him, except to be himself, and that was the problem, because no one ever really figured him out."

Ro nodded. "I've learned a lot about Garak since coming to the station."

Quark grunted. *I can only imagine. Odo must have kept quite a file on Garak. But Garak never got to Ziyal. No, I think she got to him.* Ro continued looking at him expectantly, probably waiting for him to expound further on Garak. He shrugged. "I think Ziyal's death changed Garak. Who knows? Maybe that's what finally snapped whatever loyalties he still had to the old Cardassia. You just never knew with him."

Their group reached the entrance. A security officer scanned their retinas and then waved a tricorder over them, searching for weapons. Satisfied with the results, he waved them in.

The guests wound past a wall screen scrolling through an official welcome from the Bajoran government. Whatever chatter had been underway when guests entered dissolved promptly when they were presented with the first painting. A deferential hush filled the room, more like at a place of worship than an art exhibit. Even Quark, who prided himself on being a connoisseur of any and all valuable art commodities from the famous and infamous, found himself lacking any words to describe what he felt.

Suspended from the ceiling was an oil painting on matte black canvas. Monochromatic tints and shades in juxtaposed violent and graceful brush strokes carved the one-dimensional surface as surely as a sculptor's chisel would stone. A straight-on perspective of a face dominated the center, with two sharply geometric side profiles adjoining the central face at unwieldy angles. Surrounded with tempestuous swirls of gray and whites, shiny black triangles, presumably hair, sprayed out in wakes behind the heads.

Ro had immersed herself in reading the biographical texts scrolling across the monitors lining the walls, but Quark remained fixed in front of the painting, pondering. He grabbed Ro by the elbow.

"What?" she said, puzzled.

"Look." He nudged his head toward the painting.

"I did."

"No, *look*. That's the answer to your question. Who is Ziyal. Look."

Standing shoulder to shoulder with Quark while the other guests milled about, Ro contemplated the painting. Quark watched her eyes following the eruptions of color, the soothing organic forms mingled with the stark triangles and squares. Nodding her head almost imperceptibly, she leaned closer into Quark and gave his hand a tight squeeze.

They stood together until another guest, hoping to obtain a better view, asked them to move along.

Her step buoyant, Kira passed through the security checkpoint, headed down a hallway and turned a corner . . . *Wait a minute,* she thought, puzzled. Ambassador Lang, Gul Macet and several of Lang's aides huddled tightly together. The schedule indicated that the lunch break wasn't due for another hour. Why would they be . . . unless . . . Tense with uncertainty, Kira strode toward the Cardassians. They parted when they recognized who was approaching.

"Colonel, please join us," Ambassador Lang said, opening her arms.

Kira took a spot beside Lang. "What's going on? I thought you all would be in the conference room. I'd heard opening statements were scheduled to begin an hour ago and—"

Macet interrupted her. "Minister Asarem announced that Bajor would be withdrawing from any diplomatic proceedings until after completing its probationary period for joining the Federation."

A mountaintop avalanche inundating her path might have shocked Kira as much as Macet's revelation. Maybe she was still asleep. Maybe this was some stress-induced bad dream . . . "What? That's not how things were supposed to go. At least, Minister Shakaar never said anything about postponing the talks. I thought Minister Asarem would take a more open approach, not shut things down altogether." Her head spun with the implications of Macet's words.

"Apparently, Minister Asarem believes that binding Bajor to a path independent of the one Bajor is forging with the Federation is a waste of time," Lang explained patiently, whatever shock she might have felt gradually giving way to the sadness brimming in her eyes. "Existing treaties between the Federation and Cardassia will apply equally with Bajor—there's no need to negotiate something separately."

This is ludicrous! Kira refused to accept this turn of events. "You've talked to First Minister Shakaar, Ambassador? He can't have signed off on this." She scanned the lobby, peered down the hall, hoping to see evidence of a Bajoran presence, but found none. *Cowards turned tail and ran.*

Sullen-faced, Lang said, "I'm told Minister Shakaar is currently unavailable."

Kira took a deep breath and started pacing. "All right. Let's say, just for the sake of argument, that Asarem's position really is what's best for Bajor. Why *not* wait until after the transition to settle this—why now? Why push it?"

"Ironically, our situation isn't unlike Bajor's was seven years ago," Lang replied. "The allies govern our territories while Cardassia Prime struggles to rebuild and redefine itself. A single epidemic and what remains of our civilization could be brought to its knees.

"We can't rebuild without outside help, we can't secure outside help unless we prove we can be trusted. If we fail to obtain the assistance we need, our world will revert to the same principles that led to our downfall. We are fated to repeat history unless we can prove we can move beyond the place where Cardassia began to go terribly wrong—and that's with the Bajoran Occupation. If we can start again with new Cardassia forging ties with new Bajor, my people stand a chance."

And the only way my people stand a chance, for all the same reasons. "I'll do what I can," Kira said, intending to go straight to the minister's office and demand to be seen or block Asarem's doorway until she agreed to see her. Kira tolerated the vagaries of politics because she understood that government's rigidly defined rules and protocols had to be navigated somehow, but this kind of game playing didn't serve anyone. She shot off down the hallway, back toward the security checkpoint.

"Colonel, we don't expect you—" Lang began, walking after her.

Kira stopped. "No, I know you don't expect it, I expect it of myself. Asking another generation to fix this is wrong—for both sides." In her gut, Kira knew she spoke truth. Her mind was clear, she believed the Prophets guided her. "This ends here. This thing between us will end *now.*"

After a brunch stop, Phillipa had come into her office to find that Dr. Girani had left a list of individuals he was recommending for anger management counseling. She'd encountered a few of the more surly characters during her time helping out the previous night so she had expected some referrals, but this many? If she followed standard

Starfleet protocol for anger management therapy, she'd have half her daily appointment schedule filled with Girani's recommendations alone. But because there were disciplinary and incarceration issues pending, Phillipa recognized how vital her services were. What she wouldn't give for the odd, criminally insane schizophrenic or even marriage counseling to provide a little diversity. She sighed and ordered the computer to search the database for all the latest research on anger control issues. Maybe there was something new and exciting she could use to throw a new spin on her therapy sessions. She'd just reached the good part of "Guided Imagery and Brain Chemistry," about the effectiveness of role playing in holographic scenarios, when a chime notified her that she had visitors. Knowing that she didn't have any appointments scheduled until after alpha shift, she ordered the door open, hoping yet another crisis hadn't erupted.

Hand in hand with Dizhei, Thriss entered. Phillipa smiled reflexively. Thriss had progressed from small, subtle steps like remembering her appointments without reminders and choosing to eat breakfast with her bondmates to more noticeable moves forward such as pride in her physical appearance. No longer dull and listless, her straight white hair, interspersed with small braids, shimmered. She chose elegant, attractive clothing instead of rumpled, careworn caftans and smocks. When she walked, she took long, purposeful strides instead of allowing Dizhei or Anichent to pull her along. Her antennae relaxed, responding to pleasure, not just anger. *Some excellent progress with this patient and we started after she instigated a fight at Quark's. I can only hope I have such good luck with the other night's rioters,* she thought.

"I know I don't have an appointment," Thriss began apologetically.

Dizhei maintained a placid demeanor, smiling indulgently at her bondmate's earnestness. Phillipa had discovered that while Thriss tended to be emotionally obvious, Dizhei was the opposite. Yes, she was sweet-natured, always talkative, eagerly discussing her bondmates, but more reticent about herself. But from time to time when Thriss began rhapsodizing about Shar, Phillipa observed that Dizhei's smile tightened noticeably. *There's obviously subtext here . . . I need to get her in for a session. She has the too-bright smile on now. Interesting.*

"Don't worry about it. Have a seat," Phillipa gestured for her Andorian guests to make themselves comfortable in the visitors' chairs or the therapist's couch facing her. Thriss hadn't been sitting a minute before she started wiggling her foot, twisting it around the chair leg. *Whatever it is, she certainly is anxious today.*

"This isn't really about therapy either," Thriss said. "I probably shouldn't be here, but I didn't know who else to ask and—"

Phillipa shushed her. "Ask."

Thriss exchanged looks with Dizhei and took a deep breath. "I heard a rumor that ops downloaded communications from the *Defiant* today, but with all the problems last night, no one has the time or inclination to check. Councellor zh'Thane is away with Admiral Akaar on Bajor so she can't ask."

"You want Shar's letter," Phillipa grinned. "No problem." She tapped a few commands into the computer, entered her authorization codes and was able to ascertain from the communications logs that indeed, a Gamma Quadrant transmission had been received an hour before. "It's here, but it's above my clearance level. Colonel Kira has to review and disperse the information, but I could check and see when that might happen."

"Would you?" Thriss scooted to the edge of her chair expectantly, placing her hands, palm down on the desk and drumming her fingers. "I don't want to cause problems."

"Relax. It'll be fine." Phillipa touched her combadge, "Counselor Matthias to ops."

"This is Ling. Go ahead."

"I have Shathrissía zh'Cheen, Ensign ch'Thane's bondmate, in my office. I was wondering when the communiqués from the *Defiant* would be distributed?"

"Colonel Kira reviewed them some time ago, and to my knowledge, all the personal messages went out to individual databases."

Thriss' incessant finger drumming suddenly stopped; she eased back into the chair, molding her shoulders to the curved backrest. In contrast, Dizhei remained poised, her antennae soft and flexible.

Phillipa reached across the desk and rested her hand over Thriss'. "Is it possible to check with the colonel to see if there was any word from Ensign ch'Thane?" she said to Ensign Ling.

"The colonel has asked not to be disturbed except in an emergency, but I'll relay your inquiry at the earliest opportunity."

"Thanks. Matthias out." Thriss shrunk before Phillipa's eyes. She tucked her legs beneath her and dropped her head on the armrest. Were it not for her shallow, ragged breaths, Phillipa might have worried that she'd stopped breathing.

Phillipa tightened her grip on Thriss' hand. "Don't jump to conclusions, Thriss. There might be something embedded or included in Commander Vaughn's datablock. Be patient. Colonel Kira has a lot to deal with right now."

The two bondmates exchanged a rush of whispered Andorii; Dizhei did most of the talking, finally resting a possessive hand on Thriss' knee. "Thriss has a shift with Dr. Girani. If you want to contact her, she'll be there until late this afternoon. Shall we go, *zh'yi?*"

"Wait." Phillipa looked between both Andorians, but directed her words at Dizhei since she believed Dizhei would need persuading. "Why doesn't Thriss stay here for a few minutes? We can talk a bit, and then I'll take her down to the infirmary."

But Dizhei had left her chair and was guiding Thriss along with a hand placed in the small of her back before Phillipa had finished speaking. The decision had been made, though how much input Thriss had was questionable. Once more, Phillipa reiterated her offer for on-the-spot counseling, but Thriss shook her head weakly and waved a good-bye.

Absently twirling a lock of hair between her fingers, Phillipa sat in her chair staring at the words filling her desktop screen like white noise. She filtered the last fifteen minutes through years of academic and field training, plus a healthy dose of intuition.

Not one logical interpretation of the scene she'd witnessed reassured her; every extrapolation she worked through had negative connotations. So she resolved to sit there and spin every potentiality until she came up with a positive outcome. She turned off her desk screen. There had to be a positive outcome somewhere. There had to be. For Thriss' sake. For all four of them.

Kira had no intention of calling ahead to warn Minister Asarem that she was on her way. She'd followed protocols and niceties until her mouth ached from trying to smile away her frustration. No more. The minister's office door slid open obediently on her order. Sitting behind her desk studying a tome of Bajoran law, Asarem appeared legitimately shocked to see her. Kira relished the advantage of surprise for only a second before walking right up to the side of her chair. She didn't want anything between them when she had this conversation.

"I don't recall that we had a meeting, Colonel," Asarem said, turning her chair toward Kira and offering a serene smile.

Good recovery. "We didn't. I let myself in."

"So I noticed," she said dryly.

"One of the few fringe benefits of being in command around here: there's no place on this station where I can't find you." After her conversation outside the conference room, she'd had the computer track Asarem's every move on the station.

Asarem tipped back in her chair, throwing her legs out in front of her as if she were stretching post-nap. "Manners and civil liberties never figure into your games of hide and seek?"

"Don't be clever with me, Asarem," Kira snipped. "We're both old hands at this. We can trade barbs and witticisms until we're hoarse, or we can have an honest discussion."

"I have nothing to discuss with you," she said dismissively. She snapped a law book closed and shoved it back on a shelf behind her desk where other old-fashioned volumes were stored. Thumbing a switch, Asarem made a show of pulling up her schedule. "I have state business to attend to, Colonel."

"Oh, I don't believe you do." Kira reached across Asarem's desk and turned off the desk screen. "Just what the hell were you thinking when you shut down the talks today? What's all this about waiting for Bajor to adopt the Federation's treaties with Cardassia?"

"It's a logical move," Asarem said, shoving Kira's arm off her desk. "Transitioning an entire planetary system into a completely new governmental form involves a lot more than making sure there aren't hurt feelings between neighbors."

Kira clenched her fists. She so wanted to punch something, but her hothead days were behind her. *Keep a steady course . . .* "This thing between us and Cardassia—this is our issue to resolve, not the Federation's. Passing it off for them to handle is cowardly."

"I resent that characterization." Asarem left her desk and exited down a private corridor.

Kira followed. She wished she could tie Asarem to a chair and force her to see reason, a tactic that worked effectively in the Resistance, but might earn her a court martial if she employed it here. No, she had to play by the minister's rules.

Asarem spoke to Kira as she walked. "Waiting to take on something of the magnitude of normalizing Bajoran/Cardassian relations until after the Federation is pragmatic. Why make promises we might not be able to keep once the Federation is in charge? Why duplicate efforts? We need to use our time to help Bajor." She turned into a side room, likely a records office. Pulling a stool out from beneath a desk, Asarem climbed atop it and started browsing the countless rows of padds, books, and scrolls.

Kira hopped up on the counter closest to where Asarem stood. "Bajor will never heal until we deal with the mistrust festering between us and Cardassia. We'll come into the Federation weak. We'll be hiding behind our mother's skirts."

"You're free to assume what you want, Colonel, but the decision is made." She removed a scroll and jumped off the stool. "It's not negotiable."

How could Asarem treat Bajor/Cardassia relations with the same indifferent concern that one might reserve for street signage? Kira grabbed Asarem by the shoulder. "This is wrong!"

With a swift elbow shove, the minister dislodged Kira's grip. She spun around, eyes blazing. "How *dare* you! You have no idea what this is about."

"I don't? Because it's pretty damn obvious what's happening here!" Kira shouted.

"You think you know it all," Asarem said through gritted teeth. She stepped closer to Kira. "You've always been that way. So self-righteous. Well this time, you're not even close." Turning on her heel, she half walked, half ran from the records room. Shoulder to shoulder, the women raced down the hall, surprised aides ducking out of the way right and left.

"If you do, as you claim, have Bajor's best interests at heart," Kira said, "then you and I want the same things. But from where I'm standing you and I couldn't be on more opposite sides."

"That's where you're wrong, Kira." She laughed bitterly. "The irony of all this is that you and I are on exactly the same side down to the last detail."

Kira halted in her tracks, wondering if in her anger she'd missed something Asarem had said previously, because she believed she'd just heard Asarem say that they were on the same side. *How could that be? None of this makes sense.* She knew what she'd seen during the talks, what she'd read in the transcripts.

Seeing the puzzled expression on Kira's face, Asarem laughed again. "You should see yourself, Kira. It's almost worth putting up with your attitude to see how confused you look right now." Asarem grabbed Kira by the elbow and dragged her into the closest vacant room. When she was assured they were alone, she explained, "Yes, Colonel. It's true. I want peace with Cardassia. I came to these talks prepared to negotiate—to give probably more than Ambassador Lang would ask for. And you know why I didn't? Because I was ordered not to."

Still convinced Asarem had an angle, Kira said suspiciously, "Ordered?"

"Shakaar instructed me to take a hard-line position," Asarem explained. "He told me to make it, in his exact words, 'as difficult as possible' to find reconciliation."

"Shakaar wouldn't do that."

Shaking her head, Asarem plopped down in a chair and sighed resignedly. "I knew you wouldn't believe me. Considering your history with him."

Forcing herself to consider that Asaraem was being truthful with her, Kira tried to visualize the talks from the minister's perspective. How aggravating it must be to have to sit, day after day, representing an agenda not of your own making. Kira imagined that spinning fabrications, deliberately blocking legitimate dialogue would take a toll on a person of integrity; an alibi existed for Asarem's seeming unreasonableness. *But what was Shakaar trying to do?* "If that's true—" she looked directly at Asarem.

The minister met Kira's eyes. "Then he lied to you." She let her words linger between them before offering further explanation.

A tightening in her chest made the air in the room feel too thin to breathe; the implications of Asarem's accusations were staggering. Kira rubbed her temples with the heels of her hands. Asarem waited while Kira struggled to formulate a response. Finding that quick explanations for the inexplicable proved futile, Kira said nothing. She didn't know what to say.

"If you don't believe it, go to him," Asarem said, not unkindly. "He comes back tomorrow sometime. Ask him. See if he's brave enough to be honest with you." Soundlessly, she left Kira alone in the half light to struggle through what she'd do next.

She was sitting there still when Ro's urgent page found her.

19

Talk about your circadian rhythms being off.

Not long after being snatched off the *Defiant,* day and night blended together for Nog. Constantly wearing a hood would do that to a person. He vaguely recalled being woken several times. After the gag was yanked out of his mouth, someone held up water for him to drink and shoved stale kelp cakes into his mouth. Given a choice, Nog would have passed on the kelp cakes.

While he couldn't see, his already superior auditory abilities were significantly heightened. He heard every opening door, could count the number of Yrythny passing by and understand most of the conversations. If what he picked up from eavesdropping was true, the *Avaril*'s general population wasn't aware he'd been stowed away in a storage closet near engineering. He knew he was close by engineering from the tone of the plasma coursing through the conduits, the rhythmic percussion of the warp core. The engines' presence comforted him.

Whoever his captor or captors were, they went to significant lengths to avoid being identified, utilizing different clothing, shoes, scents and never speaking when he might overhear. Consequently, he had no idea what his ultimate destination might be. Whether he was fated to be held hostage for ransom, killed, or sold to be the cabin boy for some Cheka general, Nog wasn't sure. If killed, he hoped his kidnappers would have the decency to send his body to Commander Vaughn. His father, at least, ought to have an opportunity to profit from Nog's misfortunes. The desiccated remains of the first Ferengi in Starfleet had to be worth *something*. Sobering thoughts for a young Ferengi.

While he might not know what time of day it was, Nog heard feet shuffling in the corridor at every shift change. *Vanìmel is a day away, give or take six hours, accounting for the time I was knocked unconscious. With any luck, my present circumstances are a misunderstanding and my gracious hosts will put me in touch with Commander Vaughn as soon as we touch down.*

The pitch of the warp engines vibrating through the deckplates suddenly dropped to nothing; Nog heard the impulse engine attempt, unsuccessfully, to engage. Given the back up systems on *Avaril,* impulse should be available soon, but not for another fifteen minutes or so. The *Avaril* was adrift. The expected panicked footsteps rushed up and down the corridor. Still no engine. Nog guessed at least ten minutes had passed since the warp core failed.

The storage closet door swished open. Hands grabbed at Nog, hefting him into the air. A Yrythny threw him over a shoulder, the gag stopped his protestations; his bound hands and feet prevented him from fighting his way free. The hood stayed in place, but Nog discerned the general direction his captors took him: a quick transport car downward. The air on the lowest decks had a dank, dusty quality. Hazarding a guess, he was being hauled to the *Avaril's* shuttlebay and taken . . . he had no idea. There were two Yrythny in his party; neither of them spoke. Doors opened and shut until the distinctively hollow sound of footsteps on metal gratings confirmed Nog's suspicions. A pause while the group waited for a shuttle's doors to open. Nog was thrown, like baggage, into the rear of the craft. He listened as switches flipped, engines activated, a preflight diagnostic run. He had no clue how long they would idle in the shuttlebay or where he was being taken, but he suspected it had to do with the tricorder holding the cloaking specs (actually a homing beacon—very clever). Nog put his faith in the Great River, hoping that once again it would provide in his hour of need.

* * *

With *Defiant* maintaining its cloak, Vaughn sat on the bridge, watching the pieces of the chessboard move into place. He would make his move when he was ready and not a moment before.

All eyes watched as the *Avaril* continued plodding toward Vanìmel while the Cheka ship maintained a parallel course beside her. The main viewscreen displayed a computer-generated graphic of an uninhabited planetary system where Bowers had projected the Cheka would intercept the Yrythny.

The first piece fell into place when the *Avaril,* a green ellipse on the screen, tumbled out of warp, and stalled. The *Defiant's* scans indicated internal engineering problems—not even impulse engines could be activated. She was stranded.

"The *Avaril* is transmitting a request for emergency assistance to Luthia control. They suspect internal sabotage to their engines," Bowers reported.

"Continue to monitor communications, Lieutenant," Vaughn ordered. At least initial appearances indicated that J'Maah hadn't sold them out.

The *Avaril* had only minutes to cope with their misfortune before the Cheka warship *Ston'yan,* a diamond-shaped graphic in red, rumbled into position off the *Avaril's* port side.

"*Ston'yan* dropping out of warp and powering weapons. *Avaril* unable to activate defensive shielding," Bowers announced. He looked up at Vaughn. "Showdown at the O.K. Corral."

Vaughn laughed grimly, wishing this could be settled with the sheriff and the black hat dueling with Colts at high noon. *Here we go,* he thought, rising from his chair. "Sound red alert. All crew to battle stations. Ensign Tenmei, ahead full, course one-nine-seven mark two." It was a trajectory that would place them dead center between the *Avaril* and the *Ston'yan.*

"*Avaril,* twenty-six million kilometers," Prynn announced.

"Steady as she goes, Ensign. Any sign of attack from the Cheka, Mr. Bowers?"

"No, sir. The *Ston'yan* remains on alert."

On the outside, Vaughn remained composed. No need to add to the anxiety of his crew; on the inside, he held his breath. Within minutes, they would know whether they had a chance at rescuing Nog.

"Avaril one million kilometers," Prynn announced.

"Take us out of warp," Vaughn ordered. "Maintain cloak."

Rahim looked up from sciences. *"Avaril* shuttlebay doors have been activated. Sensors detect the launch of one Yrythny shuttle."

A third spacecraft graphic, a smaller version of the *Avaril's* green circle, appeared.

"Scan the shuttle, Ensign." *This is it.* Vaughn thought.

"Two Yrythny life-forms—" Rahim paused to smile. "—and one Ferengi."

Vaughn turned to Leishman at engineering. "Transporter lock?"

Leishman studied her panel and shook her head. "Not possible. We should be able to knock out their shields, but whatever inhibitor field they were using before is now encompassing all three shuttle occupants. Looks like it's plan B, sir."

Vaughn turned to conn. "Ensign Tenmei, follow course two-one—zero mark zero and bring the *Defiant* within ten thousand kilometers of the Yrythny shuttle. Lieutenant Bowers, power phasers and prepare to drop cloak on my mark. Ensign Leishman, report to transporter bay one."

The tall engineer vacated her post and started for the exit.

"Good luck, Mikaela," Vaughn said as she crossed close to his chair.

"Yes, sir," she said with a wink. "I'll give 'em hell."

On the viewscreen, Vaughn saw the shuttle, just a little bigger than its Starfleet analog, cross the expanse between the two ships, dwarfed by the massive *Avaril* and the equally formidable Cheka warship. At the requisite distance, Prynn adjusted the *Defiant's* course, bringing her parallel with the shuttle.

"Chao to the bridge. Ensign Leishman is ready to transport to the Yrythny shuttle."

Vaughn didn't hesitate. "Drop cloak, Lieutenant Bowers. Target the shuttle's shield generators and fire phasers."

"Phasers firing sir," Bowers said.

Green circles rippled and winked out around the Yrythny shuttle, indicating a direct hit. "Shuttle's shields are down, sir," Bowers reported.

"Energize, Chief!"

"Ensign Leishman is away, sir," Chao replied over the comm.

Vaughn sat back down. *Now that we've crashed the party, let's see who tries to throw us out first.*

Sensors told Ezri that the *Avaril* was having technical trouble and that the Cheka warship had powered weapons. *Looks like an ambush,* she thought helplessly. The *Sagan*'s weapons might divert the warship's attention for a minute, but ultimately, she could do nothing to help the stranded Yrythny vessel.

"What now, Jeshoh?" Ezri said.

"We wait." He sat stiffly in the chair beside her.

"Fine. All stop, Shar."

As the *Sagan* held position, Keren left her seat, dropping down to crouch beside Jeshoh. She rested a hand on his leg and tried gazing up into his face but he twisted away from her. "My whole life's work has been about helping all of my people. Not myself. Please don't keep me from helping them," she pleaded.

"Sit down, Keren. We'll talk when this is over," he said gruffly.

"Jeshoh, we can stop this now. Let's dock on the *Avaril.* Turn in the terrorists. They'll reduce our punishment."

"Yrythny shuttle launching from *Avaril,*" Shar reported. "It's moving toward the Cheka vessel."

"Please, Jeshoh—" Keren whispered.

"Wait for a signal from the shuttle," Jeshoh ordered.

"I'm monitoring communications channels," Ezri said. A cursory survey revealed the Yrythny shuttle wasn't transmitting, but jamming the *Sagan*'s inquiry. *Something's not right here.*

"We should be receiving instructions by now," Jeshoh said, jumping from his chair and pacing. "I wonder—"

"Lieutenant, look," Shar said excitedly. "The *Defiant!*"

Keren scrambled to her feet, crowding next to Jeshoh so she could see the console screen. Keen in her focus, Ezri gasped when *Defiant*'s phasers took out the shuttle's shields.

Jeshoh slumped forward. "It can't be . . ."

"Were I to hazard a guess," Ezri said, "I'd say your deal is off."

"No!" Jeshoh slammed the console. "No!"

Anticipating the Cheka's displeasure with *Defiant*'s appearance, Vaughn made a preemptive move. "Tactical, raise shields and ready phasers." Vaughn said. "Ensign Rahim, monitor all transmissions between the three ships. Audio feed over the comm system."

"—*a direct hit to our shield generators. You have to help us!*" the panicked Yrythny voice said. "*We have the cloaking specs and an engineer who can install and replicate the technology.*"

"What about the eggs?" came the vibrating Cheka voice.

"—*the* Defiant *off starboard—*" static disrupted the transmission.

Vaughn searched his memory to place the Yrythny voice; he knew he'd heard it before.

Ensign Permenter suddenly looked up from the engineering station, where she'd replaced Leishman, recognition written on her face. "That was—"

Tlaral, thought Nog, wondering why he hadn't pegged her before. For his money, he thought it would be Minister M'Yeoh. No one in a position like his was that incompetent unless it was for show. But he hadn't had any latinum riding on the deal so he'd live with the disappointment.

I'm being traded to the Cheka. In exchange for what? What do the Cheka have that the Yrythny want? Uncle Quark always says the four hungers are food, sex, power and money, not necessarily in that order. But because money can buy food, sex, and power, money trumps them all. If I'm the money, the Yrythny are trading me for . . . Wait. Not all Yrythny are in need, Nog amended his thought. *Only the Wanderers because—*

They want weapons. To push Vanìmel into a civil war. If they can't wrangle their rights legally, they'll take them by force.

The shuttle's control panel beeped like crazy. Before he could guess what might be happening, the shuttle rocked a second time, tipping from side to side and acrid smoke filled the cockpit.

"*We've lost our shield generators. Grab hold of—*"

Suddenly he heard the whine of a Starfleet transporter beam.

"*We've been boarded!*" Tlaral shouted. "*Get—!*"

Feet hit the deck, followed by scuffling, rustling, clattering and a thud. Nog hitched along the floor toward the rear of the shuttle to avoid being dragged into the fray. Having heard the Yrythny use the word "defiant" he hoped it meant Vaughn was close by. For now, however, as much as he wanted to believe he had friends aboard, he couldn't be sure. Braced against a metal corner, he pushed his wristbands against the edge.

"Lock onto the Yrythny. Two to transport," he heard someone say. *Mikaela.*

The sound of the transporter beam filled the cabin again. Then hands pulled the hood off his head and yanked the gag out of his mouth. "You okay?" Leishman asked, performing a cursory check.

"Could be worse," Nog answered, managing a smile. "You couldn't have just beamed me off first?"

" 'Fraid not," she said, holding up two ripped armbands with little devices attached. Transporter scramblers, Nog guessed. She reached for the one on Nog's arm and snapped it off as well. "You ready?" Nog nodded, and Mikaela tapped her combadge again. "Leishman to Chao. Lock onto Lieutenant Nog and beam him out."

He didn't even get to say good-bye before he rematerialized in the transporter bay. Chief Chao informed the bridge that he was back aboard. Maybe he was imagining things, but Nog thought he might have heard applause.

Suddenly Dr. Bashir was there, hauling him off the transporter pad and sitting beside him. He unfastened Nog's restraints and checked him over to make sure he wasn't bleeding, broken, or too badly bruised.

"You had us worried," Bashir said, examining his wrists and ankles. "Welcome home, Lieutenant. I wish I could let you retire to your quarters, but we're a little shorthanded in engineering, and we still have to get out of here."

"What about Mikaela?" Nog cried.

Ensign Leishman dropped into the pilot's chair and made a cursory inspection of the controls before activating the shuttle's sensors and computer systems. The hours she'd spent with the *Avaril*'s engineering staff finally paid off. *Okay little David, we're going to make the bad guys think you're Goliath.* She took out the makeshift device Permenter had given her and plugged it into a port on the shuttle's main console. True to Bryanne's promise, it fit perfectly into the Yrythny system, and instantly initiated an information upload. As the "noisemaker" programming poured into the shuttle's computer, Leishman reconfigured the navigational system, integrating a datachip that allowed the shuttle to be remote piloted from the *Defiant*. The download completed, she reinitialized the computer matrix. Then she thumbed the switch on the transmitter, hailing the *Avaril*. "Shuttle to *Avaril*. This is Ensign Mikaela Leishman of the *U.S.S. Defiant*. Do you read?"

After a pause that was likely only seconds—but felt like minutes—the *Avaril* answered. *"We read you."*

"Power down primary systems, *Avaril*. Repeat, power down primary systems."

"Ensign, if you'd clarify—"

"Scan the shuttle, *Avaril*. Tell me what you see."

Another long pause. *"Powering down primary power. Thank you, Ensign."*

She touched her combadge. *"Defiant,* what do you read?"

"Nice work, Mikaela," said Bowers. *"If I didn't know better, I'd think there were two* Avarils *out there."*

The Cheka ought to be seriously confused by the decoy, providing the real *Avaril* a chance to restore their defensive capabilities. If *Ston'yan* decided to attack, at least the odds of the *Avaril* surviving had improved, though she doubted Vaughn would let it get that far. He'd draw the *Ston'yan*'s fire before he allowed innocents to die.

"Leishman to Chao. Beam me out." She closed her eyes . . .

. . . and opened them when she was back home. Leishman stepped off the transporter pad, nodding to Chao, who reported Leishman's safe return to the bridge.

She once again heard Bowers's cool, steady voice. "Ston'yan *targeting weapons."*

"Ensign Tenmei, prepare to engage Ston'yan. *Evasive maneuvers,"* Vaughn barked.

"Sir!" Bowers said. *"It's the* Sagan!"

"Shall I open a channel to *Defiant*—?" Shar said.

"No!" Jeshoh touched the emitter tip of his weapon to Shar's neck. "Proceed toward the Cheka vessel."

"Jeshoh, don't do this!" Keren begged.

"That's odd," Shar said, assessing the sensor data. "I'm picking up two *Avarils*."

"Why would there be two—?" Recognition dawned on Ezri. "Oh, that's clever—Vaughn's created a noisemaker." She smiled, admiring the commander's tactics.

"Sir?" Shar said.

"Trick the enemy's sensors into believing that there are two ships out there. The enemy has to guess which one to hit first. The confusion buys time."

"Giving the *Avaril* time to escape," Shar reasoned.

Ezri nodded.

"Approach the Cheka ship, Lieutenant," Jeshoh ordered.

Looking over her shoulder, Ezri recognized panic spreading over Jeshoh's face. *Should I say something . . . no. All his options need to be gone before he'll budge.* She nodded to Shar, who tapped in the commands to ease the *Sagan* toward the Cheka warship.

"Hail them," Vaughn ordered. *What the hell does Dax think she's doing out here?*

"They're not answering our hails, sir," Bowers reported.

"Who's on board?" Vaughn asked. He stood behind Rahim, assimilating the data as it came up on screen.

"One Trill, one Andorian, and two Yrythny."

"Are all their systems operational?"

"Yes, sir," Bowers said. "Full shields, weapons, communications, and life support. They've set a course for the *Ston'yan*."

What could Dax be up to? Without knowing why the *Sagan* was joining them, and because the *Sagan* wasn't answering their hails, he had to assume that this might not be a friendly visit. But he had to trust his senior officers to wrangle with the problem.

"Ensign Tenmei, proceed on course zero-nine-zero mark three," Vaughn said. "Sam, get ready to throw a punch at the *Ston'yan*. Just hard enough to get their attention."

"Aye, sir," Sam grinned. "Preparing full spread of quantum torpedoes."

Rahim said, "The Cheka have fired polaron cannons on one of the *Avarils*, sir."

"They took the bait." Vaughn expected they would. Having

failed to receive their cargo from the Yrythny, they would attack. He was certain the Cheka had planned on taking out the *Avaril* from the onset. Many who double-cross find themselves double-crossed at the end of the road. "On screen."

Yellow and blue light erupted as an engine core breached. The brilliant flare dissipated, providing a full frontal view of the *Ston'yan.*

"Attack pattern beta, Ensign Tenmei!"

"The Cheka have destroyed an *Avaril,*" Shar announced, his listeners all watching him as they awaited the verdict: "The false one."

Ezri wondered how much longer they could hover on the perimeter of the standoff. To this point, the *Sagan* didn't pose a threat to any of the parties and was easy to ignore. With one of the pieces off the board, Ezri bet that the Cheka would come after them next—either tractor them in or blow them up. Neither option pleased her.

"Jeshoh, what's to say the Cheka won't turn on you?" Keren said, reaching for him.

He jerked away. "Because I have something they want."

"And Keren? If the Cheka turn on you, they turn on her," Ezri said calmly. "You don't want that, Jeshoh. You know you don't. Let me open a channel to the *Defiant.* You and Keren can take asylum with the crew until we can negotiate with your govern—"

"The way you negotiated the colonizing compromise?" Jeshoh snorted.

Ezri winced inwardly. *I've failed the Yrythny spectacularly. All the more reason I have to figure out how to make it right.*

She pressed on toward the *Ston'yan.*

On approach to the warship, Ensign Prynn Tenmei decided she didn't like the look of it. Not because she found the Cheka to be foul creatures (though she did), or because the *Ston'yan* appeared terribly menacing. No, Prynn felt the Cheka starship lacked panache.

During the Dominion War, she had flown against (and admired) Jem'Hadar attack ships, *Galor*-class Cardassian cruisers; she'd flown in formation with Romulan warbirds and gone into battle alongside Klingon Birds-of-Prey. She might not like the Cardassians' way of doing business—or the Romulans' and Klingons' for that matter—but at least their empires had developed spacecraft worthy of engagement. The *Ston'yan,* by contrast, was a clumsy predator, more like a blind shark battering its prey with its head before moving in for the kill. No style whatsoever.

"*Ston'yan* twenty-five thousand kilometers and closing," she said.

"Acknowledged, Ensign. Maintain course," Vaughn said.

Prynn hit the touchpad for navigational reference and considered the territory ahead. A wild-goose chase through one of this system's asteroid belts might be fun. Close to the sun, maybe, or toward that gas giant . . . *Hello?* She broke into a smile when she saw the last piece of navigational data. *Now that's a nice surprise,* she thought. *Oh to be on the* Ston'yan's *bridge when I sock this one to them.* She tapped her combadge. "Conn to engineering. What's the status on the femtobots?"

"*Untested, but ready to go,*" Nog said. "*We need a 30-second window to activate the system and tactical will have to power down weapons.*"

"Captain, I have an idea—but it's risky," Prynn said, wanting to give her father and Bowers a heads-up as to what she had in mind. "Transmitting navigational data and proposed target to your stations now. I'll easily outfly the *Ston'yan,* but can we survive without weapons for half a minute?"

"I'm game," Bowers piped up.

Vaughn looked up from reviewing her data. "Proceed, Ensign."

"Thank you sir," Prynn said, speedily tapping the commands into the flight control panel. "*Ston'yan* within firing range."

"Fire when ready, Lieutenant," Vaughn said.

When Bowers let fly his spread of torpedoes, Prynn initiated evasive maneuvers. She'd covered twenty thousand kilometers before the *Ston'yan* caught up with the *Defiant.* Steady rounds firing from Cheka polaron cannons forced Prynn into a pendulumlike flight pattern.

"*Avaril* has regained impulse engines," Rahim said.

"Good. What about the *Sagan?*" Vaughn asked.

The entire crew—including Prynn—hung on Rahim's answer. The shuttle still hadn't responded to their hails.

"The *Sagan* is behind the *Ston'yan.* Not quite sure who they're trying to catch up with, though, us or them."

* * *

This may be a case of the inmates running the asylum, Ezri thought, plotting the *Sagan's* course behind the Cheka. Far in the lead, the *Defiant* led the *Ston'yan* on a merry chase at dizzying speeds. *Prynn must be in her glory.*

Incredulous, Keren asked, "What are we doing?"

"We need to keep up with the Cheka. We still have what they want. And they have what we want."

"Listen to yourself, Jeshoh!" Keren protested.

He turned away, unmoved by her pleas.

To Ezri's side, Shar blanched pale blue. "The Cheka are releasing a wake of mines. Boosting shields."

"Taking evasive maneuvers," Ezri barked. *Sagan* veered to port, avoiding a mine aimed for starboard only to fly straight toward another. An explosion rocked the shuttle.

Ezri heard the dull crunch of flesh against metal; Keren cried out.

"Jeshoh!" Ezri shouted. "Help her, dammit!" She fought the instinct to abandon the conn and rush back to tend to the wounded Yrythny.

"Shields at seventy percent," Shar said, his antennae rigid with tension. "The *Defiant* appears to be going in close to this system's star. *Sagan* isn't designed to withstand—"

Out of the corner of her eye, Ezri saw Keren slumped on the floor; she groaned, twisting her head from side to side as delirium overtook her.

"Shar, check on Keren."

"But the shields—"

"That's an order, Ensign."

Shar jumped up from his station, went for a medical kit, and started passing a tricorder over Keren. Jeshoh, still clutching his weapon, stood statue still, shell-shocked and pale.

"Change your mind, Jeshoh," Ezri said calmly. *Don't let him see your fear.* "It's not too late."

"No!" he despaired. His eyes dropped to the floor where Keren had fallen into unconsciousness.

"Ensign Tenmei, move into the final phase," Vaughn ordered.

"Yes, sir." For her plan to work, Prynn needed to keep the *Ston'yan* off its guard long enough that they wouldn't have time to back out of her trap. Considering what she had to work with, she decided on playing chicken with the Cheka around the star. *Let's see what your ship is made of,* Prynn thought.

"*Ston'yan* closing," Rahim said.

Plunging toward the sun's corona, she faked to port, before peeling out abruptly to starboard. In following the *Defiant*'s port-side fake, the *Ston'yan* cooked its underbelly. Prynn eluded their fire for a few more minutes, buying her the time she needed to set up the last leg of the chase.

"*Ston'yan* still in pursuit with weapons off-line," Bowers said. "Correction, *Ston'yan* weapons are back on-line and attempting to lock onto us."

"Target destination in fifty seconds," Permenter said. "Twenty seconds until femtobot shield augmentation activated."

The *Defiant* shuddered.

"Direct hit. Shields at sixty-five percent," Bowers reported.

Permenter looked at Tenmei. "The femtobot augmentation can be activated all the way down to fifty percent, but I strongly suggest we try not to put that to the test."

"Course locked in," Prynn said. "Here we go."

Though still hot on the Cheka's tail, Ezri eavesdropped on Shar's medical explanations to Jeshoh, discovering she had a new problem.

"According to my scans," Shar said, "she has a subdural hematoma. A blood bruise on the brain. I could attempt to treat her, but my paramedic training is limited, and I fear I don't know enough about Yrythny blood chemistry." His tone wasn't hopeful.

His calm evaporating, Jeshoh slammed a fist into a compartment.

"We can help her, Jeshoh," Ezri said. "Dr. Bashir on the *Defiant* is one of the finest medical practitioners you could ask for, and he has a fully equipped medical bay. He'll stabilize her until we can get her to your people."

"No!" he shouted, breathing ragged. "We'll never be together if we go back now."

Ezri said simply, "If we don't go back, she'll die."

"You don't know that! Shar, treat her now," Jeshoh snapped, pacing the small compartment like a caged animal.

This has gone on as long as I can allow, Ezri thought.

"Help Keren," she whispered gruffly. Her body was perilously close to caving in to stress; her shoulders ached from sitting, tightly wound, for so long. Fatigue and hunger would soon blur her ability to focus and if her calculations were right, in less than a minute, all the rules of this fight would change again. She dared to glance away from the flight controls to meet Jeshoh's eyes. "Please," she begged. "Do this for her. I've watched you stand against your leaders, your culture—all because you believed in doing the right thing. You know what you have to do, Jeshoh. *Do it now.*"

"Thirty seconds. Activating shield augmentation," Permenter said.

"Ston'yan" one thousand kilometers and closing," Bowers reported. "Weapons charging."

Trusting that her crewmates would back her up, Prynn drifted into a mental place where the conn became an extension of her fingers, responding instantaneously to her thoughts. *Just a little closer. . . .* The bridge crew snapped reports back and forth. Prynn ignored them. *Almost there . . . we should be crossing the threshold. . . . NOW.*

A blinding, brilliant flash consumed the darkness. Prynn pulled all the power she could from the engines, determined to fly through the descending web weapon's net. The tactical readout confirmed that the *Ston'yan* had been caught in the weapon's perimeter. For one terrifying moment, she wondered if the Cheka had friend-or-foe technology that would allow them to escape, but she had to hope that overconfidence would be their downfall.

"It's working," Bowers said. "The femtobots are preventing the nanobots from penetrating the ship!"

"We aren't out of the woods, yet," Vaughn cautioned. "Keep it together, Ensign Tenmei."

Because the *Ston'yan* remained tight on the *Defiant's* heels, Prynn wasn't sure the web weapon had caught their pursuer. In one last evasive tactic, Prynn piloted the *Defiant* into a sharp seventy-five degree pull-up, banking in front of the Cheka ship, flipping over and flying back the direction they'd come, over the top of the *Ston'yan.*

"The web got them!" Bowers shouted. *"Ston'yan* is no longer in pursuit."

"Status of the femtobots?" Vaughn asked.

"It worked," Permenter confirmed. "Nanobots were all neutralized."

Prynn's elation enhanced the adrenaline coursing through her veins. *What a rush.*

"Sir," said Bowers "the *Sagan* is hailing us. Audio only."

"Put them through."

"*Defiant, this is Lieutenant Dax. Permission to bring in the* Sagan."

"By all means, Lieutenant. Bring her home."

Julian raced into the shuttlebay, eager to be the first to greet the *Sagan.* Impatience wasn't his usual style, but he needed to know that Ezri was all right.

The shuttle doors hissed open with Shar jumping out first, standing aside while two Yrythny exited; the tall, handsomely dressed male cradled an unconscious female in his arms. All three passengers trudged toward him as if heavily burdened.

"Doctor," Shar called. "We have a medical emergency."

Thoughts of Ezri temporarily forgotten, Julian pulled out his medical tricorder and scanned the wounded Yrythny. "We'll need to operate. It may take me a few minutes to synthesize her blood, but she should be fine," he said to the Yrythny he now recognized as Jeshoh. "Shar, take our guests to sickbay. I'll be right behind you." Tapping his combadge he said, "Bashir to Richter. Prep for surgery. We have a Yrythny with a subdural hemotoma. I'll be there presently."

With the distraction of a new patient, Julian hadn't heard Ezri exit the shuttle. He stopped when he suddenly heard:

"Hey. Can I walk with you?"

He paused, smiled broadly and reached for her proffered hand. All of him relaxed at her touch. For a moment they said nothing. Her appearance worried him, dark circles around her eyes, porcelain skin paler than normal, her shoulders hunched with fatigue.

"What exactly happened in there?" Julian asked, concerned.

She smiled weakly. "Ask me later. I just . . . I just want you to know I love you."

"I love you, too," he said simply, deciding it would be best not to press her for explanations now. They were back together. For now, that was enough. Julian draped an arm around her waist, and together they headed for the medical bay.

20

"Computer, lights at full illumination," Shakaar ordered. He dropped his travel bag on his desk and began rooting around inside.

Kira waited for him to toss out some clothes and his other personal belongings before deciding to interrupt him. "I hope all is well on the *Gryphon*."

Startled, he spun around. "How did you—?"

"You may be First Minister of Bajor, but this is still my station, Edon."

"This couldn't wait until morning?" he asked.

"No," Kira said simply. She walked over beside him, braced herself against his desk and watched him sort through his travel bag.

Shakaar thumbed on his desk screen, perused a memo or two and replicated a glass of *pooncheenee*. Kira watched sedately, following his every move with her eyes. Finally, he motioned for her to take a seat; he dropped into his own chair, a rare occurrence since he preferred standing.

Electing to perch on the edge of his desk, she peered down at him. "Yesterday, Lieutenant Ro discovered that the Ziyal exhibit had been brutally vandalized." Brutal understated the degree of calculated destruction. Twisted, maybe. Depraved, better.

His eyebrow shot up. "Have the culprits been identified?"

"No. But the damage was extensive." Acids melting paints off canvases, water smudging delicate charcoals, knives slashing obscenities . . . as if Ziyal, through her work, had been tortured incrementally, murdered anew.

"Can the artwork be repaired?" Shakaar asked, putting away personal items from his bag.

"The curator can restore some of the pieces—it could take weeks." *Assuming she can be persuaded to stop crying at some point,* Kira thought ruefully. "But there are a few that are beyond repair. Those pieces might be holographically reproduced, but the originals are irreparable."

"Tragic," Shakaar muttered, thoughtfully rubbing his chin with his thumb. He took another sip of his juice, pausing to peer over the glass at Kira who remained fixed where she sat. "You didn't have to make this report in person."

"I didn't," Kira admitted. "But I felt like what happened tonight at the exhibit can be attributed, in part, to a station environment hostile toward Cardassians. And I think you're feeding that hatred, Minister."

Mustering indignation, Shakaar spouted off a biting retort, but Kira dismissed it. "You know what I'm talking about, Shakaar. Don't play coy with me."

Lips pursed, he glared at her. Kira had known him long enough to recognize his shift into tactical mode as he tried to ascertain whether she was friend or foe. She sat, unflinching, while he appraised her. Finally, he said, "Go ahead. Get it off your chest. You'll feel better."

"You told Asarem to back out of the talks," she said, modulating her anger by infusing her voice with syrup.

"Straight to the point, Nerys," he smiled grudgingly. "I always liked that about you."

"You don't deny it, then?"

"You've never asked me for my position on the talks, you've only complained about Minister Asarem's behavior and asked me to use my influence on her," he rationalized.

"Don't mince words with me, Shakaar," Kira growled. "You knew what I was asking."

"You wanted Minister Asarem to be nice to your Cardassian friends. I told Asarem to be less confrontational. I did what I said I would."

"You have a chance to help Bajor and you run away like a deserter."

"Part of being a leader is choosing between equally good options.

351

Forging peace with Cardassia, as a Bajoran nation, is a good choice. But a simpler path—one that recognizes that our relationship with Cardassia will be normalized when we join the Federation—is also a good choice. Why choose the more complicated option?"

"Because we aren't whole, as a people, without closure. As Bajor, sovereign and independent," she argued. "You've always fought your own battles and now you're turning the biggest one of all—the one that wins the war—over to someone else?"

Shakaar continued his oratory as if Kira weren't even in the room. "Consider their gift, even. How like them, to remind us of our humiliation."

"What?"

"All those pretty pictures, Nerys, they came from Dukat's bastard. Because Dukat took a married woman from her home and children and raped her, a great artist was born. I'm not one who believes the ends justifies the means."

"What does Ziyal have to do with peace negotiations?"

"The Cardassians don't really want peace. They came here, with their *gift,*" he spat the word, "to remind us exactly who we are to each other. They're the masters and we're the slaves. Not while I'm First Minister of Bajor. Never again."

"Ziyal was Bajoran, too!" she protested.

He laughed, dismissing her with the indulgent mien of a wise teacher amused by his student's naïve assertions. Sipping his juice, he studied his desk screen and continued to putter about his office, blithely indifferent.

He's misdirecting you. He wants to provoke you, make you lose your temper so he can discredit your accusations. Kira called on memory for strength. *Holding the soft, cool hand of her dying friend against her cheek . . . Cackling voices from her childhood hissing that Cardassians were without pagh . . . The smell of her mother's hair as she said good-bye. . . .*

Lies. *Shakaar lied.* Trembling, Kira dug her fingernails into the palms of her hands and rushed through a silent prayer. "Lending your support to the talks—giving Minister Asarem the go-ahead to negotiate—will help you let go of the past, Edon," she pleaded softly. "Let it go."

His face softening, Shakaar tenderly took her by the wrists and one hand at a time, pried her fingers off her palms, feather-tracing the remaining angry red indentations with his index finger.

A searing wave of bile scalded her throat. *Who are you?*

Jerking her hands away from Shakaar, she clenched them into fists and thrust them at her sides, sending his travel bag and the metal box he had just unpacked, clattering onto to the floor. The box opened, but nothing spilled out.

Utterly unruffled, he dropped to the floor to retrieve the empty box, gather up the bag and a few clothes, and return them to the desk. Smiling kindly, he said, "You need to relax, Nerys. I'm worried about how stressed you are. You should take some time off. Go away. Clear your head."

She stared at him, still clinging to the one idea that made sense to her. "You don't know—you couldn't have—there's no way—" she stammered.

"Yes?"

"The vandalism. The veiled threats at the Cardassian delegation. You didn't have anything to do—?"

"Come now, Nerys—this is me you're talking to," he placed his hands on his chest. "Listen to how ridiculous you sound! I'm the First Minister of Bajor. I don't deal in criminal conspiracies. Besides, I wasn't even here tonight. You *know* me, Nerys. Almost better than anyone."

Kira shook her head in disbelief. "You know, logically, you're right. And I am under a lot of stress. But I *don't* know you anymore," she confessed. And it hurt to say it. Who she was resulted from, in no small part, the time she had spent with Shakaar. To have arrived at a place where she could even fathom making an accusation against him. . . . Her convulsing world left her unbalanced, disoriented. "But if Ro's investigation uncovers even the smallest link to you, Minister, nothing will protect you from me."

"I'll submit myself to your lash if I'm found guilty of skulking around Deep Space 9 and terrorizing its residents," he said sarcastically.

The door chimed; Sirsy announced Vedek Nolan, who became distinctly uncomfortable upon seeing Kira as he entered the office. His beady eyes darted between her and the minister. "Late night shrine services, Minister. You asked for an escort?" he questioned.

"Yes, I wanted an update about how the station's religious community was faring in these troubled times," Shakaar explained to the confused vedek who clearly was wondering what Kira was doing here when business hours had ended earlier. "I think we're done here, aren't we, Colonel?" he asked Kira mildly.

Their word battles had been punctuated with dueling glares; this last round proved not to be an exception. This time, Shakaar looked away first.

Kira knew he could afford to lose because circumstances provided him the perfect snub. *He's going to services. He's actually going to services and I can't! And he enjoys that.* "Yes, we're done."

Shakaar nodded and launched into animated dialogue with the vedek as he swept past Kira and out of the room.

"For now," she said softly.

They still hadn't answered her calls, even though she'd started signaling at their door five minutes ago. And that was after three failed attempts to contact Thriss from her office, once Dr. Girani had told Phillipa about the latest incident. Phillipa believed herself to be a patient person—except in an emergency. Present circumstances certainly qualified.

Over the course of their sessions, Phillipa had pieced together Shar and Thriss's history. By calling in a few favors, she'd been able to gain access to an Andorian database that explained in academic terms the physiological processes Thriss had described. Shar and Thriss had initiated *tezha,* a facet of sexual intimacy, but not in the conventional sense that most humanoids understood. *Tezha* literally created a tangible, biochemical attachment between bondmates; bodies became tuned to each other, with brain chemistry and endocrine balances responding to the unique combination of sensory markers that identified the bondmates. It wasn't unlike imprinting between young and their parents. When bondmates ventured into intimate associations before the *shelthreth,* the overall cohesion of the bond wasn't assured. Bonds between segments surpassed bonds within the whole group. Because Thriss' attachment to Shar surpassed what she shared with the others, Phillipa worried that Anichent and Dizhei wouldn't be adequately attuned to Thriss to provide her the emotional support she needed to weather this crisis.

Phillipa rolled back on her heels outside Shar's quarters, wondering if Thriss would answer a direct call if she used her combadge. Before her hand reached her chest, the door hissed open, revealing Anichent.

"Good day, Counselor. Have you anything new to report from Colonel Kira? Perhaps a letter from Shar?" he said, his tightly tensed antennae betraying more about his frame of mind than the lackadaisical way he leaned against the door frame. *As if he's trying desperately to appear casual in order to mask his emotional state. Nice try, Anichent.*

"Dr. Girani told me what happened. I'm here to see Thriss." She took a step toward the threshold, but Anichent made no move to get out of her way. *Not being one for words, he resorts to physical intimidation,* she reasoned. *If worst comes to worst, I've mastered the Vulcan neck pinch. I could have him on the floor in a second. And Dizhei? I could take her, no problem.* Phillipa only pondered violent impulses—she never seriously considered instigating a fight. But she took comfort knowing she was equally matched with most who might threaten her. *Nobody ever expects the counselor to kick ass.*

"Thriss is resting now. You can see her in the morning," Anichent said, folding his arms. "I understand why you're here. We appreciate your concern. But this is a family matter and Dizhei and I will handle it."

"She almost assaulted a patient, Anichent," Phillipa said. "A child. That's completely uncharacteristic of her. Adults? Yes. Children? Never. Her disppointment at not receiving a letter from Shar could be triggering a serious relapse." She hadn't had time to read the whole report, but she'd read enough to worry her.

A primary schoolchild with a fracture received during exercise period had come in to have the bone mended. A routine procedure Thriss had performed many times. Busy with an OB exam, Girani had asked Thriss to assist Ensign Mancuso, the nurse. While Mancuso prepped the fracture repair kit, Thriss had grown frustrated with the child's persistent tears and had screamed at her, thrown a tray of medical tools across the room and scared the wits out of the child.

"We're all saddened by not hearing from Shar, but there's always next time. We're here for Thriss. We'll help her cope with this."

Anichent wouldn't budge. "We're waiting to confirm our decision with Councillor zh'Thane, but I believe we'll be leaving for Andor tomorrow. It's what's best for us."

Phillipa shifted her weight to one hip. "This persistent focus on 'we,' while admirable in its loyalty fails to acknowledge Thriss's needs as an individual. She might not be as well-equipped to deal with this as you are, Anichent." When Thriss had become Phillipa's patient, she had spent hours scouring the database for any helpful information. A portrait of a species intent on protecting the needs of the whole over the one had emerged. Not an easy obstacle for a therapist to hurdle when one of the parts of the whole was broken. "You're making a mistake," Phillipa reiterated, hoping Anichent would relent.

"You come from a species that has the luxury of considering the needs of the individual first. We do not," Anichent said quietly. "Our social customs are complex, Counselor. I think we're the best first line of defense for Thriss. Out of deference to you, we'll bring her to your office first thing tomorrow, before we leave for good."

Perceiving Anichent as immovable, Phillipa backed away from the threshold of ch'Thane's quarters and watched the door close in her face.

As much as she wanted to help Thriss immediately, believing that one could bleed to death as easily from a slow hemorrhage as from a severed artery, she would compromise rather than cause conflict among the bondmates. Their relationship had the deceptive fragility of crystal: smooth and hard to the touch, but quick to be crushed with any measure of applied force. Phillipa refused to push, lest she be the one to finally shatter Thriss.

With deliberate concentration, Thriss lifted her head from the pillow. "Is Counselor Matthias out there? I thought I heard her voice." The room heaved and swayed; she tried merging the two Dizheis rushing toward her with her eyes but her bondmate moved too quickly and the effort made her dizzy. Collapsing into the covers she willed her weighty limbs to float, to dissolve into boneless liquid. Her joints ached; their burning tightness cinched tighter like a thousand pinches in her hands and knees and hips and feet.

Dizhei smoothed her hair with a dry, cool hand. "It's all right. Don't push yourself. I know it's been a hard day."

She rolled her face down into her pillow and sought the anesthetic of memory. Shar came to her unbidden, and she eagerly allowed the room to recede from her senses as she willed her mind to recall the soft brush of his lips mapping her face. The tone of his voice that he reserved for quiet, dark moments when she molded herself to his back, absorbing with her own body the heat he radiated. Nestling her nose in his chest, inhaling the myriad of scents that were Shar. Breathing came easier as she drifted into dreams. She could almost hear him whispering the silly endearments that they'd invented as aliases, to avoid their clandestine meetings and notes from being discovered.

She missed him. Every part of her was meant to fit with him and without him, she felt adrift. Somewhere among the lights of a billion worlds he wandered where her net couldn't draw him in. Frozen darkness, like the void of space, extinguished any warmth she could cull from her dreams.

He was lost. He had forgotten her. Since he was far away, she had passed from his memory. He wasn't coming home. He'd never come home. Not truly. Not to her.

In the haze of sound and light, she imagined she heard Anichent and Dizhei's voices, elongated and garbled. *Home, we need to return home,* she heard one of them say. She tried to explain that Shar wasn't home so it didn't matter, but it took more strength than she could muster. And *Zhadi* was here? That couldn't be. Thriss squinted at the wall and thought she saw *Zhadi*. Only *Zhadi* wore such bright, gaudy colors, colors that Shar thought were ridiculous. But it couldn't be *Zhadi*: she was away and wouldn't be back for days. Unlike Shar, who would never be back.

She wanted sleep. She wanted the dark numbness of sleep so she pushed past the disappointment and the pain and the useless aching prison that was her body . . . her body that would never carry Shar's child . . . and willed it all to fade away into nothingness.

Kira picked her way past the crime scene barriers and into the nearly desolate gallery. A few of Ro's people and the curator's staff sorted through the disarray, searching for evidence, and gently handling the remains of Ziyal's artwork. No one smiled.

Had it been only a few days since she'd walked here with Macet as they both sought to find a workable solution for both their peoples? In spite of the brawl and in spite of Minister Asarem closing down the talks, Kira had remained hopeful until her encounter with Shakaar. Try as she might, she couldn't understand his untenable machinations. Yes, postponing the normalization of relations until after Bajor joined the Federation made pragmatic sense, but ethical sense? Though they'd had their disagreements—and Kira had found herself increasingly on opposing sides with him—she had always believed Shakaar to be a man of honor, a man who saw his role not only as a policy leader, but as a protector of the people's integrity. Kira couldn't see where the integrity was in his present course of action.

She shuffled past hateful words carved into the walls and paintings, over puddles of red paint still drizzling off benches and walls. Beneath the sadistic violence lacerating the room, Kira sensed Ziyal's spirit—it was weaker, but it lingered. Kira's eyes watered. Her friend's *pagh* had been given a chance to live anew; after a lifetime as a fugitive, she had found a place to rest, where she could be safe from the cruelties of bigotry. *And we couldn't even shield her here,* Kira thought sadly.

She wandered from space to space, lost in her thoughts, so when she stumbled upon a civilian she was slow to fix on her identity. *This is a closed area. Authorized personnel only,* she prepared to say until she recognized she stood face-to-face with Minister Asarem.

They considered each other awkwardly, neither knowing what to say or how to begin. That Asarem had chosen to come here now, to witness this tragedy, spoke well of her to Kira's way of thinking.

The dullness in Kira's chest receded, replaced by warmth. Maybe there was a reason why her feet brought her here instead of instinctively guiding her back to her quarters. After that distasteful meeting with Shakaar, she longed to shower, wash her hands of him, but instead she'd ended up taking a different turbolift and walking across the Promenade and now, Asarem Wadeen stood before her, hands laced behind her back, waiting, watching.

Kira didn't believe in coincidences.

They exchanged civil greetings, words about the shocking nature of the crime and then, again, lapsed into awkward silence. Neither woman moved to leave.

"Minister, do you mind if I take a minute of your time?"

"Do you have another lecture for me?"

"No, more like an apology. I talked to Shakaar."

"Ah," she said, understanding.

"The situation is just as you said," Kira admitted. "But you have to know that in all the years I've known Shakaar, to choose such a course isn't like him."

Asarem nodded. "We don't always come down on the same side of things, the first minister and I. He tends to be more progressive while I feel safest with a more conservative, traditional approach. But even knowing our stylistic differences, the way he chose to handle this situation with Ambassador Lang surprised even me."

Moved by Asarem's gracious frankness, Kira felt ashamed by her own hasty judgment. "I'm sorry. For what I've said. For how I've behaved."

"If I were in your place, I would likely have done as you did," Asarem said graciously.

"Shakaar did say he thought we'd find we had a lot in common if we had a chance to get to know each other."

"I believe that as well."

They continued walking, avoiding looking at each other until Kira stopped. "I know as things presently stand, talks won't resume. You can't call Ambassador Lang and start things up again without going against Shakaar's orders."

"True," Asarem conceded.

"But if you knew, in your heart, that Shakaar was wrong and that he was walking contrary to the path the Prophets have set for Bajor, would you go against him?"

"What are you asking?"

"Please. Can we sit?"

They found a small, mostly unsoiled section of carpet in front of a maintenance closet. Pushing aside a broken piece of bench and other dusty refuse, the women dropped down cross-legged to the floor. Kira fumbled around for the words, seeing her own confusion reflected on Asarem's face until she fell back on the oldest convention of storytelling: start from the beginning. Haltingly, she asked, "Have you ever heard of the *Ravinok?*"

And from there, Ziyal's story, as Kira recalled it, tumbled out. She related her own conflicted emotions upon finding Dukat's illegitimate daughter in the Dozarian system, Dukat's willingness to murder Ziyal, in cold blood, rather than risk her existence being discovered by his family or the Cardassian government, and Kira's forcing him to accept responsibility for the unwanted child. Details that faded from her recollections due to the passage of time flooded back to her and Kira found herself explaining Ziyal's uncomfortable initiation into Bajor's art community, the prylars who grew to treasure her, and her tentative exploration of a relationship with the Prophets. How Ziyal had come to love Garak, much to the dismay of her friends on the station. Of her final days, when Sisko and Starfleet prepared to retake the station and Dukat was forced to flee or be taken prisoner, how Damar ultimately completed the murder Dukat had originally intended and how it felt to see her lifeless body. And as she spoke, Kira knew her cheeks were wet with tears and that she'd shared thoughts and impressions she'd never before voiced aloud to a virtual stranger, but she felt compelled to continue. When the last words left her lips, Kira felt she'd finally arrived at the place the Prophets intended her to, and the restlessness that had haunted her since Macet's arrival finally abated.

Asarem said little in response and Kira understood why. What else could be said? Knowing she had done as she should, Kira decided to leave. She had decisions to make and now she might be able to make them with a peaceful heart. Wishing her good night, Kira started toward the exit when Asarem called after her.

"So what will you do next?"

Kira shrugged. "I don't know. Keep pummeling Shakaar until he relents. Help Ro. Go to Bajor. I'm not sure." She hovered between exhaustion and collapse—a change of scenery could allow her to refuel, gear up for the next challenge. But Ro had two critical open investigations—the Promenade riot and the still unsolved vandalism; responsibility effectively tethered her to the station.

"Walk with the Prophets, Colonel," Asarem said.

"So she finally fell asleep," Phillipa announced, flopping backward onto her bed. She ordered the lights dimmed and sighed. Punching and pulling her pillow succeeded in reconfiguring lumps, but not much else; her neck muscles felt like knotted cords. She rolled over onto her stomach, dangling her feet over the side of the bed and watched her husband undress.

"Rubbing her back works every time. Mireh drops off like that—" Sibias snapped his fingers.

"And how did you figure that out?"

"Works with you."

"You're just a little too sure of yourself, smart man. I don't think a little pressure between the shoulder blades is going to work for me tonight."

"That a challenge?"

"Maybe."

"Tough day?"

"Oh yeah," she groaned. After she'd returned to her quarters, she tried contacting Thriss several more times before her family's needs pressed her into temporarily forgoing her professional concerns. She and Sibias helped the children with homework, played Kadis-Kot and wrapped up the evening with a chapter from Arios's latest favorite, *The Adventures of Lin Marna and the Mystery of Singularity Sam.* Sibias defused Mireh's stalling tactics while she took a sonic shower and now, with the children taken care of, she allowed herself to resume worrying about her patient.

Kicking off his slippers, Sibias sat down beside her. His thumbs massaged the hollows of her shoulder blades. "Can you talk about it?"

Relaxing proved challenging for Phillipa, though Sibias kneading away her muscular stress didn't hurt. She willingly yielded to the pressure, enjoying sensations his hands produced. "Is this how it works with Mireh? You keep her talking while your hands work out every kink in her back?"

"More or less. But there aren't many kinks in her back, being two and all," he said, working down her rib cage. "Mireh isn't as concerned about saving the universe as you are—yet."

Closing her eyes, she blanked her mind, focused on his touch until . . . "I'm sorry," she said, pulling herself up on her elbows, "I can't stop thinking about my patient. I'll just find something to read. Maybe one of your architectural history journals can bore me to sleep. That research on jevonite looks fascinating."

Carefully, Sibias eased her over onto her back. "You can't make it better for everyone, Phil. You can't force people to make good choices. Sometimes, they mess up and you have to be okay with that." He toyed with a lock of her hair, mapped the outline of her cheekbone with his finger.

"I know, I know. . . ." She inhaled sharply. "But I have this feeling that if I could just see her, talk to her, I might be able to make a difference." She covered her face with her forearms. It was just so damn frustrating when you had the tools to fix something and you couldn't. She had to confess, however, that the way Sibias grazed her bare arms might fix her problem with settling down to sleep . . .

He nestled his face in the crook of her neck. "You say that every time, my wife,"

"Your beard is ticklish," she laughed.

"Think of it as a variation on massage therapy," he murmured into the hollow of her throat.

Phillipa loved how he smelled—in her imagination he was musty archeology texts and crisp autumn days and smoky tallow candles. She dropped her arms to her sides, tipped her head toward his and rested her hair against his face. He reached for the top of her pajamas and in one smooth motion, undid the first button, and then the second.

"So I'm thinking if the backrub isn't going to work . . ." he began.

"Damn straight." Twisting onto her side, she wriggled her leg between his and pulled him into her. As they kissed, a blurry thought of Thriss sleeping without the one she loved tightened her throat, until a warm fog of sensation gradually diluted her coherence, leaving her worries to be rediscovered in the morning.

Dizhei stretched awake, wondering when she'd fallen asleep on the couch. A vague recollection of a middle-of-the-night communication from Charivretha explained why she would be in the living room, but not why Anichent had left her there, instead of rousing her to return to watch over Thriss.

This latest bout of moodiness seemed to be following her usual pattern. An angry outburst followed by a verbal tirade, directed most of the time at Anichent until guilt supplanted anger and she dissolved into a quivering mass of tears. Last night, Thriss had cried herself into a migraine before sleep overtook her. Both Dizhei and Anichent had been grateful for the reprieve.

Without question, Thriss' anguish would be better dealt with on

Andor. Those of their own kind could counsel with her, provide her with the emotional support she needed to survive the remainder of Shar's absence. If needs be, she or Anichent could return to Deep Space 9 closer to the time the *Defiant* was scheduled to come home. They would insist that Shar take immediate leave for the *shelthreth*. The anxiety plaguing all of them would end. Decisions about who would stay with whom and where could be made later.

Stumbling to her feet, she stretched again. Perhaps she should check in on Thriss. See how she was feeling this morning. If they were fortunate, her mood might have lifted, allowing them to enjoy their final hours on the station. Dizhei didn't hear Anichent stirring. He'd likely gone to the gymnasium for an early workout. She hoped she could interest him in breakfast at Quark's, anything but replicated—

The door slid open. Dizhei paused. Blinked. And shook her head hoping she might be victim to a sleepy hallucination. But her quivering knees, her racing heartbeat, and the scream that leapt to her throat meant her body understood what her mind refused to accept.

21

Vaughn waited at the bottom of the stairs for Dax. He'd finished his testimony in Tlaral's hearing a little more than an hour ago. Though he hadn't had any direct interaction with the Yrythny technologist, the judicial panel had requested that he explain the situation and circumstances surrounding the Consortium trade. Over the course of the day, Lieutenant Nog and Prynn had also offered their testimonies. His sense was that Tlaral faced an unpleasant fate.

The least of her crimes had been hiding her Wanderer identity and becoming a consort to a Houseborn male. Violating those laws meant, at minimum, a life in prison. Add conspiracy charges stemming from the attempted weapon/Cheka trade and Vaughn was certain the judicial panel would have few options in determining her punishment. She had helped her case by offering to share intelligence on the underground's radical wing. Should her information prove valuable, the panel might be able to exhibit leniency, though some might argue a swift death was less painful than a lifetime haunted by bad choices. Vaughn wasn't sure they would know Tlaral's fate before they left in the morning. He almost hoped the panel would deliberate slowly, avoid succumbing to public pressure for a swift, dramatic verdict. Rash decisions were rarely the correct ones.

At last, the tall, curved doors opened. Ezri slipped through, her attempt to make a soundless getaway failing miserably when the metal handle clanged against the door panels. She swiftly sprang down the stairs, skipping every other step.

"Ready to go, Commander?" she said with a heavy sigh. She had been testifying for more than two hours.

"In every possible way," Vaughn said.

Together, they strolled silently through the long, echoing halls of the Assembly Center, where only two weeks before Ezri had been brought to speak before a joint meeting of both assemblies. Vaughn wished he could have been there to hear her triumphal oratory—at least that's how Shar referred to it. Ezri had been more circumspect in her replies to Vaughn's inquiries. Maybe once they were back on the *Defiant* she would share her account of her experiences among the Yrythny. Sensing that a more complex story lurked beneath the surface, Vaughn was willing to bide his time. "How is it going for Jeshoh in there?"

"Even though Keren's facing charges of her own, her testimony was persuasive," Ezri said. "I believe the panel accepted her explanation of her relationship with Jeshoh, that for most of their lives they'd been friends and they intended to follow the law as best they could. She came off sounding like she'd made the only possible choices in an impossible situation."

That she'd done well pleased him; Vaughn had liked her since their first day on Luthia. If he'd had his druthers, she would have come to the Consortium in Minister M'Yeoh's place. He had to pity the science minister, however. Within a day, he'd lost his consort and likely his political future. The Assembly had demanded the details regarding his union with Tlaral, assuming that he'd either conspired with her or was too easily deceived. When faced with similar circumstances, Keren had chosen the better path. Vaughn concluded, "Keren strikes me as an honorable individual."

"Who broke the law. Who's lost the position she's worked for since she was 10 years out of the water. Who may lose the one she loves. And Jeshoh, because he aligned himself with the terrorists, is facing far worse charges," Ezri noted pragmatically.

"At least you and Shar were able to persuade the panel to drop any charges relating to hijacking the *Sagan*."

"It may not be enough." She shook her head. "The panel hearing Tlaral's case and Jeshoh's will compare notes. If Tlaral shoulders primary responsibility for orchestrating the plan, Jeshoh's punishment should be reduced."

"Is he worried about the potential outcomes?"

"As always, he's more worried about Keren." She pursed her lips, wrinkled her brow thoughtfully. "For himself, I'm not sure. Losing his position as Vice Chair of the Upper Assembly didn't seem to upset him, though the leaders of House Perian were devastated that their favorite son put illicit love above duty to home and world."

"In all the wisdom and experience of the ages, no philosopher has yet found the magical formula for balancing love and duty," Vaughn noted. *God knows I've looked for it.*

They exited through the Assembly Center's main doors and into the Great Plaza. Every corner bustled with activity: vendors, government workers coming and going from their jobs, military officers and Vanìmel dwellers armed with petitions, lined up to enter the Assembly members' offices. Vaughn had been surprised how well Luthia had absorbed the events of the past day. The population appeared quite calm, considering a top Houseborn official had been brought up on treason, the Wanderer underground had attempted to instigate a civil war and news of a major scientific breakthrough had broken within the last few hours. *The business of daily life always propels us forward,* he thought.

"Commander," Ezri said, stopping in her tracks. "Before you go, you ought to try this delicacy from the Black Archipelago region. House Soid harvests massive *darro*, filets the meat into thin strips and marinates it for a year." She tipped her head in the direction of a vending cart where a long line of Yrythny waited.

Having had little time to experience Yrythny culture, Vaughn readily assented. Any regrets he had about leaving involved not having had time to be immersed in the wondrous strangeness of this remarkable world.

They procured their lunch and resumed their walk back to quarters.

"You seem to have enjoyed your time here," Vaughn said, chewing the dried fish off a skewer.

" 'Enjoyed' is how I refer to vacation," Ezri said. "I prefer to think I made the most of my time here. I learned a lot, not just about the Yrythny, but about myself."

"Over my lifetime, I've found that often the most important thing we take from exploration is a better understanding of the world within than the worlds outside."

Dax looked at him quizzically. "What are you suggesting? That the final frontier is less about exploring space than it is about exploring ourselves?"

Vaughn smiled. "Isn't it?"

"You can follow along with the model on your desk screen," Shar said to a filled auditorium of scientists, sitting in semicircle rows around the rostrum where he stood. More Yrythny sat in the aisles and squeezed in around the rear doors. The spotlight trained on him made it difficult to discern exactly how many had gathered to hear his presentation, but he sensed he had a full house. Nog was somewhere in the room, though that didn't make him feel much better. He was still outnumbered about two thousand to one. Not seeing Yrythny faces made it easier to pretend he was back on Andor, presenting his senior thesis prior to his first year at the Academy.

Shar indicated the holographic projection of the Yrythny chromosome. "Here, on the nineteenth chromosome is where the most critical deletions and mutations are occurring." He highlighted the segment in question. "The genes in this segment are responsible for frontal lobe development—upper brain functions. In this segment over here . . ." Shar continued speaking from the text he'd memorized earlier. Having reviewed his results dozens of times with Vaughn and his own staff, Minister M'Yeoh and his committee, and the senior Assembly staff, he could recite this presentation in his sleep.

No one had slept much in the two days since the *Defiant* returned from the Consortium. The whole crew had been enjoying reunions among friends, staying up late swapping stories, and those who could finally took long-overdue shore leave. The *Defiant* hadn't been back an hour before Prynn was grilling Juarez and Candlewood about any and all knowledge they might have about Vanìmel's oceans. Earlier today she had caught the first shuttle to the Coral Sea, leaving word that she would be back to Luthia in time for tomorrow's launch, but not to call her back to the *Defiant* unless the Cheka, the Borg and the Romulans decided to drop by. After hearing Nog's version of the Consortium trip, Shar couldn't say he blamed her.

Shar had spent his time working on his research, promising himself that as soon as he finished he would start analyzing the Yrythny chromosome with an eye to helping his own people. He still believed the "Turn Key" segments might provide clues as to how he might fix weaknesses in Andorian chromosomes. He would focus on his own projects later, after he'd finished reporting to this surprisingly large group of Yrythny.

"Over time, the Yrythny have selected their consorts from a narrow pool of genotypes, enabling recessive mutations to be passed down with increasing frequency," Shar continued. The holoprojection of the chromosome was replaced by a simplified graphic of a Mendelian-style flow chart, showing five generations of Yrythny genotypes. He kept expecting to be interrupted with questions; if he were at home, he'd have been answering questions every minute or so. But he suspected his audience was still reeling from the revelations in his research. It wasn't every day an alien presented a planet with information that had the potential to alter thousands of years of rigidly held social and cultural traditions. He couldn't fathom what would happen, long term, with the Yrythny. The leadership might try to dismiss Shar's work, continuing with the status quo. Already the Assembly had imposed strict controls on who had access to the data, but word traveled rapidly in Luthia and many uninvited guests had shown up for Shar's presentations. Over time, Shar was confident his discovery would have impact. The farmer-scientists on the Hebshu Peninsula would assure that.

Shar deactivated the hologram and the room lighting came up. "That concludes my presentation. If anyone desires further clarification, I've uploaded my data to the Luthia Scientific Archives and the Assembly network. Thank you for coming." He turned to collect the few items he'd brought with him, loading them into his briefcase. When he turned back around, he discovered no one had left. Before he could ask what his Yrythny colleagues were waiting for, every scientist, engineer, and ordinary citizen who had attended his lecture rose to their feet, all eyes focused on him. His antennae tingled, overwhelmed by the deeply felt emotions in the room. Scanning their faces, looking into their eyes, Shar saw mixtures of amazement, gratitude and shock greeting him. He fumbled for the right words, but Nog rescued him, springing to his feet and launching into hearty applause. The Yrythny stared, watching Nog smack his palms together, but gradually, they followed suit, until the entire room thundered.

Shar blinked back incredulity. *I am at the beginning of a path I've been searching for my whole life. I've found my mission.* He looked over at Nog, who hadn't relented, and back at his Yrythny colleagues. Lacking the wherewithal to share what this moment meant to him, Shar accepted their adulation.

Thriss will be proud.

Time to relax, Ezri thought. She splashed some perfume on her wrists that had been among the dozens of gifts she'd received, baskets and packages stacked atop the table in her Luthian quarters. Simply standing in one place, squeezing the plush rug between her toes, had an unexpected charm. Doing nothing was a nice change. She'd hardly had a chance to enjoy Julian. Studying for and delivering testimony before the judicial panel had consumed a good deal of her time, as did preparing to return to their mission and wrapping up loose ends with the Yrythny. Since it was their last night in Luthia, Ezri felt like she deserved to be idle.

Emerging from the bathroom, she yanked her crimson robe tight and plopped down on the couch beside Julian, tucking her bare feet behind her. "Have I told you how wonderful it feels to have this back?" She fingered the robe's lapels. "I should have taken it from our quarters before you all left for the Consortium, but now I have the fun of rediscovering something I missed."

"I hope you missed me as much as the bathrobe," Julian said dryly. Scooting closer to her, Julian reached around her shoulders and pulled her close. Ezri snuggled into him, draped over his lap and nestled her head in the crook of his arm. He ran his fingers through her hair, smoothing and tucking it behind her ears.

"Your hair is longer," he observed.

"It's been two weeks, not two months," she laughed.

"Yes, but did you know that a Trill's hair is capable of growing half a centimeter a week?"

Leave it to Julian to prove his point, no matter what the circumstances. "We could continue discussing my amazing follicles, or you could find other equally intriguing aspects of my anatomy to study." She walked her fingers up his neck and ruffled the hair on the back of his head.

"As much as that suggestion appeals to me, I think I want to talk to you before we further my studies of Trill anatomy." Julian linked their fingers together. Bringing her hand up to his lips, he placed a kiss on each knuckle.

"Isn't the woman supposed to be the one who likes to talk?" Ezri pouted.

"No, seriously. We haven't talked much about what happened while we were apart. You clearly have something on your mind," Julian said. "When you aren't being frivolous, you're quite pensive. I'd like you to share it with me."

Rising from Julian's lap, Ezri curled into the couch, resting her cheek on the cushions. She studied her lap while she struggled to find the right words.

"You were right," she said finally, meeting his eyes. "I still haven't found my equilibrium."

He waited patiently for her to elaborate at her own pace.

"I was so sure of myself, Julian. So sure I could do it all. And you were right. I'd started to believe no challenge was beyond me. That I had no limits. But this experience taught me otherwise. My time here wasn't what I thought it would be. It was, in short, kind of humiliating."

"That's hardly what I've heard. The Yrythny were wowed by your diplomatic savvy. The compromise you negotiated before Shar made his discovery is still going to be ratified, except now some of the inter-caste taboos will be lifted for colonists. You blazed the trail."

"See, that's the thing. I didn't blaze the trail," she rolled her eyes, embarrassed. "Technically, Curzon, Lela, Audrid, and Jadzia did. They did most of the work. Even the speech I gave at the Assembly that first day? I stole it from Lela."

"What's the benefit of having a symbiont if you don't learn from past lives?"

"I'm not supposed to *live* my past lives and that's what Ive been doing. By the time I started working on the compromise, it was Curzon doing the work, not Ezri." Ezri brought her knees up into her chest. "Being joined isn't supposed to work like that. I'm supposed to augment the symbiont's experiences with my own, but sometimes it feels like Dax has already done it all."

"Ezri, I think you're being hard on yourself—" Julian tried to hug her, but Ezri backed away.

"I'm not asking for pity, Julian," she said earnestly. "Honest. Dax's past hosts made incredible contributions to the Federation. Books could be written about Curzon and Jadzia alone! But then the superlative Jadzia is followed up with Ezri Tigan, who didn't want to be joined in the first place. I'm kind of the place-holding host until some brilliant initiate can receive Dax after I die."

Julian took Ezri's hand and squeezed it, willing her to look him in the eye. "Listen to me. Right now, you're giving Dax experiences none of the other hosts could. None of them ever ventured on an exploratory mission like this one. The things you've seen—and will see in the years to come—will be different from anything the others experienced."

Grateful for his sweet words, Ezri kissed Julian's palm. She knew, however, that she needed to own up to her mistakes. "I had no idea what was being asked of me when I agreed to help the Yrythny. Part of me thought that I needed to prove to Commander Vaughn, and to the crew, that I was good enough to be his first officer, to be a leader. That choosing the command track was the right decision at this point in my personal evolution." She sighed. "But then when I started working with all these committees . . . I'm not an ambassador or an anthropologist. It became easier to know what to do when I allowed Lela or Curzon to take the lead instead of myself."

"In the end, though, it was Ezri who triumphed," Julian pointed out. "Nothing Dax had done could have helped you. When you trusted *your* experiences and training, you succeeded brilliantly."

She quirked a half-smile. "I know. That part I feel good about. When I think back to the previous two weeks . . . not so much. I was a fool. Poor Shar, I think he knew it and he was very, very patient with me."

"All's well that ends well?"

"Yeah. I suppose."

A beep sounded from the wall console. Ezri looked over and saw the message light blinking. "I'd better check that. With us leaving in the morning, you never know what might be coming up at the last minute."

She crossed the room to pull up the message, quickly scanning the contents. "It's from the judiciary panel. They'll have a ruling on Jeshoh's case tomorrow morning. Is it a good sign that they've come back with a decision so quickly?" Part of Ezri worried, hoping her testimony had helped his case. What happened on the *Sagan* was an aberration from the Jeshoh she'd grown to like and admire in her time on Vanìmel.

"If you think about it, there wasn't that much to decide. His guilt wasn't in question, more what the consequences would be."

"I'm glad we'll know soon."

"And yet another triumph for Ezri. Without you, Jeshoh might have gone through with Tlaral's plan. You might have saved him—and Keren—a lot of heartache."

Shoving her hands in her pockets, Ezri said, "Are you hungry? I'm hungry."

Julian laughed. "Not so much hungry, but thirsty. How about—"

"—a Tarkelian tea. You're so predictable," she said affectionately. "Sorry, you'll have to wait until we're back on *Defiant* to indulge that particular vice. Tell you what, though, try this." She tossed him a self-heating bulb from among her gifts. "Local brew. You might like it." For herself, she selected a slice of a fruit torte she'd grown to like during the official dinner parties she'd attended. Someone who'd apparently noticed sent her a dozen.

"Not bad," Julian said after an appreciative sip. "We should save one for the replicators to analyze."

"That's a good idea. In fact, I should do the same with all the— OW!" Ezri dropped her plate on the table and hopped up on one foot while massaging the bruised toes of the other. Bending over, she reached for the offending item. "Your dufflebag belongs in the middle of the rug?" she said with mock annoyance.

"I was so eager to see you I didn't bother to put it away in the sleeproom."

"Yes, well explain that to my toes," she said, hefting the bag onto an empty chair. "Hey . . . what's this—" Ezri removed a padd from inside. Clicking it on, she thumbed through the contents. She read aloud, " 'Lughor pulled her close and bit her cheek, snarling, "You will be my mate, my Ngara—' Umm, Julian, what are you doing with *Burning Hearts of Qo'noS?*"

"Oh, that." He tapped his foot absently. "Commander Vaughn was finished with it, so he handed it off to me."

"Did he say if he liked it?"

"I asked him. He just rolled his eyes."

Ezri continued perusing the padd, thumbing through a few more screens. "You know, Jadzia wouldn't consider this fiction, she'd see it as an instruction manual." She raised a teasing eyebrow.

"And Ezri?" Julian said, rising from the couch.

"You want to find out?"

"Did you even sleep last night?" Nog asked, rubbing his eyes and yawning.

Shar looked up from his computer terminal. After dinner, he'd come straight back to his Luthian quarters to work on his chromosomal studies. Once the *Defiant* resumed its mission his time would, by necessity, belong to Vaughn and the needs of the mission. Returning to Deep Space 9 having made meaningful progress on his goals would go a long way to silencing those who had cast aspersions on his choices (most notably, his *zhavey*). "It's morning?"

"Morning usually is when the sun comes out. Unless this world is backward and they call it morning when it's dark outside." Nog padded over to the replicator, ordered up a root beer and collapsed on a chair.

"Adrenaline must have kept me up," Shar said. He closed the file he'd been working on and uploaded it to the *Defiant*. "Yesterday was a rather unique day for me."

"Don't let it go to your head, Ensign. Even if you solve the universe's problems, I still outrank you." Nog winked and took a swig of root beer.

"Noted, sir," Shar said, suppressing a smile. "Do you want to grab breakfast here or wait until we return to *Defiant?*

"What exactly *is* a Yrythny breakfast?"

"Fish, *shmshu* cheese on kelp cakes, sea melons—"

Nog's face puckered. "I'll eat on the *Defiant,* thanks. Grubcakes in slug sauce. That's a meal."

The door chime sounded. Since Nog still sleepily nursed his soda, Shar figured he'd better see who their visitor was.

"Keren—" he said. Her rumpled clothes and grayed complexion bespoke the stress she'd been through since they'd landed at Luthia. He hadn't talked privately with her since they'd left for House Perian to hunt the raiders.

"Try not to be so surprised, Ensign ch'Thane," Keren said lightly. "Your feelings are showing."

"What? Oh, of course. My antennae."

"I wanted to tell you about the ruling before you heard it officially." She peeked into Shar's quarters and noticing Nog, said, "Can we go someplace to talk?"

"The courtyard?"

She nodded.

As she sat down, Keren dropped a small backpack on the ground beside the bench. Both shifted uncomfortably, neither knowing how to broach the events of the previous days. Finally Keren said, "The panel issued their findings for Jeshoh and me. They let me off easy. When the first colonists leave Vanìmel I will be with them. They've decided exile is better than prison. I think they're worried that I might be a martyr to whatever is left of the underground."

"You would have tried to go off-world anyway, wouldn't you?" Shar asked. "Now that your people have a working defense against the web weapons—"

"Yes. But I have to admit that being sent away and never being allowed to return is a sobering thought. Whether the colonies are successful or not, I will live out my life elsewhere." Keren reached over, stroking the velvety petals of a trumpet flower. "This is still my home and I love it."

I wonder how I would feel if I could never return to Andor. The thought struck him as ironic, considering he'd been avoiding going back for over four years. *The time has come. I'm ready for the* shelthreth. And until the thought crossed his mind, Shar hadn't known that he would choose the *shelthreth* when his current mission was over. In a few days, he'd sit down with Commander Vaughn and negotiate the terms of his leave. The more he imagined making a life commitment to Anichent, Dizhei and Thriss, the more excited he became.

"Understandably, Jeshoh's sentence isn't quite as lenient as mine," Keren continued. "He will serve a prison sentence. The number of years will be decided after Tlaral's hearing wraps up."

"After prison, isn't he free? There aren't any more restrictions imposed on him."

"Yes. At that point, he will join me wherever I am . . ." She gripped the edge of the bench, her shoulders tense.

A sense of dread filled Shar. "What is it, Keren?"

"With his position, with his involvement in the underground, the panel decided that they couldn't excuse his relationship with me." Closing her eyes, she whispered, "He'll never be able to go into the waters."

Her bravery, her resolve in the face of these consequences, humbled Shar. After spending her life working for the right to take a consort and have offspring, she wouldn't have the chance unless she chose someone other than Jeshoh. Having witnessed their devotion to each other, Shar couldn't fathom that she would abandon Jeshoh now.

"Of course I'll wait for him, Shar," Keren said. Seeing his puzzled expression, she clarified, "You're wearing your feelings again."

"I'm sorry. I wish there was a way . . ."

"We knew the risks." With a distant look in her eyes, she said, "Jeshoh and I will have a home together someday. I know we will." She patted his leg. "I have another reason for visiting. To say goodbye, yes, but I have a gift."

"But—"

"No protests." Reaching into her backpack, Keren removed a sealed container about the size of a dinner plate. "The eggs stripped from House Perian couldn't all be saved. Most of them had been out of the water for too long under variable temperatures and became nonviable. The government destroyed them, but before they did I persuaded them to let me give you an egg pouch in thanks for your research." Reaching out to take his hand, she turned it palm up and placed the container into it, smiling gently. "I know what you're trying to do for your people, Shar. This way, you have proper samples to work with and not just computer models."

Emotion tightened Shar's throat. He swallowed, opened his mouth, but nothing emerged. Continuing to stare at her, he reached for her hands and squeezed them.

"It's a small thing, Shar. You've more than paid for the right to take these." Standing up, she lay her cheek in his hair for a moment and walked away. When he shook off his astonishment, he searched the courtyard for her, but she had vanished, leaving his life very much the way she had come into it.

The doors to his quarters opened and Nog poked his head out. "Hey, Shar. I've decided to head back to the ship. The commander called a minute ago. He said an encrypted message came through marked 'eyes only,' but apparently it was for you and not Vaughn. He's having it rerouted here."

"Thank you, Nog," Shar said, gazing at the egg container. "I'll be along soon. But I want to sit here for a few minutes longer."

"Okay. I'll see you shipboard then?"

Shar nodded.

He ran his fingers over Keren's gift, imagining that the answers he'd sought his entire life might lie within. Bowing his head, he covered his eyes, offering gratitude to whatever power in the universe had brought him to this place at this time. He would never regret the choices that brought him here; he would never be the same person after today. For a moment he meditated, savoring the gentle trickle of water spilling over the fountain, the occasional rustle of leaves. When he opened his eyes, he was ready to return to duty. Holding the gift protectively against him, he entered his quarters.

* * *

Sleeping late was a rare indulgence, but it felt nice to flaunt the routine one last time before starting up the rigors of co-commanding a Starfleet mission. Soon enough, Ezri would be stumbling into the mess, muttering her request to the replicator and feeling her way to a table. Choosing to loll about, half dressed, eating a breakfast of succulent fresh fruits and licking the juice off your fingers wasn't something she anticipated being able to do before she returned to Deep Space 9. Never mind that she had the guest quarters to herself. To provide him with adequate time to restock the medical bay, Julian had reported to duty two hours ago. Ezri stayed behind, wrapped up in her covers, relishing the warmth streaming through the courtyard windows. A check of the chronometer indicated she still had another hour before she met with Vaughn to allocate duty shifts. *A walk. A walk sounds nice.* She pulled on an old favorite pair of Academy sweats and ambled out to the balcony.

Spending these weeks on Luthia made her wonder if more nature could be incorporated into the station's auspices. Outside the arboretum and a few botany labs, assuaging a craving for trees and flowers required time in a holosuite, or a trip to Bajor. Leisurely, Ezri walked down the stairs, bending over to examine the fragrant ground cover. She took a seat on a bench, throwing her legs out in front of her, throwing back her head and closing her eyes, soaking up the light for a last few precious minutes.

"*. . . I wish there was something we could have done. Dr. Girani had no idea the infirmary was missing anything and . . .*"

Ezri sat up straight. *I swear I heard voices.*

"*—until you come home. I don't know what else to tell you. The others are too distraught to speak right now.*"

She twisted around, trying to see who might still be in quarters because if she had to guess, she'd just heard Charivretha zh'Thane. *Maybe I drank too much wine last night or those chocolate pastries didn't sit well with my stomach.* Shar's courtyard door was open, the curtains blowing. Cautiously, Ezri approached the open door. The closer she came, the more clear the voice and as she listened, the context became clear. Standing outside, Ezri braced herself on the doorway, willing her thudding heart to stop. *What can I do?* She considered walking away. Invading his privacy right now could be exactly the wrong thing—or it could be exactly what he needed. She pushed aside the curtain and stepped inside.

With his back to the courtyard door, he sat on the floor in front of the console. She had been right—the speaker was zh'Thane. The Federation Councillor sat in a chair in what looked like VIP quarters on DS9, the pain etched on her face expressing more than her words could.

"Her death was painless. I know you wouldn't have wanted her to suffer. None of us understand why she did it. She seemed—better. I am sorry, my chei.*"*

The screen turned to static and then the message replayed.

"Thirishar, I wish I could be sending this message under happier circumstances, but a great tragedy has befallen us—"

Ezri knelt down, touched Shar's shoulder. He turned with a start, his limbs trembling uncontrollably. Wide-eyed, he stared at Ezri, his pain, unfathomable. Helplessness swelled inside her and she ached for him. She opened and closed her mouth several times, searching for words. *I shouldn't be here.* Zh'Thane's heartbreaking message continued to play in the background. *What can I give him? I'm not equipped for this—I can't make it better!* From deep inside her, an answer, of a kind, came. Not so much an answer as a knowing, a knowing from Dax.

You. He needs you, Ezri.

Tears welled in her eyes. "I'm so sorry . . ." She gathered him into her arms and he yielded to her touch.

They wept together.

EPILOGUE

"I'm not an invalid!" protested Kasidy.

"No, you're not," Kira said patiently, clearing the dessert plates off the coffee table and heading off to the kitchen, "but you've spent the last half hour rubbing your arches. Your feet must be killing you after our walk today. Let me remind you that visiting every last stall at the market was your idea."

"If my feet get any bigger, I'm going to have to attach warnings to my shoes saying, 'Watch out—wide berth.'" Wincing, she threw her body forward, hoping the momentum would help her off the couch. The baby, however, had diffcrent ideas, choosing that moment to thrust its head squarely into her diaphragm. She grunted as it suddenly became hard to breathe. "I'll think I'll just stay here for a bit," she said, settling back into the cushions. From across the room, Kasidy saw Kira grin.

"Having a laugh at my expense, Colonel?" Kasidy teased, grateful that Kira had gradually unwound over the past few days; initially, her smiles had been infrequent.

Upon arrival, Kira had been so pale (Kasidy swore she'd lost weight as well), Kasidy thought she might be coming down with something serious. A more logical explanation for her condition quickly became apparent: she hadn't been on Bajor an hour before the station contacted her, with the next message arriving fifteen minutes after the first. Kasidy had quickly instituted a daily pattern of long walks—asking Kira to leave her combadge back at the house.

Kira scraped chocolate frosting off the plates into the recycler and deposited the plates in the sink to be washed later. "I was just remembering this time . . . a month before Kirayoshi was born. Sitting in Quark's with Jadzia, I'd probably had a liter of juice. The little guy decided it'd be a good time to play hoverball with my bladder."

It was Kasidy's turn to laugh, relating all too well to Kira's anecdote. Throwing her legs up so she sat sideways, Kas rested her chin on the back of the couch and watched Kira continue cleaning up. Though the meal had been simple, salads made with fresh greens and vegetables from her garden and squash soup, old-fashioned cooking tended to make a mess no matter how many shortcuts technology might provide.

"I vote we replicate breakfast," Kira said, pouring the last of the soup into a storage container. Clearing off the counters, she shuttled clean goblets into the cupboard and tossed a handful of katerpods into the produce basket. Wiping her hands on a towel, she crossed back to the sitting room and resumed her perch on Kasidy's favorite overstuffed chair.

"Cooking can be bothersome," Kasidy conceded, "but there's nothing quite as satisfying as getting your hands dirty *doing* something and then enjoying the fruits of your labors."

"You know . . . you sound like Benjamin when you talk like that," Kira said wistfully.

"I think that's one of the reasons I cook: it helps me keep him close."

"Do you—" Kira began, but hesitated.

"Get lonely?" she said, completing the question. "Miss him?" Since Kira arrived, they both had kept their conversations light. Kas assumed Kira needed the respite from her worries about the station as much as Kas needed to stop dwelling on Jake.

"I wasn't trying to be nosy," Kira apologized.

Kasidy held up a hand to stop her. "Everyone wonders and my honest answer is, of course. After the station—after being a ship's captain—the quiet around here took some getting used to. Now I actually like it." She said it and she meant it. At first, Kasidy followed through with the "dream house" project because she felt like she owed it to Ben. Gradually, she became caught up in the details, grateful to be staying busy. She was surprised how much time she spent selecting the stones for the fireplace, talking with the carpenter who carved the mantel, and finding just the right hand-thrown pottery plates that would sit on her kitchen table. Attributing her preoccupation with rugs and end tables to a maternal nesting instinct felt plausible to her. Then one day, standing in this very room she sat in now, she was savoring the warm sun streaming through the windows when she realized that she loved it here. This was *her* home. Her lullabies would whisper through its rafters. Fresh asters and Bajoran lilacs from the garden she planted would fill vases in every room. Jake—and Ben—would return here. Until then, she would make it ready to welcome them. "I have my fears," she said at last. "And I'd sleep easier knowing Jake was safe, but I'm happy."

"I'm glad you're happy, Kas. You've had more than your share of heartache since the war ended," Kira said, turning her gaze to watch the evening's first moonrise.

"We all have," Kasidy replied. "I hardly have a monopoly on suffering. I consider myself very blessed. You've shouldered your share of struggles."

"Mine are relatively small," she said lightly. Since her arrival, Kira had avoided talking about any work-related problems she might be having, focusing instead on Kasidy's baby, her search for dependable farm help, Jake, and the general political situation. Kas assumed that Kira didn't want to "needlessly worry the pregnant lady," a sentiment she'd become intimately familiar with. As the days passed, however, Kasidy began suspecting Kira's reticence wasn't solely motivated by benevolence. Perhaps, being immersed in DS9 and Bajor's needs had acclimated Kira to ignoring her own. *And that's not good,* she thought. "It's my turn to ask an impertinent question, Nerys."

"Fire away."

"Are you happy?"

Kira snorted. "Kas—"

"I'm not budging from this spot until you tell me what's on your mind," Kasidy said.

Kira inhaled deeply. She toyed with the macramé vest she wore, threading her fingers through the holes. "There's not a simple answer. I wouldn't necessarily change my life—" she lifted heavy-lidded eyes to Kasidy "—except the Attainder. That I could do without." The weak smile she offered Kas failed to offset her worry wrinkles.

Kira carries her burdens in her eyes. Shades of Benjamin, Kasidy thought, imagining she could see the mantle of command bestowed upon her friend by her husband. "Talk to me. I've been told I'm a good listener—and I know how to keep a secret."

Considering Kasidy for a long moment, Kira's brow furrowed. "Where to start? Double-dealing Shakaar, the peace talks mess, the daughter-in-law of the Federation councillor's suicide—and that's the appetizer. Believe me, Kas, you don't want to hear about this."

"Yes I do," Kasidy insisted. "You've done a great job catching me up on all the station gossip, though I'm still not sure what to make of Lieutenant Ro, um, socializing with Quark. Now I want the rest of it."

Kira rose from her chair and walked over to turn on the fireplace. Resting her arm against the river rocks, she stared into the flames. "You know I even tried knitting? And I found it incredibly frustrating. I followed the instructions from the database to the letter and no matter how meticulously I worked, I managed to drop stitches or purl when I was supposed to knit. When the yarn became all tangled up and knotted, I figured, the hell with this! And that's how I feel things are at the station right now—just like my knitting." She ran her hand along the mantel's smoothly carved curves and curlicues, pausing to pick up the amber-gold figurine given to Kasidy by Prylar Eivos. "I do the best that I know how to do and where has that gotten us? Promenade fights, vandalism, threats against the Cardassian delegation. I hate saying it, but I almost miss the war. At least then we knew who we were fighting and what we were fighting for."

"Nerys, I'm no expert on commanding a—" The door chime rang. *Oh, who could that be?* Kasidy thought irritably. In her early days here, well-meaning Bajorans seeking to "help" the Emissary's wife stopped by, uninvited, as if she were building a shrine, not a house. Gradually, as all parties came to an understanding she'd stopped being a curiosity to the locals. Now her neighbors vigorously protected her privacy, refusing to dole out the smallest tidbit to strangers seeking her, even those on religious pilgrimages. *I hope there's not an emergency. Wouldn't they call first?* Kasidy scooted to the edge of the couch, psyching herself up for whoever might be visiting.

"I'll get it," Kira said. She set the figurine down on the coffee table and vanished into the foyer.

"I'm not an invalid," Kasidy muttered, pushing up onto her feet and following after Kira. The baby snuggled into her ribs; she paused to push gently on the head, trying to dislodge it. No luck. She heard the beeps of Kira tapping in the lock release.

"You?" came her visitor's shocked exclamation.

"Not who you were expecting, Vedek Yevir?" Kira said.

Inwardly, Kasidy groaned, wishing she could become invisible; Yevir was about as welcome as a malfunctioning phaser in the middle of a firefight. While she found most Bajoran clerics to be pleasant (being the Emissary's wife meant they were on their best behavior around her), Yevir was the exception. Kasidy couldn't stomach his sanctimoniousness, how he wrapped his unapologetic quest to be kai in a cloak of piety. He'd shown his true character when he slapped the Attainder on Kira; Kasidy wasn't prepared to forgive him for what she believed to be a vindictive, politically motivated punishment. That Bajor would be better off with Yevir as kai than they were with Winn was doubtful to Kasidy's way of thinking. For a moment, Kasidy considered turning back around and hiding in the sitting room. Kira would get rid of him.

. . . But how fair was that to Kira.

Kasidy turned the corner and saw Kira had blocked the doorway, arms linked across her chest. From her posture, Kasidy surmised it would take a Klingon with a *bat'leth* to pass into the vestibule.

"With all due respect, Vedek, why not go back to town and call back in the morning? Make an *appointment* with Captain Yates," Kira said coldly.

Peering at the vedek from behind Kira, Kasidy said, "So you were in the neighborhood and thought you'd stop by for a visit?"

Her tone provoked a deep pink flush in Yevir's cheeks. His eyes fixed on Kasidy. "I know I've come without an invitation, Captain Yates, but my business is urgent. I've come to believe Bajor's spiritual health is at stake."

Kira was impressed. To Kasidy, she said, "I'll take care of this." And to Yevir, "Take it up with the Vedek Assembly."

Kasidy stopped her. "I'm not the Emissary, Vedek. Even though it seems I keep having to remind people—"

"Please," Yevir said. "Captain, I need—I assure you the situation is quite dire." Yevir took a step toward Kasidy. Kira glared at him and he promptly stepped back.

Still the master of overstatement, Kas thought, *and still unable to take a hint.* "I'm sorry, but we were in the middle of something and—"

"A moment of your time—that's all I ask. I beg of you." The look in his eyes was imploring.

Suspecting he might be prostrate on the porch at any moment, Kasidy wondered what to do next. If she shut the door on him he'd probably still be around at dawn. Kasidy sighed. *I can't put Nerys through that.* To Kira she said, "Why don't you start walking without me? I'll catch up with you after the Vedek leaves." *Please Nerys, take the hint,* she wished fervently.

Puzzled, Kira looked over her shoulder at Kasidy, raising a questioning eyebrow. Kasidy shrugged as if to say, *Let's just get this over with.*

Kira stepped aside, gesturing for Yevir to enter.

When he made a visible point of squeezing through the door frame rather than touch Kira, Kasidy began to wonder if she'd regret her invitation. She indicated she wanted Yevir to follow her to the sitting room where she and Kira had been only minutes before. Kasidy felt Kira's eyes trained on their backs as she waited for Yevir to misstep.

If Kira's scrutiny bothered Yevir, he didn't show it. Walking behind Kasidy, Yevir's apologies continued until they were both seated. Once Kasidy heard the door close—with Kira on the outside—she felt reassured that her friend would be spared any further indignities.

Dealing with Yevir should be easy in comparison to some of the tight spots she'd had to negotiate her way out of over the years. She recalled arguing with a Nausicaan who insisted Kasidy had picked up the wrong cargo. *He* was difficult; Yevir was merely bothersome.

Since Yevir had been the one to request speaking with her, Kasidy expected him to initiate the discussion. She would nod her head politely in response, tell him there was nothing she could do and send him on his way. Folding her hands in her lap, Kasidy waited.

Yevir sat perched on the edge of the chair, blinking nervously, saying nothing, unwilling or unable to meet her eyes. Uncomfortable silence followed.

At last Kasidy said, "Please get on with your business, Vedek."

He cleared his throat, shifting a few times, and licked his lips. "The present state of affairs troubles me," Yevir stammered. "I believe recent events bode ill for Bajor."

"I'm not in a position to do anything about the state of Bajor, Vedek," Kasidy said pragmatically.

"But *I* should be!" He stood up, pacing back and forth in front of the fireplace, his robes swishing as he walked. "I was chosen by the Emissary to be a spiritual leader among my people. As such, I should know how best to guide them. But for the first time since Captain Sisko set me on my present course, the way is dark to me."

Kasidy shook her head. *This was a mistake . . .* "If you're truly concerned for Bajor, Vedek, you need to have this conversation with someone else. Somebody in the Vedek Assembly, the Chamber of Ministers . . ."

"I'm not sure I know what to say to any of them. What I do know is my people have reached a crossroad on the path of the Prophets, with no arrow to point us toward the true way. They're in danger of becoming lost, and I must learn what I need to do to help make things right."

"If you want to make things right, start by rescinding Kira's Attainder," Kasidy said tightly.

Yevir frowned and looked away. "The Colonel's standing within our faith is unrelated to this issue."

"If you want to have this conversation with me, in my house, it's not."

Yevir was silent a moment. "I'm sorry," he said finally. "I know you have a close relationship with the Colonel. And in a way, Kira's situation is part of the crisis in which my people now find themselves."

Concerned by where Yevir might be headed with this, Kasidy said, "Go on." *Give me one more reason, Yevir, and I'm tossing you out on your ass. See how good that looks on your application for kai.*

"As I said, from the start, I've tried to follow the way your husband laid out for me. Or, more accurately, what I believed that way to be. I sought to destroy Ohalu's book because I truly believed that was best for Bajor. But now . . . now I'm not so sure . . ." He fell back into his chair, folding his hands tightly before him as he concentrated on what he needed to say. "The greatest moment of clarity in my life came when I spoke with the Emissary. I knew in that timeless instant he was setting me on the path I was always destined to walk, and that it would lead me to become kai."

"You sound almost as if you don't believe that anymore."

"I don't know what to believe," Yevir said softly, in tones that convinced Kasidy the admission was painful for him to make. "Nothing is unfolding in a manner I understand. The Ohalu text, the sundering of the faithful, the failure of the peace talks with Cardassia. . . . So much is happening that threatens Bajor's spiritual well-being, I no longer feel I understand the role the Emissary chose me for.

"I came here tonight—to you—hoping that whatever illumination filled him might have touched you and that you might . . ." His voice trailed off into silence. Finally he shrugged and said quietly, "I felt compelled to come."

Kasidy probed his face, searching for insincerity, and found confusion; Yevir appeared truly flummoxed. Not for the first time, Kasidy wished being the wife of the Emissary came with a handbook. "I wish I knew what Ben would have told you if he were here."

Closing his eyes tight, Yevir slowly shook his head. "I understand. I apologize for disturbing you. Forgive me." In a paternal gesture, he lifted her hand off the armrest and pressed it between his own. "Thank you for your time, Captain Yates. I'll let myself out." He backed away, bowing—and froze, eyes fixed.

Kasidy scanned herself, the floor, the furniture, for a clue as to what had transfixed Yevir. "What is it?" she said, worried.

Still staring, he appeared not to hear her.

She followed his eyes to the figurine Kira had placed on the coffee table before answering the door. Amber and gold, the flecks inside caught the firelight and shimmered with otherworldly radiance.

"What *is* that?" he whispered.

"It's from B'hala. Unearthed during the excavation," Kasidy explained. *Jevonite,* Eivos had said it was made of. *Have I missed something?*

Hesitantly, Yevir reached toward the figurine, his trembling hand hovering. He looked at Kasidy. "May I?"

"Go ahead."

Yevir scooped up the figurine, holding it in his palm, slowly turning it over and over. "I don't have the right to ask, but—" He raised his eyes, wide with childlike wonder.

"Take it. Please," Kasidy said. "If it has some significance to you, then by all means, it's yours."

He clutched the figurine tightly in his hand. "Thank you." His head dipped in a respectful nod. "Thank you truly, Captain."

"I didn't do anything," Kasidy protested, rising.

"I believe the Prophets led me here for a reason. I don't know exactly what it is yet, but this—" He held up the hand closed around the figurine. "—I think this may be the arrow I've been searching for."

Puzzling over his effusiveness, Kasidy walked him to the door. *He believes he found what he came for,* she thought as she waved good-bye. *And knowing where you're supposed to go can make all the difference.* She watched Yevir until he disappeared around a bend in the road. *I hope that soon the same can be said for Kira.*

Kira slammed her heels into the dirt with each brisk step, grimacing at the thought of that—that—of Kas having to deal with that man! Yevir wasn't Kas's problem, he was hers. Disgusted, she spat. *I know how to take a hint from the universe.*

Yevir showing up as she was attempting to untangle her snarled life had to be a sign that she wasn't meant to understand "why." Why Thriss took her life only two days before Shar's message arrived from the Gamma Quadrant. Or why some bastard felt the need to make an example out of Ziyal—yet again. And her favorite "what-the-hell-is-he-thinking" question mark, Shakaar. Sure, she had her quarrels with him on an interpersonal level. He might use their past together as leverage over her politically, but she had trusted his leadership skills. So what happened to cause Shakaar to suddenly come down with a case of blindness equal to or surpassing Yevir's? Bajor was being led on both the secular and religious fronts by blind men. And who was she to even presume she was better than them? Nothing she was doing seemed to be working out either. To expect guidance or answers when her whole world might be walking into darkness was pretty selfish of her. She needed to let go and trust that the Prophets had a plan. Surely they wouldn't let Bajor fail because of the stupidity of her servants. *Damn!* She kicked at the dirt, sending rocks skittering. Following the gentle slope down to the riverbank, her walk gathered speed, gradually becoming a full run.

The moon's wan face rippled silver on the water's surface, its pale illumination providing enough light to see by. A chilly breeze blew off the river, rattling the dry leaves clinging to the trees and numbing Kira's ears. Breathing deeply burned her lungs but she pressed on, picking her way around the clumps of river grass. She relished pushing her body until her sides ached, being driven by instinct instead of rational thought.

How long had it been since she let go? Keeping a tight reign on her emotions was part of her duty. When everyone around her completely unspooled, Kira remained in control. Take away her beloved captain. Take away her love. Take away her right to publicly practice her religion. Throw disillusionment, confusion and frustration at her and she'd bat them away, one, two, three. Nothing to it, because that's who she was. But now the rules of the game were changing yet again, and she began to doubt her ability to keep up.

Kira followed the path away from the river into the forest where gnarled, knotted trees cloaked her in shadow. She continued running. With each step, she gagged on the pungent smoke-tinged wind blowing over from the adjoining farm. She pushed through anyway.

I'll keep going as long as my body has breath, if that's what the Prophets want from me, she vowed. If she had to pinpoint what intimidated her most about the road ahead, it was the sense that she was headed straight for a cliff with only the hope that there was some good to be achieved by her jumping.

Leaping over roots, she followed the twisting path, her view of the trail ahead obscured by tree trunks and waist-high bushes, bobbing and swaying. Her blood hammered in her throat and in her ears as her feet pounded the ground, until her boot hit something hard and she slammed into the path, knees first, then her chest, knocking the wind out of her. The stinging scrapes shocked her and she rolled over, tasting peaty dirt mingling with blood, leaves clinging to her clothes. A cry welled up in her throat but refused release.

Flat on her back, Kira looked up through knobby, stripped branches at the starless sky, feeling sharp waves of pain stabbing through her knees. She clenched her teeth, focused intently on controlling her breathing.

She lay on her back, listening to the murmuring wind, the occasional crack of a breaking branch, the swish of bird wings. Staring at the sky, she pretended the wormhole was fixed above her position, promising herself that if she could see the flash of it opening . . .

She waited. She waited until damp numbness overtook her limbs and still, nothing. *I don't know what I was expecting. I should just go back. Kas will be worried.* She sighed. Kira might have witnessed her share of miracles—and had exquisite spiritual experiences in her lifetime—but she wasn't foolish enough to believe that the Prophets gave you a sign simply because you asked for one.

Grunting, she eased herself up so she was sitting with her legs stretched out in front of her. Luckily, it didn't feel like she'd sprained or broken anything, though she could feel small rocks embedded in the skin of her kneecaps.

She brushed herself off and then, placing the heels of her hands behind her, she pushed off, succeeding only in dislodging a stone she'd braced herself against. *Let's see if I can do this without cracking my tailbone, too,* she thought ruefully. But then her fingers brushed against the stone again, piquing her curiosity. *This isn't a rock.* Yanking it free from where it was wedged under an exposed root, Kira held it out in front of her, hoping a beam of light breaking through the forest's canopy would help her better see what she held.

She thought her eyes must be playing tricks on her.

Her hands began furiously brushing off the dirt encrusting the object. Muddy, frayed, and lost here among the trees of Captain Sisko's land since when, she couldn't say. But there was no denying what she held in her hand.

A baseball.

Stitching unraveling, leather stained and pocked, and so waterlogged it was unusable—but none of it changed the fact that Kira held one of the Emissary's baseballs. Her mind raced. Kas had told her he used to bat them out here to clear his head, but—

Slowly, Kira smiled. Then the laughter came, softly at first, but gathering strength until it engulfed her.

Knowing Kasidy would be waiting, Kira returned to the path and pointed herself toward home.

**MISSION: GAMMA CONTINUES IN
BOOK THREE
CATHEDRAL**

ABOUT THE AUTHOR

Heather Jarman lives in Portland, Oregon. *This Gray Spirit* is her
first work of professional fiction. She plans to return to the *Star
Trek* universe soon.

Look for STAR TREK fiction from Pocket Books

Star Trek®

Star Trek: Voyager®

Star Trek®: Day of Honor

#1 • *Ancient Blood* • Diane Carey
#2 • *Armageddon Sky* • L.A. Graf
#3 • *Her Klingon Soul* • Michael Jan Friedman
#4 • *Treaty's Law* • Dean Wesley Smith & Kristine Kathryn Rusch
The Television Episode • Michael Jan Friedman
Day of Honor Omnibus • various

Star Trek®: The Captain's Table

#1 • *War Dragons* • L.A. Graf
#2 • *Dujonian's Hoard* • Michael Jan Friedman
#3 • *The Mist* • Dean Wesley Smith & Kristine Kathryn Rusch
#4 • *Fire Ship* • Diane Carey
#5 • *Once Burned* • Peter David
#6 • *Where Sea Meets Sky* • Jerry Oltion
The Captain's Table Omnibus • various

Star Trek®: The Dominion War

#1 • *Behind Enemy Lines* • John Vornholt
#2 • *Call to Arms...* • Diane Carey
#3 • *Tunnel Through the Stars* • John Vornholt
#4 • *...Sacrifice of Angels* • Diane Carey

Star Trek®: Section 31™

Rogue • Andy Mangels & Michael A. Martin
Shadow • Dean Wesley Smith & Kristine Kathryn Rusch
Cloak • S.D. Perry
Abyss • Dean Weddle & Jeffrey Lang

Star Trek®: Gateways

#1 • *One Small Step* • Susan Wright
#2 • *Chainmail* • Diane Carey
#3 • *Doors Into Chaos* • Robert Greenberger
#4 • *Demons of Air and Darkness* • Keith R.A. DeCandido
#5 • *No Man's Land* • Christie Golden
#6 • *Cold Wars* • Peter David
#7 • *What Lay Beyond* • various
Epilogue: Here There Be Monsters • Keith R.A. DeCandido

Star Trek®: The Badlands

#1 • Susan Wright
#2 • Susan Wright

Star Trek®: Dark Passions

#1 • Susan Wright
#2 • Susan Wright

Star Trek® Omnibus Editions

Invasion! Omnibus • various
Day of Honor Omnibus • various
The Captain's Table Omnibus • various
Star Trek: Odyssey • William Shatner with Judith and Garfield Reeves-Stevens
Millennium Omnibus • Judith and Garfield Reeves-Stevens
Starfleet: Year One • Michael Jan Friedman

Other Star Trek® Fiction

Legends of the Ferengi • Ira Steven Behr & Robert Hewitt Wolfe
Strange New Worlds, vol. I, II, III, IV, and V • Dean Wesley Smith, ed.
Adventures in Time and Space • Mary P. Taylor, ed.
Captain Proton: Defender of the Earth • D.W. "Prof" Smith
New Worlds, New Civilizations • Michael Jan Friedman
The Lives of Dax • Marco Palmieri, ed.
The Klingon Hamlet • Wil'yam Shex'pir
Enterprise Logs • Carol Greenburg, ed.
Amazing Stories Anthology • various